W9-BYE-649

———————— ★ ————————

HE WALKED TO THE DRIVER'S SIDE OF MY CAR AND I COULD SEE HIS RIGHT HAND HANGING AT HIS SIDE, HOLDING A GUN.

I put my right hand to my mouth and pulled off my mitt with my teeth. With my thumb I eased off the safety from the rifle and raised the gun across my chest, ready to swing it and fire. The man stood beside the door of the car for a moment and then he fired, three times, through the side window. I raised the gun and fired, taking out the back tire on my side of his car. The man yelled in alarm and ran, across the clearing and down the road on the other side. I came out of the trees and followed him, pelting as hard as I could in my heavy winter gear....

———————— ★ ————————

"Ted Wood keeps the ball in motion with the deftness of a real professional."

—*Mystery Scene*

"Reid Bennett and his attack dog, Sam, form one of the most attractive sleuthing combinations on today's whodunit scene."

—*San Diego Union*

Reid. I'd have had to end up fighting the pair of them."

Also available from Worldwide Mysteries by
TED WOOD

FOOL'S GOLD
CORKSCREW
WHEN THE KILLING STARTS

TED WOOD
ON THE INSIDE

TORONTO · NEW YORK · LONDON · PARIS
AMSTERDAM · STOCKHOLM · HAMBURG
ATHENS · MILAN · TOKYO · SYDNEY

ON THE INSIDE

A Worldwide Mystery/July 1991

This edition is reprinted by arrangement with
Charles Scribner's Sons; an imprint of Macmillan
Publishing Company.

ISBN 0-373-26076-8

Copyright © 1990 by Ted Wood. All rights reserved.
No part of this book may be reproduced or transmitted in any
form or by any means, electronic or mechanical, including
photocopying, recording or by any information storage and
retrieval system, without permission in writing from the
Publisher. For information, contact: Charles Scribner's Sons,
866 Third Avenue, New York, NY 10022 U.S.A.

All the characters in this book are fictitious, and any
resemblance to actual persons, living or dead, is purely
coincidental.

® are Trademarks registered in the United States Patent
Trademark Office and other countries.
TM is the property of Harlequin Enterprises Ltd.

Printed in U.S.A.

For my daughter Heather

For my beautiful mother

ONE

CARS WERE abandoned on the street, lights blazing, doors open where the drivers had jumped out to see the excitement in the parking lot at the hotel.

"What's going on?" Freda asked and I grinned.

"The Friday-night fights, I guess," I said. "There's not a lot else to do in a town like Elliot except drink and punch one another out." I would have driven right by and gone on to the motel where they were keeping a room for us, but I saw that one of the cars was a police car. And judging by the tightness of the crowd around the main event, the cop was in trouble. "Better take a look at it," I said. "Wait here." Then I added "Please" when I saw the look in her eye. It was only three days since our wedding and the bit about obeying had not been part of the ceremony.

"Chauv," she said cheerfully, "take Sam with you. He'll do a better job than I could." I patted her hand and got out, hissing at Sam, my German shepherd, to follow me. He floated over the back of the seat and was beside me as I jogged toward the crowd.

There must have been fifty men there but I could see over their shoulders that the cop was down. One man was kneeling on his arms punching him, the other had the cop's gun in his hand. Somebody shouted "Go on! Shoot the son'bitch," and the man grinned drunkenly and tried to aim.

I told Sam, "Speak," and he bounced forward on stiff legs, snarling, and barking. The crowd flew apart as if I'd let off tear gas. Men yelled and stumbled out of the way, and I was through to the fight. The guy with the gun stared at me stupidly. He was too drunk to shoot right away but drunk enough to try it once he worked out his options. I shouted "Fight."

Sam grabbed him by the gun hand and he dropped the pistol, tugging back and kicking at Sam, who hung on, tightening his jaws like vice grips. The guy doing the punching ignored me, slamming his fist up and down into the cop's face like a piston. I kicked him on the point of the shoulder, his right shoulder. He was punching right-handed. He yowled and sprawled sideways, holding his shoulder in his left hand, swearing.

I knelt over the policeman. He was bloody but conscious. "Thanks," he whispered and tried to sit up.

"Lie there, I'll call the station." The crowd had backed off fifty feet and they watched me without trying to interfere. Crowds are like that, ready to respect the guy who's taken control, any guy. Ask Hitler.

I walked to the car, picked up the mike, and pressed the button. "Policeman hurt on Brock Street, outside the Headframe Hotel. Get some help over here right away."

The answer was a startled squawk. "Who the hell is this?"

"A citizen, Reid Bennett. Two men had your officer down, one of them had his gun. The situation's under control now but there's a crowd and the officer's hurt."

"Be right there." No copybook radio procedure but he was on the way. Fine.

I went back to the scene. The cop was sitting up, his hand over his mouth. The man I'd kicked was on his feet, backing away fearfully. The other one was still struggling with Sam. I pointed a finger at the guy on his feet. "On the ground and put your hands on your head." He swore but sat, putting his left hand on his head. His right hand was useless.

"Easy," I told Sam and he let go of the other man's wrist. "On the deck next to your buddy." I said and he did it, sitting next to him, his eyes rolling around at Sam, who was at my heel waiting for my next command. "Keep," I told him and he stood in front of the men, growling low in his throat, daring them to move. Behind me I heard the siren approaching. I bent and picked up the policeman's gun and handed it to him. He holstered it and then shook my hand, holding onto it and pulling himself to his feet. He was groggy but not seriously hurt. "Thanks, Mac," he said painfully, speaking with his mouth almost closed.

The police car squealed to a stop alongside us and two men got out, one of them with sergeant's stripes on his tunic, the other a constable. The constable turned and shooed the crowd away and they scattered to their cars. The sergeant walked over to the guy I'd helped, strutting, slightly bowlegged, a bully's walk, and asked "Which one o' these assholes had your gun?"

The cop pointed and the sergeant turned and kicked the man in the gut, knocking him backwards.

"Hey," I shouted. "Cut that out."

Now he whirled to face me. "Who asked for your opinion, mister?" Then turned and swung his foot back to kick the guy again.

"Don't kick him again," I said, and he paused and turned back to me, grinning quietly.

"Or what, punk?"

It doesn't pay to escalate arguments. I kept my voice calm. "Is this how Elliot does its police work? Beating up on drunks after somebody else stops them for you?"

"What're you? A goddamn lawyer?" He laughed. "Hey, guys, we got ourselves a lawyer in town."

The man I'd helped took his hand from his bloody mouth. "He's the guy who stopped 'em," he said.

The sergeant looked at him blankly for a moment and then laughed again. "Well, in that case," he said and turned to face me, a duty grin snapped into place like a holdup man's mask, "I guess the citizens of Elliot are in your debt, sir," he said, but his grin mocked the words. "Thank you very much. I'll see if we can't get you a civic commendation."

Freda had got out of the car. She came over and stood beside me, not speaking. She's the kind of woman who would stop traffic in a town a lot bigger than Elliot, and the sergeant stared at her for a moment and asked, "Are you with this gentleman, ma'am?"

"He's my husband," she said. "Do you need a statement about what happened?" Her voice was cold. She's an actress and knows how to project emotion. She didn't like this guy.

"That won't be necessary, thank you, ma'am," the sergeant said. "But I want to thank both of you for your assistance." All textbook formality now. The man he'd kicked was trying to sit up, his hands clutched to his stomach. His face was ghastly in the orange street light. Fred crouched beside him. "Are you okay?"

"I think so." He gasped it out. "Thanks lady."

The sergeant ignored him. He told the constable who had come with him, "Take Smith to the hospital. I'll take these two down the station."

"What about this man?" Freda asked. "He could have internal injuries."

"Don't worry your pretty head about him," the sergeant said. "He'll get medical attention once I've booked him."

"As long as he doesn't fall down the station house stairs first," Freda said.

The sergeant shook his head sadly. "Ma'am, there's no need to say things like that. He's in the hands of the law now. He'll be taken care of, 'kay?"

"Make sure he is," she said.

I touched her arm. "The sergeant will do like he says, Fred." Fred, not Freda. She's never liked her given name and shortened it to make it a joke. Only a woman as good-looking as she is could get away with using a man's name without raising anybody's eyebrows.

"I hope so," she squeezed my hand and said. "I'll wait in the car." She let go and turned away. All of us watched her go.

"I guess I'll need your name for my report," the sergeant said. "If that's not too much trouble, sir."

"No trouble at all, sergeant. I'll be coming in to see you tomorrow anyway. My name's Reid Bennett."

He looked at me sharply. "Bennett? Aren't you the guy who's applying for a job as constable?"

"That's right, sergeant. I hope to be working for you."

He laughed out loud. "Well, how about that?" he said. "That's really gonna be an experience." The news had given him his authority back and he showed it in his voice. "In that case, Bennett, don't bother coming in now. I'll see you in the morning. You check into the motel and have a nice night with the little woman."

It was his first attack in what I could see was going to be a war. There was no answer so I nodded and called Sam and went back to my car, wondering why I'd let myself get talked into this assignment.

Fred was angry. "That sonofabitch," she said. "Can't you nail him for what he did?"

"It wouldn't help." I started the motor and drove on towards the lights of the motel further down the street. "He'd get a reprimand, that's all. Nothing would change."

"He's going to make your life hell," she said. "Damn. Why did you volunteer for this one, Reid?"

"I had to. These guys are too cagey to accept a young cop unless he was born here and they'd watched the way he grew up. They'll accept me. I've got a reputation as a hard-nose."

She laughed. "Only with people who don't know you." She reached out and pressed the end of my nose. "See, pure marshmallow."

The motel was almost full but they'd kept a room for us and we checked in. I unpacked the car and gave Sam a comfort stop before putting him back in the car with the window down.

The room was small and overheated but having Fred in there made it as homey as I needed. She grinned when I came in with the last of the bags. "Well, we've already seen the sights. What's it going to be, TV or me?"

"This is supposed to be our honeymoon," I said, and she laughed.

"You sure pick exotic locations to take your wives, Bennett. Okay, I'm gonna shower. How about you?"

"Just what I was thinking," I said, and we kissed and got on with our honeymoon.

Later, as she slept, I began to wonder if I should have accepted the assignment. Maybe I wouldn't have, except that the request had come from a friend, Leo Kennedy. He used to be with the Ontario Provincial Police but he'd moved up, taken a job as adviser to the Provincial Police Commission, the outfit that keeps tabs on police departments across the province. He'd come to see me at Fred's apartment in Toronto where I was recuperating from a bullet wound. It was the week before we were to be married. Fred was out shopping. He'd joshed me, asking why I wasn't out with her, picking out a silver pattern. Then he'd come to the point.

"Reid, this is a hell of a time to ask a favor but we need one."

"We, meaning the Kennedy clan or the police commission?"

"The commission. We've got a problem up at Elliot. Ever heard of it?"

I nodded. "Sure, it's a mining town not far from Olympia."

"Right." He set down the drink I'd poured him and scratched his neck awkwardly. He's a chunky, good-natured guy and he looked uncomfortable. "Like I know you're getting married and you want to get away on a honeymoon an' all, but this is urgent."

"So tell me." I sipped my beer and waited.

"Yeah, well, there's a lot of talk in town about police corruption. And I'm not talking small stuff, discounts at clothing stores an' the rest of the chickenshit. I mean heavy. For instance taking a cut from the hotel. And what's even worse, taking a cut from the local hookers.''

''That could be scuttlebutt. There's always hookers in a mining town. The police let them operate. Otherwise no woman would be safe.''

''Yeah, but the way other guys do it is to turn a blind eye. They let them work out of their Winnebagos on payday at the mine and make sure nobody's pimping off them. That's the ethical way to handle the problem. Only the chief's taking a cut.''

I set down my glass and rubbed my sore shoulder. The collarbone had been smashed by a bullet and the chunk of metal they'd put in there afterward was still making its presence felt. ''How do you know?''

He frowned. ''We got word a couple of months ago from the guy who used to own the hotel. He got tired of the way they were upping the ante and he gave us a call. We sent an investigator up there to see him, but before he reached town the hotel guy, name of Lewicki, had an accident. He was dead the day after he called us.''

''How did it happen?'' I asked. If Fred hadn't come along when she did I wouldn't have asked any questions, but I knew that if I went up to Elliot on a fishing trip for the commission, she'd come along. I wasn't sure how well she would handle the drabness and boredom of a mining community in the bush.

Kennedy leaned forward intently. ''The forensics people say Lewicki was full of booze when it happened. He came down a hill outside'f town an' wiped out on a rock at the bend. Routine road death except for one thing. This guy was AA, hadn't touched a drop in fourteen years.''

''So you figure somebody tipped a bottle of rye down his throat and turned him loose on the hill.''

Kennedy nodded. ''Yeah. Understand that we're investigating this at arm's length. All we can do is monitor the reports at a distance. We can't even use a wiretap in town because we can't trust anybody local not to tell the chief.''

I stood up and walked over to the window. Fred's place is high up in an apartment block in the north end of Toronto. It's about as pleasant as city living gets, but it made me feel like a caged animal. Living here would be a penance, but I wasn't sure I wanted to go back to my job as police chief in Murphy's Harbour. It's a sleepy little resort town, and Fred is a city girl, an actress who likes to be close to the theaters and the art gallery and all the other trimmings of the big city. We still needed some time to talk things through. We wanted to be together for keeps, but we weren't sure where.

In the meantime there was no harm listening to what Kennedy had to say. I sat down again. "You want me to go up there and snoop around, is that it?"

"No." He shook his head. "Not quite. We can get closer than that. These are good times in town. The gold mine's working two shifts, the population's grown. They're expanding their department."

I laughed. "Lemme guess. I'm going to head up there and say I'm sick of being chief in Murphy's Harbour and apply for the job?"

"Would you?" His cheerful face was serious. "You're the ideal guy. You've got small-town experience. You've got a reputation for being a hard-nose who can take guys down. It's perfect cover. You can say you're tired of not being appreciated, not getting enough money. Hell, they're paying a constable in Elliot more than you make as chief. We can back that up at Murphy's Harbour. We can make sure the mayor, or is he just a reeve up there, sings from the same hymnbook. And I figure the department at Elliot would welcome you with open arms. You'd be on the inside."

He stopped and looked at me without speaking for a moment and then added, "And there's one other thing, Reid. This is a dangerous assignment. Nobody I know can take care of himself like you can."

The door opened and Fred came in, carrying a stack of packages. She looked great. "Well hi, Leo, what brings you here?" she asked.

"You may throw me out when I tell you," he said, going over and taking the packages out of her arms. "I've been offering your intended a substitute for a honeymoon."

"We'd been planning on New England," she said. "But I guess the chowder'll be just as clammy next year."

Kennedy turned to me and for once his face was serious. "You're a lucky sonofabitch, Reid," he said.

Now I was lying there in the dark with my wife next to me, and I was certain he was right, but I'd seen something of the town. I was worrying how I'd manage over the next little while until the case was cracked.

TWO

My APPOINTMENT with the chief of police was at nine o'clock so I got up at seven, leaving Fred in bed while I went for a run with Sam at my heels. In half an hour I'd seen most of what Elliot had to offer. It wasn't much. This was a smokestack town, an oasis in the bush, built as a polite kind of barracks for the mine employees and their families.

The town was flat and had no views in any direction. There was a wide main street with the motel, the bar where the fight had been, a legion hall, and a community center with a sign outside advertising upcoming hockey games. There were two churches, one Catholic, one Methodist, a couple of restaurants, one of them Chinese, a few blue-collar-looking stores and the bank. Off the main street there were two schools, one public, one Catholic.

The high-school kids were bussed the forty miles down the highway to the next town, I guessed. Aside from that there was nothing but row after row of identical homes, bungalows for the workers, and an area of two-story places for mine management and the wealthier merchants.

The police station was a concrete-block building on the edge of town, out where the trees came right down to the road. There were three police cars on the lot and one civilian car. That told me they only had one man on duty overnight.

When I got back to the motel, Fred was up, dressed in a warmup suit, doing exercises to a tape she was playing. "Good timing," she said, switching off the machine. "I was just going to shower."

Afterwards I fed Sam and we had breakfast in the coffeeshop. The menu was basic north country, bacon and eggs or pancakes, but they did have some whole wheat bread for Fred's toast. I leveled with her as we ate. "This place is going to be hard, Fred. There's nothing for the mind in the whole town."

"A girl doesn't plan to use her mind much on her honeymoon," she laughed. "But just in case, that blue bag you've been having trouble lifting is full of books I've been intending to read since college. And I've brought some conversational Spanish tapes. I figure it will be too cold to go to Cape Cod when this is over, so we can take ourselves to Mexico. On top of which, I'm your wife. It'll be up to me to keep us housed and fed.''

The waitress came over with fresh coffee. She was a chunky kid with no makeup and she was serving Fred with great respect. "'Scuse me for askin','' she said, "But have I seen you on TV?''

"Could be,'' Fred said. "I've been in some plays and there's a tortilla commercial playing somewhere that still pays me residuals.''

"Wow,'' the girl said. "You're an actress.''

"Used to be.'' Fred smiled at her, making the girl beam. "Right now I'm married to this handsome fellow, and he's going to be a policeman in town.''

That shut the girl down. "Oh,'' she said and give me a hard look.

She left and Fred frowned at me. "Looks like the cops are not the flavor of the month in this place.''

"That's why we're here,'' I said. "Can you hang tough? It'll probably mean you don't make any friends here. But I'll try to get it all done as quickly as I can.''

"I played rep in a small town for three whole months once,'' she said. "I can handle isolation.''

I patted her hand and said, "Okay, now I've got to go and see if I can get aboard. If they turn me down I promise we'll be out of town by noon.''

"Good luck.'' She stood up and kissed me lightly. "I'll go for a walk and check the town out. See you back here.''

"I'll leave Sam with you. I don't want these guys to think he's my security blanket.'' I signed the back of the bill for breakfast and went out to apply for work.

There was a civilian clerk at the desk when I got there, a sharp-featured woman who looked as if she'd come with the furniture in 1949. "Yes?'' she asked, without coming to the counter.

"Good morning, my name's Reid Bennett. I have an appointment to see Chief Harding.''

"Wait there." She got up and clicked down the corridor to the back of the station. Then she came back and unflapped the countertop. "Back there. No smoking," she said.

I bobbed my head at her, the anxious job applicant currying favor, and walked through to the chief's office.

He was a lean man in his fifties, dressed in a tunic with two stars on the shoulders. He was reading something on his desk, and I had time to check the office before he looked up. A shelf of law books, a couple of photographs of the entire force, one with a '56 Chev behind them, three men, the other with three cruisers in the background and five men in front of them, him in the middle. There were also three pistol shooting trophies.

He looked up at last. "Bennett?"

"Yes sir."

"Good. Sit down." He waved to the chair opposite to him and I sat down, saying nothing.

He stared at me for almost a minute. Then he said, "Why do you want to work up here?"

"I'm sick of the place I'm in," I said. "The pay is lousy and I don't get any respect. I've had some pretty big cases, dangerous, some of them, but instead of being pleased when I cracked them, the reeve gives me a hard time for being violent."

He didn't answer, so I pushed on, trying harder. "Sure, I'm the chief, but I can't get any more advancement. I'd do better for myself and my family starting as a constable with your department."

It was all close enough to the truth that I could say it without embarrassment.

He listened and then said, "I was intrigued by your background, Bennett. This is a tough town, a mining town. The people are good people, but they don't respect the law and making them understand it can be difficult."

I waited while he opened the top drawer of his desk and took out my application. He flicked over the top sheet and looked at my CV. "Four years with the US Marines, two of them in Vietnam. Seven years with the Toronto department, got as high as acting detective. Then you quit. Why?"

"I got into a fight with some bikers. I killed two of them and the papers made life difficult."

He had eyes the color of a northern sea. He looked at me steadily. "Yes, I read that. And then you had a number of cases in, where was it? Murphy's Harbour, which resulted in your killing more people."

"In the line of duty, sir."

"You're a bad apple," he said, but his eyes were glittering. He was testing me.

"No sir. I'm a policeman who does what has to be done. Only in Murphy's Harbour they don't appreciate the way things have to be done sometimes."

"Says you got shot, how long was it, six weeks ago?"

"It's healing nicely, sir. Doctor says I'll have a complete recovery in another month or so."

"What will you do in the meantime?" He smiled thinly. "You can't expect some drunken miner to back off because your arm's not up to speed."

"It's my left arm. I hold the stick in the right." I grinned, disgusted at myself but playing the game the way I'd seen it the night before.

"We don't want any gratuitous violence." He frowned. "I'm looking for a law enforcement officer, not a head-beater."

"I tackle every situation the way it needs, Chief." I tried to sound earnest. "I'm not a violent man, but I grew up in a mining town, Coppercliff, near Sudbury. I know you can't always cool things out with talk."

He leaned back now, looking at me carefully. I figured he was a touch long-sighted but didn't like wearing glasses. "Anything else you want to tell me?"

I guessed he'd seen the report of my activity at the hotel and was looking for me to start talking it up. It might be the only chance I got to look good here. "One thing you might keep in mind, sir. There was a disturbance at the Headframe when I got into town last night. An officer was being assaulted by a couple of miners. I assisted the officer and got the situation under control." He didn't say anything, and I pressed on urgently. "So please have a word with the officer. He'll tell you I can handle things pretty good."

He nodded primly. "Yes, the sergeant mentioned it to me. Okay, go down to the hospital and see Dr. Frazer. He'll check you out. Then return to the motel and wait. I'll call you there."

I nodded and left smartly as he turned back to his paperwork. The woman in the outer office didn't look up. I went back to my car and drove around to the hospital, a small brick building near the center of town.

I was too early for my appointment but the doctor saw me anyway. He was tall and young. He looked tired, as if he never got enough time away from the hospital. He didn't say much to me but looked my shoulder over and X-rayed it. Then he took my blood pressure and tapped my chest and the rest of the ritual and took his stethoscope out of his ears and said, "You're in good shape. You a runner?"

"Yes, doctor. Try to do three miles a day."

"Won't be easy when winter comes," he said. Not once had he mentioned the police department. I got the same feeling as I'd had about the waitress. The people of Elliot didn't like their police.

He scribbled on the form in front of him and then looked up. "I had a policeman in here last night, says a guy called Bennett helped him out in a fight at the hotel. Are you the guy?"

"Professional courtesy," I said.

He grinned tightly. "You started on the right foot for this place," he said.

He closed the file folder. "Okay, Mr. Bennett, I'll get my report back to the department. You can go now."

He walked out of the room and I dressed and left. If I'd been hungry for the job I might have been anxious, but I didn't think they were weighed down with applications. Police work isn't everybody's choice, and these were busy times at the mine. A man could make a lot more money underground if he didn't mind putting in overtime. And when he went home he knew he wouldn't be called out again in the middle of the night.

Fred was back in the motel room, reading *Crime and Punishment*. Sam was lying on the rug next to the bed, panting in the heat of the room. Fred closed the book on her index finger and stood up to kiss me. "Did they clasp you to their bosom?"

"They're going to. In the meantime I've been told to stay here and wait for the call. I figure they'll keep me on ice until the afternoon anyway."

"How will we pass the time?" she clowned and Dostoyevsky took a back seat for a while.

The call came as we were finishing lunch in the coffeeshop. The same waitress came over as we were eating pie, and told me, "Telephone for Mr. Bennett. That's you, eh?"

"Yes, thanks." I raised my eyebrows at Fred and went to the phone. It was the clerk at the police department.

"The chief will see you at two o'clock, Mr. Bennett."

"Thank you, ma'am. I'll be there," I said, and she hung up.

This time I walked down there. I was five minutes early and the clerk kept me waiting until the dot of two before telling the chief I was there. When I went back in he stood up and offered his hand. "Welcome aboard," he said.

"You mean I'm hired, chief?"

He nodded and sat down. "Yes, I checked your references and the doctor says you're in good shape. Can you start right away?"

"I surely can."

"Good." He sat forward, leaning one elbow on his desk and looking at me closely. "You've got police experience so we don't have to send you to the college, but there's a few things you need to know about Elliot."

I waited and he went on. "This is a good department, Bennett. We're respected in town. I won't say everybody loves us, but they know that when they need us, we're there. We're tough but we're fair."

"Right, Chief." I nodded firmly.

"Now I've been talking to Sgt. Ferris and he tells me you did good work last night." He paused and I said nothing. I could feel the other shoe about to drop. "However, he said that you questioned his judgment of how to handle the situation. Is that right?"

I hedged my answer. "Last night I wasn't a member of the department, chief. I know about discipline."

"Good." He nodded curtly. "Sgt. Ferris is a good man, an experienced man. When he says jump you jump. Understood?"

"Yessir. I was in the Marines, sir."

"Right. Keep your nose clean, Bennett, and you'll do all right. Sgt. Ferris is in the guardroom behind the office. Go and see him and he'll give you your uniform and your instructions. Good luck."

"Thank you sir." I stood up and snapped to attention. Might as well polish the apple to a high gloss.

Ferris was expecting me. He was sitting at a desk in the corner of the guardroom. Aside from his desk with a manual typewriter and a telephone on it, there were a couple of file cabinets, a table where the guys ate their lunch, and half a dozen lockers.

He looked up when I came in and said, "Hi. Ready for work?" a neutral question. He was smiling except that it didn't reach to his eyes. He stood up and I studied him as I crossed the room. About fifty-five, a couple of inches under six feet tall, sandy fair hair and pale blue eyes. He was heavy, not fat, but chunky with muscle he had developed young but didn't work on anymore. His face looked almost jolly, except for those eyes.

"Sure am, sar'nt. I've been off a couple of months with this shoulder. I guess the chief mentioned that."

"Yeah. He told me. Got yourself shot. What happened to the other guy?"

"He's not around anymore," I minimized.

"Good," Ferris said. "Now you can't expect the other guys to carry you while you're mending. If you can't hack it, you're out. Got that?"

"Sure." I nodded and he went over and opened one of the lockers. A constable's uniform was inside, still in the dry cleaner's plastic bag.

"Try this one," he said. "Belonged to a guy who quit. Should fit."

I wondered if he was going to play games, handing me something that looked like a clown suit, but he hadn't. The tunic was snug across the shoulders but not a bad fit. The pants seemed the right size as well. "Seems fine, sar'nt." Using his rank all the time was clumsy, but I was moving carefully until I saw how formal the other guys were around him.

"Hang that up and I'll show you around," he said. Nobody would have guessed we'd already met and that he might be harboring a grudge.

He took me out to the office first and introduced me to the clerk. "Marcie, this here's our new officer, Reid Bennett. Bennett, this is Mrs. Sheridan."

I shook hands with her. It was like clutching a bird's claw.

"Nice to meet you, ma'am."

"Likewise," she said and turned back to her typing. Not the motherly type.

"See Marcie later and she'll give you the forms you have to fill in," he said. "First, get the lay of the land. In here we got the teletype. We're gonna get a fax machine soon. These are all our files, criminal occurrences here, accidents here." He slapped two of the file cabinets. "The blanks are in the file cabinet in the guardroom. You do your own paperwork, of course. Use the typewriter out back.'' There was a large-scale map of the area on the wall and he went over to it. "This is our district. We cover the town and the township. Most of it's just bush, but the gold mine is inside the limits and we're responsible for it, too."

I studied the map. The township extended about ten miles across, ten miles deep. The town itself sat in the southeast corner. There were only two roads outside of town, the one Fred and I had taken in, and one crossing road that led to the mine and then swung back through town to the west of us. There was a cluster of buildings at the end. I asked, "What's this place?"

"That's the old pulp mill. It's abandoned now but there's a few homes out there, retired couples mainly. We don't get trouble out there."

He turned and pointed at the radio setup in the corner. "That's the radio. Marcie handles it through the day. At night we have one guy here or else we couple the phone lines to it so you get phone calls when you're in the car. The senior man will be in the station so you don't need to learn how to use this set for a while."

"Looks like the set I had at Murphy's Harbour," I said but he didn't answer. "Now, weapons," he said and his voice had a grim pleasure in it. He liked guns. "I understand you've got your own pistol, right?"

"Right. It's a .38 Colt Police Special, six-inch barrel."

"Okay." He nodded. "We carry a Winchester pump in all the cars. We've also got tear gas equipment an' rifles. They're out back."

He led the way out of the office to the cells. There were four of them, all empty. The area smelled of carbolic.

"Generally full on Friday nights," he said. "Two in each cell sometimes."

"Miners love to drink," I said.

"And fight." He faced me and he had no trace of a smile now. "Those guys last night were out to kill Smith. Goddamn magistrate let them out on bail but they're going inside when they come to trial. And let me put you straight, Bennett. The only thing they respect is force. This isn't some candyass resort town. This is a tough place. We don't have a bunch of civil rights people lookin' over our shoulders all the time. You act tough at all times. And I mean tough. I don' want none of your bleeding-heart bullshit when I'm talking to a suspect. You got that?''

"Yes, Sergeant." I got myself onside right away. "I know the rules, only my wife was in the car. She's from the city."

"She'll have to learn or you'll have to go," he said. "Do we understand one another?''

"Yes." I nodded again and he matched me.

"Good. Now I'll show you the town."

We went out to the cruiser and he drove back into town. He didn't say much, pointing out the sights I'd seen for myself on my run. "Do you have any trouble spots?" I prodded.

"Naah. Just the Headframe, Fridays, Saturdays. There's a lot of drinking at the legion but it's under control. We don't get trouble there, 'less there's a dance an' some of the rowdies come in." He turned and grinned at me. "Guess you know how it is. Somebody gets the hots for somebody else's wife. Guy with a wife as pretty as yours, you'd see a lot of that."

I said nothing. I already knew he was a creep.

He stopped at the Headframe Hotel. "This is action central," he grinned. "There's a new guy running it. The last owner was a booze hound, got drunk and crashed his car. This guy's only been here a few months."

We went in through the side door into a corridor that opened on one side to a storeroom filled with cases of beer and on through to the taproom. It was like a thousand others in small towns. The furniture was rudimentary, vinyl-covered tables and chairs, rough paneling on the walls and a few pictures, locally done oil paintings of the mine and the bush, and a shuffle-board with burn marks all along the rim. The place smelled of old cigarette smoke and beer. The big color TV was playing soundlessly—some game show.

Ferris looked around and grinned. "It ain' fancy, but I worked out one time he has to do twenty grand a week in here, easy. More when the hockey playoffs're on, or holidays."

"Seems high," I said.

"These miners drink," Ferris said, "An' I mean drink."

The manager came out of his office. He was a pale, thin man in his forties. He smiled when he saw Ferris. It didn't look forced.

"Hi, sarge, nice to see you."

"Hi, Bill." Ferris walked over in his roosterish strut and shook hands. "Got a new guy for you to meet. Name's Bennett. He's one of us."

He turned his smile my way. It was less enthusiastic, I thought. "Bill Berger," he said. "An' I've heard all the jokes."

"Reid Bennett, Bill. Glad to know you."

We shook hands and he let go quickly and turned his attention to Ferris. "Thanks for gettin' here so quick last night, sarge. I'd a'ready called the station an' I didn't go out. The guys generally take care of things with no trouble. Sorry to hear young Smith got himself beat up."

"He'll survive," Ferris said heartily. "Might've been different if Bennett hadn've come into town when he did. Young Willis took Smitty's gun away. He was gonna shoot him."

"I heard about that, but not until later." Berger looked anxious. "It happened outside, like I said. I called."

"No sweat. You did the right thing. Just dropped by to introduce the rookie," Ferris said.

Berger went back behind the bar and poured a double Canadian Club. He shoved it over to Ferris who nodded thanks and drank half of it down. "What's your pleasure?" Berger asked me. His smile had gone.

I hesitated. I couldn't refuse, not when Ferris had already broken the rules. "A Coke'd be good thanks. I'm on the wagon, doctor's orders."

"Not the drink for a growing boy," Ferris said. "How long're you on the wagon?"

"Till the shoulder mends." I accepted the Coke and thanked Berger.

"What happened?" he asked. He didn't seem any more pleased to be serving pop than he would have been pouring me a shot of rye.

"Injured in the line of duty," I said.

Berger cocked his head. "You been a cop before?"

"Yeah." I didn't want to give him more, not with Ferris listening to my every word, every tone of voice.

"Got shot," Ferris said loudly. "Shot the guy who did it. He don't screw around, this guy."

"Oh." Berger looked at me nervously. "Yeah, well, I guess it happens." He poured himself a cup of coffee from the machine behind the bar and sipped it, black. "I heard you had a dog with you last night, jeezly big shepherd."

"Yes, that's Sam. He was all the help I had on my last job. He's pretty good."

"He won't be usin' the dog in here," Ferris said. "This is the police department, not the humane society." He snorted to himself and finished his rye. "Well, gotta get on. See you, Bill."

I nodded to Berger. "Nice meeting you, and thanks for the drink."

"Any time," he said automatically. Then to Ferris. "Smitty in the hospital, is he?"

"Naah, he's at home, takin' a couple days off until his eye gets back to normal," Ferris said.

We left and I thought about what I'd seen. Ferris didn't mind breaking the rules—two of them, accepting gifts and drinking on duty. But it was all small stuff. There was nothing to report to Toronto.

THREE

FERRIS WAS a little more talkative after his drink. He drove me around the rest of the town pointing out the details of properties that had to be checked at night. It was the usual list. Only three of them had safes for the cash and in each of them the box sat in the front window where it was easy to see. Nothing complicated. I could see that night duty in town would be a drag.

When we got back to the station he turned me over to Marcie who had me complete a bunch of forms for health insurance and pension. I found that if I stayed in Elliot until I was sixty-five I could retire on a pension that might just keep Fred and me in popcorn, if we still had teeth.

When I'd finished, Ferris told me to report to the station at midnight for my first shift. "You'll be nights for the first month," he said with the same grin. "That wife o' yours better get used to sleepin' on her own." Listening to him talk about Fred made my flesh creep, but I said nothing. I just went back to the motel, leaving the uniform in the locker.

Fred was out with Sam, so I didn't stay. I left the motel and strolled back along the main drag to the community center and went in. As in most Ontario towns, its main feature was an ice surface with bleachers around it. Hockey is a big number in the north. For a lot of kids the NHL offers the only chance they'll get to make big money. They play hard, the way ghetto kids in the States play basketball. I glanced through the window and saw a crowd of ten-year-olds skating. One of them was pretty good, and I watched pleasurably while he deked the puck past the defenseman and slapped in a goal.

The rest of the amenities were all off the front hall, the other side from the arena. The library, small by city standards but looking fresh and appealing, and two other rooms. One of them was a gym with basketball hoops and a badminton net. The other was an auditorium, and that's where I found Fred, talking to a guy in a good shirt and a pair of cord pants. He was around thirty and handsome. They were deep in conversation, but she glanced around and saw me and waved me over, smiling.

"Reid, this is Jacques Lafleur. He's the director of the center. Jacques, this is my husband, Reid Bennett."

We shook hands and sized one another up. I got the impression he would rather have found that Fred was single, but I was going to have a lot of that to contend with. I didn't hold it against him.

"Delighted to meet you, Reid," he said.

"And you, Jacques. You have a really nice place here."

He shrugged modestly. "We got some money from the government lottery foundation, and some from the mine company. We've got all the standard things. I've lined up some good courses for the winter months, yoga, dancercise, and crafts. I was delighted to find your wife is an actress. She could really give us a boost."

"Jacques has asked me if I'll coach a drama class," Fred said happily. "We'll do a play and I get to direct."

"Hey, that's perfect." I was delighted. It would keep Fred involved if the investigation dragged on. "What will you do?"

"I should warn you, you'd best pick something with a lot of female roles," Lafleur said. "Most guys around here would die rather than appear on stage."

"My dad was a hardrock miner and he'd turn in his grave if his son said 'Tennis, anyone?'" I grinned to show I was a good sport. "And anyway, I'm going to be working shifts, so I wouldn't be able to get to the rehearsals."

Fred gave me a quick kiss on the cheek. "You can be the prompter," she said. "I'll be out in a couple of minutes."

I gave her arm a squeeze and smiled at Lafleur, then went back out to watch the kids.

The game ended a couple of minutes later. Fred and Lafleur came out of the auditorium and she and I left.

"I'm excited, Reid," she said. "I can make a real contribution in this town, give some people a real boost."

"You give everybody a real boost, just walking down the street," I said and she laughed.

"Thank God you're blind." She unlocked the car door. Sam was in the back seat and he whined and nosed at my hand as I reached back to fuss him.

"Good boy," I told him. "You're going to be Fred's dog for a while. The station is off-limits to you."

Fred paused with the key in the ignition. "Won't you be taking him with you on duty?"

"No, that sergeant says not."

She looked concerned. "But how will you manage? Your arm's still weak. What will you do when something like last night happens?"

"I will demonstrate my powers of persuasion," I said, and she hugged me.

"You're a tough sonofagun, Bennett."

"And I'm also a working man. I start at midnight. I'm going to have to put in an hour or two in bed."

She laughed. "You wicked man."

I did manage to get some sleep and reported to the station around eleven-fifteen. Ferris was there, in plain clothes.

I nodded to him. "Hi, sarge. You put in a long day."

He said, "Yeah," in a surly tone. I changed quickly for my shift.

He was watching me. "You sure got a lot of scars. How'd you get that one on the arm there?"

"In 'Nam," I said.

He grinned. "Wounded were you? How'd it happen?"

"A boobytrap. It killed the guy in front of me." I don't like reliving old battles.

He shook his head. "What made you go to Vietnam?"

"It seemed like a good idea at the time." I smiled and sat down at the table. "I didn't get a notebook this afternoon. Do you have one for me?"

"Sure." He reached into his drawer and tossed me a leather binder and a new notebook, standard police issue with the cutoff covers. "There's a couple notes," he said. "I'll give 'em to you when Scott gets here. He's gonna ride with you tonight. Tomorrow you're on your own."

"Fine." I opened the book and wrote the date and time and "paraded for patrol. Sgt. Ferris on duty," closed the book and waited.

Ferris sat looking at the teletype messages he had compiled into a sheaf on his clipboard. At eleven-thirty another constable came in. It was the man who had come to Smith's assistance the night before. He nodded to Ferris. "Evenin' sarn't," then stuck his hand out to me. "Hi. Frank Scott. You're the guy helped Smitty last night."

"Yeah. Reid Bennett. That one was on the house. Starting tonight they're paying me."

He laughed. I liked the look of him. He was tall, well built but pale. He looked as if he didn't get much sunshine, and I guessed the men worked more nights and evenings than they did day shifts. Ah well. This wouldn't be forever.

He was already wearing his uniform and he sat down at the table and leaned back. We chatted about nothing, the night's hockey game, the weather.

At eleven forty-five exactly Ferris said, "Okay, let's have you."

We stood up and went round in front of the sergeant's desk, unflipping our holster flaps to show our guns and holding up our sticks, handcuffs and notebooks. He nodded at us and we put our equipment away as he read out the messages he'd gathered. There were a couple of stolen cars, taken from towns close by. "Watch out for the one taken in Olympia. Marvin Luik on Sparrow Road had his license suspended last week for drunk driving. He likes to drink in Olympia. He could've taken it to get home in," Ferris said.

He glanced down the list. "Escaped convict, from Collins Bay. That's a long way from here, but he's been out three days now and he worked here once." He gave us the name and description and then looked up. "Nothing else that affects us on here. Only things are local complaints. Mrs. Lenchak reports noisy motorcycles behind her place at the end of Mallard Street. And the school principal's concerned some of the kids might cel-

ebrate Hallowe'en early. Little buggers oughta be in bed
by now, but this is Saturday night so take a drive around
the school. And the last thing—Delaney. What's his first
name, Scott?''

"George," Scott said.

"Yeah, George Delaney. Saturday night's his night to
howl. Check the Headframe when you go out. Have a
word with him, if he's there. Otherwise you'll be called
up to their place later.''

I wrote the complaints in my book. Scott didn't bother.
This was the ritual of working here. He knew the people
like I knew my crowd at Murphy's Harbour. Ferris said,
''Scott, show Bennett the ropes. He's on his own tomorrow.''

Scott nodded and Ferris said, "Okay, Scott. I'm going
home. You're in charge. Set the radio and get on your
way.''

"Right." Scott replaced his equipment and went over
to the radio. "You couple the phone lines in like this," he
explained and flipped the necessary switches. It was the
same system I'd used in Murphy's Harbour, but I nodded and said nothing. Ferris watched us as he put on a
heavy checked coat and left, not speaking.

"Okay, the evening guy should be back by now," Scott
said. He led me out to the back of the station and we
found the evening man in the car, writing up his notebook.

Scott whisked the door open. "Hey come on, Jeff, you
can do that inside. It's cold here.''

"In a rush, are you?" The other man got out and
handed over the car log on a clipboard.

"This is Reid Bennett, the new guy," Scott said.
"Reid, this is Jeff Walker, makes the shakiest pinches you
ever saw.''

"Shaky, hell," Walker said. "My pinches stand up.''

"On crutches." Scott laughed.

I shook hands with Walker. He went into the station as
Scott walked around the patrol car checking for damage, the usual signing-over routine.

We got in and drove into town slowly. "No sense
rushin'," Scott said. "You can cover the whole place in
half an hour, gives you seven an' a half more to fill.''

"Sounds like the place I used to work," I said. We spent a couple of minutes getting our backgrounds out of the way. Then I asked him, "What're the guys like?"

"Shaky, you met him. He's been here the longest, ten years. He's pretty quick to take people in. Any arguments an' he books them for obstruct police. If they don't like it he'll give 'em a shot in the head and charge them with assault."

"Nobody stops him?"

Scott shook his head. "Naah. The magistrate's a local guy, kind of a law-and-order freak. If a guy's charged, he's guilty."

"And there's been no complaints? Hell, if a magistrate tried that around Toronto some civil liberties outfit would have him removed from the bench."

Scott laughed. "This is a mining town. We got a lot of guys here hardly speak English. Those're the ones Shaky locks up. Anybody else knows enough not to argue, anybody who might get his civil liberties in an uproar."

We reached the school and drove around it. A cluster of teenagers were standing in the yard smoking, and they stepped on their butts when we drove up. "Grass probably," Scott said. "Comes in from the Soo. I figure it's smuggled across by guys on the lake ships. We won't see as much of it during the winter."

He stopped next to the boys and spoke to them. They listened in silence and then walked out of the schoolyard, shoulders slumped rebelliously. We sat and watched them go. Scott shook his head. "Not hard to understand why they're smokin' up," he said. "If you don't play hockey there's not a hell of a lot for a young guy to do in town."

He let in the clutch and we drove out past the boys, who glanced sideways at the car and laughed as we went by. "So, where was I? There's Smitty, you met him. He's been here three years. This is his first job, he was born here. His dad's a miner. Walker you met, me, then there's Levesque, he's our show Frog. He's mean. And the last one is George Thomas. He's the station stick-man."

"Sounds like a typical station," I said, staying neutral. "Couple of good guys, couple of bad apples."

"Typical?" Scott snorted. "You mean to tell me it's like this in the OPP or Toronto?" He shook his head. "No. The guys aren't the best cops you ever met. Couple of 'em would never have made it onto a good department."

"If you hate it, why'd you stay?"

"I joined in eighty-one," he said. "That was bad times up here. All the mines were laying off. You couldn't buy a job. I took this one and glad to get it. Now I've got a wife an' three kids. I'm too old to join another department, too old to go back underground. They've got me for life, but I don't pretend to like it."

"My problem exactly." I wasn't lying. "I've been a cop so long I couldn't do anything else. This was the only chance going when I left the Harbour."

"Think they'd consider me?" He asked, only half joking. "Got to be a lot better for my kids than staying in this place."

"The money's lousy. Worse than here," I said. "But go ahead if you want to try."

We were back in the town center now, and he stopped outside the hotel. "May's well check the bar," he said. I got the feeling he was uncomfortable about talking. It was not the right time to pump him about the chief.

I got out of the car with him. "You get much trouble?"

"Some," he said. "You saw what happened last night."

This time we went in through the front door. The place was full but it seemed orderly enough for a town of this kind. A couple of guys were playing shuffleboard and all of the tables were filled with men, the tops covered with beer bottles and glasses. At a quick glance it looked as if half the guys were too drunk to drive.

Scott walked through the crowd to the bar where the barmen were filling orders, moving as if they were on piecework.

Scott nodded to Berger. "Evening, Bill. How's it goin'?"

"Busy." Berger nodded at me, his hands busy filling another tray. "No trouble though."

"Good. Willis in, is he?"

Berger glanced around. "No. Haven't see him or Cassidy all night. Guess they're dryin' out for a while."

"Likely drinking in the legion," Scott said. He stood with his back to the bar, looking around the room. I'd already noticed one bad drunk at a table in the corner. Scott walked over to him and I followed.

The man looked up at us owlishly. His buddies drank their beer and pretended we weren't there. "Hi, George," Scott said. "Looks to me like you're about full. One of these guys drivin' you home?"

"Yeah. Don't worry," the man said.

"I'm not worried. It won't be me havin' aspirin for breakfast," Scott laughed. "One thing though, I don't see your missus in here. Don't be giving her a hard time when you get home or this time you're going away. Understand?"

"That bitch," the man said. He reached for the cigarette pack in front of him and drew one out with clumsy fingers, spilling the pack on the floor.

The other men laughed and Scott said, "Just so's we understand one another. Got that, George?"

"Yeah, sure," the man growled.

Behind us there was the crash of a table going over. We turned and saw two men facing one another angrily. I waited for Scott to take the initiative. He did, shoving through the crowd and confronting the men. "Okay, that's it. Outside, the pair of you."

The crowd was on its feet now, shouting encouragement. I sized the situation up. The men were young and fit and angry and just drunk enough to want to make a case out of it. I went and stood beside Scott. "Hey," I said to the bigger of the two. "Did you know you left your lights on? You're gonna have a dead battery."

He dropped his fists and turned to look at me. "My car? Naah. I turned 'em off."

"Come and see," I said. He frowned and turned away, leaving the other man looking foolish with his hands still up. A waiter bustled over and set the table back on its legs. Then another one brought a brush and a dustpan for the broken bottles. The second battler looked down at them in disgust and followed us out the door.

Outside the big guy started across the parking lot then stopped. "My lights aren't on," he roared.

"My mistake," I said cheerfully. "Come on now, head for home. You've had enough for one night."

The man turned and saw Scott with the second guy. "I'm gonna kill him," he said.

"Yeah. No contest," I said. "Why mark your hands up on a guy like that. Go on home."

He stood and looked at me for a minute. "I'm gonna kill him," he said again but the anger was evaporating.

"Why bother? I know you could do it. The hell with him," I said, grinning like a fool.

"Yeah." The tension went out of him. "No sweat. No goddamn sweat."

He got into a pickup truck and backed out. He was roaring the engine and I knew he was as near drunk as he could be without my having to lock him up. But he drove carefully and I went back to Scott.

"Randy here is going home," Scott said. "He's kinda drunk, so we'll drop him off."

"Fine." I opened the rear door of the cruiser and the man got in, moving carefully, as if he were walking in his sleep. I shut the door and Scott drove down the main street and turned off into one of the streets of bungalows. He got out and opened the door and the man got out.

The door of the house opened and a woman came out, wearing a housecoat. "What happened?" She ran down the walk to us. "Randy, what happened?"

"Nothin'," he said irritably. "Go on inside for crissakes."

We watched them walking up to the door, him stiff-legged, sullen, the woman bending from the waist, talking at him in an angry hiss. The door closed behind them and Scott laughed.

"Hey, that was quick thinking," he said. "I'll have to remember that one."

"May not work next time. But it took the big guy's mind off killing people."

Scott laughed again. "I like the way you do business, Reid. I'd have had to end up fighting the pair of them."

"Use the head to save the hands," I said. "I've got a sore shoulder still. I can't afford to get into any donnybrooks."

"Come on," Scott said. "Let's see if there's any coffee left at the Chinaman's."

We had coffee and patrolled the town again, checking the lockup properties this time. Then the crowd left the bar, and the place went to sleep all around us. I pumped Scott carefully all night, pacing my questions, finding out a lot more about the other men but nothing about the chief or the sergeant. I went off-duty at eight, wondering how long it would take to get close to the problems of the town.

FOUR

I WASN'T used to working the night through. My practice at Murphy's Harbour had been to stay up until both bars had closed and people had gone home, then check my properties and go to bed until dawn. Occasionally I would get up around three and check out the properties again, in case anybody was watching my routine, planning to commit a break-in while I slept. I had not regularly worked through the long gray stretch from four A.M. until six for years.

I went back to the motel and had breakfast with Fred who said she was looking for a place for us to live. She told me with a laugh that Jacques from the community center had volunteered to rent us half his house. "Don't worry," she laughed as I looked up, "I told him thanks but no thanks."

"He's really taken with you," I said.

"I know," she said. "Star-struck, if I can exaggerate a little. I don't think he's ever met a professional before."

"Nobody's ever met anybody like you before," I said, and she reached over and squeezed my hand.

"With eyesight as bad as yours I don't know how you passed your physical. But in any case, I thought we'd be better off somewhere else. I've got a couple of leads from the manager of this place."

I let her go looking while I hit the sack and slept until she came back at noon and told me about the house she had rented. The owner was a widow. Her husband had been killed in a mine cave-in and she had fitted out her house with a basement apartment for herself and was renting the upper level to stretch her pension.

"It's sort of fifties, I guess is the best way of putting it," Fred explained. "Vinyl-covered kitchen furniture. The rest of the stuff looks as if it came from the Eaton's catalogue the year they got married. But what the hell, she's asking a reasonable rent."

"I'm going to get reimbursed when this is over," I said. "Keep the receipts."

"Don't worry. Acting is almost all deductible. I'm an ace at bookkeeping on expenses," Fred said. "Now finish your fish and chips and we'll move in."

Mrs. Schuka was a motherly little Ukrainian lady. She was skeptical when she saw Sam. "I've never had a dog in the place before."

"He's not a dog, he's a pussycat," Fred said. "And he's trained. Nobody's going to bother us while Reid's out at night. I can promise you that."

"Does he bark?" Mrs. Schuka asked anxiously. "I don't like noise."

"Doesn't make a sound unless he's working," Fred said. She bent and fondled Sam's head. "Do you Sam?" Sam whined low in his throat and thrust his head against her hand.

"Well, all right." Mrs. Schuka smiled. "But keep him off my furniture, eh?"

"I promise," Fred said. "He's the best-behaved dog you ever saw."

The house was as she'd described it. But it was spotless, and with the October sun shining in, it seemed enough like home to suit me for a month or two. Fred paid the first and last month's rent. When Mrs. Schuka left us and went downstairs, Fred made coffee and we unpacked the few things we'd brought with us. Then Fred led me into the bedroom and sat on the bed. "I wonder if this thing works?" she said.

I was rested by the time I reached the police office at eleven-thirty. Fred was at home, watching the late movie with Sam beside her on the floor, and I was free to concentrate on the reason I'd been sent here. I took over from the afternoon-shift man who had come in early from patrol. He was tall and dark, in his thirties. He had a thin mustache, the kind old movie stars wore. I could tell from the way he moved that he thought he was God's gift.

He nodded to me. "George Thomas. You're Reid Bennett, right?"

"Yeah. Pleased to meet you, George." I remembered Scott's description—the station Romeo.

"How'd you like Elliot so far?" he asked.

"Seems like any other place. Scotty showed me around last night."

"Dudley, you mean." He laughed. "Dudley Do-right. Goes to church every Sunday, coaches the hockey team. Wouldn't say shit if he had a mouthful."

"Seems pleasant," I said, grinning to show I wouldn't disagree.

"That's what half the rounders in town think," Thomas said. "He don't uphold the law the way I like to see it done."

He was testing me, but I shrugged. I'd get more out of friends or neutral people than I would out of enemies. "Just met him last night. Seemed friendly. That's all I ask."

Thomas shoved the message board across to me. "Nothing much on the wire," he said. "Sundays this place is dead. Not that you noticed, I guess. I hear you're a newlywed."

I looked him in the eye. "Yes," I said, and whatever he had been planning to add shriveled up.

"Okay. So you know how to turn this thing to the phone, do you?" He hooked his thumb back over his shoulder at the radio.

"Wouldn't mind going over it again, please." I grinned at him now we were back on police work. "Wouldn't want Ferris calling in and not getting me. What's he like, anyway?"

"Tough sonofabitch," Thomas expanded. "Good cop. If anybody tries anything on with the guys, he takes them out back and shows them it was a dumb idea. We don't get much trouble anymore. Used to have lots of it."

"Suits me," I said.

Thomas let the subject drop and showed me how to couple the radio. When he'd completed the procedure I undid it and did it again. "Yeah, you got it." He put on his cap, tilting it over one eye. "So, I'll find some hay to hit. You're in charge."

He left and I locked the station and drove around town. Sunday night everything was closed, so I checked all the properties, putting the time of the inspection in my notebook. I drove by the house we'd rented. The light was still on in the living room. Fred was seeing *Double Indemnity* through to the end. I considered going in but decided against it. Mrs. Schuka might be the town gossip for all I knew. Tales of the honeymooners having a tryst while I was supposed to be on duty would soon filter back to Ferris, and I didn't need trouble with him. I had work to do.

As I'd done with Scott the night before, I took a run out to the gold mine. There was a watchman on the gates in a shack, listening to the only radio station that reached Elliot, rock music and commercials. I stopped in and asked him how everything was going, and he made me a cup of coffee, glad of the break. Then I drove back and rechecked my properties. It was one o'clock. I had seven hours left to fill.

The radio sounded a few minutes later. As I'd expected, it was Ferris. "Who's this?" he asked when I picked up the mike.

"Bennett, sergeant. I'm on Main Street, opposite the Headframe."

"Anything going down?"

"Quiet as a church. I've checked the properties and the mine. Everything's normal."

"Stay out there," he said. His voice sounded a little slurred. I wondered whether he was whiling the night away with a bottle of Canadian Club. "Police work is unpredictable."

"Right, sarn't. I'm planning to take my lunch at three-thirty."

"Half an hour's all you get," he said. "Don't be goin' in there an' sackin' out. You hear me?"

"Loud and clear, sergeant."

"See you at eight," he said, enunciating very carefully.

"I'll be there. Good night."

He didn't answer and I hung up. I sat for a minute, wondering why he had called. Why was he even awake now? Was he with a woman? That thought niggled at me. I wondered who she might be. The only likely candidate was Marcie from the station. They were very friendly, more friendly than either of them was with anyone else. I wondered whether she was married. Finally I decided I didn't care. It was better for me that he should be somewhere else—anywhere.

A few minutes later I had another call. It was a woman.

"Come quick, he's drinking an' he's beatin' me up."

"Address?"

"Sixty-one Finch," she said, then I heard the clatter at the other end and a squeal and the line went dead. I'd already made a note of the layout of the town. Finch was about three blocks away. I drove around to Sixty-one and stopped outside. It was the house I'd brought the drunk home to the night before. The lights were on and when I got out of the car I could hear shouting. Probably the neighbors could hear it too, but they had shifts at the mine to face in a few hours. They were ignoring it.

The front door was open and I knocked loudly and called, "Police."

A man's voice shouted "Get lost," but I heard a woman sobbing, so I went down the hallway to the kitchen. The man I'd brought home was standing over a woman who was sitting on a kitchen chair holding her hands over her ears. She looked up at me and I saw that her face was bruised.

"Okay buddy, that's enough," I said.

He straightened up and shouted, "Get outta my house. I didn't send for you."

"Your wife needs a doctor," I said. "Sit down."

He told me where to go and whirled to open the kitchen drawer. I figured he was going for a knife, so I stepped forward and kicked him behind the left knee, hard enough to fold it for him. He fell and I rolled him onto his face and held one hand behind his back.

"That's enough," I said. But he kept on struggling.

My left arm was weak but I managed to unsnap my handcuffs case and pull out the cuffs. I got them on his right wrist and knelt on it while I tugged his other arm free. He wrestled and almost threw me off, but he was uncoordinated and after about a minute I was able to snap the other wrist into the cuff. He swore and kicked, but he was out of action.

I stood up, rubbing my aching left shoulder. "What happened here?"

The woman sniffled and reached for a paper towel to wipe her face. "He was drinking. All day. I just told him he had to get up at six for work and he got mad, started hitting me. He kicked me as well. Look." She pulled up her skirt as innocently as a child and showed me a bruise on the front of her thigh. She let the skirt hem drop again. "I don't have to put up with this," she said, but she had the whine of a perennial victim.

"I'm going to charge him with assaulting you," I said.

The man on the ground squirmed over so he could look up at her. "You say one word about me in court and you're dead," he hissed.

She covered her face again and sobbed. I'd seen it all before but it didn't make it any easier. It was time for a little creative police work. I bent down and smiled into his face.

"You ever been in jail?" I asked him.

He frowned, startled. He'd been expecting a shot in the head, not words.

"'Course not," he shouted.

"Those guys are tough. They're not women, they're rough sons of bitches and they hate guys who beat up on women," I said. "Kill me and they'd respect you; bruise your old lady and they'll make you sorry you were born."

His mouth worked but no words came out. "I don't think you'd survive," I said. "And if you did it would be on account of letting the toughest guy in there have you for a girlfriend. Do I make myself clear?"

"Girlfriend?" The beer he'd drunk was evaporating now. "Girlfriend?" he said again, lying back down.

"Think about it," I told him. "And think quietly."

I touched the woman on the shoulder. "Do you have any children in the house?"

"No, there's just us."

"Okay. Get your coat, I'll take you to the hospital."

"Will you?" She looked up at me wonderingly. "Okay. I'll get it." She had been pretty once, I judged. Now she was heavy and poorly dressed. Any disposable income in the house went to the bar, not the clothing store.

She came back in an old quilted jacket. I levered the man to his feet and steered him to the door.

In the streetlights I could see a couple of curtains along the street pulled sideways as neighbors watched the drama. His wife came with us, pulling the door closed, not stopping to lock. I put him in the backseat and opened the front for her. She turned and smiled up at me, as if she were Cinderella going to the ball, the shadows accentuating the bruises on her face.

I took her to the hospital first. There was a nurse in emergency and she looked up when the woman came in. "Jean," she stood up, ignoring me. "Did that bastard hit you again?"

The woman nodded and the nurse came around the desk and hugged her. Over her shoulder she spoke to me. "This is my sister, officer. I'll take care of her."

"Good. I just need to get a statement. Could you get her a cup of coffee and give me a couple of minutes, please?"

"Sure. You want one?"

"Thanks, black."

The nurse left and I sat the woman down and asked her. "Now, can you tell me your name, please? And what happened."

"Jean Wilcox. That's Randy in the car. Like he was mad last night when he came home from the Headframe. He didn't get up till late this mornin'. Didn't eat nothin'. Just sat and watched TV an' drank beer. An' then when I reminded him he had to be at work in the mornin' he hit me."

"Does he do this all the time?"

Her eyes were full of tears. "He never used to. Not before the accident."

"He had an accident?"

"Not him, no. The one he seen."

I frowned. "Which accident? I've only been here a couple of days, I don't know anything about the town."

"The accident that the guy had who used to run the hotel. Like Randy was out that night, and he came home mad. An' he's been mad ever since then. Like drinkin' more, beatin' on me all the time."

"You don't have to stay with him. Why don't you stay with your sister for a couple of days, cool him out."

"He'd kill me," she whispered. "You don't know him, how he's been this last couple of months."

"I'll talk to him. You saw what happened at the house."

"Will that stop him?" She wanted to believe me.

"It already has. You saw it."

The nurse came back with coffee and I took mine and excused myself and went back to the car. I had some talking to do.

Randy had passed out in the backseat. He wasn't unconscious and he roused himself when I prodded him, but he wasn't making any sense, so I drove him to the station and put him in one of the cells. He sprawled on the bunk and was snoring before I could even take away his belt and bootlaces.

I stood and looked at him for a while, wondering what part he had played in the accident. I wished he was still in control, but he wasn't. I would have to wait to question him. In the meantime there was paperwork to do.

I took an occurrence form out of the file. His wife would have to be the principal witness, but for now I charged him with obstructing the police. No sense claiming assault, he hadn't got his hands on the knife, fortunately. I sat back in the chair and flexed my fingers. I'm a lousy typist.

When I'd typed the form I went to the file cabinet that Ferris had pointed out and checked the accident occurrences, looking for the one dealing with the death of Lewicki. There was nothing unusual about it. Sgt. Ferris had investigated. Lewicki's car had been speeding down the hill outside of town. Another driver had seen it swerving towards him and had hit the shoulder on the other side. Then Lewicki's car had swerved back and continued down the hill, failing to negotiate the bend at the bottom. It had smashed into the rock face, and Lewicki, who had not been wearing his seat belt, had been thrown out and killed.

Ferris's statement included the fact that the accident had been reported by Randy Wilcox. He had called the police and Ferris had investigated along with the officer on patrol. Ferris had noticed a strong scent of liquor on Lewicki's body and had asked the doctor at the hospital to check Lewicki's blood. He had been deeply drunk. The level of alcohol in his blood had been three times the legal limit. There was an inquest, and the coroner had returned a verdict of accidental death.

I put the file away and sat and thought. Wilcox was involved. Whatever he had done had changed him. You didn't need to be Sigmund Freud to realize that he had done something serious.

There was a coffee maker in the guardroom and I made a pot, extra strong, and filled two cups. I took them back to the cells and unlocked Wilcox, slamming the door noisily so that he groaned and woke up, holding his head. "Here, drink this," I said.

He was at the low point in his hangover, still drunk enough to be feeling queasy but with enough sense to realize the trouble he was in. He groaned again and held out his hand for the cup. I gave it to him and he sipped, then closed his eyes and shifted the cup to his other hand. "Lookit, I'm sorry, eh," he said.

"Too late for that now. You should have thought about it when you were beating on your wife."

"I din' mean no harm." His voice was a whine. "She knows that."

"You blacked her eye, you kicked her. That's harm, Randy. You're a punk."

His face began to shrivel and I saw tears in his eyes. "Y're right," he said. "I'm no goddamn good to nobody."

"You used to be a nice guy," I said. "What the hell happened to you?"

He blinked and swallowed. "I don' know." He shook his head. "Like I was always, like wild, ask anybody. But jus' drinkin', I never used to hit her."

He must have been around twenty-seven, I thought, in the prime of his natural vigor, but now he was sounding like a penitent old man on his deathbed.

"The way I hear it, you were okay up until July fourteenth." I was forcing the pace but I wanted answers while we were alone.

"Was it then?" He looked up at me, round-eyed over his coffee cup. "Like I'd've said three months."

"Three months since what, Wilcox?"

I spun around. Ferris was standing behind me, smiling. I smelled the whisky on his breath from six feet away. I straightened up. "Hi, sarge. I'm just getting a statement from my prisoner."

Ferris ignored me. He passed me in the doorway of the cell and stood over the prisoner who hunched down. "What was it this time, Wilcox? Wife-beating again? Remember what I told you last time you started that nonsense, do you?" Wilcox opened his mouth to speak and Ferris backhanded him, sending him sprawling across the cot, the enamel coffee cup clattering against the wall.

I scrambled to pick it up, coming between Ferris and the prisoner. "No, he wasn't beating his wife, sarn't. She says she fell. But he was ornery when I went in. I'm charging him with obstruct police."

Ferris was breathing harshly and he looked at me angrily. "Don't you ever try to come between me and a prisoner again," he said.

"Wouldn't dream of it, sarn't. Just want you to have all the facts, that's all. How about I go and get you a cup of coffee?"

He looked at me without speaking for about twenty seconds, then he grinned. "Yeah, that's a good idea. Why'nt you do that? Bring it out here, in two minutes time."

"Sure, sarn't." I grinned obligingly. "Oh, there's one other thing, sarn't."

"You are starting to seriously piss me off, Bennett," he said.

"Yeah, well, I wouldn't say anything except that it's important." I scratched my head ruefully. "Like I took his wife to the hospital, and while we were there the nurse took a look at this guy. She knows he isn't hurt at all."

"Out," Ferris said. "Get the hell out and stay out. Understand?"

"Sure." I left, closing the door to the cells behind me. I felt like a traitor to everything I believe in about doing police work. Ferris was going to beat my prisoner. But I couldn't do anything else without being fired from here and leaving Ferris and Chief Harding in charge for the rest of their lives. My only consolation was that if Wilcox was alert he would have heard the lie I told and would save himself any more pain by threatening to show the nurse the bruises.

It didn't work out that way. Maybe Wilcox felt guilty, felt he deserved the punishment. In any case it took about ninety seconds of thudding before Ferris joined me in the guardroom where I was sitting with two cups of coffee in front of me, reading the occurrence report I'd typed.

Ferris was breathing hard. "Which one's mine?"

I pointed to his cup and he picked it up. "They must've loved you, the last place you worked." He slurped a mouthful of coffee and sat down, putting his feet on the table.

"Why's that, sergeant?"

"You're a candyass," he sneered. "That sonofabitch was beating up his old lady. Guys like that don't hear you when you say things like arrest and assault. All's they hear is violence. I just taught him a lesson. It's easy. Wanna hear it?"

There was no choice. "I think I've got it," I said.

"Make sure you have," he said. "Lemme see what you've charged him with."

I passed over the occurrence sheet and he read it through without speaking. He was a slow reader. Then he put the coffee cup down and tore the form in two. "Garbage," he said.

"You don't want him charged?"

"No. I want him cured of beating up his wife. I just took care of that. Now why don't you finish your coffee and get back on patrol. I'll take him home."

"Whatever you say, sarn't." I drank the last mouthful of my coffee and stood up. "I'm on my way."

He watched me until I reached the door then he called out. "You're gonna be okay, you just have to learn."

"Thank you, sarn't. I'm trying." I grinned at him like the court jester and went out to finish my shift, feeling disgusted with him and with myself.

FIVE

THE NIGHT was endless. I went through the empty motions of checking all my properties every hour and drove out to the mine site, this time finding the gateman asleep in his shack. His dog woke him up and he was embarrassed and grumpy. After that I went back through town and out to the cluster of homes around the deserted pulp mill. It was a tumbledown ghost town and all of the houses were dark. Only eight of them out of the forty or so still looking habitable were apparently occupied. By the light of one streetlamp still working it was a depressing place.

In town, the Chinese restaurant opened at six, in time for any miners who didn't like getting their own breakfast to eat before work. I dropped in and got a coffee from the owner's wife, an endlessly smiling little woman who laughed loud and long at my few words of Mandarin and rattled away at me as if I were a linguist. The coffee was good and I paid for it, ignoring her protests, thanking her in my lousy Chinese and leaving her convulsed.

At five minutes to eight I drove back to the station and filled out my log while I waited for the day men to come out. There were two of them. Smith was there, his black eye turning yellow now. He shook my hand and thanked me awkwardly for helping him the night I'd arrived. He was taking another car but he also introduced me to the man taking over from me.

"This is Al, Alphonse Levesque. Al, this is Reid Bennett, the new guy. He gave me a hand at the Headframe on Saturday."

"Good thing you were there," Levesque said. He was short, only about five eight, and muscular. He had the broad face and coal black eyes of an Indian, but his droopy French-style mustache was completely Quebecois. My mother was French, from Calander in Ontario, and I speak the language well, but I didn't tell him. I just shook hands and passed the car over.

He checked the mileage. "Shit. You been drivin' all night," he said in disgust. "Eighty-six kilometers. I don' do' 'alf that in a night."

"Getting to know the area," I said, but I was learning. One trip to the mine site and none to the old mill was all the driving required. I would have to disconnect the speedometer if I did any prowling.

Ferris was on duty. He looked bandbox fresh, his uniform newly pressed, his boots gleaming. I'd known drunks like him in the Marines. No matter how hard they hit the bottle at night, not a trace of it showed during working hours, if you didn't count the slight tremor in the hands.

"Bennett," he said. "The chief wants a word with you."

"Me?" I was surprised. "Something the matter?"

"He'll tell you."

I went through to the chief's office, nodding at Marcie Sheridan, who had come on duty at eight. Harding was behind his desk, writing. I tapped on the door.

He looked up. "Ah, Bennett. Come in and shut the door."

I did so and he waved me to the chair. "Sgt. Ferris tells me you arrested Randolph Wilcox last night. What happened?"

"I got a distress call from his wife and went around there. He was drunk and abusive. He'd been assaulting her and he opened the knife drawer in the kitchen when I came in, so I didn't wait. I arrested him before he could get a knife and let it turn nasty."

Harding sucked his teeth. "Sarn't Ferris didn't say anything about a knife."

"I charged him with obstructing, sir. He didn't have time to get the knife out, or I'd have booked him with assault."

"Then you did right," he said. "Understand that we're not interested in running up our arrest counts in this town. We judge our performance by the lack of arrests, the lack of incidents that require official reports."

"Understood, sir. I know better than charge him with assaulting his wife. They never press charges; it wastes everybody's time."

The comment was about twenty years out of date. These days women have established their right to protection. I would have pressed the charges myself. Not in Elliot, it seemed.

"That's what I was going to tell you," Harding said. "In this town we get our share of domestic complaints. Our practice is to go out and shake down some frightening powder. If neces-

sary, take the guy outside and have a little talk with him to
reinforce the message. But don't bring them in unless it gets
heavy. You understand?"

"Perfectly, sir."

"Okay, then, get on home," he said.

I stood up and he grinned. "You're going to be all right," he
said. "You've got a lot to learn about the way we do things, but
if you handled Wilcox with one hand, you'll be okay."

I nodded, acting as if I were at a loss for words, and left.

Fred was up, making breakfast. She kissed me and asked me
how it had gone.

"Boring," I said. "One domestic complaint and seven and
a half hours of driving around. At least in Murphy's Harbour
I would have been in bed half the night."

"This isn't forever," she said. "Can you stand it?"

"I can stand anything, with you here making pancakes for
me when I come home."

"Chauv," she said. "I'd insist on your doing some of the
cooking but you're lousy at it. How you managed on your own
without getting scurvy or beriberi is beyond me."

"Tell you what. I'll do the dishes, if you promise not to tell
the guys at the station."

"Deal," she said. "Then what? You going to bed?"

"Depends," I said, and looked at her until she laughed out
loud.

WHEN I TOOK the assignment I hadn't expected it was going to
be easy. I'd told Fred it would only be a matter of weeks, but I
guess I'd known that it would take time for me to get at the
truth as the guys in the department came to accept me. In a way
it was like the war again. I settled down to endless patrol work,
knowing I had to be alert the whole time, on guard for the
sudden tiny signal that warned me of trouble. The only difference was Fred. She made the assignment not only tolerable but
the best time I'd ever spent working. She was endlessly cheerful. Another woman might have resented the smallness of the
town, the poor selection of fresh vegetables in the one store, the
ignorance of almost everyone here of the subjects that interested her. But not Fred. She's one of nature's enthusiasts. I
guess if she hadn't been that way she wouldn't have taken me
on.

One thing that did disappoint her was that none of the other policemen asked us over for a meal. It didn't surprise me. We'd been in town less than a week. We were all working different shifts, it would be hard to coordinate a visit, and besides, cops are not social animals. However, Fred didn't complain. She worked hard preparing the course she was going to give at the community center, starting the following week. About fifty people had already signed up for it, the most students they'd ever had for one offering, Jacques told her. She made several calls to Toronto looking for suitable scripts and was down at the bus stop in town every day picking up the material her friends sent for her to read and select.

Me, I went on checking the silent town at nights. Weekdays were easier than Sunday night had been. There were people in the bar at the Headframe until one, then drivers to caution when it closed. The Chinese place stayed open until then, and I got my coffee there and learned a few words of Cantonese from Wang Luk and his wife, whose name I still didn't know. But nothing broke about the case until the following Friday night.

I was in the car at a few minutes after midnight. Levesque was on duty at the station from seven P.M. until three in the morning. He told me that was the practice. One man stayed at the radio while the other patrolled on his own. That way there was backup if somebody called in with a problem. It made sense I guess, but I knew that the main trouble would occur at the Headframe. All those miners would be drinking their way into the weekend and there were going to be fights. For that reason I had brought Sam with me.

It had been a bit of a charade, breaking Ferris's order to leave him behind. I'd brought Sam to the station and left him in my own car until I'd taken over from the afternoon man. As soon as he had gone into the station I had moved Sam into the front seat of the police car. My left arm was still not working well and I knew I wouldn't be able to handle a couple of fit young drunks any better than Smith had the week before.

When I reached the hotel I could hear the uproar as soon as I got out of the car. I called Sam to heel and went in.

Two guys were hammering away at one another, big round-house swipes I'd have had no trouble with if both arms were working. I walked over to the back of the crowd, slowly. You never run into a fight, you give them time to let one of the guys realize he's getting the worst of it. That way you only have one battler to deal with.

The crowd was beery and excited but not hostile. I worked my way through to the center and said, "That's enough, guys."

I had to speak up to be heard, but as I'd expected, one of the fighters was glad to see me. It didn't make him stop, just gave him fresh energy to take another few swings at his opponent. But I could tell from the way he glanced at me that he was waiting for me to step in.

"I said knock it off," I repeated, and the crowd roared.

The only words I made out were, "The hell with him, you can take him, George. Finish the Polack first."

Somebody ran at me from behind, shoving me towards the fighters and the tougher of the two, then both of them, threw punches at me. It was the perfect out for the weaker guy. He would team up with the other guy in punching my lights out. Their own argument would be forgotten.

I shouted "Speak."

Sam barked his way through the crowd like a knife through butter. They scattered but the two fighters were too fired up to stop swinging at me. "Fight," I shouted, and Sam lunged at the man nearest me.

The guy roared with alarm and backed up and Sam turned on the other one until he quit.

"Now hold it right there," I commanded and they stood, meek and scared while Sam raged at them.

"Easy, boy," I said and he relaxed, standing beside me, watching the two men. A waiter scrambled to pick up the tables they'd knocked over. Another one appeared with a dustpan and a mop to get the broken glass. I ignored them.

"Okay," I told the biggest of the two fighters, "Let me see some ID."

He didn't argue. He pulled out his wallet and I said, "Just the ID."

He pulled out his driver's license and I stood and wrote down his name and address.

"You too," I told the other one and he did the same. I copied it down and then stood and looked at the pair of them without speaking. The crowd had gathered on the far side of them, still swigging their beer from the bottle, watching, silently.

"Couple of champions, eh?" I said and laughed. "You couldn't punch your way out of a paper bag."

One of the men swore but the other said nothing. I laughed again. "Still wanna finish it? That's good. Come on outside, the pair of you."

"What for?" the smaller one asked.

"You're going to fight fair where you won't smash anything. No kicking, no gouging, just a good clean fistfight." I laughed. "That's what you wanted, wasn't it?"

"That bastard said something about my old lady," the big one said.

"So come on outside, get your coats off and settle it." I waved at them.

They turned and looked at one another, like two schoolkids singled out by a teacher.

"Come on. I haven't got all night. Get on with the entertainment," I said.

The big one broke first. "The hell with him. He ain't nothin'."

The shorter one hesitated. His pride was hurt, but he knew that something more serious might be damaged if he argued.

"The hell with you too," he said and turned away.

"Hey," I called, and he stopped and turned back.

"You're a couple of dorks," I said. "I want you out of here and home. If I see either one of you in the hotel again tonight you're answering to me. Understood?"

They stretched the pause as long as pride demanded, then each of them nodded and they walked away towards the door. I followed them out and watched until they got into their cars and drove off. Then I stooped and fussed Sam, rubbing his head and telling him he was a good boy. I put him in the front seat of the car and went back inside.

The crowd was hooting with laughter, slapping one another on the back, reliving the battle. I said nothing, just walked up to the bar where Berger was handling the draft-beer tap, running it nonstop as his waiters filled their trays with new glasses.

He looked up and nodded to the barman who was dispensing the hard stuff. He was doing some business but not so much as his boss.

"Take over, Charlie," he said and rang up the order he had just completed. Then he spoke to me. "Thanks, off'cer. Come in the back."

He lifted the flap on his counter and I walked through and followed him into his office. It was like any bar office, small and cluttered, cases of liquor on the floor and the desk littered with invoices and business papers.

He sat down and indicated the other chair. "Take a load off. You like anything?"

"No thanks."

He looked at me levelly. "You AA or what? I'm not gonna ring up the chief and tell him you took a nip."

"No. But I'll be stretching to stay awake after you've been in bed six hours. Thanks, but not now."

"You sure don't drink much," he said. His tone was mild, he was as anxious to find out about me as I was about him. I made the first move.

"I'm a Black Velvet man," I said. "Off duty at this time of night I'd sink a couple with the best of guys. I just don't need to get any sleepier than I am."

"Oh." His mouth was a perfect circle. "You sure didn't look sleepy out there when the fight started."

"I don't have to do much, not with my dog along. He's a better cop than I am."

"Thought the sergeant said you wouldn't be using him."

"Yeah, he did, but I've still got a bum shoulder. I figured I'd need some backup."

"What's Ferris gonna say when he hears about it? Because you can bet your ass somebody's gonna say something."

We were fencing. I had a feeling that he didn't like Ferris but I could have been wrong. I couldn't force the pace.

"I guess I'll find out soon enough," I said. "But I figure I'll have a word with the chief. He's hard but he likes things cooled out. If my dog does a good job it's dumb to leave him behind."

"Good luck," he said. He paused and I sat and smiled, weighing him up. He had a worried face, leathery but pale. He looked like one of those tiny statuettes that Quebec woodcarvers make, deeply chiseled lines each side of his nose, long chin, receding hair.

"The chief seems fair," I said.

"You could say that, I guess."

He seemed to want to say something else. I wondered if he was carrying a grudge about the money he had to pay out to the police or if he was some favorite of the chief's, glad to have the license to run the bar in this town, a license to print money. I played it right down the middle.

"I couldn't say anything else, could I? Even if I didn't like the guy. He's the boss. I do like he says."

"You were a chief yourself, weren't you?" He opened his desk drawer and took out a pack of Old Port cigars. He offered one to me but I shook my head. He grinned and shook his own head at my refusal, then lit up. "Any bars in the place you worked?"

"Couple. One hotel where they had a cocktail bar, that was where the tourists drank, or the locals on anniversaries and birthdays. The other one was mostly a beer joint—they did the blue-collar trade, what there was of it."

He waved out his match and laid it carefully in the ashtray. I could tell from his precision that he wanted to probe me.

"You have any arrangements with them?"

"Nothing special. I used to drop in a couple of times through the week, more on weekends. If they had trouble, they'd call."

"And what was in it for you?"

"Company mostly, the odd beer or shot. Both of them used to give me a pretty good Christmas present."

"Yeah?" He was leaning forward, his face wreathed in smoke. "Like what would it be?"

"The beer joint used to send me a case or two of Labatt's Blue. The bar usually sent rye. Usually Crown Royal, pretty upmarket for me."

"Yeah?" He said nothing else, and I made the next move in the chess game.

"No big deal. Of course, we were pretty close to the highway. The OPP was just outside the door if they needed any extra support."

"The nearest OPP post to here is a hundred miles away," he said softly and again he waited.

I looked at him and grinned. "Does that mean we have different rules in Elliot?"

"You could say that." He puffed his cigar.

"Like what?" I asked cunningly.

He took his cigar out of his mouth and looked at me levelly for about a minute. "Why do I get the feeling that you're not as dumb as you sound?"

"Maybe you've got second sight." I laughed. "Hell, if I was bright would I still be a constable at the age I am?"

"You're married to a class lady," he said. "A bright woman. Yeah, I heard, an actress. She's gonna turn all the broads in town into Farrah Fawcetts or whatever. I don't think she'd've gone for a dummy."

I changed my tack. "Listen, if you've got a point to all this, let's get to it."

He picked up his cigar and tapped the ash off the end very carefully. "You're bright," he said. "And you're experienced. I did my homework. You were in the T'ronto department. You've been a chief."

"In a one-man band," I said. "I did exactly what I'm doing here, only for less money."

He changed his tone, conversational now, not so serious. "How'd'you like this place?"

"So far so good. I was born in Coppercliff. Mining towns are my stomping ground."

"And how does your wife like it? I mean, no theater, not even a movie house, just weekly flicks in the community center, sitting on hard chairs. No bookstores, none of the big-city stuff a woman like her is used to."

"You don't have to worry about my wife. I'll do that," I said.

He shrugged. "Of course. So you plan to settle down here and live happily ever after?"

"That's it. Have some kids, maybe get back into hockey."

He sniffed. "How would you like to be the chief?"

I straightened up and stared at him, then laughed. "An' who's gonna vote me into the job? Bounce the chief, put me ahead of Sgt. Ferris on the application sheet?"

"Think about it." He stood up and stuck out his hand. "I like you, Bennett. Thanks for the good work tonight."

"I'll tell my dog," I said, shaking his hand. "Thanks for the vote of confidence. It's nice to be appreciated."

I went back out and resumed patrol, chewing over what I'd heard. The most sense I could make out of it was that he was tired of paying off the chief. He figured it would be cheaper or easier to work with me in the job. Well, if that was the case I would go along with him until I could put a wire on him and get the evidence I needed.

But on the other hand, I thought gloomily, as the town quieted down for the night, maybe he was testing me out on the chief's behalf. Maybe Harding had asked him to see if I was on the level. I would be well advised to move slowly with him, I decided. I didn't want to tip my hand.

I spent an uneventful night, booking off at eight in the morning. Ferris was not on duty, he came in late on Saturday to cover the seven-to-three shift, so I didn't get any flak about using Sam. I drove home and parked my car. When I got to the back door there was a box sitting there, a plain cardboard container that had held paper towels. It was open at the top. When I looked in I saw another box inside, gift-wrapped, with a card on it.

I lifted the whole bundle indoors and Fred greeted me in surprise. "Hi, honey, been shopping this early?"

I set the box on the table and kissed her. Then she peered in. "Gifties," she said. "Who's it from?"

"An anonymous friend, I figure," I said. I tore the card open. It was one of those all-purpose greeting cards with just a picture on the front. Inside was written. "Thanks. Let's talk again." There was no signature.

"Curiouser and curiouser," Fred said. "What's in the package?"

"Unless I miss my guess it's a case of rye." I tore the paper off it and found I was right. A dozen Black Velvet.

Fred looked at me, her eyes wide. "What happened?"

"Let's just say I'm starting to get myself on the inside," I said. "This is our secret."

She shook her head sadly. "I don't like this, Reid."

"No more do I, but it's the first opening in the maze so far."

SIX

I CHECKED the case all over. "What are you doing?" Fred wanted to know.

"Making sure it hasn't been tampered with," I said. "If this is a setup they may have marked it some way so the chief could waltz in here and prove I've been taking favors." I satisfied myself there were no secret symbols on the sides and then opened it. Twelve bottles of Black Velvet, in the familiar black cylinder. I opened one of the cylinders and checked the bottle. The government bond seal was intact, but there was a tiny squiggle from a felt pen tip at one end of the label. I checked all of them. They were all marked.

"That's it," I said. "The sonofabitch is trying to find out if I'm on the take. If I accept these, he's going to tell the chief and they'll come here and find them and I'll be thrown off the force."

"Then that means he wants you to be honest," Fred said. "He's testing you. If you pass he'll come clean about the chief and try to have you promoted. I hear he's on the town council. He could probably swing it."

"This could be the break I need," I said. "I'll run it back down there right now, and he'll know I'm straight."

"What will you say?" She had her long red hair pulled back with a strand of thick wool. She looked about eighteen and beautiful, but this was work and she was all business.

"I'm not sure. I don't want to scare him off by coming on too sanctimonious."

"Won't he trust you more for it?" she frowned.

"It needs phrasing very carefully," I said, then kidded, "Come on, you're the drama expert in this house. What do I say?"

She sat down and folded her hands in her lap thoughtfully.

"It seems to me that he wants you on his side. That doesn't mean he wants you straight, just that he wants to be sure where you stand."

"So what do I tell him?"

"How about this?" She grinned suddenly. "Yes, this would be good." She told me the line she'd thought of.

It sounded good to me. She ran me through it a couple of times. Then I left, putting the box in the trunk of my car and driving back downtown to the hotel. It was closed at this hour. The cleanup man was slopping his mop around. He looked up in surprise when I came in the back door, carrying the box. "We're closed," he said.

I kept my voice low, angry. "Where's Berger?"

"In bed," he said in surprise. "Who're you?"

"My name's Bennett. Go and tell him I'm here to see him. And hurry." Fred had gone over the scene with me, playing it like a drama. "Remember, action is character," she'd said. "It's not just what you say, it's how you say it that's important."

It worked. The guy leaned his mop against the bar and went up the stairs behind the door marked Private. He was down again in a minute. "Boss says he'll be right down. Wait in the office."

I nodded curtly and went into the office, scooping up a bottle of Black Velvet and a shot glass as I passed the bar. The cleaner looked at me in surprise but said nothing.

I poured myself an ounce and a half, sipped off the half ounce and gargled in it before swallowing, to make my breath as boozy as possible. The bottle was already half empty; he wouldn't know how much I'd had.

He came in a couple of minutes later, dressed but unshaven and rumpled. "What's going on?" He sounded angry.

"Sit down," I said and he did, falling silent. I slugged the other ounce of rye and looked at him. "I wanna know what's going on. Last night you made a funny kind of speech to me. Sounded to me like you were trying something on for size. Then this morning there's a case of my kind of booze on the doorstep."

Now he nodded. "Yeah. Call it a gratuity. I don't mind what you call it. A gesture of friendship. Whatever."

"You know the rules about cops taking payola," I said. "You think I'm gonna put my job on the line for a lousy case of rye?"

That was the line Fred had come up with. And it worked. I could almost see the wheels turning behind his eyes.

"You said you took gifts from the bars where you used to work."

He had no tone at all in his voice. We were sparring again.

"This isn't Christmas and I haven't done you favors to warrant a case of the stuff. For all I know you're about to call the chief and tell him to look in my closet and find a marked case of rye. The chief comes in and I go out. Is that it? You the local testing facility for crooked cops?"

"You're being paranoid," he said, but he licked his lips.

"You figure I'm paranoid? If I'm going to risk my job its not for something I could buy myself if I wanted." The second half of Fred's line, the invitation.

He looked at me without speaking for a long time. Then he spoke, and he smiled as he did. "Don't screw around, do you?"

"Not for nickels and dimes."

"Then for how much?"

I laughed scornfully. "I'm not paranoid and I'm not stupid. I'd like to be out of here by the time I'm fifty, able to set up somewhere, do something else." It was still open-ended. The ball was still in his court.

He rubbed his hands over his uncombed hair. "That sounds heavy," he said at last.

"You said last night you wanted me to be the chief. On his pay I could probably save enough living here to cut out on schedule." I paused, but he waited until I went on. "So I've brought back the case of liquor. It's on your bar, still in the box you sent it in. If you want to talk about promotion, I'm here to listen."

I heard voices outside—a couple of men—and I saw Berger's eyes flick towards the door. "I'm being squeezed," he said. And then there was a tap on the door.

"Come in," he called.

The door opened and Harding came in, followed by Ferris. "Morning, Bill," Harding said evenly. He nodded to him and turned to me. "What are you doing here, Bennett?"

"Talking to Mr. Berger, sir."

"Your wife said you would be," Harding said. "Right before we searched your house."

"If you were looking for a certain case of liquor that turned up on my doorstep, look behind you," I said.

I stood up and shoved past him into the bar. He looked surprised but said nothing and came with me.

"There must have been a wrong delivery," I said softly. "This came to my house and I've just brought it to the only place in town it could have been addressed to."

Harding looked into the box and opened the case of liquor. "It's been opened," he said.

"Right. It was wrapped when it arrived. I thought maybe someone had left off a box of books for my wife. When I saw what it was I knew where it was intended to go, so I brought it here."

Harding looked at me out of cold eyes. He didn't speak for a long time. Then he said, "You did the right thing. We got an anonymous call that you were receiving payoffs from the hotel."

"I'm new in town but I'm a longtime copper," I said coldly. "I know the rules on gratuities, chief. Not that I knew it was a gratuity. I haven't done anything to earn one. But I figured it had been misdelivered, so I brought it down here. Mr. Berger thanked me and poured me a drink." Fred would have been proud of me. This was all improvisation.

Harding said, "Okay, that takes care of it. You can go home now."

"Right," I said. I leaned back into the office. "Thanks for the shot, Mr. Berger."

Ferris was standing in the office door and I spoke to him next. "And sergeant, you're probably going to hear that I used my dog last night to cool out a fight. I would appreciate the chance to take him on patrol with me at nights. He can do things a man can't. He's good, and he's free."

I turned to Harding. "Chief, this isn't the place to make the request, but with respect, I would like you to listen to what Mr. Berger has to say about my dog and give me permission to use him. He gets the department a lot of extra respect."

Harding was grinning—a thin, satisfied tightness around the mouth. "I'll listen and I'll give Sgt. Ferris his instructions," he said. "Now get to bed."

"Right sir." I stood to attention and then turned away. I was frustrated. Berger had been on the point of giving me the information I needed. He wanted out of his bind. I could see that much now. But I still had no evidence. When I finally got his confidence I would have to wire him and have him meet with the chief and tape the payoff procedure. Then I could call in the police commission and head out of town. For now I could only wait and hope he would talk to me the next time I came in.

I slept badly but was back at the station at eleven-thirty for duty. I was surprised to find Harding there, dressed in civilian clothes. He was in the guardroom, talking to the afternoon man, Al Levesque. When I came in Harding turned and I nodded, "Good evening, chief."

"Good evening, Bennett." That was it. Neither of them spoke as I slipped into my uniform and checked the teletype pad for messages. Then Harding told Levesque. "Your turn on the street, Levesque. Bennett can handle the radio this evening."

Levesque looked surprised but he said nothing, just put on his down-filled parka with the police crest and nodded to me. "No calls so far, but you can expect Mrs. Frazer to call around one. That's when her 'usband gets in from the 'otel."

"You usually go down there?"

"Sometimes." He shrugged. "Nineteen Falcon Street."

I nodded and he left. Harding looked at me, not speaking.

There was nothing much to do but wait for the phone to ring, so I picked up the empty coffeepot. "Think I'll set up for the night. Like a cup, chief?"

It broke the tension he was trying to build. "No," he said shortly. Then he said, "You did well, this morning, Bennett."

"Just going by the book, chief. I know a lot of hotels like the police on their side. I don't mind accepting the occasional drink, but when they start wrapping glass around it and sending it to the house, they're trying to own you. I don't want that."

"You would have been out of this town by noon if you'd taken that liquor," he said. Except for what I knew of his own dealings he sounded like any normal police chief, straight down the middle.

"I don't want to screw up," I said. "My wife's settled in. I like the town. We can make a life here."

"You can," he nodded. "And it's not a dead-end job. They're looking at a mining prospect in the bush, not fifteen miles from here. If that comes on stream we'll be growing. The town will grow, get a proper shopping mall maybe, another couple of thousand people. The department will expand. We'll need a second sergeant."

I looked at him, trying to seem cunning. "There's a lot of guys ahead of me in seniority here."

"But not in experience," he said. "You'd be my first choice."

I grinned. "That would be great."

He nodded. "There's only one thing to look out for."

"What's that?"

"Corruption," he said. I widened my eyes a little and he nodded. "Oh yeah, it happens. We had one guy, we fired him. He was shaking down the hookers, or trying to. They come into town on the fifteenth and the last day of the month—paydays. They park their Winnebagos and go to work."

"It's the same in a lot of bush towns."

He nodded dismissively. "It happens. If you don't let the single guys get laid a couple times a month they'd be out screwing schoolkids. I don't like it, but I turn a blind eye to it. I just make sure there's no slimebag in a red hat taking a cut off their earnings. And then this so-called officer of the law tried his shakedown. I had him out of here by morning. He was lucky not to go to jail."

"Sonofabitch," I said musingly. "He must've been crazy as well as bent."

Harding nodded. "So, as your superior, and, in a way, as a friend, I want to warn you about Berger at the Headframe."

"He tries to set guys up?"

"Some of them," he said. "He tried it on Constable Scott and he's tried it on you."

"But not the others? Why us?"

Harding shrugged. He was a good-looking guy for his age, around fifty-five, good lean face, a typical Rotarian. Butter would not have melted in his mouth. "I don't understand the man. I'm just giving you the facts. He's trouble, and I suggest you stay away from him. No going into the place except off duty, during business hours. No more drinks in the office. It's for your own good. Understood?"

"Yes sir." I could see what he was doing. He wanted me neutralized. My honesty that morning had made him more suspicious. He was warning me off the track.

"Okay. I just wanted to have a talk with you, explain how things stood." He got up. "So that's it. Keep your nose clean and you're looking at a good future in Elliot."

"I'll do my best, chief." He turned away and I said, "Oh, just one thing, sir."

"What's that?" He was frowning as he turned around.

"My dog. He can cool out a fight faster than a couple of men can do it. He can run a suspect down. He can track. He's trained and he's docile, but he's a real authority. I'd very much like your permission to take him with me on patrol."

He tightened his frown up a notch, thoughtfully. "I don't want anybody coming to me with a complaint about being bitten," he said.

"He never bites. If somebody tries to fight he holds onto their hand. If they've got a weapon he grabs that hand. Just clamps on it, doesn't sink his teeth in."

Suddenly he grinned. "Why not?" he said. "I've already spoken to Sgt. Ferris, but in light of our conversation here, I'll bring him up to date in the morning. Yes. Use the goddamn dog. Now I'm going home."

"Thanks, chief. Good night."

He left and I sat thinking about what he had said. It seemed to back up the story I'd been sent here to investigate, that he was corrupt. If it was true, he was being careful. I was from outside, and he knew now that I was straight. Maybe he already suspected I was a plant. That's why he was stringing me along, offering the faint chance of a promotion as a way of appearing pleased with what I'd done. But he would be more careful than ever in his dealings now. I would have to be extra cautious.

It was quiet in the station. There wasn't so much as a phone call until three o'clock. Levesque didn't bother calling in. For all I knew he was in bed somewhere. But he returned on time, grumpy and tired. "Why's the chief givin' you the easy job? You're new."

"Wanted to see I could do it right, I guess."

He swore, then grinned. "Not your fault, eh?"

"It's a tough job but somebody's gotta do it." I matched his grin. "How'd it go? Any trouble at the hotel?"

"Nothin'. When I come in there a couple guys ask where's the dog. I t'ink dat dog a' yours do a good job."

He left and I set the phone-radio connection and went out in the car, taking Sam with me. The town was settling into a Sunday night. By this time everything was closed and the lights were out. There was a party going on, in one of the bungalows. Cars lined the curb and the rock music was audible from the roadway, but nobody was complaining. I made a note of the address and drove on around town, then out to the mine site and back, still wondering how to make my next move.

The answer came to me as I got back to the party scene. It was after four by now and the people were going home, trickling out, a couple at a time. They were saying noisy farewells at the door and a lot of them looked the worse for wear, so I parked the police car at the end of the block where they could see it. It was a simple drunk test. If they were sober enough to recognize that I was watching and drive carefully, they were sober enough to drive. You couldn't do that in a city, but here nobody had more than a few blocks to go and they were the only things moving.

I recognized one of the couples. It was the Wilcox family. Randy was pretty drunk. His wife was trying to persuade him to give her the keys but he was refusing. I waited until he got into the driver's seat then drove up nose to nose with him and flicked my headlights to high beam. I could see him squinching up his face at the brightness, trying to work out what it was.

He sat there, and I got out and opened his door. "Hey," he said and tried to close it.

"Out of the car, Randy. Jean, you take over."

"She ain' gonna drive," he said, but his voice was dull. His wife was in no danger of another beating tonight.

"Yes, she is." I had hold of his wrist and I squeezed until I had his full attention. Like a lot of drunks, he was smartening up now he was in trouble.

"I want to talk to you," I said.

"What about?" His voice was less slurred, he was concentrating hard.

"I'll tell you. You be at the hockey arena at four this afternoon. Got that?"

"What for?"

"Just be there. Otherwise I'm going to have to give you a Breathalyzer test and you're going to lose your license."

"When'dja say?" He bent forward like an old man, putting all his concentration into hearing me.

"Four o'clock this afternoon. Be there."

"At the 'rena. 'kay." He nodded at me and I kept my grip on his wrist, pulling him out of his seat and around his car to put him in the passenger seat. I fastened his seat belt and leaned down to speak to his wife. "Drive carefully, okay?"

"Sure will." She sounded bright and cheerful. Maybe Sgt. Ferris's old-fashioned message had gotten through to her husband. Randy was keeping his fists off her. Good. I shut his door and went back to the police car. Jean backed up neatly and slipped around me, driving quietly away. Now all I had to hope was that Randy would remember my message when he sobered up.

SEVEN

FRED AND I walked up to the arena around three that afternoon. Fred had a couple of plays with her and she wanted to show Jacques her choice and get his opinion. Like a lot of other people in the recreation business, he worked just about every day. He was single, Fred had told me, and he had nothing more exciting to do.

We went into his office and they were soon deep in conversation. I excused myself and strolled out to stand by the glass wall that overlooked the ice surface. There was a hockey game in progress, and one of the teams was being coached by Scott. The kids were around fourteen. One or two of them were very good, but I noticed Scott gave each one of them equal ice time even though his side was down one goal. It pleased me. The more I saw of Scott the more I liked the way he did things.

He was too busy to notice me, so I opened the door and sauntered in, catching him bending over the boards, bellowing at one of his defensemen. "Keep on him! Check him!"

He looked around and saw me. He grinned and waved then turned back to his kids. One of them got a penalty, and Scott roared as loudly as any fan at the ref, then turned to me. "He should have skated harder. Then he wouldn't have had to hook him from behind."

It was pleasant to be there in the chill of the rink, and I watched until the end of the period. When Scott went into the dressing room to chew out his team, I went out to the coffee machine. It was quarter to four. Randy Wilcox came in with his wife.

He said something to her and she left, nodding pleasantly at me but getting lost. There was a volleyball game going on in the gym and she went in to watch.

"You wanted to see me." He was uptight. He looked hung over but there was no booze on his breath.

"Yeah. I wanted to talk to you about the accident."

He looked around, nervously. "Here?" I noticed that he didn't ask which accident. He knew what I was talking about.

"Why not?"

"Somebody might hear."

"Let's go sit in the stands." I shoved the door open and we went out to sit high up in the seats, behind the few supporters, who were all sitting front and center.

I handed him my untouched coffee. "Here, I don't really need this."

"Okay, thanks." He took it and cracked the lid, dropping it casually underfoot. He sipped and said, "What's this about? I told the sergeant everything I seen the night it happened."

"I'd like you to go over it for me, okay?"

"What for?" He didn't look at me as he spoke, and I knew I was onto something important.

I just smiled at him.

He gave in and asked, "You been talking to the sergeant?"

"No. I just heard you were there, that's all. And your wife mentioned it that night."

"None of her goddamn business," he said angrily.

"She said it turned you into a mean mother," I said. "As a cop, I don't like mean mothers. I want to know what happened. If you're in any kind of trouble, maybe we can sort it out, let you take life easy again."

"Why'd you wanna do that?"

"I've been a cop a long time. I figure it's better to have friends than enemies. Okay?"

He said nothing for almost a moment. The teams came out again and started to play. I saw Scott glance up at me once then turn back to his coaching.

"Yeah, well I was there. I was comin' back from seein' my dad. He lives out by the old mill, you know."

"What did you see?"

"I saw the other vehicle coming after me in the wrong lane. I hit the shoulder an' it swerved back an' then missed the curve an' hit the rock on the side of the road."

I knew he was lying. Ordinary citizens don't say vehicle, they say car or truck. He had been coached in his story, by a policeman.

"Bullroar," I said, and he turned and stared at me.

"'Makes you say that?" He was scared, not angry.

"That's not what you saw. Is it? Come on Randy. I wasn't born yesterday. Somebody told you to say that."

"No, that's what happened." He shook his head then buried his nose in the coffee cup. His hand was trembling.

"I heard that Lewicki was dry. Hadn't had a drink in years."

"Well, he fell offa wagon that night, I guess."

"Did he? Or did somebody push him off?"

"It wasn't me," he blurted, then checked himself.

"But you saw who it was?"

"I don't know," he said miserably.

"Then what did you see?" I kept my tone conversational, not threatening him. I figured he'd had his fill of threats.

"I seen the cop car at the top of the hill. An' then I went by I seen Gus's car there as well."

"And that's all you saw?"

He shook his head again. "No."

"What else? Come on Randy, this is eating the guts out of you. Get it out."

"I seen Sgt. Ferris there, like beside Gus's car. The light was on in the car, like the door was open. An' I saw him holdin' up a bottle. I couldn't see what he was doin'. Not prop'ly. Looked like he was tippin' it was all."

"Then what?"

He folded both hands around his coffee. "Well I'd had a couple beers with my ol' man, right. So I din't stop. I went on down the hill an' then I seen a car comin' down after me. Like it was Gus's car. I foun' that out later. Right then I just hit the gas an' got outta the way. It was barrelin'. Then I heard the bang behind me when he hit. But I din't stop. I wen' right home."

"Then what happened?"

He looked at me. "Listen. I gotta know why you wanna hear all this. Like, this was a while back."

"It's not going any further. Let's just say I'm a nosy sonofabitch, okay?"

"I never told anybody," he said. His breath was gusty but there was no booze on it. He was sober, and he was telling the truth.

"I can guess," I said. "You got a call from the sergeant. He said you'd been drinking and he was going to lock you up for impaired driving, right?"

His eyes widened. "He told you?"

"You made a deal with him. You reported the accident and he let you go, am I right?"

He nodded respectfully. "That's the God's honest truth, off'cer."

"Okay, thanks. That's all I needed to know. I owe you one. Do yourself a favor, forget the whole thing, okay. There won't be any drunk driving charge."

"There won't?"

"No, it's too late now. But keep your nose clean. Stay out of the hotel a bit more. Spend more time at home."

"Yeah." He frowned at me, as if he suspected I had a thing for his wife. "Yeah, my dad's been sayin' the same thing."

"Listen to him. He knows what he's talking about."

"Okay." He switched hands with his coffee and stuck out his right. I shook it. His hand was like leather. "Thanks," he said. "I think I'll go see what the wife's doin'."

"Good idea." I grinned at him and he left, not looking back.

I stayed where I was until the game finished. Scott's guys had tied but they couldn't score the clincher. I went down as he was seeing the last of them off the ice.

"Good game. When are they playing again?"

"Tuesday night, here—a league game. Against the Olympia Titans. Eight o'clock."

"I'll be here. It was a good game."

The last of his boys clunked past on his blades and Scott looked at me intently. "What was Wilcox on about?"

"Seems like I made myself a friend the other night," I said lightly. "When the sergeant let him go he thought it was on account of me. Wanted to thank me."

"I've known him for fifteen years," Scott said doubtfully. "He never spoke to a cop before unless he was in trouble."

"How many times has he thought he was going inside?" I laughed but I was careful. Scott was a good guy but he didn't have to be involved.

"Well, I guess there's a first time for everything," he shrugged. "Anyway, I've got to talk to my guys. See you."

He walked away into the dressing room and I went back out to the office and checked on Fred. Jacques was on his feet, acting out a part from the play. He was putting everything into it, but even I could see how hammy he was. When he saw me he closed the book. "Yeah, I could do that," he said to Fred. "I'd like to."

"Great. That just leaves three more men to find." She was all business. "Do you think we'll get that many at the class?"

"None signed up so far," he said. "Maybe you can round up your husband."

It was a joke and we all laughed and they broke up their meeting. Fred held my arm as we walked back alone on the street as the few lights came on. It had begun to snow lightly, and she stuck out her tongue to catch a flake. "Delicious," she said. "Like the thought of having you at home tonight for a change."

"I'm glad you're taking to the place." I squeezed my arm down on hers. "Tomorrow we're going on an outing."

"Where to?" she asked in surprise.

"Thunder Bay. You'll like it after this place. It's a big town."

"Hey," she tugged at my arm. "Would that mean staying over in some motel?"

"It could, if you played your cards right," I said and she laughed. A car passed us, driving slowly through the swirling snow.

My real reason for leaving town was to get a chance to call Kennedy in Toronto. This had been his idea. He wasn't sure how secure any phone in Elliot would be. So we drove to Thunder Bay and I made my call and filled him in. Then I went with Fred while she shopped and we had dinner and went to the theater. It was good to be able to relax for twenty-four hours. The following morning we drove home, stopping off for lunch along the way. We got back around three in the afternoon, and I took Sam for a run. It was difficult, running on the snow, but I went out to the highway and put in three miles before coming home. I was hot and pleasurably tired but Fred's face brought me back to reality. She was looking horrified.

"What's up? Bad news?" I asked.

"Terrible," she said. "Mrs. Schuka came up while you were out. She says there was a cave-in at the mine. A miner was trapped and they just got his body out this afternoon."

"Someone you knew?" I asked.

She shook her head. "No. But that doesn't matter. They're all such good square people. I feel terrible." She paused. "Maybe you knew him. You've met more of the men than I have. His name was Wilcox."

I was heading for the shower but I stopped in my tracks. "Randy Wilcox?"

"Yes, I think that's what she said." Fred frowned. "Did you know him?"

"I had the pleasure of locking him up for beating his wife," I said. "But he was a reasonable guy aside from that one time. It's a pity."

She looked at me almost coldly. "You take this kind of news very casually, Reid. Is it because you're a cop?"

I didn't want her to know what I was thinking. If someone had arranged Wilcox's accident they might have the same thing in line for me. She didn't need to know that.

"I'm sorry, pet. It's just that my dad died the same way. The memory is still painful."

She softened at once and came over to hold me. "Poor old Reid," she said and kissed me. "I'm sorry. I'd forgotten about that. I was so shocked about this man."

I kissed her and said gently, "It happens in mines, Fred. These guys and their families live with that. It's one of the things you have to accept when you live in a town like Elliot."

I showered and slept and had a late snack with a strong cup of coffee. Fred had cocoa. She yawned when I left. "All that high living yesterday is telling on me," she said. "I'm hitting the hay the moment you leave."

"Sleep tight," I told her, getting my coat. "See you at eight."

"Right." She came and hugged me. She was barefoot and seemed tiny and fragile. I kissed her, hoping nothing was going to cause her any pain, ever. "Take care," she said.

I put my finger on her nose and said, "You too. Don't fall out of bed."

She laughed and I went to work.

There was a coffee can on the table in the guardroom with a hand-lettered sign: For the Wilcox family. It contained a number of five-dollar bills and I put one in while Thomas watched me.

"That's three this year," he said, yawning. "Gettin' expensive, workin' here."

"What happened? I heard it was a cave-in."

He yawned again. "It ended up like that, but I heard it was a screwup with the blasting. Like he was a blaster and he was setting the charges. His partner had gone back to the safety room for something and then, boom." He clapped his hands together. "From what they found they think he screwed up with a detonator, set off all the charges before he'd put 'em in place.''

"And that made the stope collapse?''

"Yeah.'' Thomas stood up and got his parka. "Shouldn't have, but maybe some of the securing bolts weren't in deep enough. There's gonna be an investigation, I know that much.''

"Are we involved?''

He shook his head. "Naah. The Workman's Compensation people handle it, coroner's office. They both got representatives in town now.'' He shoved the teletype list towards me. "Listen, I got a date. There's a couple stolen cars on the list, nothing else.''

"Okay, you can split.'' It was a few minutes before twelve and he came out with me and signed the car over. I put Sam into the front seat and drove into town. Wilcox's death was eating me up. It seemed to me he had been killed because he spoke to me. Murdered! For the sake of one conversation. It was a burden I would carry all my life. I tried to make sense of the sequence of events. I was surprised to hear that his assistant had been in the safety room. All mining safety procedures are carefully worked out so that no one man has to remember everything. He works with a partner. Both of them go through all the steps together. If Wilcox's partner had left the scene early it could mean he knew in advance that something was going to go wrong. It could even mean he had sabotaged the charges in some way. The thought chilled me. The only reason I knew of to kill Wilcox was that he had talked to me.

EIGHT

FERRIS WAS on duty when I came off duty in the morning. "I want you back at seven tonight," he said. "It's payday at the mine, and we generally get a gang of hookers in town. Also the guys can get kind of rowdy, paynights. We put two men on patrol together."

"Right. I'll be here." I nodded and left.

I was back at quarter to seven that evening. It happened to be the night of Fred's first class at the community center. I drove her over on my way to work. "I'll get one of the women to drop me home," she said when I let her off at the door.

"If Jacques offers, have him out of the house by three; I'll be home then," I said.

She laughed. "Don't worry your pointed little head, Charlie Brown," she said and kissed me. I watched her trot up the three steps to the front door. She turned to wave and smile and disappeared. I waved back and drove on to the station. I found that my partner was going to be Walker.

We chatted as we checked the teletype for messages, waiting to be paraded out. He seemed casual, a normal-enough copper, except for Scott's words of warning. "Bringing Rin Tin Tin with us?" he asked.

"Yeah. The chief gave permission."

"Good." Walker grinned. "Last payday there was a rhubarb. Some horny Polack tried to jump the line."

"What's the routine?" I asked.

He shrugged. "Nothin' clever. We just keep the peace, if you'll pardon the pun. It generally clears up by midnight, just after. The girls go through the guys like a dose of salts."

We went out to the car and I put Sam in the backseat and we drove past the hotel. "No sense stopping in," Walker said. "All the action's at the other end of town, for a while anyways."

We found the two trick trucks set up on a wide lot where someone had excavated gravel. The resulting flat area had been bulldozed out to serve as a campsite for any visitors in recreational vehicles. The township kept the snow plowed out, and the place was jammed with cars and trucks parked every which way. At the back of the lot stood the pair of Winnebagos.

The other police car was there. We got out and spoke to the two men on duty, Scott and Levesque. "Nothin' 'appen," Levesque said. "The girls got 'ere aroun' five. Guys started comin' out after the shift. Been steady. No trouble."

"We didn't check the Headframe," Walker said. "Take a look in on your way back to the station."

"Will do," Levesque said. "I could sure use a beer. Makes me t'irsty watchin' all these ashes gettin' 'auled."

Scott said nothing, just nodded at me and smiled sadly.

Walker and I got back into the car and he lit a cigarette.

"Great, huh?" he said, blowing smoke. "Join the p'lice force an' sit around a parking lot watching illegal activity takin' place under our noses."

"The chief figures it's easier than not getting the guys fixed up." I was testing the water, wondering how he would respond. It was possible that the chief had put him with me to make sure I didn't talk to the girls, see if they had an arrangement going.

"I guess he's right," Walker said. "He's got the authority. What the hell do we know? Right?"

I watched as a man came out of one of the campers. He was walking slowly, as if his feet were barely making contact with the ground. Another man passed him before he was ten feet from the camper. I noticed when the first guy opened the door of the car that it was full of men, joshing one another like teenagers.

"All these cars full?" I wondered out loud.

"Gen'rally," Walker said. "These two broads take on half the goddamn town. All the single men an' some of the married ones." He sat back, yawning. "Wouldn't mind a piece of that myself," he said as the other camper door opened and a woman stood there, outlined against the light as she saw a customer out. She was wearing something sheer, and every line of her body showed through. Another man came to the door immediately and she closed the door after him, rubbing her arms against the cold.

"What's the price?" I asked.

"Fifty," he said. "You thinkin' of takin' a stab at it?"

"No. That was fine when I was in the service," I said. "I was just working it out. They must be moving a couple of grand apiece out of here at the speed they're working. Ever have any trouble?"

"You mean holdups?" Walker turned to stare at me. "You gotta be joking. Anybody tried to rip one of 'em off, the other guys would kill him. These women are important around here."

"Then why are we here? Other places I've seen this kind of thing, the police stay out of sight. They're on call if there's any trouble, but they don't monitor the action like this."

"Beats the hell out of me," Walker said. "I did hear that they had trouble once. Some john broke a girl's jaw. That was before my time. But since then the chief makes sure we're here every time."

"They must be glad of that," I said carefully. I was wondering what his response would be. If he was on the take, or knew about it, he would be suspicious.

He didn't sound it. "Yeah," he said easily. "Makes me feel like a pimp sometimes."

"What happens when they're through? Do the women hang around or take off?"

"Take off right away," he said. "I guess they're on a circuit, like ball players."

He leaned back and shoved his hat forward over his eyes, like any policeman on a boring stakeout anywhere. I stayed alert, disliking the duty but doing it. I figured there would be a disturbance somewhere along the way. Some guy would figure he'd waited long enough or someone would want to go to the wrong Winnebago when his turn came and someone else would get antsy.

What happened was different. The Winnebago nearest to us suddenly erupted with noise, a man's shouting and a woman's shrieks.

Walker sat up alertly and we got out. I let Sam out of the backseat and he came with me. The cars were opening and men were crowding towards the camper. Walker got there first. He threw the door open and we stepped inside with Sam at my heels. There isn't much room when you get two tall men in one of those things and we were jammed but I could see the struggle. A man was holding on to the woman, who was naked. He had her by the arms, and her hair was every which way as if he had been shaking her.

She turned and screamed at us. "Stop this bastard. He's beatin' me up."

"Outside, asshole," Walker said.

"This is a whore," the man roared. "You gonna take her word against mine? I'm a taxpayer."

"You're an asshole," Walker said. "Outside."

The man threw the woman away from him contemptuously and she sprawled across the bed, bouncing as she fell. Walker grabbed the guy's arm and pulled him out of the wagon. I let him by and spoke to the woman. "What happened?"

She stood up, ignoring her own nakedness, looking around for her wrap only because of the cold air that was pouring in through the open door. "He's one o' them wimps that can't get it on unless he gets rough," she said. "There's one in every goddamn crowd."

"What did he do?"

"When he came in he didn't talk. Just threw the money on the bed an' grabbed me." She pushed her hair back out of her eyes, and pulled a pack of Viceroys off the dresser beside the bed. She lit up, moving in quick angry jerks, tossing her head. I waited. She said, "Like I don't mind that. Lots of guys don' talk. An' sometimes they can't wait. That goes with the territory. But then he started squeezin' me an' it hurt." She opened her robe and exposed her breast. "Lookit. Fingermarks, for Chrissakes."

"Has he been in before?"

"No. An' he won't again," she said, her anger still boiling. "It's tough enough without guys like him."

"You get much of this, do you?"

Now she slowed her pace and looked at me, her eyes full of contempt. "Not in this town," she said.

She was about thirty, pretty but tough-looking. I looked back at her evenly. "You do in other towns?"

"Some of 'em," she said and dragged on her cigarette, then stubbed it.

"What makes this place different?" I asked.

She looked at me again, grinning crookedly. "You really want me to tell you?"

"I'm new here. I do."

She pulled her robe tighter around her. "Didn't the chief tell you?" she asked.

"He doesn't talk to me. I'm just a rookie."

"Yeah, an' I'm the Virgin Queen," she laughed harshly.

"You mean you're paying for the protection?" It was a bald question, but this was no time for subtlety. Walker would be back in with me in a matter of moments.

"What do you think, sweetheart? You figure we get a couple of cops baby-sitting us everywhere we go?"

"Who are you paying?" I demanded.

Her face was cold. "What's it to you?"

"I need to know."

She tugged her wrap tighter around her, regaining her control. "Why? You lookin' for your share?"

"I can put an end to it," I said.

She laughed, scornfully. "You an' who else? Think I want to spend paynight in the goddamn tank? It's worth every penny."

"What's your name?" I insisted.

She laughed and opened her housecoat and squirmed her body towards me. "What would you call it?" she sneered.

"Name?" I repeated, but she only laughed, and then Walker was back at the door.

"Come on, fer Chrissakes. We got a problem."

I turned and went out, Sam behind me. Outside a crowd of men had gathered around the guy we'd evicted. Two of them were holding him by the arms while another one punched him, his fist moving like a metronome, back and forth, into the face.

"Speak," I commanded and Sam sprang forward, barking.

The big man looked around at the noise but ignored Sam and drove his fist into the first guy's face again. It was a mask of blood by now and the man was barely conscious.

"Knock it off," I said and the big man lowered his fist and turned around.

"I heard what happen'. This is not what a man does to a woman. I show him." He had a rich Russian voice like you hear in an Orthodox Church. Out here among the parked cars and the shadowy trees at the edge of the lot it sounded theatrical.

"She's okay," I said. "Go and see for yourself."

Sam was still barking. I told him, easy, and he stopped. I could hear the clamoring voice of another man. "Hey, I'm next."

"After him you're next," I said.

The big Ukrainian turned away and went into the Winnebago. I noticed that he took off his hat as he entered, closing the door behind him.

The two men with the victim let go of him, and he reeled and almost fell.

Walker grabbed him. "You all right, Jack?"

"Yeah," the man said thickly. "No goddamn thanks to you."

"You wanna charge that guy with assault?"

The man turned his head and spat. He muttered something I didn't catch and Walker said, "You got two choices, buddy. You charge him or you go home. Which is it going to be?"

"I'm goin'," the man said. He took out a handkerchief and wiped his face. "I'm goin'," he repeated, and he stumbled over to his car. There was nobody else in it and he started it with a clumsy roar and backed away.

Walker spoke to the other man. "I don't want any more trouble. You got that?"

"Yes, officer." Only one of them understood. The other one spoke to him in an anxious whisper and he turned his head and answered in a low closemouthed hiss that sounded Slavic. Then they walked back to their pickup truck. The other men standing around did the same. Walker watched them go, then said, "Come on. Let's si'down."

I put Sam in the backseat and got in. Walker was lighting up another cigarette, moving angrily. "Where the hell were you?" he demanded. "I was out there tryin' to sort out the heyrube an' where's my goddamn partner? Inside, makin' nice."

"I figured you had it under control," I said.

"You figured you might get your goddamn head handed to you by that bohunk," he said.

"I wanted to know what happened."

"Did you?" He puffed on his cigarette, his anger still flickering. "You figured she'd make a complaint and lose the night's business while we took her down to the station to make a report? You figured she'd show up again for the hearing?" He shook his head impatiently. "Don't you know anything?"

His anger seemed genuine. Either he was one hell of an actor or else he had no part in Harding's payoff scheme. He was just a simple guy caught in the bind of having to work at something distasteful.

"The hooker told me something important," I said.

"What was that?" he sneered. "Did she tell you that she gives Harding a cut? Was that it?"

"Does she?"

He lowered his cigarette carefully and turned his head to stare at me. "You don't need to be a goddamn Einstein to know that something's goin' down. What it is don't matter. We're cops. These guys with hard-ons are citizens. We stop any breach of the peace. Period."

"Yeah, but we'd be doing it even if there wasn't any arrangement," I argued. "Hell, you know as much law as me. If she's paying him off, that's illegal."

He drew on his cigarette again, using it as a tranquilizer. "Big deal," he said. "An' diggin' gold out of the inside of a rock that's liable to come down on your goddamn head is a hard way to feed your family. Baby-sitting a couple of whores is a whole lot easier. Which do you want to do for a living?"

"My father was killed the same way young Wilcox died. I'm not going down any more mines if I can help it."

Walker relaxed, turning to look ahead of him, out of the steamy windshield. "Then quit makin' like Sherlock Holmes," he said. "We're both in the same boat. I got a wife an' three kids to worry about." It was cynical but maybe nothing more. I couldn't tell so I made the last comment I could, choosing my words carefully. "I don't like working for a crooked boss. It's liable to rub off."

"You mean you're gonna start asking for presents?" He was still angry and his voice was dull. "Or will you take it out in kind?"

"If he goes down we're all tarred with the same brush," I said. "I'm thirty-eight. There's not too many places want a cop with a bad smell to him, not the age I am."

"Exactly," he said. "Now drop the subject, will ya."

"Okay." I sat silently until the big man came out of the Winnebago. The woman stood in the doorway behind him and he turned and bowed to her. I could hear the catcalls of other men through the closed windows of our car and of theirs. Cheerfully the big miner turned and bowed to the crowd and went back to his truck, passing one of his buddies as he walked. They did not speak.

"One last question and I'll wrap up," I said.

"Yeah?" I could tell from his tone that the whole subject was eating him up.

"What's the woman's name? Any idea?"

"Calls herself Loretta. Could be a phony but it's a saint's name an' that goes down good with the guys. Most of 'em are Catholic."

I nodded and he asked, "Why'd you want to know?"

"Don't you want to know everything that goes on in your patch?"

"Most of it," he said, and he grinned. It was too dark to see his face properly but I could tell from the change in his voice. "Some of it, no thanks. The rest of it, yeah, I wanna know."

"If Harding got bounced, who'd take over?"

"Me, if there was any justice, which we all know there ain't," he said. "So it'd probably be Ferris. That means out of the frying pan into the fire. Now do me a favor. I'm gonna catch some zuzz. Don't wake me unless there's something you can't handle. Like maybe an illegal left turn or somebody asking directions."

I snorted out a laugh and said nothing. He slid further down in the seat, resting his head against the side window, his hat canted awkwardly. He was asleep in thirty seconds.

Nothing else exciting happened. After a couple of hours I let Sam out and walked around the lot to stretch my legs as well as his. I noted the number of Loretta's vehicle and the other Winnebago. I also kept a tally of the licenses of the customers.

By midnight, most of the cars had gone and no new ones were turning up. When there was only one car on the lot I woke Walker. "That's it. Securing from baby-sitting detail."

He yawned and looked at his watch. "Twelve-ten. That's fast. Okay. Let's head back to the barn, have our lunch."

He picked up the microphone. "Unit one, leaving campsite. All visitors gone. Over."

Ferris answered. "Roger unit one. Return to station code four. Out."

We drove back without speaking. The parking lot of the Headframe was full but the other police car was outside so we didn't stop. Walker nodded towards the place. "Big business tonight. It's the Wilcox wake. Last one we had took in three grand what with booze and sweep tickets."

"We expected to drop a few bucks there?"

He shook his head. "Nah. I guess you hit the collection at the station, did you?"

I nodded and he said, "Yeah, the chief generally rounds it off with a C note and then gets his picture in the paper handing over the contribution like it was his own."

"We could use the good will," I said. "We're not the most popular guys in town."

He shrugged. "Suits me. If I'd wanted to be popular I'd have joined a rock group."

We got to the station and found Ferris on duty.

"Any trouble?" he asked. He looked tired and sounded as if he didn't care what the answer was.

"One guy got a little rough with Loretta," Walker said. "We pulled him off before she was hurt. She didn't want to lay a complaint and then some big miner punched out the guy who'd been rough but nobody wanted to complain."

"Good," Ferris said. "I'm goin' off now. Walker, you're the senior man. Thomas is on the night shift. He's alone in the car. You stay in the office. Bennett and his dog can handle anything that comes up. You're both off at three, right?"

"Right, sarge," Walker said. He grinned at me. "You get to do the walking. I'll do the sitting."

Ferris went to his locker and took out his parka. He put it on over his uniform, then shoved a toque on his head. "I'll see you at midnight tomorrow, Bennett. Walker, I'll see you Friday."

I nodded to him, noticing that he was showing his age. His skin looked slack and his eyes were red. I had thought he was in his fifties, but tonight he looked ten years older. He had worked eighteen hours of the last twenty-four and he was tired.

When he'd gone Walker made a fresh pot of coffee and we ate our sandwiches and played a hand of dominoes. Then he checked his watch. "Best get out there," he said. "Take a good look around the properties. Especially the drugstore. Some of those guys are into uppers and downers. They may make a pass at the store."

"Will do. I'll see you at three."

He dug into his lunch pail and pulled out a paperback novel.

"Yeah," he laughed. "That's soon enough. I got a book to read."

The town was beginning to close down. There were a couple of dozen cars on the lot of the Headframe and the restaurant was half full. I made my rounds, checking everything quickly. The bar in the Headframe was busy and I guessed there would be a high absentee rate next morning at the mine. Someone had brought in an enlargement of the wedding photo of Randy Wilcox and his wife and it stood over the collection tin on the countertop. The box was stuffed with money. There were even a couple of twenties visible. But the reason for the benefit had not slowed anybody down. Men were pretty drunk and I decided to hang around outside later. For now I just made a quick inspection to see there was no trouble and left. I wanted to get to the campground if I could before the two women left.

I arrived to find one vehicle gone already. But the one we had been in was still in place. The light was on inside and I went over to it and knocked on the door.

There was no answer and I called out, "Hello? Anyone home?"

Again there was no answer and all my reflexes tickled. If the woman had been inside she would have called out, probably telling me to go to hell. When she didn't, I tried the door. It opened and I stepped up inside. And then I stopped. Loretta was lying on the floor, her robe spread awkwardly over her.

I crouched to check her. She was cold to the touch and without disturbing the robe I could see that the sleeve had been knotted around her throat.

NINE

THERE WERE no signs of life that I could detect, but for all I knew she still had a chance. Before I started I ran back to the car and called in, "Car two, emergency."

Walker answered at once. "Yeah. What's up?"

"I'm at the campsite. The hooker who had the fight has been strangled. I'm going to give her CPR. Call the doctor and the chief and get some help up here, pronto."

"Right." The radio clicked and I left Sam in the car and ran back to the RV, taking out my clasp knife as I ran. I had to save the knot, in case it told us anything about the man who had tied it.

It wasn't easy to slide the blade under the fabric. It had been pulled so tight that it was below the normal level of her flesh. I nicked her throat as I shoved the knife down but it didn't bleed, evidence that I was probably going to be too late to help her. It was hard to find a space beside her to kneel, but I squeezed in and began breathing and pumping, listening for signs of life. There was no response, but I kept on, keeping one ear open for the sound of an approaching car.

I persevered, still in my heavy parka, with the sweat running down my forehead and dripping onto her naked shoulder until suddenly I found a faint pulse in her throat. As I held my finger there the nick I'd made in her neck started to ooze blood. Good. The circulation was reaching her head.

She still was not breathing. I quit pumping her chest and concentrated on artificial respiration, inflating her chest like a child's toy with every breath. Then, far off I heard the sound of a siren. A minute later Walker burst in. I looked up between breaths. "She's got a pulse. Is the ambulance coming?"

"The doctor's on his way," he said. "You want me to take over?"

"No, it'll waste time changing places." I bent and breathed into her mouth again, then listened at her nostrils for sounds of breath.

"Okay, keep at it," Walker said. He put his hands into his pockets. It looks sloppy but it's professional. It prevents you from touching anything, leaving extra prints for the lab guys to find, or moving something that might be critical to the investigation. I kept on, but she still did not breathe. Her pulse was slow and irregular and I checked it constantly between breaths. "She may not make it," I said. "And if she does she could be a vegetable the rest of her life."

"Don't quit," Walker said. "Keep going. Soon's the chief gets here I'll head down and talk to the guy we kicked out."

"Good." I went back to my breathing as another vehicle pulled up outside. A moment later the doctor I had met at the hospital came bounding in, carrying his bag in one hand and a big hard case in the other.

"Keep on," he told me, shoving past Walker. He set down his bag and pulled out a stethoscope. I watched out of the corner of my eye as he tapped the girl's chest while I kept breathing into her.

"She's still going," he said as I came up for air.

"There was no pulse when I started. It's been ticking about the last five minutes."

He nodded and unsnapped the other case, bringing out an oxygen mask. "Okay, I've got her," he said and put the mask over her face. I stood up gratefully and undid my parka. I was hot and out of breath. The doctor said to Walker, "Go to my car, there's another bag on the front seat, bring it in, please."

When Walker returned the doctor took the bag and extracted a small bottle and a syringe. He filled the syringe and injected whatever it was into the woman's arm. I noticed that he took the time to wipe the spot with antiseptic before he did so.

"Close the door," he told Walker.

Walker did. In the closed room I was suddenly aware of the smell from the woman. Her sphincter had failed her when the sleeve had been tightened around her neck. It always happens that way. A new set of headlights bounced towards us over the lot, flashing over the windows of the camper. "That could be the chief," Walker said.

"Let him in, but you wait outside," the doctor told him. He put his stethoscope into his ears and listened to the woman's chest again. I watched his face relax as he listened. "That's better," he said. He stood up and looked at me. "How long have you been here?"

I checked my watch. "Around ten minutes. I found her, called in and started CPR. It took about five minutes for her heart to kick in."

He nodded, breaking out a small smile. "Congratulations. You've saved her, I think."

"Will she be brain-damaged?"

He cocked his head doubtfully. "That's the bad news. She may be. We'll have to wait until she comes around."

The door opened and Harding came in. He nodded to the doctor, then me. "What happened?"

"I came over about ten minutes ago," I told him. "The other vehicle was gone so I banged on the door to see if this woman had a problem. She didn't answer and I tried the door. I found her like this with the sleeve of her kimono tied around her throat. I called the station and started CPR. The doctor says she's going to make it."

He nodded. "Don't touch anything, either of you." He took a piece of chalk out of his pocket and quickly drew a line all around the woman's body, lifting the kimono to do it. Then he looked up. "Doctor, when will the ambulance be here?"

"Any time." The doctor checked his watch. "They were on a call from the other side of town with a patient on board, heart attack. I told them to drop him at emergency and get over here."

"Good." Harding turned and walked out.

The doctor said nothing. He knelt again and checked the woman's chest. Then he looked up, smiling grimly. "She's breathing on her own now."

"She's all yours, doc," I said. "I'll go talk to the chief."

I squeezed by him and went outside. The chief was talking to Walker, who was standing by the scout car. I joined them.

"Who was the guy?" the chief was asking.

"Josh Maynard. He's a supervisor in the smelter," Walker said. "The other guy gave him a good going over. I asked if he wanted to press charges and he said no. So, following standard procedure, I sent him home."

He sounded nervous. It made me even more sure that he was not on the take. If he was in the chief's pocket he would have been more relaxed.

"And what about the bohunk?" Harding snapped.

"He spent time in the trailer. Then another guy went in. We stayed on duty until just before twelve when the last car left."

"Did you check the vehicles before leaving the site?" The chief was coldly furious. His tone was rigid.

"We never do, chief," Walker said unhappily. "You know that. We wait until everyone's gone and then we leave."

"How do you know the last man here didn't do this to her?" Harding snapped.

I spoke up. "It couldn't have been the last guy out, chief. Otherwise the woman would have been dead. As it is she's hanging in. That means she was strangled a few minutes before I got here. Any longer and she wouldn't have come back like she did."

"Possible," Harding said. "But I'd still like to know who her last customer was."

"I've got the license number of the car, chief." I unflapped my notebook and squinted at the last page in the light from the revolving flasher on the police car. "YXJ 392, maroon Chev."

"Good," Harding snapped. "I'm glad some bastard was alert." He spoke to Walker. "Go and get Sgt. Ferris and call on Maynard. Take a full statement. Also, get the name of the owner of that Chev and get it back to me. I'll be here."

"Yessir." Walker slid behind the wheel and drove off, switching off the lights on top of the car as he reached the roadway.

Harding looked at me. "You did well, Bennett, bringing her back like that. But tell me, what the hell were you doing here in the first place?"

"Checking there was no trouble, chief." I was surprised by the question. "After the attention we'd been giving these women all evening I figured the job wasn't complete until they were gone. Isn't that the way it's done?"

"Very diligent," he said coldly. "I wonder why none of the other men has done this before, and none of these unfortunate women has ever been strangled before."

"Maybe they check routinely. Have you ever asked them?" I was angry. I know that the prime suspect in any murder case is the guy who finds the body. That's standard. I've been caught in the web a couple of times in my career, but I didn't like his tone. He was carrying things too far.

"Don't be impertinent," he snapped. "Did you touch anything inside?"

"I cut the knot off her neck. It's lying next to her. I guess it will have my fingerprints on it, if that means anything."

"It may mean a great deal," he said. "Have you ever been involved in a homicide investigation before?"

"Yes. I've been the investigating officer on most of them."

"Good," he said. "I'm going to need help. Not that this is a homicide, thank God. But until she comes around and tells us what happened I'm going to treat it that way."

"She may never come around." I said it innocently but I was testing him. He seemed too fresh, too alert to have been pulled from bed to come here. I was beginning to wonder if he had tied that knot around the woman's neck.

He stood silently, thinking. Then we saw the flashing light of the ambulance approaching. It squealed to a stop beside us and the driver jumped out. "Where's the problem?"

"In the camper." The chief pointed. "The doctor's in there. See him."

"Right." The guy hustled to the back of the ambulance and he and his partner pulled out the stretcher. The chief and I stood in silence, watching, until they came out of the van with the woman on the stretcher, wrapped in a blanket. The doctor was walking beside them, carrying the oxygen equipment. He got into the back of the ambulance with her, then ran back and picked up the rest of his equipment. He climbed into the back again, then spoke to one of the ambulance men who nodded and got into the doctor's car. Both vehicles backed up and headed out, picking up speed as they hit the road.

"Right," the chief said. "I'll take a look. You go get the photographer. D'you know where he lives?"

"No," I said.

He told me and I left to get the photographer out of bed. It turned out that he was an accountant at the mine, an amateur. He had been to the wake at the Headframe and he was a little the worse for wear. But he snapped back to life when I told him what had happened and grabbed his equipment bag at once. "I'll follow in my own car," he said. "No sense tying up the police car. You may need it."

I waited while he started his car and he followed me to the camper. By that time there was another car there. I recognized it as Ferris's. I knocked on the door and announced the photographer. Ferris stepped down from the vehicle as the photographer went in. "Okay, Bennett. We got work to do," he said. "We'll take the police car."

I went ahead and put Sam in the rear seat. He lay there, looking up at Ferris without moving his head as the sergeant got behind the wheel.

"Where are we going, sarge?"

"To talk to the last guy there. Walker got the name. He's a driller at the mine."

"Right."

Ferris said nothing, just drove out to the mine site at the limit. His hand movements were slow, as if his arms weighed him down, the motions of a man running on empty. It explained why he did not speak and I didn't push him for conversation.

But I was thinking as I drove. The Winnebago had been parked at the west end of town. That was on the road leading to the abandoned mill site. The woman had been attacked only a minute or two before I got there, but I had seen no car driving away from the place back into town. That meant that the attacker had either gone on to the old mill or had driven into some house at the same end of town, getting off the road before I drove by. Nothing concrete, but it would help when we started our house-to-house canvass the next morning.

At the mine site the watchman's dog barked for about a minute before the man came to the door of his shack and let the barrier up so we could drive in.

We both got out. Ferris did the talking.

"Where can I find John Peterson?"

The watchman blinked at us. "What's he done then?"

"Where is he?" Ferris repeated. "Come on, this is important."

"Just a minute." The watchman went back into the shack and we followed as he opened a ledger. I noticed the pages were computer printouts. In my father's day they would have been hand-written, filled with crossings out and overwritings as the endless turnover of men changed the mine's population week by week. Today it was easier to keep track.

The watchman turned a few pages and Ferris got impatient. "It'll be under the P's for Chrissake."

"Yeah, I'm gettin' to it." The watchman turned a couple of pages more rapidly and then ran his finger down the names. "Yeah, here we are. Unit four, room twen'y-seven."

"Which one is unit four?" Ferris snapped.

"The middle one. Like there's seven units. Go past the headframe of the mine and you'll see 'em." He frowned. "You know it. You've been here before."

"Too many times," Ferris said. "Bunch of assholes, all of 'em."

We got back into the car and drove up past the tall entrance to the mine and a hundred yards further to the housing units. They were all the same. Raised four feet from the ground, rows of mobile homes, like you see in retirement villages. Only these were in seven groups, each group connected into a single unit. The lights were on in the fourth unit and we went inside.

The interior was as I'd expected. Around the rim were the men's rooms. A couple of doors were open and I noticed that each one was about ten feet square with a window, a bed, a chest and a wardrobe built in. Each had a mini-bathroom that probably contained a toilet and a handbasin. The center of the space was divided into a big recreation lounge with Ping-Pong tables and a couple of television sets and lots of comfortable chairs. There was a shelf of books that looked as if it was never touched. Beyond was a doorway that led to the mess hall and the showers and any other facilities. A few guys were sitting in front of one of the television sets with cans of pop beside them. They looked up when we came in. Nobody spoke.

"John Peterson here?" Ferris asked. The men looked at us without answering.

"Thanks a lot," he said. He looked around the numbers on the doors and saw they went only as high as twenty. "Through the door," he said. He went through and we found ourselves in similar space, only this time the mess hall was in the center. It was deserted at this time of night but I could see that there were enough places for about fifty men. That meant there would be about 350 men in the seven units. I wondered how many of them had spent time with Loretta that evening.

"There it is." Ferris pointed to the door of one of the rooms.

He went over and opened it without knocking. The room was in darkness and he flicked on the light. I was behind him and saw the man in bed sit up, startled.

"What's this?" he asked.

"Outta bed," Ferris ordered.

"What for? What the hell's wrong with you guys?" the man said. He was frightened but puzzled. He had been sleeping. It didn't look to me as if he knew anything about the attempted murder.

"Out of bed," Ferris said again and he reached over and whisked the covers off the man.

The guy was wearing a pair of boxer shorts and he stood up and reached for his pants, which were hanging on the back of his chair. He was slimly built with a few well-defined muscle groups. He looked stringy and durable.

"What the hell's goin' on? I haven't done nothin'," he mumbled.

"Where were you tonight?" Ferris asked.

The man looked at us and rubbed his hand over his hair, still puzzled. "I wen' into town. Why?"

"Where did you go?"

"I went to the hotel. Then I went to the campsite an' got laid." He could have been a Cub Scout talking about his latest pack outing. He stood and looked from one to the other of us. "What's this all about? The cops were there. There was lots of guys there, like always on paynight. What's goin' on?"

"Were you the last guy to visit Loretta?"

"Could've been," Peterson said. He was still blinking himself awake. His face was pitted with tiny marks. I guessed he had been a blaster and had not always been careful about getting far enough away from his explosions.

"This officer saw you there." Ferris hooked his thumb at me, not turning around.

"So what? Big deal," Peterson said angrily. "So was half the goddamn guys in this camp. What's so special?"

"How was she when you left?" Ferris asked. He was handling the whole thing differently from the way I would have done. I would have started more softly, lulling the guy. This way there was no shock in the question. But from the way Peterson answered I knew he was telling the truth.

He grinned, almost apologetically. "Same as always. She must've been wore out but she din' look it. Said she'd see me again on the thirtieth."

"So why did you strangle her?"

"Strangle her?" The man's voice gave out into a squawk. "What the hell are you smokin'? I didn't strangle her. Why would any sonofabitch strangle her?"

"For her money," Ferris said. He glanced around the room. "Mind if we take a look through this place?"

"Help yourself." Peterson threw up his hands. "Strangle her? That's unbelievable."

Ferris nodded grimly. "Believe it," he said. "Who all was in the car with you?"

"Why?" Peterson asked.

Ferris straightened his forefinger and stuck it an inch from Peterson's face. "I ask the questions. You answer them. Got it?"

"Yeah, okay." Peterson shook his head slowly, clearing it. "There was Jeff an' Bill. Jeff Watkins, Bill Lesnevich."

"What rooms they in?"

"Fourteen and thirty-four. Why?"

Ferris glanced around at me. "Get the pair of them in here, lock their rooms after them."

"Right." I went to the other rooms and brought the men back. One of them was in bed when I got there, the other was in the shower. They wanted to know what was going on and I told them the sergeant wanted to talk to them.

When we got back to Peterson's room, Ferris was conducting his search. The bed was wrecked, the covers peeled apart, one by one, the pillow out of its case, the mattress on its end. By the time we got there he was going through Peterson's closet, examining each item. There was a leather holdall in the bottom of the closet and he checked that last. It was empty.

When he had searched everywhere he turned out all the pockets in Peterson's clothes. There was $170 in his wallet. The two men with me watched in silence, looking more and more puzzled. One of them asked at last, "What's goin' on here?"

"Some bastard strangled Loretta," Peterson said. "We was the last guys there. They figure I done it."

"Come with me," Ferris said to him. "Bring your coat, we're gonna take a look at your car in a minute."

One of the men started to splutter. "Lookit. You ain' gonna go through my stuff like this. Where's your warrant?"

"Right here," Ferris said and he patted his holster and grinned.

"This is illegal," the man said.

"We're in hot pursuit of a wanted man," Ferris said. We weren't. Technically we were breaking the law and anything he found could be dismissed in a court of law. But he was like a terrier, hanging on to the best chance he had. I figured the worried guy had a stash of grass in his clothes so I stepped in.

"All we're looking for is anything that came from that woman's RV. We're not looking for illegal substances, anything like that. We're not going to do anything if we find any. We'd like your cooperation so we can clear you of suspicion in this attempted homicide and we can all get to bed."

Ferris turned his head sharply, narrowing his eyes. But he didn't overrule me. He knew he was overstepping the mark.

The two men looked at one another. The one who had not said anything shrugged, and the complainer nodded. "Okay. Like I had another guy in my room before me. He could've left somethin' I don' know about."

"As long as it's not a pile of money we won't ask questions," Ferris said.

"It sure as hell ain't." The man walked away. "Come on, come an' see."

We went to his room and he unlocked it. Sure enough he had a plastic bag of grass in his chest of drawers, tucked away in a spare pair of socks. Ferris dropped it on the floor. "Did he leave the socks as well?" he asked drily.

But there was nothing there to tie the man to the murder attempt. No money, no souvenirs from the Winnebago. And it was the same with the third guy. They were just three more of the ships that had crossed her path that night. We took them out to Peterson's car, which was also empty except for a bottle of rye in the trunk. Alcohol was forbidden in the single men's quarters.

Ferris held it up, without speaking.

Peterson gulped. "Hey, I'd forgot all about that. Sorry, off'cer."

"Get rid of it," Ferris said. "Pass it around, drop it on a rock, whatever. If it's still here in the morning you'll be off the site by noon."

Peterson nodded. He unscrewed the cap and offered it to the others. One by one all three of them took a deep drink. Then he screwed the cap back on, swore softly and smashed the bottle against the tow hitch on the back of his car. The cold air was filled with whisky fumes and he stood for a moment, crushing the broken bottle under his work boots. Then he said, "'preciate you not reporting this, off'cer. I need this job, eh."

"Thank you for your willing cooperation," Ferris said coldly. "Now we got work to do."

We went back to the scout car and drove off. The watchman was alert this time and he swung the barrier up as we approached. I waved to him as we passed.

"Wasn't them," Ferris said as he drove, more alertly now.

"It had to be somebody from that end of town. I didn't see any cars moving as I came up to the campsite. The woman had been attacked only a couple of minutes before I got there. Should we look at the houses out by the mill? See if anybody's come home late?"

"All o' the folks out there are old," Ferris said. "We'll go back to the site, check with the chief, see what he says."

When we got to the trailer we found the chief and Walker. Ferris reported to him and the chief nodded grimly. "Okay. There's not much more we can do tonight. Take Bennett back to the station and get his statement. I'll join you there."

I drove the police car back. Ferris followed in his own car. When we got there I put Sam in my car and went inside. Ferris was waiting at the typewriter with a statement form in place. "Okay," he said, almost cheerfully. "Let's have the sordid details."

I gave him the facts and he typed them up and gave me the form to sign. I signed it and he checked his watch. "Three-fifteen, you might as well call it a night."

I thanked him and handed over my notebook, then began changing into plain clothes. I was almost finished when the chief walked in. He stood without speaking while I buttoned my shirt. Then he picked up my lunch pail.

"Mind if I look inside?"

I glanced at him in surprise. "In my lunch box? What for?"

"Do you mind?" he repeated coldly.

"Help yourself, chief," I shrugged.

He opened it and looked in. The sandwich bag I had emptied and folded flat was puffy, full. He opened it and pulled out a handful of money, in big bills mostly, fifties, hundreds.

"Where did this come from?" he asked.

TEN

"THIS IS a plant," I said softly. "I don't know where this money came from."

Harding was suddenly angry. "Well I do," he said. "It came from that woman's Winnebago. Did you take it before you strangled her or after?"

I was angry enough to accuse him, to tell him I knew about his arrangement with the girls, about his cut from the hotel. But I didn't. I said nothing. Ferris spoke first. To Harding.

"Do I charge him with the attempted murder as well?"

"Not yet," Harding said softly. "Count this money and charge him with theft."

Ferris nodded and turned to me, pulling out the card from his notebook that contains the caution and the Charter of Rights formula we read to prisoners, the equivalent of the American Miranda.

"Okay," Harding said. "Do you have anything to say?"

"Not to you. I want to make a telephone call to my wife."

"One call," Harding said.

I dialed the house, and after eight rings Fred came to the phone. "Hello."

"This is Reid. I've been charged with theft. I want you to call my buddy in Toronto and tell him. Then can you come down here and see me please."

Her voice was sleepy, puzzled. "Reid? What's happening?"

"It's a frame-up, love. But they've charged me. Can you do what I asked, please?"

"Of course." There was a pause and she came back, her voice clearer as she woke up completely. "They're evil, Reid. Don't worry, it won't stick."

"You're right." I wanted to tell her how much she meant to me but Ferris and Harding were either side of me, listening hard. "I'll tell you all about it when you come in."

"Take care, love," she said and I hung up.

"Very touching," Harding sneered. "What's she going to say when she knows where the money came from?"

I said nothing. With me in the cells and Sam still outside in my car, Freda was on her own. I didn't want to put her in any danger from these two. I'd seen the way they worked.

"I'll take your gun," Ferris said.

I drew it, broke the action and tipped out the shells. Then I passed it to him. He swung the cylinder shut and rattled the shells in his left hand. "And your spares," he said.

I handed them over, then my stick and cuffs. "Take that belt off, and the laces outta your boots," Ferris said.

I was arrested once before, in Toronto, when I killed a couple of bikers. That time, like now, I had been arrested by men I worked with. They had given me a cup of coffee and sat and talked to me until my lawyer arrived and arranged for me to go home. Harding was different.

"Put him in the cells," he said.

Ferris laid my pistol and shells on the guardroom table and nodded to me. "You heard."

I walked in front of him, through the doorway to the cells and into the first one. He clanged the door shut behind me and I sat down on the wooden bunk and looked at him, not speaking.

Ferris looked at me in silence then left, slamming the outer door behind him. I heard voices from the other room. Then a typewriter began to click, and I sat there listening to it and to the hissing of the central heating system, getting more and more tense. I couldn't help thinking what life would be like for me and for Fred over the next little while. The people of Elliot didn't like the police anyway. As a crooked cop, arrested by his own partners, I would be an outcast. Fred would come in for her share of the local anger. She had to get away, I decided. Probably I would be forced to stay in town, but she didn't have to put up with it. She could head back to the anonymity of her apartment in Toronto.

The second thought that nagged me was so unpleasant that I couldn't face it. Would she think that I was guilty? The first time I was arrested it broke up my marriage. That marriage had been rocky anyway, but I wondered whether Freda could find herself believing I had done what they said.

I knew it was nonsense, but alone, in the small hours, sorry for myself, I almost enjoyed thinking the worst. The thought made me stand up and pace, shuffling in my unlaced boots, back and forth, from the bars to the toilet and back, three paces each way like a big cat in a cage.

It must have been only twenty minutes before I heard her voice outside. She was calm and her voice was strong. I couldn't hear the words, only the tone, steady and firm. She talked back and forth with Ferris for about a minute before the door opened and he came in, a nasty half grin on his face.

"Visitor for you," he said and stood there as Fred brushed past him and reached through the bars, pressing herself against them.

I took her hands in mine and poked my face as far through the bars as it would go to kiss her. She had tears in her eyes.

Ferris stood watching us, the same sneaky grin on his face.

She spoke first. "Are you all right?"

"I'm okay. You don't think I did this, do you?"

She tried a little grin. It was lopsided but it cheered me. "You? Come on, you're too much of a Boy Scout."

I squeezed her hand. "Did you make the call?"

She nodded. We had pulled apart, just holding hands through the bars. "The lawyer will be here around ten. There's a flight to Olympia at eight-thirty and he'll drive up."

"They'll probably keep me in until then." I squeezed her hand. "Listen. The whole case is ugly. I found one of the prostitutes strangled. I called in and gave her CPR. She came back, heart and breathing. When she comes to she'll be able to say who attacked her. Tell the lawyer to go to the hospital. I'm worried about her."

She said nothing, just tightened her grip on my hands. Ferris spoke up. "Okay, that's long enough."

"No it's not," I said. "I want my wife to have my dog. She has to bring him in."

"I'm not doing any goddamn animal tricks," Ferris exploded.

Fred let go of my hand, winked at me and walked out. "Wait here," she told Ferris. I watched him stand, spluttering, but her show of confidence had startled him. He turned and looked at me, mouth open, searching for words, and in about thirty seconds Fred came back in, leading Sam.

I reached through the bars and patted his head. "Good boy," I told him. "Easy." He relaxed and stood looking at me until I told him, "Go with Freda."

His stance didn't change but after she had reached in and held my hand again he left with her, oblivious of me.

Ferris banged the door shut behind her and I sat on the bunk, feeling easier in my mind. Fred didn't need any warnings. She knew how I felt about the chief. She would keep Sam close to her until I got out. She was safe. That was the thought that finally let me put my own problems out of my mind and sink into a deep, dreamless sleep.

I woke up when the morning shift man arrived. I heard a car drive up outside and then the banging of the outer door. A minute later the door to the cell block burst open and Levesque came in.

"Jeez Christ. I don' believe it," he said. He waved back over his shoulder towards the guardroom. "I just seen the book, eh?"

"Somebody stuffed a bunch of money in my lunch box," I said.

"You the only one got a key," he said. He wasn't firm about it, just spelling out the facts as he knew them.

"It seems not," I said. "Did you guys get called out again last night when I found that woman strangled?"

"No." He shrugged his shoulders. "First I seen of that was on the sheet. Nobody call me."

"What time did you get off?" I asked.

"Twelve," he said. "Me an' Scott. We was workin' four to twelve." He looked at me, narrowing his eyes. "You din' take that money, eh?"

"Of course not." I didn't want to make a song and dance of it. It wouldn't help. I figured the lawyer Kennedy was sending would be able to get me off within minutes. I hoped he would. Prison is tough for ex-cops.

Levesque scratched his neck, puzzling. "What's goin' on?" he asked.

"I've been set up," I said.

He shook his head. Not disagreeing but uncertain. "Listen, you wan' some coffee?" His tone didn't ring true. It had the same kind of phony brightness you hear in people's voices when they're visiting a terminally sick friend.

"I'd like some, please."

"'Kay. I'm gonna make a pot." He went out, pulling the door closed quietly behind him. He brought me a cup a few minutes later, not saying anything except "Careful, i's 'ot."

He left me and I sat down and drank it and thought. I was concerned about the prostitute. If she recovered completely she would clear me of any charge of attempted murder. But she might never regain her wits a hundred percent. She might only make it back far enough to be a robot, going through the motions of living, unable to think properly or even to take care of herself.

But the guy who had strangled her might not know that. He might think she could finger him. I wondered if she was being kept under security at the hospital. And who would be watching her anyway? If it was one of Harding's friends she was going to die.

In any case, I decided, my attempt to save her had saved my own neck. No jury would believe I had strangled the woman and then brought her back from the grave. But the alleged theft of the money would stick tight. There had been nothing to stop me grabbing her cash before I started giving her CPR. From what I'd seen of the people in town they would enjoy believing that about a policeman.

The time stretched on. At nine o'clock the door opened again and Harding came in, with Ferris behind him. Both of them looked strained. Harding did the talking.

"I just had a call from Toronto, Bennett. They tell me a lawyer is coming up this morning. I'm going to delay your bail hearing until he gets here."

I nodded and he looked at me for a moment then turned away, not speaking. Ferris let him out and then slammed the door behind him. I lay on the bunk with my hands behind my head and waited.

Around ten-fifteen I heard a car arrive outside. The door slammed and then after a couple of minutes, the cell-block door opened and Harding came in with a man I knew. Irv Goldman, a sergeant of detectives from Toronto. I've worked with him a number of times and he's a good friend. He'd been at my wedding to Fred. He fixed me with a frown as he walked behind the chief and I kept quiet. He was undercover.

"Here's your lawyer," Harding said. "He's going to talk to you while I phone the magistrate, check on when we can have a bail hearing." His tone was brisk and businesslike; he would not be faulted by this intruder. "Might not be possible until tomorrow."

Goldman spoke then. His voice was polite but cold. "He had better be out of this rathole by noon, chief, or I am laying charges of unlawful detention."

"You couldn't make them stick," Harding snapped.

"Try me," Goldman said. "But if you enjoy running this department you'll have that bail hearing within the next thirty minutes."

Harding said nothing. He drew his mouth tight and left, pulling the door shut behind him. I reached through the bars and shook hands with Irv. "Thanks for coming up. What happened?"

He tapped his ear with one finger and waved around the walls. I got the message. There might be a bug. Then he answered. "Your buddy asked me to come. Here's my card."

He opened his wallet and pulled out a card, he took out a pen and wrote on it before handing it over. When he did I read the name, Walter Baker, Baker, Strauss and Karpus, Solicitors. He had added the words *my cousin*.

"Thank you for coming, Mr. Baker. Has the chief told you what I'm charged with?"

"Theft over two hundred dollars," he said. "What's the story?"

I told him, starting with the hours spent watching the hookers catering to the miners. He didn't interrupt, and when I finished he just nodded. "I'll go and see how the bail arrangements are coming," he said. "Wait here."

"What else?" I said and sat down. He grinned and winked at me and went out. Another car arrived a minute or two later and then, after another ten minutes, Harding came in and let me out. He was angry and he did not speak to me, just opened the cell door and beckoned.

I followed him to the front office where Irv was standing talking to an elderly man in a dark suit. Irv said nothing while the other man asked me if I would abide by the rules he was going to set. I said I would. He told me I could go free on my own recognizance so long as I remained in town and made no attempt to contact Alice Forsythe, also known as Cynthia, Frenchie, and Loretta. I agreed and signed the bail form and they let me go.

Fred had taken my car when she left in the night so Irv drove me back to the house. As soon as we were out of sight of the station he grinned. "Hey, this legal racket is okay. Just make a noise and they listen. Not like bein' a cop."

"Thanks for coming up, Irv. How did it happen?"

He laughed. "I don't get no respect," he said. "I must be the only detective in Ontario with a goddamn law degree. Broke my mother's heart when I went into the department instead of hanging out a shingle."

I was not up to joking about the way things stood. "Did Leo Kennedy know that?"

"No. But the computer did," Irv explained. "When Fred called the Provincial Police Commission last night, they contacted Kennedy and he had someone in the office check the records. Then he got the Metro chief out of bed with the request to use me and here I am. I can give you a hand with the investigation."

"It's ugly, Irv," I said. "They haven't charged me with attempt murder. I guess that would have come if I hadn't managed to get her heart started again. But the theft charge will stick no matter what."

"Worry not," Irv said. "Before you come to court we'll have these bastards locked up for corruption and the whole story'll come out."

I was too tired and depressed to think it would be that easy, but I grinned anyway and sat back, pointing out the turns to the house.

Irv pulled into the driveway and Fred had the front door open before we could get out of the car. She ran down the steps and hugged me. "Are you all right?"

"Large as life and twice as ugly," I said and squeezed her. "Irv's my lawyer."

"Great. How are you, Irv?" she said and they exchanged kisses. "Come on inside."

We went in and thrashed the case out over breakfast. I was weary. Depression, I guess. Being charged with a crime I hadn't committed gave me the same sense of futility you get when you're wounded. You haven't done anything different from normal but suddenly your life has changed. You're out of commission.

Irv looked at me as he finished his second cup of coffee. "Best thing you can do is sleep, Reid. I'll go into town, ask about Loretta at the hospital, then take a look at the campground, see if there's any footprints into the trees. I'll come back this afternoon.''

''I'll come with you.''

He shook his head and stood up. ''You'll be sharper after a few hours in bed. See you later.''

He reclaimed his coat and left, Fred taking him out to his car. When she returned she was looking more cheerful. ''He's right, Reid. Go and get some sleep. You can work later.''

She was tired too. I could see it in the smudges under her eyes. She was worried, wishing we had never come to town. I was with her on that one, but the job had gone too far for me to turn back now.

''Okay,'' I said and went to bed.

I was asleep almost at once and didn't wake until she came in quietly in the early afternoon. ''Irv's back,'' she said and kissed me.

I sat up. ''Good. I'll grab a shower and a shave and join you.''

He was sitting at the kitchen table writing up his notes when I came in ten minutes later. He looked up and grinned. ''I guess that's as close to human as you get,'' he said. ''How are you feeling?''

''About normal for the third week of night shift.''

''That good, huh?'' He laughed and indicated his notes. ''Well, I've done some digging and found out a few things, about the town mostly. They aren't in love with the boys in blue up here.''

''They have good reason.''

''Yeah, well I had a good talk with the doctor. He thinks I'm a lawyer and he was complaining about the way Ferris in particular clobbers prisoners. He's laid charges a couple of times but nothing came of it. The police have the magistrate in their pocket apparently. Anyway, he says he's keeping the woman in a coma, keeping her body temperature down to lessen the chance of her brain swelling. Seems that can happen sometimes. He figures she won't come around for a couple of days yet, not until the weekend.''

''Is she under guard?''

''No. He says that Harding didn't even suggest it. They don't have the manpower to spare a man for full-time surveillance so they're waiting for her to come around and then Harding will go over and take a statement.''

"Does the doctor think she'll be making any sense?"

Irv shrugged. "He's not sure. She was without oxygen for a few minutes, he's not sure how long. She could be a cabbage or she could be bright. He's got his fingers crossed."

"Me too," I said. "Is he going to call you when she does come out of it?"

"Yeah. I want to be there for the statement."

"Did you take a look at the site?"

"Yeah," he nodded. "It could have been too late. There were all kinds of thrill-seekers up there. I guess there's nothing else in town to think about, except the soap operas. People were all over the place and there were some footprints, but they all ended up against trees, where guys had gone to take a leak. That could have happened any time."

Fred came up behind me and put her arms around my neck. I reached up and squeezed her hand. "What do we do next?" I wondered.

"Well, I've been thinking about that." Irv stretched luxuriously. "If this was my department I'd order a house to house canvass, check if anyone up that end saw a car coming back from that end of town. If we could backtrack the car that left the scene we might be on to something."

"If we're going to do that, you and I will have to do it," I said and he shook his head.

"I hate to be the bearer of bad tidings, old buddy, but your name is mud around town."

I turned to look up at Fred. "This is going to get ugly, honey. I figure you'd be better off at home."

"This is my home for the moment," she said softly. "I knew when we came here that it wasn't going to be easy. I'm staying."

"Attagirl," Irv said. "The old ace here is going to need some moral support."

She rested her hands on my shoulders, patting me lightly, almost absently. "I know," she said.

She went to the stove and started making coffee. Irv looked at her and nodded appreciatively. "You're a lucky guy, Reid."

I knew it but I said nothing and he looked back down at his notes. When he looked up he said, "Do you know where the chief lives?"

"No." I shook my head.

"Thought not," he said cheerfully. "Well, that's the good news, if we can make it account for anything. He lives on Hummingbird Terrace. That's one of the fancy houses for the mine management." He tapped his notes with one finger. "And the interesting thing is that it's just in town from the campsite. He could be the guy who went up there and strangled that woman. I timed the driving. He could have been back home within two minutes forty seconds. It would have taken you five minutes to drive there from the center of town."

"Then that's what happened." I stood up, excited. "He went out there to collect his cut, got mad at the girl and choked her. He went home and I went back and found her. He didn't get to the scene for twenty-five minutes, something like that. He had lots of time to drive down to the station and plant the cash, then come on to the trailer site."

"Agreed," Irv said as Fred set down a coffee cup in front of him. "But now comes the difficult part. We have to prove that, beyond the shadow of a doubt."

ELEVEN

"THERE ARE two things we can do," I said. "I'll talk to Randy Wilcox's father. Maybe he knew what his son had seen. If he does, we may have a case. And you could go talk to Berger at the hotel. If we can blow Harding out of the water, the job is done and the case against me collapses."

"Okay." Irv nodded and stood up. "I'll take Berger. I'll tell him you want to talk to him. He may be suspicious of me." He stood for a moment with his hands on the back of his chair. "The only thing is, I have to leave here tonight. I've got a case in high court tomorrow, a homicide. I have to appear."

I nodded. "Okay. If you set it up, I can take care of things from there on. Thanks, Irv."

Fred was looking thoughtful. "What about the other woman? Perhaps she saw something."

"I took her license number but it's in my notebook, at the police station," I said.

"Pity," Irv agreed. "But I'll call the provincial police, see if they can get hold of her. After what happened to her buddy she may be ready to give them a statement."

"In the meantime, she's in danger as well," I said. "If Harding or whoever it was tried to kill one of them, he'll do it to the other one to make sure she stays quiet."

"Yeah." Irv nodded. "I'll get on to the OPP right away."

"How can I help?" Fred asked.

Irv shook his head. "I think it's better if you stay out of it, Freddi. I'm sure everyone in town knows you by now. If they see you they'll know we're talking about Reid and that may clam some people up tight."

She grinned without amusement. "One thing I could do is keep in touch with the hospital, check on the woman's progress."

"They'll probably be the same," Irv said. "They don't want to talk to Reid or you, as his messenger."

"No." I snapped my fingers. "No, we may have an ally. There's a nurse, she's Wilcox's sister-in-law. She was happy about my locking him up. She'll probably give you information, Fred."

"I'll talk to her," Fred said. She looked pleased. She's not the type to twiddle her thumbs while men do the work.

Irv left, promising he'd be back to tell us about Berger, then head for his flight. I saw him to the door and got my parka.

Fred watched as I put it on. "You think this man Wilcox will know anything?"

"Maybe, maybe not." I shrugged. "I can only ask."

She reached up and grabbed the lapels of my parka and kissed me. "Take care."

"You too. I won't be long." I winked at her and left. Sam watched me go and it seemed that there was reproach in his eyes. But I wanted him with Fred. I wasn't sure what would break, but I knew he could take care of her if something did.

The curtains along the street dipped like flags at a regatta when I came out into the driveway. Harding would not have to tail me, I thought. Any one of the neighbors would tell him whether I was in or not.

The road to the old town had not been plowed as carefully as the streets in town and I drove carefully. The sun was low and when I rounded the corner and came down the slope to the mill the place looked almost beautiful. Snow had drifted in over the abandoned buildings and they had a forlorn look, like some castle in a kid's fairy story.

There was smoke rising from the chimneys of some of the houses and I stopped at the first one and asked where Mr. Wilcox lived. The old lady who came to the door was surprised. "Who wants him?" she asked.

I smiled. "I used to know his son."

"Oh. In that case." She came out onto the step and pointed to one of the houses further down. "He lives there. Him and that yappy dog of his."

I turned to thank her, but she had already closed the door behind her so I got back in my car and drove the last fifty yards. The house looked in better shape than most of the others around. It had been painted recently and there was a good big greenhouse built into the south wall. I could see a man inside, through the steamed-up windows. He was tending flowers. I could hear a dog barking, a small, yappy dog. After a moment the man came to the glass and peered out, shielding his eyes against the sun.

He saw me and waved me around towards the front door. He opened it as I got there.

"Couldn't open the greenhouse door," he said. "One nip of this air and everything's gone."

"That's a beautiful show you've got," I said. Now I was here I wasn't sure how to proceed with him. There was a good chance he would throw me out once I'd given him my name.

"For sure," he said. "Come on in." He was a rangy man in his late sixties, dressed in work clothes that were old but well kept.

I came in and slipped off my overboots. "Here, I'll show you," he said. He led the way through the kitchen. It was spotlessly clean. So was his living room. Beyond it, where the window would have been, there were glass doors. He opened them into his greenhouse. It was eighty degrees in there and moist.

"Reminds me of the boonies," I said.

He looked at me very hard. His eyes were a pale blue.

"The jungle, you mean. That's why I got into it," he said. "I was in Burma."

As he spoke more I could hear his faint British accent.

I looked around. "You don't have the same kind of plants but the color's just as strong."

He grunted. "Ever price an orchid?" He waved his hand at his plants. "This is what you can afford when you're on a pension. Geraniums, African violets, a few hibiscus, wandering jew."

"Price isn't everything. These are beautiful."

"You're Bennett, aren't you?" he asked softly.

I looked into those pale eyes. There was no expression there. "Yes, I am, Mr. Wilcox, and I'm here to say I'm very sad at what happened to Randy. My father died the same way."

"Then you understand," he said. He turned his head away and fiddled with the leaves of a geranium plant. I waited until he had composed himself.

"I got a pot of coffee goin'," he said.

We went back into the kitchen where he plugged in his coffee maker. It was half full. Neither of us said anything until it had come almost to a boil. Then he poured two cups. "What do you take in it?"

"I like it black, please," I said.

He handed me the cup and nodded towards the living room. "Sit down. An' take that coat off."

I slipped out of my parka and hung it over the back of a chair and then went into the living room. He took the armchair opposite the TV. I sat on the couch.

"Did you take that woman's money?"

"No sir. I didn't. Somebody put it into my lunch pail."

He sipped and nodded. "I believe you, after what happened to Randy." His lips were pursed, tense. "He told me what you said to him."

"He told you what was going on?"

"Yeah. He told me." He looked older as he huddled with his grief. "You want to know when he told me?"

"Let me guess: last Sunday," I said.

Wilcox nodded. "Right. He sat right where you're sitting, with Jeannie next to him and he told me. Told me he'd spoken to you and he figured you were a good guy or he'd never have said anything."

"What do you make of it?" I kept my tone brisk. He was that kind of man. He would be ashamed of letting his sorrow show.

"I think that Lewicki was murdered. By the cops," he said. "And now I think that my son was murdered to shut him up."

"What did the inquiry say? I've been working nights, I didn't get to the hearing."

He set down his coffee cup next to a big fern on a stand beside him. "They said he must have been careless with the charges."

"Would he have been?"

Wilcox shook his head. "For sure not. He's been drinking, heavy, since his run-in with the police. There must have been mornings he went into work with the shakes. But Monday he was cold sober. Didn't even have a beer with me on Sunday night. Said he was off it, for keeps. So his hands were steady Monday."

"Where was his helper when this happened?"

"That's the queer part," Wilcox said. "He says he had a headache. He went back to his lunch box to get some aspirin. Very convenient."

"If he was that hung over he'd have stayed home," I said. "Guys don't work with explosives unless they're up to par."

Wilcox cleared his throat. He didn't meet my eyes. "Yeah, well that came up. This guy, his name's Nunziatta, he said that lots of days young Randy had been hung over. Only he'd always come in, so he came in as well."

"Did he say how Randy was that day?"

"Said he was normal, didn't seem like he'd had anything at all to drink. Said it was Randy's idea that he went and got an aspirin. He was in the lunchroom when the blast came."

I sat for a moment, trying to remember the procedures my father had told me about, years ago. "Was all the explosive accounted for, all the detonator caps, everything?"

"Everything was buried. What wasn't blown up in the blast," Wilcox said harshly. "They dug out everything they could, but it's not like going over somebody's parlor. You know what it's like in a stope. Miners did the looking, not police."

"What do you know about this Nunziatta?"

"Nothing much. He'd worked with Randy for a year. They got on pretty good. They used to drink together a lot over this last while, since Lewicki got killed. But from what I hear, Nunziatta used to quit earlier than Randy. He'd have a few, then go home. Randy'd stay till closing most nights."

"Did you talk to him after the hearing?"

"I didn't want to talk to anybody," Wilcox said. He cleared his throat again and when he spoke his voice was louder. He was working to control his emotion. "Like my wife died two years ago. My daughter married an accountant at the mine. They moved to Toronto and she never calls me or writes anymore. Randy was the only one I had left."

"I'm sorry, Mr. Wilcox."

"It happens. I suppose," he said. He picked up his coffee cup and gulped the rest of the contents down. "I came home and sat right here and thought about what I could do. And there didn't seem like a hell of a lot. Even if I can prove somebody murdered my boy, he's still dead."

"Nothing can change that. But if there was a proper inquiry, the guy who did it could end up in jail. And the police could be convicted. That would be a monument to him."

He looked at me coldly. "Then you're home and dried. No charge against you. Is that it?"

"The charge is phony. It isn't going to stick."

"But it's there."

I looked at him, wondering whether I could trust him. Most likely I could. He didn't seem like a blabbermouth. But on the other hand, he didn't need to know. I compromised.

"My future isn't in this town," I said. "I'm here to do a job; when it's done, I'm gone."

He narrowed his eyes. "That could mean anything."

"I'm not saying any more. But you can trust me."

He got up and went over to the dresser. He took out a can of Players cigarette tobacco and rolled himself a smoke before he answered. When it was lit he said, "I've been wondering how long it would take to send somebody like you up here. We're a long way from Toronto. Things can go wrong for a long time before the government gets around to doing anything about it."

I said nothing and he sat down again. "I take it you're here to put an end to the corruption in the police force." I didn't answer but he raised one hand. "Don't say anything. I guessed that when Randy told me you'd had a word with him at the arena. So I was thinking, if Randy had spoke up when it happened, none of this would've happened. Now what happens if I come forward?"

"It will create a scandal. But that's all. You're not an eyewitness. People will believe you but a court wouldn't. Things will go on like they are now. Only you'll be in danger."

"Then you're in danger as well," he said.

"That's part of the job. And anyway, they think they've got me in a corner, with this charge hanging over me."

"How can I help?" he asked. "I want to find out what really happened to my son and why."

"You could talk to Nunziatta. Just as Randy's father. See what he says, see if you think he's as clean as he sounds."

He nodded and smoked the last of his thin little roll-up. Then he stubbed it and said, "Okay then, that's what I'll do. But in the meantime, you're in danger. I've got something for you."

"For me?"

He stood up. "Wait there." He went through the kitchen and I heard him patter down the basement steps. When he came back he was carrying an old Lee-Enfield rifle. I recognized the military stock, a war-surplus weapon from World War Two. He snapped the bolt open and handed the rifle to me.

"This thing is accurate at four hundred yards."

I took it, frowning. "You want me to have this?"

"For two reasons," he said. "It'll give you some firepower, and it'll get it out of the house. I've been thinking a lot about using it."

"Who on?" I looked at him. He didn't seem the type to commit suicide.

"On that bastard Ferris," he said. "Since Randy died I've been sitting here thinking of getting him in my sights and pulling that trigger. I've done it before on guys I didn't know. I'd just been told to hate them."

"Do you have any shells?"

"Yeah." He opened the dresser and took out a box. Three were missing. When I looked at the gaps he said, "Three shells, three moose. One a season when I was still hunting. I'm good with that thing."

"Then I'll take it, and thank you. They took my gun when they arrested me."

He took the rifle from me and slipped out the magazine. "Let me load it," he said. I watched as he lovingly filled the mag. It was something he had done often. He handed it back to me. "Carry this in your pocket. You ever use one of these things?"

"My dad had one. The Mark Four, U-sights, just like this. He'd carried one in the British Army."

"I like the sound of him," he said and when I'd put the magazine in my pocket he shook my hand. "Thank you for coming over. I'll talk to Nunziatta and call you."

"The phone calls have started," I said. "My wife's disconnected the telephone. I live at Forty-six Bluejay Street."

"Then I'll be in touch," he said.

He walked me through to the kitchen and I transferred the magazine to my parka pocket and draped the parka over the rifle. It didn't hide it but it made it less conspicuous. "Thanks for the help," I said and left.

I stopped the car halfway back to town, put my parka on and laid the rifle, complete with magazine, on the backseat, under the blanket I keep there to catch most of Sam's hair when he rides with me. Freda didn't need to know I was armed, I decided. It would only make her more anxious.

By the time I got home Irv Goldman was back. He and Fred were in the living room, having a drink. Irv is not much of a drinker. They were sipping sherry. "Grab yourself a cold one," he commanded. "I've got news."

I pulled a Labatt's Blue out of the fridge and joined them.

"How did you get on with Berger?" I asked after I'd given Fred a quick buss.

"Very productive," Irv said. "He wants a meeting with you, tonight."

"Where?"

"Out of town." Irv grinned. "He's in real Dutch with these clowns, I could tell that. He was jumpy and evasive. When I suggested you come over there, he just about had a kitten. So he said he'd see you outside town, on the old logging road that runs west from the highway. He says it's plowed out and there's a cleared spot a mile in, where they used to store equipment."

Fred frowned. "Sounds kind of remote."

"Privacy's hard to come by in Elliot," I said. "If we meet in a public place we'll be seen, and everybody knows both of us. Word would get back to Harding. Out there we're not likely to have a car come by. Maybe the odd couple heads out there for a spot of Mom and Pop, but otherwise we're on our own."

"What time?"

"Eleven," Irv said. "By then the hotel'll be busy enough that nobody's gonna notice if he leaves. He's jumpy, Reid. I think he knows how rough these people play."

Fred spoke next. "If he's so aware of what's going on, he must have some reason for putting up with it." She shrugged. "I mean, a guy with nothing to hide would have gone to the authorities as soon as the chief moved in on him. He knows it's not legal. Why has he been putting up with it?"

Irv nodded. "I thought of that one, too. I've called Toronto to see if he's got a sheet. I'll know tomorrow." He stood up. "Now I've got to catch that flight. The case should be over by Wednesday of next week, and I'll come back up."

I stood up and shook his hand. "Thanks for the help, Irv. Left to these bastards I'd still be inside."

"Worry not. You've got friends in high places." He grinned and we shook hands, then he bussed Fred and we saw him out and waved him good-bye.

Fred shut the door and said, "I've got a butterflied leg of lamb. How does that sound?"

"Great," I told her. She was still looking tense. I hugged her. "Once I've met with Berger and set him up, this is winding down. We could be out of here by the weekend."

"You're forgetting about my class," she said, trying a smile. "What's going to happen to all my actresses?"

"You can sign them all up with your agent," I said and she grinned, glad to have the subject changed for a while.

Our evening was quiet. We didn't talk about the case. Instead we sat pretending to watch television. There was a hockey game on but it didn't hold the interest of either of us and finally I switched the set off and we played cribbage. I was glad when the clock crept up to ten-thirty.

"Well, I'm on my horse," I said. "The last act is about to begin."

"Let's hope so." She stood up. "Should I come with you?"

"No. He won't want any witnesses. But thanks anyway." I put a sweater on over my heavy shirt and then my parka and overboots. It's a maxim of mine that in winter you always dress as if you're going to have to walk home. Fred watched me, then asked, "Are you going to take Sam?"

"No. I thought I'd leave him here with you. I'm just going to talk, there's no reason for having him along."

She grinned at me crookedly. "You wouldn't lie to me, would you Reid?"

"I'm a lousy liar," I said, squeezed her hand, winked and left. I drove out of town to the logging road. As Berger had told Irv, it had been plowed out. I drove in for a mile and found the clearing, a place about an acre in extent, slashed out of the scrubby trees. It too had been plowed and I pulled in. There was no other car there.

I sat for a minute in silence, enjoying the warmth of the car. Then I checked my watch. It showed five to eleven. I felt tense. For too many days I had been the guy on the low end of the totem pole, the one unpleasant things happened to. I felt uncomfortable, and now my discomfort became too much for me. I wanted an edge, the way I would have arranged things if I were in charge. I got out of the car, taking the rifle with me, leaving the car motor running. I inserted the magazine into the rifle. The weight of the spare shells in the pocket of my parka felt comforting. I was probably overreacting, but it felt good to be in charge of my own activities again. With my heavy mitts on I couldn't use the trigger on the rifle, I would have to shuck them to fire, but I worked the bolt once to feed a shell into the chamber. It seemed like overkill, but the old tingling I had experienced so often in 'Nam was in my blood.

I walked across the clearing and into the trees, forty yards from the car. It was cold for mid-November, ten below. Later in the winter this would seem like a mild spell. After the warmth of the car I hugged into the collar of my parka and breathed through my mouth, stopping the hairs in my nose from freezing. In the spillover light from my car headlights I could see my breath like a cloud beside me. I stood still and listened.

A car came up the road. I heard it a moment before the headlights flickered through the trees on the roadside. Then it pulled into the lot. It drove up nose to nose with my car and a man got out. He walked to the driver's side of my car and I could see his right hand hanging at his side, holding a gun.

I put my right hand to my mouth and pulled off my mitt with my teeth. With my thumb I eased off the safety from the rifle and raised the gun across my chest, ready to swing it and fire. The man stood beside the door of the car for a moment and then he fired, three times, through the side window. I raised the gun and fired, taking out the back tire on my side of his car. The man yelled in alarm and ran, across the clearing and down the road on the other side. I came out of the trees and followed him, pelting as hard as I could in my heavy winter gear.

TWELVE

I WAS gaining on him and he stopped suddenly and pointed his gun. I reacted instinctively, diving to my left, rolling away so his shot sailed past me, yards wide. Then I crouched up and blazed off a round just over his head. "Halt! or the next one's going through you," I shouted.

He wailed, like a child. "Don't shoot me. Please."

"Drop the gun. In front of you."

He tossed it away from him as if it were hot. Maybe he thought this would be like a Western movie, the pistol would go off and shoot me neatly through the heart. It didn't. The hammer was down on a dead round. I stood up, keeping the rifle on him. "On the deck," I told him. He looked at me helplessly, not understanding, his hands on his head. "On the ground. Sit," I said. He sat down and I came up to him, keeping the rifle aimed at his chest.

"Don't shoot me. Please." He was babbling. "Please. I didn't mean nothing. I knew you wasn't there."

I bent and picked up his gun. It was a Colt police special, like the one I had handed to Ferris that morning.

"Who sent you?"

"Whaddya mean?" He squirmed around to look up at me, his voice pleading. I glanced back up the road where the head-lights were blazing through the trees, but there was nobody there. He had come alone.

"Whaddya gonna do?" his voice was high and frightened.

"I'm going to find out why you wanted to kill me," I said and prodded him with the gun muzzle. "Who sent you?"

"Ferris."

"Sgt. Ferris?"

"Yeah. That's him. He sent me. Gave me the gun, told me to come out here, pull up at the front of your car like I done, an' shoot you."

"Where did you get the gun?"

"He gave it to me." The voice was still high and frightened. He could have been lying but it didn't sound like it.

"Who else came with you?"

"Nobody. He said not to bring nobody else. Said I was to shoot, then get back in the car and come back to town."

"And then what?"

"Nothin'." He almost squawked it. "Just go home. That's what he said."

"What's your name?"

"Frank Nunziatta."

"Well, Frankie, you're in a whole mess of trouble," I said. "You just tried to murder a man. You'll get ten years for that."

"I knew you wasn't there," he pleaded.

"That's not going to cut any ice when I turn you over to the OPP," I said, keeping my voice angry.

"The OPP?" His voice was still fearful but it was puzzled too.

"Yeah, the OPP. You don't think I'm going to give you back to Ferris, do you?" I laughed. "Hell, you should thank me for it. You'd be found hanging in your cell tomorrow morning if I did that."

I was thinking as I spoke. Going direct to the OPP would be smart. Drive right down there and let them sort things out. Only it bothered me. So far only Ferris was implicated. They might investigate the shooting and even put pressure on Berger at the Headframe and still not catch Harding. And he was the man I was trying to uncover.

I prodded Nunziatta with my toe. "Did Ferris tell you to kill Randy Wilcox?"

"I never done that. That was like I said at the inquiry." He was still panicky but the tone of his voice had changed again. It sounded to me as if he had lied about this before. He was on familiar ground. I tried a different tack.

"How come a nice Catholic boy comes out and murders somebody on the say-so of a police sergeant? You always try to kill everybody somebody tells you to?"

"Of course not." The fear was back.

"So why now?"

"Like I had to. I owe him." His voice was almost a whisper.

"How much can you owe a cop that you promise to kill a guy?" I laughed harshly. "What's he got on you, Frankie? And don't bother lying to me. It's all going to come out when you go to court.''

"Court?'' He looked up at me and lifted his hands from his head. It must have been killing him not to be able to use them as he pleaded.

"Court,'' I said. ''What did you think? I was going to kiss and make up because you've said you're sorry?''

"Lookit, I know it was bad, what I done to your car, but I never shot you, did I? Like I knew you wasn't in the car. I just done what I was told an' I was goin' home. Then when you came back to town I was gonna tell him, 'Hey, I din't know he wasn't in the car.' That's what I was gonna do.''

"You think he'd have let you off what you owe him for a story like that?'' I prodded him with my toe. ''If you think you're in trouble now, wait until he hears what's happened.''

For the effect, and to check that there was still no one else hiding, I walked around him. He tried to follow my movement with his head, swinging it first one way, then around to the other side as I circled. ''Hey, please, you won't let him near me, eh?''

"Who else knows about this?''

"Howd'ya mean?''

"Come on,'' I snapped. ''Was Ferris the only guy you spoke to? Was he alone? What?''

"He called me at home. Said to come and see him outside the Headframe. When I got there he sat in my car, gave me the gun and told me what to do. He was on his own.''

"And what's he got on you? How come he can casually walk up and say, 'Hey, Frankie, doing anything tonight? Good. I want you to off a guy for me.' ''

"Of course not.'' In the winter stillness I could hear him swallow nervously. It sounded like somebody clearing the bolt on a rifle.

"You're into something heavy and he can send you down. That's it, isn't it?''

"Not really.'' The same whine in the voice.

"What is it? Gambling? Drugs?'' I sneered. ''Come on, Frankie. You're into something sleazy and Ferris knows. Does Harding know as well?''

"The chief?'' Nunziatta seemed surprised. ''No. I don' think so. Like I fix the guys at the mine up with pills, okay? Nothin' heavy. I wouldn' touch nothin' heavy. Just pills an' grass an' that. An' Sgt. Ferris found out an' him an' me, we got an arrangement.''

Ferris again. I was beginning to wonder whether Harding fitted in at all. I hadn't seen enough of the way he worked to know whether he just sat back and drew his pay and let Ferris run the town for him. I've known chiefs like that in other small towns. They give the speeches at the Rotary dinners while the police work is conducted for them. Perhaps Ferris was the only bad apple in the barrel. But I had to be sure. The thought gave me an idea.

"Frank, how would you like to make a deal?" I said.

"Yeah? What can I do?" He was tiring. His arms were slipping down and he was relieved when I told him, "Okay. On your feet."

"Where're we going?" he asked nervously.

"You're going to get yourself off the hook," I told him. "Come with me."

"Can I take my hands down now, please?" His voice had dropped to its normal pitch but he was still worried.

"No," I said. "Keep them up there till we get back to your car, then lean on it."

"Okay." He struggled to his feet. It's hard in winter clothing, with your hands out of commission. I didn't help him, just followed as he walked ahead back to his car and put his hands on the hood.

"Further back, and spread your feet," I told him and he did it, moving as if he had done this before. I patted him down. He was clean. I pulled his wallet and checked his ID. Francis Nunziatta was the name on his driver's license and his union card. He also had a couple of hundred dollars. I handed him back his wallet and said, "Okay. Change the tire on your car."

He got out his spare and changed the first one without saying a word. While he was doing it I checked the gun he'd used. It was mine. I wondered whether Ferris had made an official record of taking it off me that morning. If he hadn't then it would look as if I had committed suicide. The investigation done by Ferris would have ignored the holes through the glass and the multiple shots and the entry angle of the wound.

Nunziatta straightened up and put his blown wheel in the trunk.

"Get that coat off," I told him.

"How'dya mean? I'll freeze," he said.

"Do it," I told him and he did. He was wearing a heavy flannel shirt and I opened it. He had an undershirt and I tugged it up. "Hands on your head again." He did as I said and I leaned the rifle against his car and took out the tiny microphone from my pocket and the roll of surgical tape. I taped it on his chest. "Dress up again and sit in the car," I told him. "The driver's seat."

I picked up my rifle again, then switched off his car lights and took the keys out of the ignition. He watched me, then got into the car. "Wind the window up," I told him. "And start talking."

"Whaddya want me to say?"

"Your prayers might not be a bad idea," I said. I took the receiver out of my pocket, and stuck the button in my ear and held the tape recorder in my hand. "Go on, talk."

I walked away listening. Nunziatta was talking almost to himself, a low mumbling that I could make out as baffled swearing. I could see he was watching me and he began to speak louder. "I can see you. I'm talkin'. What more you want me to say?" I checked the playback on the recorder, then switched it off and put it into my pocket.

"Okay," I called and nodded to him, then walked back and got into the car next to him. "Here." I gave him the keys. "Start the car." He did, turning the heat up high. "Now I'm going to caution you on a charge of attempted murder."

"I thought we had a deal," he blustered.

"We do, but this is one of the conditions."

He swore, but under his breath, and I gave him the caution and his rights. "Okay Mr. Nunziatta, tell me what happened tonight, the sixteenth of November."

I switched on the tape recorder and led him through the facts, asking a couple of polite questions so that the tape would be clean enough to use in evidence, then thanked him and switched the machine off.

"Right, Frankie. Let's go." I could see he was angry with me for using the diminutive for his name. That was my reason for doing it. It gave me control, treating him like a naughty child.

"We're going to call on the chief," I said. "Drive."

We drove into town and I gave him his instructions. He was to pull up on the street, somewhere out of the lights, where I would not be visible from the house. He was to open his parka

and go to the door and ask for the chief. He then had to get the
chief alone and tell him what he had done.

"What if he asks me for the gun?"

"Tell him that Ferris said to leave it in my car," I told him.
"Let's go."

He drove up to the house and I crouched in my seat as he got
out and walked to the door. I turned the tape machine on and
waited.

On my earplug I heard the ringing of the doorbell. Then the
clatter of the door and a woman's voice. "Yes?" she asked
curtly.

"I need to speak to the chief. It's important," Nunziatta
said.

"He's at the police station. Why didn't you go there?"

"I din' think he'd be there this time of night. Sorry to bother
you." I heard the door close and then Nunziatta came back. He
got into the car. "He ain't in."

"I heard," I told him. "Drive to the police station and park
on the street. If there's any policemen around, go up to them
so they don't come and look in the car. Tell them you're looking for the chief. Otherwise, go right on in."

"Okay. You're the boss." Having me crouched out of sight
had given him back his normal cockiness. When we reached the
station he said, "There's two p'lice cars here, an' the chief's car,
an' Sgt. Ferris's. What if the sergeant's there?"

"If Ferris asks you what you want, start making a commo-
tion, make sure the chief gets into the room."

"Lookit, I ain't no goddamn actor," he blustered.

"No, but you're Italian. Just start waving your arms around,
talking loud—that ought to do it," I said. "And get it right,
Frankie. If we don't nail the chief on this one, all bets are off,
you're going inside. So remember that and be goddamn con-
vincing."

He swore but he didn't argue. He got out and walked into the
station. On the monitor I heard the door slam and then a man's
voice asking, "What do you want?"

"I have to see the chief. It's important. His wife said he was
here."

"The chief's busy," the voice said. I recognized it; it was
Walker speaking.

"This time of night an' he's busy? Hell, it's after eleven. I
figured he'd be home, gettin' ready for bed."

"He ought to be," Walker said. "We all ought to be. Only something came up."

"What happened, for Chrissakes?" Nunziatta was acting natural, the indignant citizen.

"It'll be on the radio in the morning, I guess." Walker's voice was tight and high, anxious.

"Yeah, well I can't wait for the morning. I have to see him now, this is important. I told you."

"Way to go, Frankie," I murmured.

"You're a pain, Nunziatta," Walker said. Then there was a clattering and a short wait and I heard Harding's voice.

"Yes. What's this about?" he asked.

"It's private, chief. Like I'm sorry if you're busy but I have to talk to you on your own."

"Go ahead then. Walker, you go through to the guard-room. Don't touch anything, put your hands in your pockets. Understand?"

"Yessir." More noise and then it was Harding's voice. "This had better be important."

"It is important." Nunziatta sounded nervous. He cleared his throat, it was explosive in my earpiece. "Like it's something I done for Sgt. Ferris."

"Indeed?" Harding's voice dropped its anger, becoming almost playful. "And what would that be, Mr. Nunziatta?"

"Yeah, well, like he asked me to kill a guy. He gave me a gun and told me where the car would be an' that. I had to go up there and walk around next to the car an' shoot 'im through the window."

"When was this?" Harding's question took me by surprise. He should have acted startled, not matter-of-fact.

"He called me around nine-thirty. Said to meet him at the Headframe, which I done. Then he gave me a gun an' told me to go out to the clearing on the old logging road. Said there would be a car there with a guy in it. I was t' go up beside it an' let 'im have it."

"And did you do it?" Harding's voice was still smooth, almost a purr.

I had coached Nunziatta on his answer and he played it perfectly. "I did what he said." Even the grammar was correct.

"Then I have to tell you that you're in a whole lot of trouble," Harding said.

I frowned and straightened up. Nunziatta's voice was spluttering in my ear. "How'dya mean? Like this guy's a cop, a sergeant, for Chrissakes. He told me to do somethin' an' I did it. It's him's in trouble. Not me."

"I think you'd better come and see him for yourself," Harding said. "This way."

There was a clatter as the countertop flap was raised, then Nunziatta was walking a few paces. I heard a door open and then Nunziatta gave a half scream. "Mother o' God, what happened?"

"Suicide," Harding said. "It seems that Sgt. Ferris felt so bad about what he'd asked you to do that he came back into the station, went into the guardroom and blew his brains out with his service revolver."

THIRTEEN

I SAT listening to Nunziatta's babble, not even taking in the words. Ferris was dead. What did it mean? And what did I do next? The confession I'd taken from Nunziatta meant nothing now.

He was babbling, but making sense. "Listen. I didn't kill nobody," he was saying. "Like it was Offic'r Bennett in the car only he wasn' in the car. He's outside now. He said to come in."

"Then we'd better have a word with him," Harding said smoothly. "Walker, go and bring Bennett in, will you."

I took the earplug out of my ear and put it in my pocket, then I turned off the tape recorder and sat up, innocent as a baby, waiting for Walker.

He came to the side of the car and I opened the door. He looked anxious.

"Reid, what the hell's goin' on? Nunziatta's in there sayin' he tried to shoot you."

"He did, with my own gun yet. Ferris sent him. That's why I brought him back to talk to the chief."

"Yeah. That's the other thing." Walker was almost frantic, the words exploding out of him. "Ferris shot himself. I found him when I came in for work. He's in the guardroom, on the floor."

"You're kidding." I wasn't married to an actress for nothing. I got out of the car and shoved my arms apart speechlessly.

"True," Walker said. "Really. I nearly threw up when I saw him. Anyways, all hell's breakin' loose. The chief's down here an' when Nunziatta came in an' said he'd been sent to off you, Harding said he wants to talk to you."

"I guess he does. Let's go." I slammed the car door and followed Walker. He was half a pace ahead of me, almost running to get back inside.

He led me through the guardroom. Harding was standing by the door and he held one hand up. "You can't come in, Bennett."

"You wanted to see me?"

"Yes. Mr. Nunziatta says he was sent out to meet you and shoot you. Says he did what he was told, and yet here you are, large as life. What's going on?"

"You'd better ask the sergeant. He's the guy who sent Frankie out there."

"I'm afraid that's not possible." He turned and stepped back a pace so I could see into the room. "Look."

I craned forward to see. Sgt. Ferris was lying on his left side on the guardroom floor. There was a pool of congealed blood under his head, and I could see the neat black entry wound in the right temple, just forward of the ear. On the floor behind him was a service revolver where it had fallen from his sprawled hand.

"Who found him?"

I expected him to snub me, but he answered at once. "Walker did. When he came in for the midnight shift."

"What time was that? Nunziatta tells me he was talking to Ferris around nine o'clock, outside the Headframe."

Now Harding collected himself, drawing himself up taller, putting his own horrors behind him. "I want to know where you were between then and now."

I could see Nunziatta staring at me, ready to break into a babble of denial if I said anything he didn't feel comfortable with. I adjusted the story slightly. "I wanted to talk to him about the cave-in at the mine. He said he'd meet me outside town. Sgt. Ferris must have heard about it because he gave Nunziatta a gun and told him to look out for himself. I wouldn't have known except I saw the bump in his pocket and took it off him."

Harding held out his hand. "Where is it?"

I took it out of my pocket, emptied the shells into my hand and gave him the weapon, broken open. He took it and snapped it shut. "A police weapon."

"Yeah. It's mine. That's why I came back here with Nunziatta, I wanted to know how come Ferris had handed him my gun. Didn't he keep a record of taking if off me this morning?"

"I'll check," Harding said. He turned his back on me and walked over to Nunziatta, digging him in the chest with a stiff forefinger. "What did the sergeant say to you?"

Nunziatta was a gifted liar. He picked up my story and embroidered it.

"He said he'd heard I was s'posed to be meeting Mr. Bennett an' he said that Bennett was mean. I needed some protection. So he gave me the gun." He did a beautiful Neapolitan headshake. "Hell, I don' know nothin' about guns. I done like he said. I took it, put it in my pocket, only Mr. Bennett guessed an' he took it offa me."

"I want a formal statement, off both of you," Harding said. "Walker, take a statement from Mr. Nunziatta. Bennett, you come with me."

He turned away and marched in front of me, down the corridor to his office. He went inside and shut the door. "Sit," he ordered and I sat.

He paced up and down once behind his desk, hands behind his back, thoughtful.

"You're not what you seem, are you Bennett?"

"I don't know what you mean," I said. Playing dumb is always the best thing to do, people explain themselves and you get an idea of their motives.

He sat down abruptly, putting his elbows on the desk, hands clenched, staring at me. "Let me spell it out for you. I had a nice, well-run department until you arrived. We were doing a good job of keeping the peace in a place where it's not always easy. Then you arrive. Suddenly I've got a bar owner who thinks you're trying to shake him down. I have a prostitute murdered, or close to it. Then her money turns up in your lunch pail. And now this."

I shrugged. "None of this has anything to do with me, chief. I was just trying to do the job the way you outlined it for me."

He unclasped his hands and laid them on the desk carefully, as if they were evidence in the case. "I am not a stupid man, Bennett, and I don't think you are, either. It occurs to me that someone sent you here to investigate the department."

He looked at me levelly. I returned his gaze, frowning slightly as if I were puzzled, until he went on. "I know there have been rumors, stories of corruption in town. I've heard them, followed up on them, but never found any substance. Just the anger and hatred that most police departments generate among the criminal fringes of society."

I shrugged. "Nobody likes cops."

He suddenly slapped his right hand on the desk startlingly. "But since you came here, everything has escalated." He stood up again, rigid with anger. "Who sent you, Bennett?"

I sat back, acting startled. "I don't know what the hell you're talking about. I came up here looking for a job and a quiet life. I fill the job description. I do my work, I go home. Now you're talking about conspiracies. You're not making any sense."

He glared at me, then ticked off on his fingers. "One, you talk to Berger at the hotel and the next thing he's calling and asking me to get you off his back. Two. You arrest young Wilcox, and the next thing I know there's been a very suspicious accident in the mine. Three, you find this whore with a kimono sleeve around her neck and I discover her money in your lunch box."

It was time to counterattack, before he got too close to the truth. "Okay." I stood up and shouted at him, "I didn't put that goddamn money in there and I want to know who did. Was it Ferris? And why did Ferris interfere in my meeting with Nunziatta this evening? Why did he give him a gun? And why did he come back here and blow his brains out on the guard-room floor? He's the guy you should be investigating. Have you checked his bank account? Have you ever thought for two seconds that the corruption stories might be true, that maybe your sergeant was ripping off the people in this town? Have you?"

He sat down carefully, as if his bones were very brittle. He looked old and tired. "Yes," he said softly. "I've thought that, once or twice, but nothing ever substantiated what I was thinking. Sgt. Ferris had enemies. He was too quick to hand out physical punishment, but he was straight. I had tips, anonymous mostly, and when I followed them up there was nothing in them."

"More than one anonymous call? About the same guy? Didn't that make you suspicious? How many of the other guys were accused?"

"The other men didn't have the same reputation for toughness," Harding said. He sounded weary.

"He was crooked," I said angrily. "He gave my gun to some rounder. What's all that about?"

"That's something I intend to find out from our friend Nunziatta," he said.

"And where do I fit in?"

He sniffed, staring down at his desk. "I am going to make a public statement in the morning saying that Sgt. Ferris's suicide is conclusive proof that you did not take that money and that you are forthwith reinstated."

"Well thank you for that, chief."

He nodded, tight-lipped. "We'll have a total housecleaning in this department. You can be in charge of it."

"Me? What are the other guys going to say?"

"They're going to call you sergeant and do what you tell them." He grinned briefly, a courtesy.

"You're promoting me?"

"Yes." He nodded to dismiss any thanks. "You've got the experience. None of these guys could detect a bad smell if they were standing in it. I'm making you the sergeant and giving you the responsibility for digging into whatever it is that Ferris was doing in town."

I stood up and thrust out my hand, grinning. "Hey, thank you, chief. I'll do the best job you've ever seen."

"You'd better," he said, giving my hand a perfunctory shake. "Right now I want you to investigate the killing. Then go over to his house and take it to pieces, find out if he had any money squirreled away, any drugs, anything."

"I'll need a search warrant."

"You'll have it." He was enjoying being decisive. "You've got a free hand."

"What about Nunziatta? He says he saw Ferris at the Headframe parking lot. He could be lying, he could have seen him here, shot him and then come up to try to shoot me."

"Work on him, as well. I want this whole thing resolved."

"Yessir." I nodded. "I'll get on it right away."

"Good," he said. "Send Walker in here and start."

"Right." I came to attention and turned smartly. If I was his man, I'd better start acting the part.

Walker was in the front office, pecking away on the office typewriter while Nunziatta sat opposite him, smoking and sweating. Walker looked up when I came in. "Heading home?"

"No. I'm back on the job," I said.

He grinned and stood up. "Hey, great. I didn't think you'd taken that broad's money."

"Thanks." I shook hands with him. "The chief wants to see you. I'll baby-sit Frankie until you get back."

He put his hat on and walked down the corridor. I leaned over the typewriter and checked the statement he was taking. It was essentially the story I had come up with on the spur of the moment. I looked up and found Nunziatta grinning at me. "I got it right?" he queried.

"You're going to have to do better than this, Frank. I want the truth."

He exploded. "Shit. I was jus' doin' like you said, coverin' your ass."

"And your own." I tapped the typewriter. "When Mr. Walker comes back I'm telling him to tear this crap up and start again. This time I want the truth, the whole truth, and nothing but the truth."

"Where'd you get off ordering me around?"

"You surrendered your license to lie when you took that shot at me," I said.

"We had a deal," he spluttered.

"We still do." I leaned across the desk and smiled into his soul. "That's why you're sitting here instead of on a bench in the cells. But I want the whole truth in that statement. That means you're out of the dope business for keeps."

He swore and scrubbed his hand over his head, ruffling his hair. "I'll take that wire as well," I said, holding out my hand.

He opened his shirt and pulled it off his chest, hissing as a chunk of his chest fur came away with the tape. I took the device and stuck it away in my pocket. Then, as he was buttoning his shirt, we heard footsteps in the corridor, and Walker came back, looking startled. He came up and stuck out his hand. "Congratulations, Reid. The chief just told me."

"Told you what?" Nunziatta asked in a squawk.

"Mr. Bennett is the sergeant here," Walker said. His voice was high, full of pep, but I could read his bitterness. He was the man who should have got the job, he thought.

"Thanks, Jeff," I said. "Now I'm going to have a look in the other room. I've had a talk to Mr. Nunziatta and he's going to tell you the truth. You'll need a new statement form; this one is incorrect."

Walker pulled the paper out of the machine and laid it aside. "Right, sarge," he said and I grinned.

I left them sitting there and walked back to the guardroom, closing the door. First I went over and crouched by the body, making sure I wasn't obscuring any evidence. The entrance wound had powder burns around it. He had been shot from within inches. It didn't automatically mean he'd done it himself, it just meant that the gun had been close to his head. I squatted lower and peered at the other side of his head. I could see there was massive damage, the kind that would be caused by a hollow point round. I stood up, standing where I thought he must have stood and crouching slightly so I would be the same height as he had been in life, and pointed my finger at my temple. It gave me an approximate entry angle. I stepped over the body and inspected the far wall.

I found the hole, up close to the ceiling, punched through the drywall covering. I made a circle around it with my pencil and walked back to the body, very slowly, looking up at the ceiling for bloodstains. The ceiling hadn't been painted for a long time and there were flyspecks everywhere, but I saw a few spots that might have been cranial matter and I penciled each of them. There were a few more on the floor, which was waxed every week and was cleaner.

Then I checked the location of the gun. It was lying where it would have fallen from his lifeless hand, blown backwards by the recoil. I didn't touch it but went back down to Harding's office and tapped on the door. He was on the telephone, and he waved me in. "Yes, I'm sorry doctor, but it's an emergency, a fatality. Could you come over right away?"

He waited, then thanked the person at the other end and hung up. "What does it look like?"

"Looks kosher to me, chief. I want to fingerprint the weapon and the rounds, and I'd like permission to dig out a chunk of the guardroom wall."

"Right. The photographer will be here in a few minutes. Wait until he's taken his pictures before you change anything. Anything else?"

I needed a statement from Walker. After that I wanted to backtrack the sergeant's movements to see if anyone had seen him since he spoke to Nunziatta.

Harding looked startled. "You think Nunziatta did it?"

"It would fit with his having my gun," I said. "But he's not acting like a guy who just blew a man's brains out. I'm going to talk to him."

"Lean on him," Harding said. "I want the truth."

He waved, dismissing me, and I went out to the front office. Walker looked up. "Is this right? He says Ferris gave him a gun and told him to shoot you."

"Seems that way." I stood beside Nunziatta. "What I want to know, Frankie, is where you were between nine o'clock, when you say you got this gun, and eleven, which is when you tried to kill me."

"I had things to do," Nunziatta said.

"Like what? A house call in your pharmacy business?"

He shrugged, pursing his lips. "Yeah, well."

"Where did you go?"

Now he was uncomfortable. "Look, I saw some guys, okay?"

"Which guys, where? In case the thought hasn't crossed your mind, you're the number-one suspect in the death of Sgt. Ferris," I said.

He stood up, half shouting his answer. "Are you crazy? I told you, I saw him in the parking lot outside the Headframe Hotel. That was two hours before I saw you on the side road. He was alive then, drivin' his car."

"We only have your word for that, Frankie, until we check with these customers of yours."

Walker took over smoothly. "No big deal, Frank. You tell us who you went to see, we check with them, you're in the clear."

Nunziatta sat and thought for a moment, frowning with the effort. "Yeah, well, I did see a couple guys."

"Where and when?"

"The first one was outside the community center."

"What's the guy's name?"

He swallowed hard. "Look, I don't want no trouble."

"You've already got all the trouble you can handle. Who did you see?"

"Jacques, you know, the guy as runs the place."

The news surprised me. I wouldn't have expected Jacques to be doing business with Nunziatta. I had pegged him as squarer than that. "What time was this?"

"Around nine-thirty."

"What took you so long? You could have been there in two minutes."

"I had to go and pick up the merchandise."

"Where from?"

"From my stash." He became excited again. "Listen. Do I have to go over all this?"

"For sure. Where's your stash?"

"Over in the old town."

"Where exactly in the old town?"

He got cunning again. "Somewhere safe." He looked up at me with a smug half grin. "You gotta be careful."

"I told you, you're out of business, Frankie," I said. "When Mr. Walker is through with this statement he'll go there with you and pick up your supply."

He opened his mouth to argue but thought better of it and said nothing. I dropped the next question on him. "What did you sell to Jacques?"

"Grass," he said. "I see him every week. He gets a bag, that's all."

"Then where'd you go?"

"Out to the mine site."

"And saw who?"

"Couple guys from my shift in the mine. One's called George, the other one's Vlad. I don' know their last names."

"Okay, so you used up about an hour. Where else did you go before you came to see me?"

"I went to the Headframe. I was kind of shook. You know, what he asked me to do an' all. I had a drink."

"What time was that?"

He shrugged again and his voice was impatient. "I don't know."

"Don't give me this macho garbage, Frankie. I was up there when you were crying, 'Don't shoot, please don't shoot me,' like a kid. You're gutless and we both know it. Just answer the question."

"Awright. I'm sorry. I don't know what time I got there. I left at ten to eleven. I know that."

I stepped back a pace and nodded to Walker. He got up and followed me as I retreated down the corridor into the guard-room. I stopped, out of earshot of Nunziatta, who was strain-ing to hear us. "When you're through with his statement go with him. Pick up his stash, then check with all three of his customers on time and place of their meetings. They'll lie, but tell them you'll search their places and lay charges if they don't talk. Then charge Nunziatta with trafficking and put him in the cells."

"Right, sarge." The rank came more easily this time.

I patted him on the shoulder and went into the guardroom. There were still a couple of things to do before I surrendered the body. But first I had to wait for the photographer. He arrived a few minutes later. He was shaken by the sight of Ferris's body, and he didn't say much, but once he got behind his viewfinder he became professional and took the shots I needed. Harding came in and watched the photographer work. He didn't speak. He looked out of his depth. I wondered how much he had depended on Ferris for support.

When the photographer had finished and gone, Harding stayed there, still not speaking, as I blackened Ferris's fingertips and rolled each one on the appropriate place on the page. After that I lifted the gun, using a pencil inserted into the barrel so I wouldn't disturb any prints. It was meaningless, probably. If somebody else had shot him they would have wiped it down. Otherwise I would find his prints.

A few minutes later the doctor arrived, the same man who had attended the strangled woman.

He looked at me oddly. "I thought you were suspended," he said.

"Not anymore," I said, and the chief came alive suddenly and explained for me.

"In case you're wondering what's happening, doctor, I believe that Sgt. Ferris was responsible for the attack on that woman, last night. When she survived, I think he panicked and did this to himself. In the meantime, the charges against Officer Bennett have been dropped and he is reinstated with promotion to sergeant."

The doctor grinned and gave me his hand. "Glad to hear that, sergeant. My wife is attending the drama class your wife's started. She was very upset when she heard you'd been suspended."

"Thanks. So was I."

He nodded, tightly indicating that playtime was over, then crouched by Ferris's body, looking at the head injury as far as he could without moving anything. "Well, he's dead. They don't come any deader."

"Thank you, doctor. If your men can move him, please. There'll be an inquest."

He smiled wryly. "More work."

"That's your job, too?"

"There's only two of us on staff at the hospital, and I'm the senior man."

"How are you with forensics, doctor?"

"I'm no expert, but I know the fundamentals."

"Good. Can you test his hand for me, please? See if there's any powder traces on it."

He narrowed his eyes. "Don't you think he shot himself?"

"Routine," I said, for the chief's benefit. "I'd like to be sure."

He stood back, motioning down the corridor to the ambulance attendants. They came in and looked at the body. One of them was young and hip with his hair long enough to cover his ears and his cap tipped sideways. The other one was older and squarer. They were startled when they recognized the body, but only the younger one spoke. "Well, well," he said knowingly.

We all watched as they loaded Ferris into a body bag and put the bundle on their gurney. As they trundled it out I turned to the doctor. "How soon do you think you can check the powder deposits, doc?"

He sucked his teeth, thinking. "The materials have to be flown in from the forensics center in Toronto. I won't be able to do anything until they arrive."

I nodded. "If you would do it when you can, please, we need to know." I was sorry he didn't have the materials at hand. It would have been good to test both the chief and Walker as well as the corpse.

He left and I got out my pocketknife and chipped away the drywall around the bullet hole. I was lucky. The stud was right behind it and the bullet was embedded in the soft pine. I cut it out and put the bullet in an evidence bag for comparison with the shells in Ferris's gun. Then I stuck the bag in my pocket and turned to the chief, who was still watching me, doing nothing, like any spectator at an accident. He was not acting the way a policeman, especially a senior officer, should act. He seemed empty, useless.

"I'm going to backtrack the sergeant's movements since nine," I said. "Walker is going to take Nunziatta over to pick up his drugs and question some guys he dealt with tonight. I'll radio from wherever I get to if I need help."

Harding pulled himself together. "Right. Will you need extra men?"

"Who's available?"

"Levesque is off at midnight. I can keep him on if you need him."

"Thanks, chief. I'll let you know."

I put my parka back on and took the keys to one of the cars from the board, nodded at Harding and left.

The first thing I did was drive home to give Fred a two-minute update. She was anxious. "You've been ages," she said, holding me. "What happened?"

I filled her in quickly and she gasped. "One day you're arrested, next day you're the sergeant. Hell, Reid, it's like a game of Snakes and Ladders."

I gave her a quick kiss on the cheek. "It's good to be working again. I have to check some things out. Don't wait up—I'll probably be most of the night."

She clung to me for a moment and I kissed her and left, leaving Sam with her. Then I was on my way, debating priorities. Did I need to check on Ferris's movements, or to talk to Berger? I still hadn't worked out why he and Ferris would have set me up for an ambush.

FOURTEEN

THERE WERE half a dozen cars at the Headframe. I parked and went in. Business was slowing, there were only three knots of drinkers at tables and a couple of men at the bar. The same thin barman was on duty. He stared at me curiously but said nothing, just turned away to look at the big TV, which was showing an old Clint Eastwood movie. I went up to him, feeling the eyes of all the men on me. None of them knew about my miraculous reinstatement. I was still the guy who robbed whores, and they were waiting for their chance to despise me out loud.

I canceled the idea right away. "My name is Bennett, Sgt. Bennett, Elliot police. Was Sgt. Ferris in here tonight?"

I spoke loudly enough to reach the other tables, and I caught the buzz of surprise.

The barman frowned disbelievingly. "I heard you was off the job."

"I've been promoted to sergeant," I said curtly. "This is an investigation, so let's have some answers, please. Have you seen Sgt. Ferris in here tonight?"

The barman flopped his cloth on the bar top and swirled it back and forth, taking his time answering. "Yeah, he was in," he said at last.

"What time?"

He shrugged and gave a sly little grin. "Hell, I don't know. I don't keep tabs on the customers."

I trapped his hand and he looked up startled. "I'm not playing games. Ferris is dead. What time was he in here?"

That shook him. His face lost its grin, his mouth fell open. "Dead? What happened?"

"You'll read about it in the paper. What time was he here?"

He glanced up at the clock on the far wall, licking his lips. "An hour ago, something like that."

"How long did he stay?"

The barman cleared his throat. I knew he was going to lie. "I'm not sure. Like we were busy then, you know how it is."

"Did he talk to anybody?"

His eyes darted away from me, then back as he gained whatever courage he needed to stretch the truth. "I didn't see him talkin' to anybody. He came in for a drink. I poured it. He sat down there, at the end of the bar."

"How many drinks did he have?" It was easier than asking him to remember times. I'd seen Ferris drink. One per ten minutes would have been about right.

"Couple," he said, but again it was too quick.

"How about a guy called Frank Nunziatta, Italian, around five seven, one-seventy, thirty-five."

He frowned. "I don't remember him."

I changed my tack. "Where's Berger?"

Now the grin came back, clouding his face like five o'clock shadow, blurring his hostility. "Out for the evening."

"Out where?"

He widened the grin. "Now he's a grown boy, ain't he. He don't tell me everything."

He had freed his hand and moved back a few inches from the bar, but I reached out and grabbed his shirt, tugging him forward so he was leaning over the bar, off balance, struggling to keep his feet. "Where? Tell me before I find you've been serving booze to drunks and lock you up." I threw him away from me lightly and he staggered back, his hand at his throat, readjusting his shirtfront.

"'Re you threatening me?"

"Now you're smartening up." I beamed at him. "Where's Berger?"

"With his woman." He spat the word out disgustedly.

"Where?"

He opened his mouth to make some quick reply but I smiled at him and he coughed nervously. "She lives on Grackle Court. Number eighteen."

I nodded to him. "Right. I'm going over there to see him. If, when I get there, I find him expecting me, you are going to wish you'd never come to this town. You got that?"

He didn't speak, and I stood there looking through him until he nodded. "Right."

Grackle Court was part of the two-story enclave in town. By city standards the houses were small and unimposing but they were the best Elliot could offer, and Number eighteen looked cared for. There were a couple of small floodlights in the snow, giving a bluish cast to the front of the house. Inside it seemed dark. If Berger was there, his R and R was underway.

I rang the doorbell and waited, standing to one side of the door. After a long pause a woman's voice called, "Who's there?"

"Sgt. Bennett, p'lice. Open up." I clipped my name short and kept my voice gruff so that she might think I'd said Ferris. I wanted her and her date off balance.

The door opened three inches. I could see a thin slice of the woman inside. She was blond, wearing a black kimono. "What is it?" she demanded.

"I want to talk to Berger." Politeness would be a waste of time. I kept up the pressure.

"He's not here," she barked and moved to shut the door.

I shoved my foot against it and said, "Let me in. This is serious."

She spluttered as she heaved her shoulder against the door. The usual irate citizen speech. Then I heard another voice behind her, and she disappeared from sight. My foot took up the extra inch of slack and then another face appeared in the crack.

It was Berger. "Bennett?" His voice went up an octave.

"Surprise, surprise," I said. "Open up."

He backed off a half pace and I stepped in. The pair of them stood looking at me without speaking. The woman was blazing angry but silent, Berger was trying to decide what kind of face he should be showing. He was wearing a shirt and slacks with his suspenders dangling. Both of them were barefoot.

I shoved him in the chest with a forefinger. "Shook up, huh? Thought you'd seen the last of me."

"What is this?" The woman spoke first. She was short, her forehead came only as high as my chin, but she had more guts than Berger. "Who in hell d'you think you are?"

"I have to talk to your friend," I said. "In private. I can do it here or I can stand him outside in the snow."

Berger looked at her, smiling weakly. "It's all right, Belle. This won't take long."

She swore but she flounced off into a bedroom and banged the door shut behind her.

Berger tried to get his act going. "What's this all about?"

"It's about sending a boy to do a man's job," I said. "Your friend Nunziatta blew it. I arrested him and locked him up."

"Nunziatta?" He shoved his fingers through his hair open-mouthed. "What's going on?"

"Why did you send him?" I moved in on him, crowding him, making him aware how ridiculous he looked in his thrown-on clothes.

"Send him?" He tried to sound baffled, but I shoved him through the open door of the living room and followed him in, switching on the light at the door. "Sit," I ordered as if I were giving a command to Sam.

He looked startled but he did it without arguing.

"Right," I said. "Now I want some honest answers and I want them fast. Why did you send Nunziatta to shoot me?"

"Honest to God I don't know what you're talking about."

"Right. Let's take it one step at a time," I said. "My lawyer came to you with a request for a meeting between me and you. Is that right?"

"Yes, that's right." Now his words tumbled out. "I wasn't sure what to think. I asked him what for and he wouldn't say, said you had a proposition for me. That could have meant anything at all."

"So what did you do?"

"I didn't know what to do. Then Sgt. Ferris came into the hotel and I told him what had happened. He asked what time the meeting was supposed to be and where."

"You'd already picked the spot. Remember? A nice discreet little spot for a back shooting. Don't con me, Berger. I want the truth. And for a start, I know that Ferris came into the bar after nine, after he'd spoken to Nunziatta."

He ignored the second part of my statement; he was still working on his own involvement. "For Chrissakes, I knew you wouldn't want to be seen with me, in case Ferris was having you watched. That's why I picked the clearing. Where else could we meet?"

"What's wrong with your office? What are you hiding, Berger?"

He made a move to stand up, but I put my hand on his head and shoved. He swore but subsided. "It's complicated," he said.

"That was yesterday." I grunted a laugh. "Today it's worse than that. You've got an attempted murder charge standing against you."

"Attempted murder? Who of?" His voice was as shrill as nails on a blackboard. He was stretched to breaking point, but I didn't let up on him.

"Of me. If Nunziatta was better at his job I'd be dead. Instead of that he's inside explaining who sent him."

"It wasn't me." His voice had the same screech, but I read the double meaning in it.

"No. It was your buddy Ferris. Is that why you went down to the police station and blew his brains out?"

"What?" He almost whispered it. "What did you say?"

"I came down here from sweeping his brains off the guardroom floor." It was deliberately brutal. I wanted him horrified.

He sat and looked up at me, struggling to make sense of the news. "The sergeant's dead?"

"Thirty-eight through the head will do that to a man," I said. "But don't worry. The department carries on. I've been reinstated, with the rank of sergeant."

"Jesus Christ, I don't know what's going on." He jammed both hands through his hair.

"I do," I said. "I know that you set me up to be killed. What I want to know is why."

He opened his mouth to speak but I overrode him. "You're paying off the police department. I want to know details. How much are you paying and who's getting the money?"

"I don't know where you got that idea," he said. He smoothed his hair with his fingers, getting control of himself again. Maybe it was the mention of money, but he was becoming what he had been in his own office, the big frog in a little pond, the kind of guy that small-town people have to tiptoe around.

"Talk fast," I said.

He smoothed his hair with his hands. I noticed for the first time that the roots were slightly lighter than the even darkness of the rest of it. Then he spoke, his voice composed. "I can understand how you feel, but I had nothing to do with it. Nothing." He waited to see if I was going to question him, then went on. "What I've told you is the truth. I was surprised when your lawyer wanted to set up a meeting. But he sounded like it was important so I said 'sure.' I knew you were in trouble for taking that woman's money so I suggested a private place."

"Smooth as silk," I sneered. "Then you set up the guy with the gun."

He shook his head and his voice was reasonable, unshaken, the way it would be on the witness stand. "No. It wasn't anything like that. I began to worry. You're under investigation for a pretty bad crime. I'm a respectable businessman. I started to worry, like I said. Then Sgt. Ferris came in and I told him about my concern and he said he would see to it."

"Beautiful. All I need is violins and I'll cry," I said. "And then you went around to the police station and blew the sergeant's brains out with his own gun and all your troubles are over."

His face was expressionless. He looked out of his pale blue eyes and said nothing. He was practicing for court, and I was beaten.

I made the best move I had left. "A couple of days ago you gave me to believe that you were paying off the police in town. I want to know if it's true."

"Are you trying to shake me down?" He was in full control now, the surprised citizen.

"Are you paying off the police department?" I kept my voice even, staring at him, but he just looked back, blandly.

"What gives you that idea?"

"Just say I'm psychic."

He took his eyes off me and began doing up the buttons on his cuffs. "I have an excellent relationship with the police in this town."

"Where were you before you owned the Headframe?"

He frowned now, another courtroom gesture. Whatever he was, this guy was used to acting honest for an audience. It was the most damning thing about him, and it meant nothing to anyone but me. "How do you mean?"

"Where did you come from, to buy the Headframe?"

"I previously owned a hotel down south. I've been in the business for twenty years. Why?"

"When did you buy this place?"

"It came up for sale in July after the previous owner died. I bought it then."

He had beaten me. I had nothing on him but the fact that he had told Ferris about our meeting. It was enough to make the hair on my neck stand up, but in a courtroom it was no more than conversation. I cut my losses. "I'll be in your office at nine in the morning to get a full statement. You can go back to bed until then."

His poise slipped one degree as he said, "I'll be there." His tone was pushy; he was exulting in his win.

I left. He followed me to the door and saw me out without saying another word. I was off balance. I'd been certain I had all the answers to the puzzle, but none of them fit the slots I'd expected. Ferris's death had changed everything. Before that I had known what to do. I could have charged Ferris and let him put everything together for me in his plea bargaining. Now he was gone and Berger had closed ranks with the chief. I had no doubts about their relationship. The mystery was, why was Berger so anxious to maintain it?

There was nothing to do but trail back to the station and check what was happening there.

Walker was in the guardroom with the chief and Nunziatta. The chief was examining a plastic bag of grass, a pretty small bag, I thought, for the only dealer in town.

"Is this all he had in his stash?" I asked.

Walker nodded. "Yeah, this an' some pills." He held up another bag that was lying on a chair. It was filled with plastic envelopes of pills. "Uppers an' downers."

The chief looked at me. "Any idea what the street value of this is?"

"Not much," I said, picking up the grass. "What were you charging, Frankie?"

"Ten," he said. He was nervous and quiet.

"About four hundred bucks for this, about six hundred for the pills," I told the chief. "Are you charging him with trafficking?"

"Of course." Harding nodded briskly. "I dislike drugs more than just about any other form of crime." He could have modeled for a recruiting poster for honest lawmen.

Nunziatta squawked, "I got a deal goin' with Mr. Bennett."

"My deal with you is that I'll drop the charge of attempted murder. Aside from that, you're on your own."

He swore, but under his breath. I looked at him sharply. He was rolling over too easily. It gave me the feeling that there was a conspiracy here that was outside my knowledge.

"Where was the stash?" I asked Walker.

"In the boiler of the old pulp mill," he said.

I frowned. "There must have been a trail through the snow a blind man could follow. Sounds like a dumb place to leave drugs."

"That only led to the door," Walker said. "Inside there's a thousand places you could've hid something this size. Naah, it was safe enough."

Harding said nothing. His silence bugged me. He should have been taking charge, ordering the investigation.

"Okay, book him, if that's what the chief wants. I've got work to do." I nodded to Harding and went through to the guardroom and took out the evidence bags with Ferris's gun in it. I got the fingerprint kit and went over the gun, lifting one set of prints. They were Ferris's.

Harding had come through and he watched me as I compared them.

"What do you see?"

"The sergeant's prints are the only ones on the gun," I said and he nodded.

"Figures. It's his gun. Looks like he did it himself. No question."

I didn't say anything. To me the prints meant something else. A policeman handles his gun every day. There should have been a jumble of prints on the weapon. Instead I had just one textbook set. It looked to me as if someone had wiped the gun, then wrapped Ferris's dead fingers around it. It was the indication I needed that he had been murdered.

FIFTEEN

I BROKE the gun and printed the rounds. They were hollow points. One of them could have caused that wound to his head.

I put everything back in the evidence bags. The gun I kept. The rounds I gave to the chief to lock in his safe. He was in the front office with Walker, who was typing. "I'm going down to the hospital to check the body," I said. "I want to search the pockets and then search his house. If you could come with me, please, chief, I need a witness."

Harding shook his head. "I'll stay here. The media will be all over us when word gets out. Take Walker with you."

It was another cop-out but I nodded to him and spoke to Walker, who was sitting at the typewriter, head hunched forward, rattling away with two fingers. "Okay, Jeff, we're on. Can you come with me, please?"

He nodded, pulled his arrest report out of the typewriter, and got his parka, not saying anything. Harding broke the silence. "Do a thorough job," he said. "I'll check the properties. See you when you get back."

Walker didn't talk as we walked out together. My promotion was rankling. I almost wished I could tell him that it was temporary, that I would be off down the highway as soon as my assignment was completed and by that time the chief's job would probably be up for grabs. But there were more important things at stake than my popularity, so I kept my mouth shut.

There was an elderly porter on duty at the hospital. He looked as if he had been born for the job. He was thin and paper-white and silent. He recognized Walker and nodded to him, ignoring me. Walker said, "This is Sgt. Bennett. Where's the doctor?"

"In the delivery room. Maureen Cassidy's havin' a baby. Bin in here all day," he said, ignoring me.

"We're here to examine Mr. Ferris's body," I said and he glanced at me as if surprised that I knew how to talk. He didn't answer but led us down to the basement where Ferris's body was installed in their tiny morgue, in one of their two cool compartments. The porter's eyes flickered when I pulled the sheet back off Ferris and unzipped the body bag. I could tell that this was the part of his job that he relished most. "Thank you, we can manage now," I told him, but he didn't take the hint, so I reinforced the message. "If you don't mind, this is an investigation. It's confidential."

He scowled at Walker, challenging him to overrule me, but when Walker said nothing he left. When he'd gone I laid out a couple of evidence bags on the table beside the body and began going through Ferris's pockets. Walker watched and made a list of contents. In the top right pocket I found Ferris's notebook and I called out what it was and then silently read through the most recent entries. They were routine and ended at the time he had last gone off duty the night before. He also had a pen and a couple of loose summons cards. I went to the other pockets. In the left top pocket was a letter from a small town in British Columbia. I opened it and read the first words. It began, "Dear Dad." The signature was *John*. I flicked through the pages, getting the gist of it, which was all personal. Apparently Ferris had a couple of grandchildren out there. The letter made no reference to any other family members.

I noted the name and address in my book and put the letter in the evidence bag. Walker asked, "Who's it from?"

"A son in B.C. Did he have any other family?"

"Didn't know he had anybody." Walker shrugged. "He didn't talk about any. Not that he talked much anyway."

I checked his equipment. The holster was empty. His cuffs were there. Next I opened the side pockets. In one was a can of Copenhagen snuff and a wad of tissues, all clean. In the other there was a container of blue pills.

"Uppers," Walker said.

"Looks like it. I'll have the doctor check them."

That was it for the tunic. I dug into his pants pockets. He had his stick in the right back, the special long pocket all policemen used to have before the new two-handed sticks came into use. In the left rear he had a billfold, and I drew it out and opened it.

"Driver's license," I said, checking the number. The last digits of the number give the driver's date of birth. I saw that he was fifty-eight and that his first names were John Simon.

He also had his police ID, his social security card and a Visa, plus $438, all but the thirty-eight in fifties, which made me wonder if it had come from Loretta's stash. That was all. He had no photographs, none of the trivia that most other men carry with them.

I listed everything and went to the front pockets. In the left he had more tissues, used. In the right he had a pocketknife, his pouch of spare shells and sixty-six cents in change. That was everything. I looked up at Walker. "Did you see his keys anywhere at the station?"

He looked surprised. "No. 'Course, I wasn't looking. I was too shook up with finding him like I did."

"We'll check after," I said. "He sure hasn't got them with him now."

The fact surprised me. Every cop carries keys, more so than an ordinary citizen. You have your handcuff key with you at all times on duty, plus the key to your locker and any other keys needed for the job. Usually you keep them all on the ring with your house and car keys.

To complete the search I made a quick check of the other places a man would hide anything. I looked in his shoes and his socks. He had nothing there and he was not wearing a money belt. Except for his wristwatch, which was what seemed to be a genuine Rolex Oyster, he had nothing else but his clothes.

"Pretty fancy watch," Walker commented. "Hell, I've bought cars for less than he must've paid for that."

"If it's real," I said. "Okay, that wraps it up here. Let's go get his keys from the station and search his house."

"What about the pills?" Walker asked.

"I'll leave them with a note for the doctor," I said. "We'll check if he's out of the delivery room."

He wasn't, and the only nurse on duty was in the delivery room with him, so I kept the pills and Ferris's gun, which I had brought with me. "We'll bring them back later. I don't want to leave anything with Frankenstein," I said.

"He's all right," Walker said. "Kind of creepy, but I guess working around dead people all the time'll do that to you."

I didn't argue. I was a little angry with myself for not checking Ferris's locker while I was at the station. It was a routine kind of action I would have taken automatically if I hadn't been thrown off balance by the speed with which Harding had reinstated me.

Harding was not in the station when we returned. The door was locked and we found the radio adjusted to accept telephone calls. I assumed he had gone out on patrol to check the properties. Again, it was unprofessional. He should have given Walker the job and come with me. I dismissed the thought and checked Ferris's locker and found his keys. He had left the key in the padlock, which was hanging open on the hasp. I frowned when I saw it, trying to recreate what had happened before Ferris was shot. On impulse I turned to Walker, who was standing a pace behind me, and asked him, "Could I see your gun, please?"

"What the hell for?" His voice rose angrily and I smiled politely.

"No, I don't think you did it, but I'm in charge of the investigation. I'd do it to anyone."

He pursed his lips bitterly but drew his weapon and broke it and handed it over. It was clean and smelled of gun oil. I glanced down the barrel, which was shiny bright and had two pits in it. Without being obvious about it I glanced at the tips of the rounds which were visible with the cylinder open. They were hollow points. "These are illegal rounds," I said.

"We all carry hollow points. The chief gave permission," Walker said angrily. "A car hit a bear on the road to the mine one time. It was madder'n a snake, dangerous—and the first guy on the scene put four rounds into it before it dropped. After that the chief said we should carry hollow points."

"I see." I handed his gun back and he flipped it shut with an angry snap.

I turned away and searched the locker. Ferris had another vial of the same kind of blue pills and a mickey of rye. Aside from that and his civilian clothes there was nothing. I closed the locker again and took Ferris's keys. "Now we come to the hard part," I said. "Can you grab some more evidence bags, please?"

"Sure." The word was almost a hiss. He was bitterly angry.

Before we went out to Ferris's house I made sure that his car was locked. I had to search that as well but wanted to do the job in daylight when I wouldn't miss anything. Then we drove out to his house, Walker taking out his anger on the car, driving too fast, cutting the corners, fishtailing once or twice on icy patches, generally acting like a teenager. I ignored the display, using the time to check Ferris's key ring. It held the keys to his

cuffs, his house, his locker and his car. Nothing else. I had been
half expecting a safety deposit box key and decided to be extra
careful looking for one at his house.

Finally Walker squealed to a stop in Ferris's driveway. He
made to open the door, but I sat still for a moment. It surprised him and he turned to look at me.

"Okay," I said. "I know my promotion has got up your
nose. I know you're teed off because I checked your weapon.
Let's establish right now that I've been given a job to do and I
want to do it right. Okay?"

"Yeah." His tone was tight but then he got hold of himself.
"Yeah," he said again. "I'm sorry, sergeant."

I could have told him to knock off the rank and use my
name, but it would have looked condescending. So I just got
out of the car and crunched over the uncleared snow to the
front door.

Walker opened it and we went in. The layout was identical to
the house I was living in. Even the furniture was similar in age
and style. The only differences were those a woman's presence
would make. The few pictures in the place looked as if they had
come from Woolworth's, bad prints of northern scenes that
gave you the feeling they had been hung only to cover stains on
the walls. And even though the house was tidy it had an air of
neglect that lay like a film of dust over everything.

"This is going to take a while," I told Walker. "Stick the
coffeepot on, if you can find it."

"Will do," he said. He was speaking in a more normal voice
now, over his tantrum, ready to bide his time and do as he was
told. I heard him clanking in the kitchen as I looked first in the
living room, checking for anything that might have served as a
desk.

I found a sideboard with one drawer filled with papers. I
lifted the drawer out and started going through the contents.
They told me nothing. There were the obvious domestic papers, the lease for the house, insurance policies, a couple more
letters from his son, bills and receipts. Nothing to point to any
corruption. Even his bankbook was innocent. I checked and
saw that he had deposited regular amounts every two weeks.
They were always the same, always put in on paydays and no
more than he could have afforded out of his pay. There was a
big brown envelope and I opened that last. It contained photographs. I spread them on the table.

Looking at them made me sad about Ferris's death. They were the first indication that he had once been an ordinary guy. His wedding picture was there. He was in army uniform, with medal ribbons, something that's unusual in the Canadian or British service. He had the striped pair that indicated he had fought in Korea. His bride was a tiny, pretty girl, smiling into the camera as if the sunshine of the day would last forever.

Walker came in with the coffee as I was examining them. He set the cup down clear of the pictures and looked over my shoulder. "Nice-looking lady," he said.

"You never met her?"

"No. He came here on his own, five, six years ago," Walker said, slurping his coffee.

I shuffled through the photos, finding a couple with a child in them. Then I found a death certificate made out for a Joan Ferris, dated 1982. The cause of death was stated as cancer. That helped to explain Ferris's unpleasantness. Seeing your wife die from a painful disease would sour any man. He hadn't recovered. That was all the difference between him and other widowers I had known.

"Did he have any women friends in town?" I asked.

Walker pursed his lips thoughtfully. "None I ever heard about. Kind of funny when you think about it. There's a slew of widows his age."

"Do you happen to know if he saw any of the hookers when they came to town?"

He shook his head. "I don't think so. I was on duty with him a couple of times up there. He used to close down the detail and move out as soon as the girls were through."

I checked everything—the contents and then the bottoms of the drawers. There was no key anywhere, no stash of money. It was the same in his bedroom. There was a tin in one of the drawers and I opened it with excitement. Perhaps it held his stash of money. But it didn't. It had his personal treasures, the trifles you find in every home. There were his medals from Korea and his regimental cap badge. And in a little jeweler's box, the wedding ring and the engagement ring with the tiny stone that his wife had worn in the wedding photograph.

After checking the contents of the drawers and closets, we were able to wrap up the search in an hour. We found fishing tackle and a Remington hunting rifle in the basement but nothing else. There weren't even any books in the house.

At last I said, "Okay, I guess that's everything. Let's go back to the station."

Walker nodded without speaking. He seemed depressed, but it was understandable. First Ferris's death, then my promotion over his head. It had been too much to handle. He opened the door and stood waiting while I looked around me one last time. That was when I noticed the kitchen calendar. It had come from a service station, and it featured a pinup dressed in a bikini and a nice shiny wrench. On impulse I walked over and glanced at it. There were a couple of notations written down for certain dates. On the fourth of the month he had a date with the garage to get tires rotated. On the fifth he had seen the dentist. And on the twentieth, two days from now, he had a simple X in red ink.

Walker watched me from the doorway. "Anything important?" he asked wearily.

I kept the news to myself, if it was news. "We know he died with his teeth in good shape. He was at the dentist this month."

"That's good," Walker said. "Where he's gone there's a whole lot of wailing and gnashing. He'll need teeth."

I laughed with him, showing we were both tough cops. He drove me back to the station. Harding was there and I reported my finding, not mentioning the calendar, and he nodded. "What do you want to do next?" he asked.

I sat down opposite him and thought. "We might ask if anybody was in or around the station at the time it happened, if they heard or saw anything. But we can't do that until the morning."

"Are you saying you don't think this was a clear-cut suicide?" He was quizzical, almost amused, one eyebrow raised slightly. It looked like a gesture he practiced while shaving.

I answered carefully. "It looks cut and dried, but that would wrap it up properly."

He inclined his head doubtfully. "I guess so," he said.

"Anyway, I'm going down to the hospital to get the doctor to look at the weapon and the pills I found. Then I'm going home. I'll be in at eight o'clock."

"Good idea." He yawned and stood up. "I'm going home too." He reached for his hat and we walked out together. He stopped to tell Walker to take over and to hold off any calls from the media. Then we went out. As he approached his car, he asked, "Why are you taking the gun to the hospital?"

"The doctor is the only guy in town with any scientific training," I said. "It looked to me as if it had been fired recently, but that was as much as I can tell." I wasn't giving him the whole truth. There's more to it than that and he should have known. When a gun is fired into a body from close range it sucks some of the blood back into the barrel. I wanted the doctor to check the barrel and see if he could find any traces.

He got into his car, nodded once and drove off. I stood for a minute, breathing deeply, enjoying the cleanness of the cold air. Then I told myself, Okay, Bennett, hospital, then home.

I found the doctor sitting at the nurse's station. Both of them were drinking coffee, still wearing their operating-room greens. He looked up at me wearily when I came in. "Hi, what's happening at the station?"

"Nothing new, doc. How'd the woman make out with the baby?"

"Fine big boy, nearly six kilos," he said. "No wonder it took her so long."

"Good." That was the formalities over. I recognized the nurse as the one who had been on duty the night I brought Mrs. Wilcox in. I nodded to her. "Busy night?" I said.

"Busy enough." She was a cheerful type, around forty, running to fat but without the narrowness around the eyes that makes some chubby people look sly. "I hear you're the new sergeant," she said.

I nodded. "Yeah, surprised me too."

"Good thing," she said. "I had you figured for a good guy when you brought Jean in here that night. Want some coffee?"

"No thanks. I just have to see the doctor, then I'm heading home. By the way, how's the woman from the trailer?"

"Still out," the doctor said. "I'm keeping her body temperature low and maintaining her coma. It should help to minimize the chance of brain damage."

"When do you expect her to be able to talk?"

"Forty-eight hours more, then we'll bring her out of it." He yawned and stood up, setting down his cup. "Thanks, Rosie. I'll go talk to the officer, then go home myself."

"Right." She swallowed the last of her own coffee and took both cups off to wash them. The doctor looked at my packages.

"What's on your mind?"

"I'd like to know if there are blood traces in the muzzle, hair, anything else that could have been pulled in there from the implosion after the gun fired."

He hefted the gun in his hand. "You mean you don't think he did it himself?"

"Just eliminating alternatives. Can you do that here?"

"Blood, yes," he said. "I can even type it if we get any. What else?"

I handed him the bag with the pills in it. "I found these in the sergeant's pocket. They look like uppers. I wondered if you could identify them for me?"

He yawned again. "Will it do in the morning? The pharmacy's open then."

"That would be fine. Thank you."

He stood there with a bag in each hand, looking at me. "Glad to help," he said. "I'm glad you're around, Mr. Bennett. It's time this town got some proper police protection."

"Thank you for the vote of confidence, doctor. I'll see you in the morning."

He nodded and turned away and I went home, my mind racing around and around the facts. Freda was awake, and even though I didn't make any noise, she got up and came through to the kitchen where I was getting a glass of water. "Are you all right, dear?"

"I'll be a lot righter after a night in bed," I said.

She took my hand and led me back to the bedroom.

SIXTEEN

I WOKE with a start and found Fred gone. The light was on in the kitchen and I padded out there, blinking at the light. She was standing at the stove and there was a good smell of coffee in the air. She looked pale and when I held her she seemed distracted. "It's seven-fifteen, but you were sleeping so peacefully I didn't want to wake you," she said. "Can you handle a big breakfast?"

"Please. It's probably going to be a long day."

She turned me around and gave me a gentle shove in the back. "Right. You shower and shave and I'll do my thing here." I went through to the bathroom with Sam following like a shadow. I'd handed him over to Fred the night before, and he would have obeyed her ahead of me, but he's bonded to me over the five years we've been partners, and despite his training he feels lost unless I'm in charge.

Ten minutes later I was back at the table and Freda set bacon and eggs in front of me. She was eating toast, dry. "Dieting?" I asked.

"I guess it's all the stress," she said, "but it was as much as I could do to cook that bacon, let alone try to eat it."

I reached out and squeezed her hand. "It's over now, honey. I'm the sergeant and it means I can get closer to the investigation. We should be out of here in a month."

She put her toast down and sipped her milk. I noticed that as well. She's a coffee drinker by choice and doesn't usually function until about eight-thirty, after she's had a cup. "I'm glad to hear you say that," she said. "What are you going to do first?"

"Search Ferris's car. That's routine. Then I want to check a few things, find out if he had any women friends in town, any semblance of a private life outside of his rye bottle. It seems to me that Marcie, the office clerk, was friendlier with him than she is with anybody else. Might be nice to see if they had anything going."

"Leave that to me," she said. "I'll talk to Mrs. Schuka. She's one of nature's gossips. She'll know."

"Good." I got back to my bacon and eggs. "There was another thing. He had a date on his calendar, just an X in red, for tomorrow."

"Yeah," she said. "I wonder what that was about."

"I'll let you know. But you try to relax. I'm in the clear now, so you can hold your head up again at the supermarket."

She smiled awkwardly. "I'm glad about that, Reid. I didn't want to bother you, but this is a very small town. My reception was pretty chilly yesterday when I went down to the bus terminal to collect my books. When you were suspended everybody assumed you were guilty. They took it out on me."

I reached out and squeezed her hand. "I'm sorry, love."

"No problem. You're a big wheel now. They'll probably give me a discount at all the stores."

"This isn't forever. Another few weeks and we're on our way home, in time for Christmas, probably."

"Good," she said, "although I'll miss my class. I've never had star billing before."

I finished breakfast and she handed Sam over to me. He frisked around me like a puppy until I'd fussed him and told him he was a good boy. Then he slid in behind me as I left and went out to the scout car I'd driven home.

Walker was on the desk at the station. He looked weary, more tired than you normally get after the night shift. "Are you okay for another hour?" I asked. "I'd like to take a look at the place you found Nunziatta's stash."

"Sure." He nodded bleakly. "He's in the cells right now. Whining sonofagun, wanted us to have a bail hearing last night."

"He'll be out by ten. Have you spoken to him this morning?"

"Took him a cup of java. He's fine. Mad, but fine."

I went back to the cells to check for myself. Nunziatta was lying on the bunk. He sprang up and stood at the door, holding on to the bars. "How much longer I gotta stay in this hole?"

"As soon as we get the justice of the peace here you'll be out on bail." There was a chair in the hallway and I pulled it up in front of his cell and sat down. "First, a couple of questions."

"I already told you guys everything I know," he said.

"Tell me, did Ferris have any friends in town? Any girl-friends?"

He slammed one hand against the bars angrily. "Hell, I don't know. I'm not his goddamn keeper."

"You knew him better than anybody. Did he have any friends, outside of your charming self?"

"I never heard of none." He shoved himself away from the bars and flopped back on the cot.

"Okay, that's question number one. Question number two is, where's the rest of your stash?"

That brought him off the cot again, banging the cell door in frustration. "Christ, what is it with you? I took the cop to my place, he took everything as was there. Ask him."

"You're lying to me, Frankie. You have more than that, hidden somewhere."

He didn't answer, just muttered something and sat down again. I sat and looked at him and at last he spoke again. "How much stuff d'you think I can afford to carry? This isn't T'rannah. There's only so many people want what I'm sellin'. I'm just small time. Look, Mr. Bennett, I ain't stupid. I wouldn't cross you up. Believe me."

I stood up without speaking. I didn't trust him, but it didn't matter. I'd had all the help from him I was going to get. I went back out just as Levesque walked in. He looked at me in surprise. "Hey, Reid. What you doin' here?"

"I'm back on the job. Ferris committed suicide last night."

"Suicide?"

"Yeah," Walker said. "Shot himself. I found him when I came on at eleven-thirty, layin' right there on the floor."

Levesque frowned, thinking. "You know what that says?" He looked at us both questioningly. "It means he strangled that hooker. When she din' die he couldn't take it. He shot him-self."

"That's what the chief thinks too," I said. "He's appointed me sergeant."

He smiled, distorting his big mustache so it looked like a small animal, writhing. "Hey, tha's great. Congratulations." He reached out and shook my hand and I nodded thanks. "Shoulda been me." He laughed. "How's your health, sarge?"

We all laughed. I said, "Okay, we'll get you on duty, then I want you to take care of things while Jeff and I tidy up the de-tails."

I opened the duty book. It's standard, in one form or another in any department, a daily calendar with coming events in it, things that have to be covered. There was nothing for this day, or for the next. I noted that carefully. Whatever the cross was for on Ferris's calendar, it didn't relate to police work.

I handed the whole sheaf of teletype messages to Levesque. "Nobody's had time to go through them. You do it. Anything important, put it on the board. Got everything with you for the shift?"

He drew himself up and opened his holster and pulled his stick. "Jus' need my notebook."

I nodded and opened the top drawer. It held his notebook and those of the other men who were off duty. I opened it and saw Ferris's initials. The sergeant had been through it. I read the report of the previous day's work, all routine.

"Good. Here you go. You're in charge until the chief gets here. We've got a prisoner in the cells, Frank Nunziatta, charged with trafficking. Look in on him and take care of the phone. If anyone wants to know about Sgt. Ferris, refer them to the chief."

Walker and I searched Ferris's car. It was clean except for a bottle of Canadian Club in the trunk. I even took up the rubber splash mats to check for a safety deposit box key, but there was nothing under them but rust stains coming through the carpet. The only thing that didn't make sense was the fact that he had a couple of pieces of old lead pipe in his trunk, scrap from some old plumbing job. There was about fifty pounds of it, in a sack, and I checked it and left it there. Probably he'd been using it to give his rear wheels more grip on the road in winter.

I put Sam in the back of the police car and then Walker drove me over to the old town and we checked the mill. I brought Sam with me as we tracked into the place, our feet squeaking on the snow as we walked, a sign that the temperature was well down. There was a clear trail in the snow leading to the side of the main building. It looked as if it had been used a number of times, which jibed with Nunziatta's story of having picked his stuff up here before he came out to shoot me. Inside it was dreary and neglected looking; the big presses and cutting machinery had been taken out. There were holes in the floor where they'd been, as unsightly as missing teeth. In a few places windows had blown in and snow had drifted across the floor so that whole areas of the echoing old space were like blank sheets of paper waiting for somebody to draw me a clue on them, only nobody had obliged.

I checked inside the boiler room where Walker told me. The door was four feet square. The owners had economized on costs by using the bark and sawdust and waste from the mill to fire it, and you could get right inside if you chose to. Walker still had his night-duty flashlight with him and I flashed it over the interior. It was dirty but empty, not even a trace of ashes. The last man on duty had done his job well, cleaning the firebox out to the last cinder.

"Well, that's it. Drop me back at the station and head on home," I said.

"Good," he said shortly and led the way. He turned in the narrow part of the roadway that had been cleared of snow and headed back up the hill. As we drove I saw Wilcox out walking his dog.

"Stop the car, please," I said. I got out and walked up to Wilcox. He was smoking one of his thin little cigarettes, watching his dog romping in the snow.

"Morning," he said. "How's it going?"

"I want you to know your rifle came in useful. Nunziatta tried to shoot me last night, and I was able to outgun him."

"No kidding." He crushed out his cigarette on the sole of his overshoe and tossed it aside. "What happened?"

I filled him in briefly, and he shook his head. "I figured there was something shaky about him."

He looked at me out of his keen blue eyes and I knew the question that was burning in him. "I asked him about Randy. He didn't say anything different, but I haven't finished with him yet. I've locked him up for drug trafficking. He kept his stash in the mill."

"Yeah?" He shook his head. "I wondered who it was usin' that place. Been someone going in there lots of nights. I figured it was a guy and a girl maybe."

The question came to me without thought. He had lived here most of his life, perhaps he would have heard something. "Tell me, does tomorrow have any special significance to the town?"

He thought about it, and shook his head. "No. Don't think so."

"Thanks anyway." I nodded, then realized I owed him more than a dismissal. "Sgt. Ferris shot himself last night. Keep it to yourself, but there was a mark on his calendar for tomorrow. I can't see anything in the duty book to account for it.''

''Killed himself?'' It was the obvious reaction. I took the necessary minutes to fill him in.

He shook his head again. His dog had noticed Sam sitting up in the back of the police car and had started yapping at him, small and bossy and safe, with the window up.

''By the way, I'm reinstated, with Ferris's old job,'' I said and he laughed out loud.

''Well maybe that chief knows a good cop when he sees one,'' he said. ''Congratulations.''

We shook hands and I left him having to pick his dog up so it didn't try to chase Sam out of town.

We went back to the station and Walker booked off. Then I took Levesque out with me to retrieve my car from the clearing and turn it over to the garage in town to have the side window replaced. Fortunately they had a replacement in stock and promised to turn it around by afternoon.

The chief had arrived by the time I got back to the station, and the JP was there for the bail hearing. I didn't take part in it. While they were in the guardroom I spent a quick few seconds checking whether Ferris would have been off the next day. He wasn't due for a day off, and he was working the four-to-midnight shift, so the cross probably didn't mean a date with some secret girlfriend.

The others came out of the guardroom. Nunziatta was angry but under control. Harding smiled. He still looked drawn even in the bright morning sunshine, but he was lean and handsome in his uniform and white shirt. He was wearing his amiability like a badge of office. ''Ah, Bennett. I was telling His Worship about your reinstatement,'' he said.

The JP smiled and stuck out his hand. Yesterday I had thought him a sour old man. Today he was a pleasure to talk to. ''I'm delighted to hear the news,'' he said. ''I really hated to think one of the men was corrupt.''

''Thank you, sir.'' I smiled and the chief saw him to the door. Nunziatta stayed for a moment while he signed for his property, then snorted and left without speaking.

The chief paused briefly at the front desk. ''Anything new?'' he asked.

"No sir." I told him what Walker and I had found in the house and the car, essentially nothing. I also asked him if he knew anything about Ferris's private life.

He shook his head. "No. He was a very private man."

"Thank you, sir. I'm going to wait for the photographer to bring in my shots, then go and talk to the doctor."

"Right," he said. "Oh, by the way, Marcie won't be in. I stopped by and told her about Ferris and it upset her. She'd worked with him for seven years, longer than any of the other people. She took it hard."

The news didn't surprise me. It reinforced what I'd been thinking: that she and Ferris had been more than workmates.

The photographer came in half an hour later, and I opened the countertop and led him through to the guardroom.

"They all came out well," he said nervously, tipping the photos into my hand.

"Great. Thank you." I stood and studied them. Sometimes the photograph will make some detail you've missed jump out at you. I guess I'd been hoping for that kind of miracle, but it didn't happen. I went through them all twice, trying to think if there was anything else I could have done. There wasn't.

"Thank you, Mr. Roberts. I really appreciate your trouble. I hope it hasn't caused you any problems at work."

"Oh, no." He beamed, a little proudly. "No, I run the department. There's a whole staff to take care of the routine stuff. I just concentrate on the major projects and supervise the rest of the work."

"You're the head accountant at the mine, aren't you?"

"Yes." He was a small man with a gleaming bald head that flashed under the lights as he nodded to me. Under his topcoat he was wearing a suit and tie, one of the few people in town who bothered to dress with any formality.

"Tell me," I said, thinking hard about how to phrase my question, "is tomorrow a special day for any reason? At the mine, or in town?"

He looked startled. "What makes you ask?"

"I have a suspicion that tomorrow is important in this investigation," I said. "I can't tell you any more than that."

He worked his lips nervously. "Well, this is strictly confidential," he said. "We don't normally tell anybody but the chief himself."

I felt my excitement rising but stayed calm, nodding to him. "Believe me, Mr. Roberts, your confidence is safe with me, and I really need to know."

He looked around, checking the closed door behind him, then lowered his voice.

"Tomorrow is the day we move out our refined product."

"Your gold?" It was hard not to take him by the shoulders and shake the details out of his mouth.

"Yes, not five nines pure, but about ninety percent. It goes to the mint in Ottawa."

"And how big is the shipment?"

He licked his lips now, as nervous as an old-line Catholic about to eat steak on Friday. "This won't go any further?"

"You have my word, Mr. Roberts." I resisted the temptation to raise my right hand. "One thousand pounds," he said. "Depending on market price, and bearing in mind that it's not fully pure, only about ninety percent, that's about six million dollars' worth."

The news jolted me, as if I'd touched a live wire. Six million dollars! Ferris must have been involved. I knew he was corrupt. Perhaps he had seen this as his big score, the caper that would have set him free.

My face must have stayed calm because Roberts went on explaining. "That's approximate, as I say. Gold closed at four-twenty-four U.S. last night, that's five hundred and change Canadian, times fourteen ounces per troy pound, times a thousand. Seven million, less the ten percent for impurities that they take out at the refinery in Ottawa, say six million plus."

"And it's all conducted in secrecy, the move?"

"Yes." He glanced around again and nodded. "It's moved in an unmarked bullion van they send up from Toronto. It's armored, and the crew carry weapons but they're not in uniform."

"Do they take it all the way to Ottawa?"

He shook his head. "No, only to Olympia, to the airfield. There's a second security team there with the aircraft. They fly it the rest of the way."

"What's the department's responsibility?"

"We always notify the chief and there's an escort out of town as far as the township line. The provincial police take over there."

"I see." I nodded. Probably all the men who had ever taken the escort duty would have guessed what was going on, but none of them would have needed to be told the contents of the van. It was just another duty on the day shift.

"How often does this happen?"

"It varies. About every two months, usually."

I was thinking. This detail wouldn't crop up on the station calendar. The request would be on some private document the chief kept to himself in his own office.

"This won't go any further?" Roberts asked. He was frowning, almost sweating with tension. He would have made a lousy witness.

"No. Thank you, Mr. Roberts. The information stays within these walls. One other question. Who's in charge of security at the mine?"

"Jack Sheridan." Roberts half turned and pointed towards the door behind him. "He's the husband of Marcie, your secretary."

SEVENTEEN

ROBERTS STOOD looking at me, fiddling with his big fur hat. "You're quite sure you won't let this go any further."

"I won't tell a soul. And please forget we ever had this conversation."

"Good." He nodded nervously. "And now I really should be getting to the office."

I thanked him again for the photographs and let him out. Things were beginning to make sense. Marcie and Ferris were close; maybe they were lovers, or maybe close friends, good enough that she had talked to him about the bullion van, passing on confidences her husband had let slip at home. Six million dollars would have tempted people a lot more honest than Ferris.

The most frustrating part of any investigation is the time when answers start to come. It's like doing a crossword puzzle and having a couple of letters in place in a word which spoil your first guess at what the answer should have been. Why, if Ferris was this close to a grab of this magnitude, would he have taken his gun to his head? And if he hadn't done it, who had? And why? And was the chief involved in some plan to lift the gold?

I needed help. There was only one thing to do. I had to contact Toronto and get advice, and even more important, some solid help from guys I could depend on. Then if the bullion van was heisted, the whole problem I'd come here to unravel would be ended.

The chief came back in as I was musing. I had spread the photographs on the table in front of me and he came and leafed through them as casually as any bystander. As he moved his arm I got a whiff of an expensive cologne. If he was mourning Ferris's death it wasn't upsetting his daily routine at all. "Roberts does good work, doesn't he?" he said.

"Very professional." I nodded. "But they don't show me anything new. How about you?"

He picked up the shot of Ferris's body and looked at it again before shaking his head. "No. They'll make a good show-and-tell for the inquest but there's no surprises in them." He dropped it and stood looking at me. "What do you propose to do next?" He might as well have been a visitor for all the help or direction he was giving.

I shrugged. "Seems open and shut, chief. I'm going to talk to the doctor, see if he's conducted his examination. Then I guess we can wrap things up and go on, business as usual."

"Good," he said. "We'll have to notify his family, see if they want the body shipped somewhere for funeral arrangements. Otherwise, we'll do it here. His insurance with the department will cover the expenses."

"Right." I stood up. "I'll go see the doctor and make the arrangements," I said. "I think it would be best if you were to call his son, chief. It would sound a sour note if I did it, since I've taken over his job."

He gave a dutiful little tut, holding his head erect. "It shall be done," he said and walked briskly back to his office.

I took Sam with me to the hospital. It was only ten o'clock, but the doctor was back on duty, wearing a white coat, his stethoscope hanging around his neck. "Just finished my rounds," he said. "I slept in this morning. We don't have any operations to take care of."

"Sorry to clutter up your day, doc, but the chief's asking if you've had a chance to examine Ferris's body."

"Doing it at noon," he said. "I try to have at least some time for myself. Right now I'm going for my workout." He paused. "And don't worry. I'll check the muzzle of the weapon first. That's your first priority, right?"

"Thank you," I said. "If it comes up clean I'll know what kind of case I'm working on."

He nodded. "Anything else?"

"Not medically, but I wanted to make a long distance call and I'm a little concerned about privacy from the station. Could I do it from your office, please?"

He looked at me quizzically. "Not cheating on that gorgeous wife of yours?"

"Are you kidding?" I laughed with him.

"Come with me," he said and I followed him back to his tiny office. It had a couple of bookcases stuffed with drab-looking textbooks. The walls were hung with packages of X-ray plates and there was a little plastic figurine on his desk, a demented looking man with the inscription "Lord, give me patience, and hurry."

He indicated the phone and then lingered at the door. "Look, this is none of my business, but can I ask you a question?"

"I'll try to answer."

He came in and shut the door behind him. "I've been watching you. You're not the kind of head-beater the chief usually hires. I'm starting to wonder if you have an agenda that's not been made public."

I stood and looked at him, seeing him clearly for the first time. He was a year or two older than me and fit-looking but tired. His hair was fair and thin and it stuck up at the back. I could feel in my bones that he was an honest man. He deserved an honest answer.

"I do," I said. "I haven't told anyone else in town, doctor, but I've got a job to do here that doesn't involve my paycheck from the department."

"Ah." He picked up his little figurine and tossed it in his hand. "I don't think you need to say anything else. But if I can be of any assistance, please call on me. If you're doing what I think, I'd be very happy to assist."

"I may need some help, perhaps tomorrow," I said.

He smiled, a real smile that warmed his eyes. "Tomorrow. Jam tomorrow, jam yesterday."

"Never jam today," I completed for him. "Only this is serious. I think something is about to happen. That's why I want to call Toronto."

"I hope it won't mean you and your wife will leave," he said. "I've never seen my own better half so happy as she is with this play business."

"Fred won't let you down," I said. "The play must go on. She'll make whatever arrangements necessary."

"She's a very special woman, sergeant," he said, and I wondered where he'd met her. Perhaps he had picked up his wife from the rehearsal.

"I know," I said. "I'm a lucky man, and I don't intend to change that. Like I said, this is business."

He put down the figurine and nodded. "Good. It's all yours."

He left and I dialed the number of Leo Kennedy's office at
the Provincial Police Commission. He wasn't there. The clerk
he'd left responsible for his movements was new. She had been
given the usual speeches about security and would tell me only
that he was on assignment in a police department somewhere.
She wouldn't even say where. I asked who his boss was and she
told me that he reported directly to the assistant deputy minister. "That's direct?" I asked and she said it was, surprised that
I didn't recognize a big wheel when it ran over me.

I asked to be put through to him, but he was in a conference
in Washington and wouldn't be back for a week. "I can contact Inspector Kennedy and have him ring you," she said at last.

"When?" I asked.

"He's in transit at the moment. I can reach him tomorrow."
She was genuinely trying to be helpful. It was like watching
Nureyev trying to dance in leg irons.

"Please tell him to call me at exactly noon tomorrow at this
number," I told her. "Please. It's vital."

She promised and I hung up, having to restrain myself from
breaking the telephone. It wasn't her fault, I reminded myself.
Kennedy had a full slate of jobs on, he couldn't sit in his office
for a month at a time waiting for me to rub the lamp like
Aladdin.

I sat and thought for a minute longer. Should I call in the
OPP? On the face of it, that was the thing to do. But I had
nothing more than a suspicion to go on. I couldn't talk to a
senior officer. I would have to talk to an inspector at most in the
nearest contingent to Elliot, and once I'd alerted them my cover
would be blown. Harding would know why I was in town and
my investigation would be over.

I went out to look for the doctor, but he had already gone,
so I left. Sam was waiting patiently in the front seat. I started
the car and sat for a minute, trying to see into the future, rubbing Sam's head as if it were a crystal ball. No, there was
nothing else for it. I had to work this one through myself.

The obvious thing to do was to see what else I could find out
about the gold shipment. I drove out to the gold mine and the
security man stopped me at the gate. "Sgt. Bennett, here to see
Mr. Roberts in accounting," I told him.

"Sergeant?" He bobbed his head in wonder. "Well sure, go
up to the main office, I'll call and tell him you're coming."

I drove up to the office, a single-story brick building beside the refinery. All around me was the coming and going of a mine in full operation. The stack at the smelter was rolling out a plume of white steam, and I wondered how much acid it contained. More than it would have done if it had been located down south where the environmentalists could see it.

Next to it, connected by an overhead brick bridge, sat the refinery which took the extract from the smelter and purified it a little further, not all the way to the "five-nines" gold, 99.999% pure, at which gold is traded. The final step is always taken at the mint, which is the only place empowered to mark it with the purity sign. It's a pretty good safety precaution. The final ten percent of the refining process is complex and expensive. Confining that stage to one center cuts down on the risk of theft. Cuts it down, but not out. A load of gold concentrate had been hijacked a year before at Kirkland Lake.

A smartly dressed young woman met me at the door of the accounting section and led me in to Roberts's office. It was in a corner of a big bullpen where about forty people were working. Most of the other men were in shirtsleeves, but he was still wearing his full three-piece suit, frowning at a computer printout.

He stood up when I came in, nodded to the woman and stuck out his hand. "Hello again, sergeant. Something wrong with the photographs?"

"No, they're excellent, Mr. Roberts. You do very professional work." It's always wise to start off by flattering.

"Oh?" He sat down again, waving me to the other chair.

"Yeah. The reason I came is to find out a little more about the other subject we discussed."

"Why? Do you think we're in some sort of danger?" A good accountant, identifying with his company's money.

"It's too early to tell." I stopped and looked at him. I knew nothing about him except for his job and the fact that the chief had introduced him. I wondered how well he knew Harding.

He sat back, pursing his lips in impatience. Here in his own office he was more sure of himself. "That's a very ambiguous statement."

"It's a very difficult situation," I said. I was debating with myself how much to tell him. For all I knew, he and his wife went bowling with the chief every Thursday.

He looked at me without speaking for a couple of seconds, then he said, "I have heard rumors in town, you know."

"What kind of rumors?"

He smiled without humor. "I think you know what I'm talking about."

We were going to play catch. "Perhaps I do, Mr. Roberts, but I'm new in town and even newer in my job. I'll show you mine if you'll show me yours."

That made him chuckle. "Haven't heard that since I was yea high," he said happily. "No, what I mean is I've heard that Sgt. Ferris was not to be trusted."

"Exactly," I said. "But as the new kid on the block, I can't very well go to the chief and tell him that. That's why I'm playing hard to get." He was ready to believe me. Fred must be right. I have an honest face.

"And you think he might have been planning something for tomorrow?"

"It's a faint possibility," I said. "I'm almost sure he wasn't, but I want to do a good job without getting the chief mad at me for speaking ill of the dead."

He nodded and sat silent for a moment, leaning back in his chair, important and happy. "Smart," he said at last. "You seem to be very professional, Mr. Bennett."

I shrugged modestly. "It seemed to me that the best thing I could do would be to familiarize myself with what happens tomorrow and be on my toes. Like I said, it's probably nothing, but I had my own suspicions of the sergeant."

His phone rang. He frowned but ignored it. Somebody else picked it up outside. "What can I do to help?"

"I'd like to know what the shipment will be moved in, and when it's due to leave. There's nothing on the duty roster."

He reached into his desk and pulled out a file folder. He checked it and said, "Seven A.M." He sat back in his chair. "I don't know the number of the vehicle, but it's a plain brown van. It sits kind of heavy on the road. All the armor, I guess." He was enjoying himself now, thinking about his gold. "One man sits in the front, the other in the van itself. They're both armed."

"And the men themselves are in plain clothes."

"Yes." He was clear about this one. "They wear suits."

"And when does the van get here?"

"They spend the night at the motel in town. They check in there as representatives of one of the companies we do business with in Toronto, a firm that supplies drill bits."

"Thank you. You've been very helpful." I stood up and he did the same.

"You don't want to meet with our security people?"

"Frankly, no. This is all supposition on my part. The fewer the people that know about it, the less foolish I look tomorrow when everything goes off as usual."

He smiled and shook hands. "I think I'm going to enjoy working with you," he said.

"If everyone were as helpful as you, there'd be no need for police departments at all," I said. I nodded and turned toward the door as he sat down again and picked up his printout.

My next stop was the hospital. The nurse on duty steered me to the morgue and I went in and found the doctor, wearing rubber gloves, holding a test tube.

The morgue attendant was there with him. I caught the doctor's eye and he said, "Hi. Would you like a cup of coffee, sergeant?"

"Yes, please." I can take a hint.

"George, would you mind? There's a fresh cup at the nurse's station."

George frowned in disgust. He was waiting for the fun to begin—when the doctor started slicing up Ferris's carcass. "How'dya take it?"

"Black, thanks, George."

He left and the doctor held out the test tube. "It's as you thought," he said. "I can't find any traces of blood or tissue in the muzzle of the gun."

I met his gaze. "You know what that means, don't you?"

"Yes." He nodded. "Yes. It means your sergeant didn't commit suicide. He was murdered."

EIGHTEEN

I HANDED the test tube back to him. "There's no possibility you could be wrong?"

He shook his head and put a rubber stopper on the test tube. "No." He shook his head a second time. "No. No blood, and I carried out the test twice."

"Thank you. Can I ask you, please, to save that sample? If this thing comes to trial we're going to need evidence to back up your findings."

"Don't worry." He peeled off his gloves and got a strip of self-adhesive labels out of the drawer under his bench. He wrote one out and stuck it on. It formed a seal over the top of the tube. "There. That's all it takes."

"Do you have any sealing compound you can put on it?"

He looked at me blankly, then nodded. "Oh, I see. So it can't be tampered with. Yeah. I'll secure it with some Scotch tape. That should do it."

"Okay. If you could, please." While he dug around for the tape I initialed the sticker. Then he covered my signature with the tape. "That keeps the evidence intact. Now I'll get back down to the station and tell the chief."

He frowned. "There's no alternative, is there?"

"No. It makes him a suspect, and Walker. They were the people to report the body."

"Damn." The doctor sat back on the edge of the bench and crossed his feet. "I like Walker. I don't think he's responsible, do you?"

"No. I share your feelings. But it looks as if somebody blew Ferris away, probably with a .38, although I won't know until the report comes back from Toronto. I'll take the weapon now, if you don't mind, and ship it and the bullet down there today."

He got the gun and handed it to me by the muzzle. "How do you account for the fact that his gun was fired?" he said. Like most people he was enjoying being part of a murder investigation.

"That's easy," I said. "Whoever did it took his gun and fired it off somewhere, out the door most likely. Then they wiped it and dropped it back by the body."

"Have you seen the guns on the other guys?" The obvious question.

"Walker's gun, yes. It was clean. But that doesn't mean he didn't clean it before notifying the chief what he'd found."

George came back in with the coffee. He had hurried so as not to miss anything, and it was slopped into the saucer. I nodded thanks and finished talking to the doctor. "Can you conduct the autopsy, please? Should be straightforward, I'd think. I'll get back to you after I've had my talk with the chief. In the meantime..." I let the sentence hang.

He nodded. "Gotcha. Not a word."

I walked around George, who was watching us both carefully, struggling to catch up with whatever he had missed. "Thanks for the coffee. Something came up," I said, and he scowled.

The chief was in his office, fiddling with the following week's duty roster. He looked up and said "Yes? What did the doctor say?"

"He says Ferris's gun was not the one that killed him."

"What?" He stood up abruptly, scraping his chair back across the floor with the kind of screech that drives parents crazy. "How can he tell?"

"There's a straightforward test they can do, looking for traces of blood or tissue in the muzzle. He didn't find anything."

"But what would he expect to find?" Harding was white. Shock maybe. Or guilt?

"When a gun fires there's an implosion that replaces the space left behind in the blast of the bullet. If the weapon was close enough to burn the hair when it fired—as happened here—there would be tissue from the wound in the muzzle of the weapon used. Ferris's gun has nothing in the barrel but powder residue. It did not fire that bullet through his head."

He sat down again, shaking his head. "If you say so. I've never heard of this technique, test, whatever." He sat for a few seconds, his hands resting limply on the desk. "Where does that leave us?"

"It means we've got a murder on our hands. The obvious suspect is Walker."

"Now just a minute." He lifted both hands in protest.

I lifted my own in return. "I agree, chief. Walker's a good clean guy. He couldn't have done it. But look at the facts. He found the body. He also has a gun similar to the one used to kill the sergeant."

"Let's go over there right now and check his weapon." The chief was on his feet again, ready to rush right over and drag Walker out of bed.

"No need for that, chief. I did last night. It was clean."

He shook his head. "You mean you suspected him last night?"

"I mean I closed out one more possibility. It was the obvious thing to do."

"Good God. This is a disgusting business we're in," he said.

"I don't like it any better than you do. We just do it, that's all." I was watching him carefully to see if he gave anything away. But he didn't. He was a blank, shocked spectator.

"So what do we do now?" He looked like one of those aging movie stars who play the U.S. president in movies about an atomic crisis. Only nobody had written him any lines for this part. "I've been giving out the information that it looked as if the sergeant had shot himself accidentally."

"The media is the least of our worries, chief. We've got a murderer on the loose." He didn't answer and I took charge. "The most obvious possibility is Nunziatta," I said. "He had a police gun. It happens to be mine. He said the sergeant gave it to him. With the sergeant dead, we can't be sure what happened."

"That bastard." Harding looked brighter. Here was a suspect who was already unpopular. He could get indignant about this.

"I'll go down and bring him in," I said, then hesitated. "Oh, chief, I hate to mention it, but just for the record, has your gun been fired recently?"

"What?" He jumped up again. "Are you saying I did it?" He had his hand on his chest as if I'd stabbed him. He wasn't insulted, he was horrified—the way a civilian would have been.

"Of course not, chief. But if I'm in charge of the case I should be able to state categorically at the inquest that it couldn't have been you or Walker because if I don't, tongues might wag.''

He was wearing his tunic. Like any officer above the rank of sergeant he wore no gun belt, but he had his pistol in a holster in the back of his waistband. He reached around wordlessly and produced his gun. He didn't even break it, just handed it to me.

I broke it and checked the barrel. It was shiny clean, but there were dust flecks in it, an indication that it had sat around for years possibly without being fired. I noticed his own rounds were conventional, the same as my own.

''Thank you, sir. I apologize for any suggestion of impropriety.''

He took his gun back and snapped the chamber closed. ''Thank you,'' he said. ''You're a very good policeman, Bennett.''

''I try,'' I said. ''Would you like to come with me to Nunziatta's house?''

''Perhaps I should,'' he said. He picked up his hat and came with me. ''You'll need a topcoat, sir.'' I was treating him like an elderly relative, but he didn't seem to mind.

''I think not.'' He looked very military in his uniform. A topcoat wouldn't have improved his appearance, and I was certain that he lived by the impression he was making, not the job he was doing.

''Right.'' I went out to the radio and switched it to its telephone connection, then waited until the chief joined me. We walked out to the car and got in. Sam was still in the rear seat and he keened when I sat down. ''Good boy,'' I told him.

We drove to Nunziatta's house in silence. There was no car in the driveway and like all the single-story houses in town, the place had no garage. ''Looks as if he's gone,'' I said.

''We'll see,'' the chief said grimly. We went to the door and rang. A pretty young woman answered the bell. She had a baby on her hip and a three-year-old boy peeking around her skirts. She had a feeding bottle of orange juice in her hand. The chief touched his cap formally and asked, ''Is Frank in, please, Mrs. Nunziatta?''

''No.'' She looked anxious. ''Is there trouble?''

The baby started to wail and she jiggled her hip nervously.

''Do you know where he's gone, ma'am?'' I asked.

''Out,'' she said, shrugging. ''He din' say.''

"Thank you. May we come in?" The chief was acting now, I could read it. His chin was higher and he was imperious, back in command, until he saw Nunziatta, then he would let me take over and do the police work.

"Sure." She stood aside nervously and we went in. I was in plain clothes so I took off my toque. The chief kept his cap on. He was in costume.

The house was overfurnished. There was thick carpet on the floor and lots of heavy ornate furniture, including one standard lamp that still had the plastic wrapped around the shade. I let the chief do the talking.

"Do you mind if we check that he's not in?" he asked.

"He's not in. I told you," she said. I felt sorry for her. The whole fabric of her life was coming undone.

"It won't take a moment, ma'am," I said.

The baby started to yowl again and she sat down and gave it the orange juice. "Okay," she said grimly. "You don' believe me, you look around."

It took a minute. He wasn't there. "Thank you very much, Mrs. Nunziatta," I said and the chief took over. "Tell Frank to call me as soon as he gets back," he said.

She was concentrating on feeding the baby. "I wish somebody would tell me what's happening," she said softly.

"Ask your husband," Harding said. "Thank you for your assistance. We'll see ourselves out." He touched his cap curtly and turned away. I followed, feeling guilty. This is the side of crime that hurts the most, seeing what it does to innocent people.

We went back to the car and the chief got in. "He's taken off," he said. "I'll call the OPP and tell them to be on the lookout for his car. He's halfway to either Thunder Bay or the Soo, right now."

"If he is, we'll know he's guilty," I said. "But I'm not sure."

"Where else could he be?" Harding was cocky again. It looked as if the case was all wrapped up.

"Perhaps he's got another drug stash somewhere. He may have gone to check it out." I backed out of the drive and headed to the station. "Perhaps if you'll call the OPP, chief, I'll take a look around town. I'll call Levesque as well, have him on the lookout for the car."

"Good thinking." The chief nodded, then laughed shortly. "There's also the possibility that he's gone to the mine."

"If he'd gone to work, his wife would have known. He would have been dressed for it."

"I suppose so." Harding stared out of the car window, looking at the familiar scene of low houses and snow. Nothing was moving except us. It was a cold day with the smoke from the chimneys rising straight up. All the miners' wives would be in front of the television watching what life was like in Hollywood, wishing they were there.

At the station I took a few minutes to parcel up the sergeant's gun and the round I had dug out of the wall. Then I contacted the express agent in town and arranged for him to pick it up for shipment to Toronto. After that I went back to the car and put Sam in the front seat, where he could be immediately useful if I needed him. I drove back through town, looking for Nunziatta's car. I half expected it to be on the lot of the Headframe. That would have tied things together a little more neatly. I still felt that Berger was involved in all that had happened.

But Nunziatta's car was not there. I drove all around town without seeing it and then turned and headed over to the old town to check for it at the old mill. It wasn't there either and I stopped for a minute, thinking. Then, on impulse, I pulled into Wilcox's driveway and went up to the door. I could see him in his greenhouse. He peered out when he heard me drive up. He opened the front door as I reached it.

"Hi. What's up?" He seemed cheerful. I think the news of Ferris's suicide had given him a bleak satisfaction.

"More developments," I said. "Can I come in?"

"Sure, please." He stood back and I went in. His dog yapped around me until he told it to be quiet.

"Looks like the sergeant was murdered," I said.

"What?" His chin dropped. "I thought you said he shot himself."

"His own gun had been fired, but it wasn't fired near a body. I think somebody blew him away, then fired his gun out of the door and dropped it by him."

He sat down, then shook his head and waved me to another chair. I sat. "Who did it? Any idea?"

"Nunziatta's gone missing," I said.

"Sonofabitch." His dog jumped up into his lap and he stroked it absently.

I looked at him and wondered. Everyone thinks that they're a pretty good judge of character. I'm no exception. I was asking myself how far I could trust him. I plunged.

"Look. I shouldn't be asking you this, but I think I'm going to need some help."

"What kind of help?"

"There was a mark on Ferris's calendar. That's all. Just a mark, for tomorrow."

"And?" He bent down and lowered his dog to the floor. It stood there nervously, wagging its tail. He sat back and it jumped back into his lap. He ignored it.

"I've found out since that there's a gold shipment going out tomorrow."

He whistled. "You think he was gonna grab it?"

"I'm not sure but I don't want to go to the chief with the idea, in case he's part of the same scheme."

"What are you planning to do about it?" His eyes were bright with excitement. I had picked the right man.

"I'm not exactly sure, but I'll need some help. Are you game?"

He stood up, ignoring his dog which jumped down with a yap of alarm. "You bet," he said happily. "You bet your boots."

He made a fresh pot of coffee and we sat and talked. When I had laid out the few facts I had he scratched his chin and said, "Looks like we have to identify the truck, when it gets to the motel, then ride shotgun until it's out of town."

"That's not enough," I said. "First question: How could anybody get away with a half ton of anything? The road can be sealed at the highway. Nobody could get off this stretch of it without being stopped in an OPP road check."

"They couldn't," he said. And suddenly I saw how I could be wrong. They might not have to.

"What if they don't take it out of town? What if they disperse it, hide it all over town? Hell, half a ton of gold isn't that big. A piece the size of a house brick would weigh maybe eighty pounds, more probably. They'd have to hide a dozen bricks. That's all. If they sat on them for a while, until the heat was off, they could smuggle them out of town easily. We couldn't search everything that went down the road."

We sat and looked at one another like a couple of astronomers who had just discovered a new star.

NINETEEN

"OKAY. So it could happen," Wilcox said. "What can we do?"

I set down my cup and slipped into my parka. "We can be there and follow them. That's about it. Right now I have to get back to the station. Thank you for the offer of help. I'll come by this evening and let you know what's breaking."

He saw me to the door, scooping up his dog to keep it from rushing out into the cold. "Good," he said. "This beats the hell out of 'Wheel of Fortune.'"

I bumped him on the shoulder as I passed and went to the car. I fussed Sam, who sniffed me with interest, picking up the scent of Wilcox's terrier on my jacket. I drove and called the station. "Unit one. Any messages?"

Levesque answered. "Yeah, sarge. Nunziatta's wife called. He's back and he's barricaded himself in the house. You just caught us. Me'n the chief're headin' down there."

"Be right there."

The scout car was at the end of Nunziatta's street. I got out, bringing Sam with me, and went to the other car. The chief was sitting in it, talking into the radio. Levesque was standing beside him.

"Is Nunziatta home?" I asked.

"Yeah." Levesque was excited. "So's his wife and kids. He's crazy. He slapped the hell out of her when he found her on the phone." Levesque pointed down the street at a car in the driveway opposite Nunziatta's house. The back window was gone. "He's been shooting. He's on the phone now, talking to the chief."

I took charge. "Okay. He can't shoot while he's on the phone. It's in the kitchen where he can't see the street. Take my car and go around the block to the other end of the street. Stop anybody coming in."

"Right." He ran to the scout car I had been driving.

I opened the door on the other car and heard the chief talking. "Look. You're surrounded. Just cut the crap and come on out. You'll go away for years if you hurt your family."

Nunziatta's voice was a squawk. The chief was trying to cut in but I tapped him on the shoulder and indicated the receiver. He gave it to me, his face tight. "See if you can get some sense out of the sonofabitch," he said.

I waited until Nunziatta's voice died down, then cut in. "Hi, Frank. This is Reid Bennett. What's happening, man?" I drawled a little, laid back to the point of torpor. I figured he'd been into some drug or other, probably his uppers.

"You're the goddamn cause of all this," he shouted. "You said we had a deal."

"We do, Frank. You know that. You want to talk terms?"

"Terms?" His voice rose an octave. "You already told me your goddamn terms. You got me busted."

"Listen, Frank. Nothing's happened yet," I said. "Hell, we can still negotiate what's gonna happen." I've been in a couple of situations like this. The first rule is to stay calm.

"I'm tellin' you what's gonna happen. I want a car and I want clear passage to Toronto. That's what I want."

"Well, hell, why didn't you say so?" I kept a smile in my voice. "Jeez, Frank. You want it. You got it."

I let go of the microphone and glanced around. "Where the hell's his own car?"

The chief shrugged. "It's not here. I don't know where it's gone. That's why he wants another one, I guess."

Nunziatta's voice came back on the air. "You're shittin' me," he said. He was still as angry but the pitch of his voice was lower.

I took over again, explaining calmly, "Look. I told you. We don't want any trouble. All we're concerned about here is the town of Elliot. You want to go to Toronto, fine. Why don't you come on out and I'll hand you the keys to the police car."

"Great," he sneered. "How goddamn dumb do you think I am, Bennett? Might as well drive a goddamn fire reel."

"Well what's wrong with your own car? It was going fine yesterday?"

"It ain' here," he shouted. "Somethin' wrong with your eyes? See my car out there do you?"

"Whoa. Sorry, Frank. Just asking." I put a chuckle in my voice. "Wasn't thinking, that's all. Anyway, how about my car? Nice dark Chev. It's only got sixty-thousand K on the clock, goes like a bird." I released the button on the mike and the chief bent down to bluster at me. "You can't promise him immunity. Give me that microphone."

It was showdown time. I lied. "Chief. I once took the FBI course on hostage negotiations. I don't think you have. If anything happens to those kids while I'm negotiating, you're covered."

The chief worked his mouth convulsively but didn't say anything. Over his shoulder I saw Levesque wheel across the other end of the street and get out. Good. Now if I could just keep the chief occupied I might have a chance.

"When did you take this course?" He was weakening.

"About five years ago." More lies, vital lies.

"Very well." He nodded grimly. "But do not make any bargains with him without my permission."

"Thank you, sir." I buffed the apple to a high gloss.

At the other end of the radio I heard a tinkling of glass, then a shot. I glanced up and saw the car across from Nunziatta's house buck then sink. He had shot one of the tires out. It was my cue. "Good shooting, Frank. You're pretty good with that thing."

There was no answer at first, then we heard a burble of voices, then Nunziatta was speaking. "I've got a .3030 deer gun here. I want you to know that, Bennett."

"Hey, I know that. And you're goddamn good with it. Do much hunting, do you?"

It wasn't a frivolous question. You have to break the guy's concentration, it gets him off balance.

"Hunting?" He sounded startled.

"Yeah? I've got one of those things, a Remington. They're great for deer. Bit light for moose though, unless you're a real pro. Ever get a moose, did you?"

There was a mystified silence, then more anger. "I don' wanna talk about guns. I got a woman and two kids in here and they're gone if you don't give me what I want."

"Lookit. I've already told you. I'll get the car. We can't do it at the moment because I need this one to talk to you. But if you'll come out——"

He didn't let me finish. He laughed, a shrill cackle. "You think I was born yesterday? Get that goddamn car here. Okay?"

"You want a car, you got a car," I said. "Just hold the phone a second."

I turned to the chief. "We should send Levesque to get my car."

"All right." He nodded, tight-lipped. "But he's not driving out of town. I want you to be very sure of that."

"He's softening," I said. "Once he sees the car he'll be fine."

I could hear a baby crying at the other end of the line, then his wife's voice, then a slap. I took up the receiver and waved to Levesque at the other end, indicating the speaker, then my ear. He nodded and got into his car.

"Okay, Frank. This message is for Officer Levesque. Officer, please come and see me, in your car, and pick up my car keys. Then go to Haley's Garage and get my car. Fill it up and bring it here."

"Right." Levesque hung up and wheeled away around the block.

"Okay, Frank. I did what you said. That thing'll get you to the Soo without even stopping for gas."

"Good," he said. "Now you're thinking."

He sounded a little calmer, so I worked on him. "Listen, Frank, I'm sorry you're acting this way. I thought you were a nice guy."

"I am a nice guy. Ask anybody," he snapped.

"Well what's making you so mad? I promised you wouldn't get a lot of trouble out of this business thing of yours."

"Juliana says you was here. You an' the chief, askin' where I was. I'm sick of it. Understand?"

"Yeah, well I can see how you would be. That's reasonable." I might have been talking to a restive horse. The words didn't matter, just the tone, sweet and calm.

He didn't answer but I could hear his breathing, amplified over the speak of the radio.

"I guess you heard me telling him to fill the car up," I said. "It'll take him a couple of minutes extra but it was pretty low on gas." I wanted him talking. While he was using the phone he wasn't using the rifle.

"I heard. That was smart," he said. Then he laughed. "You're a smart sonofabitch, Bennett. Not like them other dummies."

The chief was leaning down through the open door of the car, listening to every word. I saw his face darken at the comment. "Smug little prick," he said. "What does he know about anything, but pushing dope to kids?"

"Ignore him, chief. Right now he thinks he's in charge." I wanted to talk to Nunziatta, but not like this. I had a feeling he was connected with everything rotten in town, but I wasn't sure how. If he broadcast his secrets over the radio, my cover was gone.

"No, Frank. They do their best. They just don't know how to handle a guy in the big time. Me, I've worked in Toronto. I've seen how the big-time boys do business."

He chuckled. "Yeah. That was pretty smart, what you had me do last night. Pretty smart."

"What was that?" the chief snapped.

I improvised. "I wanted to get a confession out of Sgt. Ferris. I gave Nunziatta my tape recorder and sent him into the station to tell Ferris what he'd done. I was out to get the sergeant for what he did."

"Why didn't you report this to me?" The chief's lean face had the white marks of anger flashing each side of his nose.

"It went right out of my mind when I saw what had happened to Ferris," I said easily. "It was too late for a confession."

"I don't like this," he said. "We'll discuss this later."

"Yessir. I'm sorry. I should have mentioned it but I've been going full tilt investigating the sergeant's death." I got back on the air. "Listen, there anything we can do to make you comfortable? Can I call anybody in Toronto for you?"

"Stay out of it," he barked. Then he laughed harshly. "You'd like that, wouldn't you? Know where I'm going and have half the goddamn Metro cops waiting for me."

"Hey, Frank. I'm sorry you feel like that. We've got a deal here. No strings, okay?"

"Don't forget it," he said. "I'm gonna get something to eat."

He let the phone drop and the clatter filled the car.

The chief bent down. "Did he hang up?"

"No. He's getting some chow. Looks as if he really thinks he's heading for Toronto."

"What will you do when the car gets here?"

"I'll deliver it. My dog is here. We'll get the gun off this guy and lock him up. That's not the hard part. The hard part is waiting."

In the end it took another twelve minutes before Levesque got back with the car. I called Nunziatta on the radio, trying to get his attention but he wasn't listening. I guessed he was having his wife prepare food for the trip.

"Okay. I'll drive up to the door. Leave it to me," I said. I got out of the police car and led Sam along the block, on Nunziatta's side of the street, where he could not see me from the front window. I sat Sam at the house next door and went back to my car. The chief moved the scout car and I drove through and parked in front of the house. Then I got out and beeped the horn.

The front window was shut and the lace curtain inside was flapping in the draft as cold air rushed in. It was impossible to see anything inside.

Nunziatta called out, "Okay, Bennett. I see you. Put your hands on your head and back off."

"Whatever you say, Frank." I had the car keys in my hand, but he didn't notice as I backed away an inch at a time.

There was a clatter at the front door and his wife came out, carrying the baby, pushing the little boy in front of her. Her face was streaked with the red and white marks of a recent slap. Then Nunziatta came out, his gun at the ready, pointed at her.

"Any shit and she gets it," he called.

"Hey, Frank. No problem. Take it easy, man." I kept my voice calm. "Just get in the car and go. You've won."

"Back off." He made a shooing motion with the gun but didn't swing it far enough from her to make it safe to rush him.

He came out of the door, leaving it open, and shoved his wife in the back with the gun. She half screamed, then sobbed, but she ran, pushing the boy in front of her, and got into the car in the front seat, sliding over to the far side.

He got in right behind her, then stood up, shouting, "You bastard. Where's the key?" His gun was held loosely, pointing up somewhere behind his wife's head.

"Hey. I forgot. I always take it with me," I said and took a step towards him, holding out the key in my left hand, ready to grab the gun with my right. Nunziatta looked at me with a snarl on his face, reaching his left hand over the gun to get the key. And then he slammed back against the open door, his face smashed by a bullet.

I whirled and saw Levesque lowering a hunting rifle. "You crazy bastard," I roared. "What did you do that for?"

Nunziatta slid down the door of my car, the gun clattering from his dead hands. His wife screamed and clawed herself out of the car, bending to cradle his shattered head in her arms. The child wailed. I swore silently.

Levesque was almost babbling with shock at what he had done. He had given up on English and was speaking in heavy Quebecois French. "The chief said to do it. The chief said. I thought he was going to shoot his wife. Honest to God."

"It's done," I said, in French. "If it makes you feel any better, it's as if the chief himself pulled the trigger. You're clean."

Levesque lowered the rifle and dashed his cuff across his eyes. The chief came forward, a tight little smirk on his lips. "It had to be done," he said. "The woman's life was in danger."

There was no sense arguing. I stooped and picked up Nunziatta's rifle, slipping the magazine out and working the bolt once to extract the last round. Then I dropped the gun and patted Nunziatta's wife on the shoulder. "I'm sorry, Mrs. Nunziatta. Your children were in danger."

She turned, tears steaming down her face and reached out to rake my face with her nails. I caught her hands and brought her to her feet. She struggled for a few seconds, then collapsed against me. I put both arms around her and held her for a moment, patting her back gently as she sobbed. Levesque was at the far door of the car, picking up the baby, taking the little boy by the hand.

Nunziatta's wife pushed herself away from me and went to stop by her husband again. I crouched with her, speaking softly. "Let's get the children in the house. It's cold for them."

She blessed herself and closed her eyes for a moment, tears squeezing out of the corners. Then she straightened and looked around in panic for the children. She took the baby from Levesque and touched her son on the shoulder and I shepherded all of them into the house.

The chief was a pace behind me but he stayed silent. I led Nunziatta's wife into the sitting room and she collapsed on the couch, pulling the little boy to her, bending her head so her hair spilled out over both the children. Her shoulders shook.

I turned to the chief. "We have to get the coroner over here."

"I know." He lifted his chin in a little physical show of authority. "I'll thank you to remember who's running this department, Bennett."

Good. I had more to do than pick up after him and the mess he was making. "I know that, sir. What are your orders?"

He glared at me, wondering whether I was being insolent. "Carry on," he said and waved one hand.

Levesque was at the door. He had composed himself but he looked shaken.

I turned to him. "Al, are you okay?"

He nodded slowly. "Yeah." His voice had the hard, tight ring you hear in people with heart problems, the vibrato of tension.

"Right. I want you to get back to the station and call the hospital. Tell the doctor what's happened and have him come out here. Then call Mr. Roberts, the accountant at the mine, and ask him to get down here with his camera. Tell both of them it's urgent."

"Right." He stopped for a moment, moving one foot nervously. "What about the rifle I used?"

"Put it on the backseat of the scout car that you're not driving. When you've made the calls, come back here and seal off the other end of the street."

Mrs. Nunziatta raised her head and looked at him without speaking. He lowered his own gaze and turned away.

The chief said, "Do you have a friend nearby, Mrs. Nunziatta?"

"Natalie Foster is my friend." She was deathly calm. I wondered how much she had hated her husband.

"Where does she live?" Harding was speaking crisply, articulating every word with great care.

"Thirteen Swallow Road. It's around the corner," she said.

"Bennett, go and get her," the chief said.

"Right." I left the house. Sam was still sitting where I'd placed him, but when he saw me he keened at me and I patted my leg to bring him over. Then I walked around the corner between the four-foot high drifts of snow that the plow had left against the curb and on to Swallow Road.

Natalie Foster was a round-faced blonde about the same age as Mrs. Nunziatta. She was at her side window and she came and opened the door as soon as I got to it.

She was wearing expensive-looking clothes, a bright green sweater and a pair of good soft corduroy slacks. She didn't look as if her husband worked in the mine. "What's going on? I heard shooting. I called the station but no one answered. Then I saw the police car at the corner.''

"There's been an incident at the Nunziatta's. Juliana asked me to bring you around. She needs help.''

She reached inside the door and hooked her coat off a peg. "What happened? You still haven't said.'' She pulled the coat on and shut the door, then walked with me, taking quick little steps.

"There's been an accident. Her husband has been seriously hurt,'' I said before we could turn the corner.

"Serves him right,'' she said viciously. "He treats that woman like dirt. She's worth ten of him.''

"It's a fatal accident,'' I said. "Be prepared, Mrs. Foster. We have to go past him.''

She pressed her lips together as we came around the corner where a knot of women was gathering, their breath puffing white plumes in the cold air as they speculated about the car and Nunziatta's dead arm. One of them had just noticed it sticking out to one side.

They turned and glared at me as I passed. One of them, a woman in her fifties, asked me, "What the hell's going on here?''

"There's been an accident,'' I said.

"Like hell!'' She looked around at the others. "Accident my foot. I saw that cop with the mustache shoot Frank Nunziatta in the head.''

I ignored them and walked on, steering Mrs. Foster around the outside of the car, crossing to the inside so I would mask her view of the body. She glanced down at it fearfully but didn't push to stop and examine it. Behind me I saw the woman who had spoken advancing on the car. I opened the house door and ushered Mrs. Foster in. Then I took Sam back down the step and walked him around the car. "Keep,'' I told him.

He stayed there, watching the older woman coming towards him. When she crossed his invisible barrier he barked. She gave a yelp of alarm and backed off. Sam fell silent again.

I went into the house. The two women were huddled together on the couch with the children on their laps. Mrs. Foster had her arms around Juliana. I left them there and went into the kitchen, where the chief was putting a kettle on.

"Tea is good at times like this,'' he said as if he'd just discovered something important.

I looked at him sharply to see if he was being serious. "We have to investigate, sir," I said. "There's no reason why the guy should have gone off his trolley the way he did. If he just wanted to get out of town he could have done it."

"His car's missing," Harding said, speaking patiently, as if I were handicapped.

"Right, but he could have got it back. This isn't making sense to me."

"Nor to me," he said grimly. "I think I'll call Scott and Walker in, have them search the town for his car. It might tell us something we don't know."

"Good idea." I nodded. "For now, can you tell me what happened? What brought all this on?" I was pushing again, acting as if he were only a witness and I was the one in charge of the investigation. But he didn't seem to notice.

"Nunziatta called the station. I took the call, and he asked me what was happening. I told him you wanted to talk to him about Ferris's death. He just flew off the handle. He called you down and then me. Then his wife started talking and I heard him hit her. I warned him not to do that and he told me to go to hell. Said he had a gun and he didn't have to take any more crap from me or anybody else. Then I heard glass break and the rifle went off and we came on down here, Levesque and I."

Outside I heard Sam break into his warning bark. "Thank you, sir," I said. "Sounds like the ambulance or the photographer is here. I'd better get outside."

"Right." He stood at the sink, then slowly turned the tap and started filling the kettle as I left.

The doctor was outside, trying to approach Nunziatta's car. Sam was patrolling the area I'd marked out, keeping him away. The doctor looked up and saw me. "Can you call him off?"

"Easy," I commanded, and Sam fell silent. I came down the steps and walked the doctor to the car, stooping to pat Sam as I passed him.

The doctor squatted and took one look at Nunziatta's head. "Did you do this?"

"No. I nearly had him cooled out. Then Levesque shot him from back off by the police car. Said the chief told him to."

"Was it necessary?" The doctor stood up, grim-faced, tugging his gloves on a little tighter.

"Not in my opinion. I'd talked him out of the house, offered him this car, my car. Nunziatta had this rifle trained on his wife, but I was close enough to grab it safely. Two seconds more and it would have been all over. This was totally unnecessary.''

"This may be enough to get Harding out of his office and out of town," the doctor said. "Anyway. This guy's dead. The ambulance is on its way."

"Thank you, doctor. I'd like you to take a blood test. It sounded to me as if he was high on something, speed maybe."

"I'll check." He shuddered and shrugged deeper into his down jacket. "I don't like the things that are happening," he said.

"Me neither, but I think tomorrow will see us through it all."

"I hope so. I'd better talk to Nunziatta's wife." He paused. "Widow, I guess now, poor woman. How's she taking it?"

"She blew up at first, tried to attack me. But she's kind of numb now. The chief had me bring her friend around to sit with her."

"Well at least he's done something right," the doctor said. He nodded at Nunziatta's body. "You can move him any time you want. He's gone."

"Thank you. I've got the photographer coming."

"Good." He nodded and walked up the steps and into the house. I bent over Nunziatta, seeing if there was anything more than his death to surprise me. I'm not sure what I expected to find. His face was caved in. There was blood in his nose and more had leaked through the wound into the corner of his right eye socket. Nothing I could see told me anything valuable.

I crouched by his body for about half a minute, checking everything I could about his appearance. His right hand was sprawled back into the snow, the left was folded across his chest where he had fallen. And the pockets of his blue down jacket were heavy with something. Ammunition for his rifle I thought, and patted one of them.

I was wrong. It was filled with something else, something heavy enough to drag the pocket sideways, something smooth to the touch as I ran my gloved fingers over the shiny fabric of his jacket. I tugged off my glove with my teeth and reached into the pocket, pulling back the Velcro that held it closed.

The object I touched was chilly to my fingers and I could feel that there were a number of them there. I pulled one of them out and whistled with surprise. It was a little yellow metal billet the diameter of a quarter. It was about half an inch thick,

flat on one side and lumpy on the other. I recognized it as a
billet of partly refined ore. I had never seen gold in this form,
but from my experience at the nickel mines I knew that this was
the form in which nickel is shipped. This looked like the out-
put of the smelter at the gold mine up the road.

TWENTY

I SLIPPED the gold back into his pocket and secured the Velcro on the flap, then checked the other pocket and found it was filled the same way. I stood up and thought hard. He had about thirty of the billets, each one weighing about three ounces and worth roughly 1200 American dollars.

A car squealed up behind me on the street and Roberts got out, carrying his camera. Sam bristled as he approached us, but I said "easy," and Sam relaxed. Roberts gasped when he saw Nunziatta. "Good God! Did he do that to himself?"

"No, unfortunately. One of the constables shot him, on orders from the chief. He was threatening his wife and children with that rifle there."

He gasped, then blew out a quick controlled gust of air and calmed himself. "Right. What can I do?"

"Take a picture of his face, then a shot that shows him and the car as well. Try to cover everything you think of. Then go back to the police car there and take a couple of shots over the top of it. After that, take his front window, and the rifle down there and one or two of the damage to the car across the street."

"Okay." He flipped his light meter open, adjusting his lens and started. I walked with him as he worked. Today he was more confident around the body. The horror of confronting violent death was not novel anymore, and he moved easily, clicking like a news photographer. Another couple of scenes like this and he would be cracking jokes like a veteran homicide officer.

When he had finished he stood rewinding his film and I spoke to him carefully. "Come and have a look at his pockets."

"Pockets?" He looked up, surprised. "You want a shot, I'll have to change the film."

"No. I want this news kept quiet," I said. "Come and see."

He walked back with me and I opened the pocket and took out a billet of gold. I was careful to keep my back to the front window so that the chief would not be able to see. Roberts gasped. "That's ours," he said. "Where did he get it?"

"I'm not sure. But he's got a bunch of them as far as I can tell by patting him down."

"He didn't get them legally." Roberts was shaken now, more than he had been by the sight of the body. "This is serious," he said. "I don't know how this could have happened."

"Maybe it's connected with the move tomorrow. Maybe the load is short. When was it made up?"

"Last night." He handed the gold back to me, and I replaced it in Nunziatta's pocket. "I was present. So was the mine manager and the chief of security. That's the procedure. We checked it and put the proper seals on the cases."

I stood up and he did the same, slowly, as if the weight of the knowledge were crushing him. "What do we do?" I asked him.

"Report it," he said instantly, and I relaxed. If he was part of some scam he would have made an excuse of some kind.

"That's what the book says. But I think you know what my own suspicions are about this town." I looked at him carefully. He returned my gaze calmly.

"You think the police are involved in this case?"

"I'm not sure who's involved and who isn't. But I do know that the chief had this man shot unnecessarily."

"Good God." He tightened his lips into a hard line. "That looks mighty suspicious to me. What can we do?"

"The first thing is for you to accompany me back to the hospital with the body when I search it," I said. "We'll talk about it as we drive."

"All right." He removed the film from his camera and put everything back into his bag. "Can I do that? Shouldn't another policeman be there?"

"I'll see what the chief says. Can you wait here?"

"Right." He shivered suddenly and hunched deeper into his coat.

I went into the house. The chief and the doctor were talking in the kitchen.

"Ah, sergeant," the chief said. "I've been talking to Dr. Frazer. He says you want an autopsy done on the body."

"Normal procedure, sir. I figure he was high on something. The doctor can make the necessary tests."

The chief's face relaxed a fraction. "Of course. Yes. That would be a good idea." He had taken off his gloves but was holding them in his right hand. Now he slapped them into his palm a couple of times. "Right. If the doctor goes with you I won't need to send one of my men. I want them to search for Nunziatta's car."

"Good." I nodded and waited for the doctor to move. He was thinking. He spoke after a moment or two. "I've given Mrs. Nunziatta something to keep her calm. If her friend can stay with her, I'll go." He turned away, then stopped. "Oh, and chief, perhaps you can call the builder in town and have him fix that front window. The family needs to keep warm."

"Of course," the chief said. He picked up the telephone in the hand that held his gloves.

The doctor and I walked out and found the ambulance waiting at the end of the street. "I want Mr. Roberts, the photographer, to come along, doctor. And I'd like it if you got rid of the civilian who helps you in the morgue. I'll explain why."

"Fine," he said. "I'll get back and finish my afternoon rounds. When you arrive let me know."

He walked briskly off to his car, exchanging a few words with Roberts, who nodded and waited for me to join him.

Together we supervised the loading of the body into the ambulance. The two men on duty exchanged glances when they saw Nunziatta's face but worked smoothly and had him out of sight in the ambulance in a couple of minutes.

"We'll follow you," I told them. Then I nodded to Roberts. "Would you care to drive me?"

"Right." He took me back to his car. I paused to put Sam in the front of my own car, then followed Roberts. He backed up and turned towards the hospital. I waited for him to start the conversation. At last he said, "I take it you think the chief's involved in some way."

"I guess the easy answer is yes," I said carefully. "What I mean is that a lot of very strange things have been happening since I came to town. I had thought that Sgt. Ferris was behind them, but now he's been shot."

"Suicide, surely?" He looked at me in horror, then turned forward again as the car swerved under us.

"No. The doctor says not. On top of which you've told me that the security chief at the mine is married to the woman at the police station. Also, the sergeant was linked to Nunziatta. You put all that together and it looks as if Ferris was involved with a leakage of gold from your storeroom."

"But where does the chief come in?"

"I can't be sure. But if he's involved, something is going to happen to your shipment tomorrow."

The ambulance signaled ahead of us and turned into the hospital's parking lot. We followed it to the rear doors.

"But surely, if he was involved in something tomorrow he'd cancel that now," Roberts said.

"He would if he heard that Nunziatta was carrying gold," I said. In front of us the two ambulance men were unloading the draped body. We sat and watched as they wheeled it into the doors.

"What do you want me to do?" Roberts asked nervously.

"I want you to make sure that the load that's going out tomorrow is intact," I said. "If it's not, it explains where Nunziatta got the gold. Do you think your manager will go along with us?"

"Yes." Roberts straightened up and answered without hesitation. "He'll listen. He's a hands-on manager. He's involved in everything that happens at the mine. Something like this, he'll want the best thing possible done." He paused anxiously. "You'll go along with what he says, will you?"

"Of course," I said. "Let's go through the procedures inside and head on over there with your gold."

He nodded briskly and we went in. I nodded to the nurse on duty. "Sgt. Bennett, Elliot police. We're here to complete our investigation on the guy who just came in. Tell Dr. Frazer we'll be in the morgue, please."

"Right." She was looking at me oddly. I guess the late-breaking gossip hadn't reached her yet. As far as she was concerned I was still under a cloud.

We got to the morgue as the ambulance men were wheeling out the empty gurney. We exchanged nods, not saying anything. White-faced George was on duty, and he was about to pull the sheet down from Nunziatta's face. "Don't touch the body," I told him and he looked up, startled.

"I wanted to make sure he was dead," he said in a whining voice.

"George, you're like something out of a Dickens novel," I said, smiling to show it was all in fun. "We'll wait here for the doctor to arrive. He won't be long."

"Okay. If you say." He sat down at his old wooden desk and pulled a paper towards him as if he were working on something. I kept him off balance. "You put in a lot of hours at this place."

That pleased him. He looked up, baring his yellowish teeth sociably. "I live close," he explained. "I'm always available to give the doctor a hand."

"How the hell would they manage without you?" I gave him another gee-whiz smile. I'd already given him warning I didn't want any interference. Now I had to get him back onside a little.

He went into a long rambling dissertation, which I prodded along with nods and the odd question until the doctor came in. He nodded to us and told George, "Time for you to get some rest, George. These gentlemen will help me. Thank you for hanging in like you have."

George tried: "It's no problem, doctor."

"No. We'll be fine. You go and get some rest and I'll see you in the morning," Frazer insisted kindly.

"Well, I have been working a long time," George said grudgingly.

Frazer checked his watch. "Since midnight last night. That's sixteen hours. I appreciate the help, but I don't want to break the back of a willing horse. See you tomorrow."

George lingered over getting his coat on but finally left.

Frazer shook his head. "He's nine parts werewolf, but we don't pay him much and nobody else would take the bloody job."

He opened the door and checked that George was out of earshot. Then he turned back and looked at me, slipping his hands into the pockets of his long white coat. "What's going on?"

"Nunziatta is carrying a couple of pocketfuls of gold from the mine," I said. "You know where I stand. So does Mr. Roberts. We'd like you to search the body with us."

"Gold?" Frazer shook his head and whisked the sheet back from Nunziatta's dead face. He rolled the sheet and tossed it on George's desk. Then he patted the pocket nearest to him. "Feels like you're right. Let's do it."

"First, I'd like a plastic evidence bag, or whatever you've got, anyway. It should be strong and transparent."

"Right." He moved off to a cupboard and brought out a small plastic sack. "This do?"

"Fine. Now, Mr. Roberts, would you go through the pockets please and drop any gold you find in here?"

I'd already removed my parka. Now Roberts took off his topcoat and started unloading Nunziatta's hoard. As he took each billet out he examined it and dropped it into the bag. He took out thirty in all.

"There are other things in here," he said when he had reached the bottom of the right pocket.

"I'll get to them later. If you'd just search all the other pockets please and check for a money belt."

He did it but found no more gold.

Frazer had watched without speaking. Now he whistled. "What are those things, pure gold?"

"Almost," Roberts said primly. "Altogether he's carrying a thousand grams of ninety percent gold. They still have to be refined up to five nines purity, but they're worth about forty thousand U.S. dollars. That's just on fifty thousand Canadian for what he's carrying."

"He didn't make that working for you guys," Frazer said softly.

"This is a straight rip-off of the mine," I said. "Now, I'm going to write down what we've found and I'll ask both of you to sign it. Then we seal the paper into the bag with the gold and go see the mine manager."

We all signed the paper, then the doctor wrote his name on a narrow strip of paper and sealed his signature under the scotch tape he used to close the bag. Nobody could open the bag without destroying his signature.

After we'd done that we quickly searched the body, turning all Nunziatta's other pockets inside out. He had nothing unusual on him, no drugs. He did have ten fifty-dollar bills in his wallet, and I had the doctor sign to verify the amount. Then I took all the possessions into my custody and picked up the bag that contained the gold and handed it to Roberts. "This is yours now. Can you hide it until we get into your boss's office?"

It was too big for his pockets, but he put on his topcoat and slipped the bag into the front of it. Then he stood with his arm across his waist while I finished with the doctor. "If you can do whatever's necessary, please, doctor. And I'd like the blood analysis made for drugs. We're going to see the mine manager. I'll let you know what happens."

"Right." Frazer nodded and pulled on a pair of rubber gloves. "And one other thing. I'm pleased with the progress on the woman who was strangled. I'm going to bring her around tomorrow morning, about nine A.M. Can you be here?"

"Unless this gold business prevents it, yes," I said.

We thanked him and left with Roberts clutching his abdomen like an appendicitis patient.

When he got into the car he let his bundle slip down into his lap. We drove out to the mine site and parked in his reserved space next to the front door of the office building. Roberts got out, clutching his stomach again, and hustled us into the executive area. The manager's office was the biggest and it occupied the corner. Other than that it was no fancier than any other office in the complex. It had the name John Kemp on the door. I could see in through the glass walls and liked what I saw of Kemp. A tall lean man with sandy hair and black-rimmed glasses, he was in shirtsleeves, talking on the phone. When Roberts tapped on the door, Kemp waved us in while he finished his call. He hung up the phone and held out his hand. "John Kemp."

It was a working hand, hard and strong. "Reid Bennett. I'm the new sergeant on the Elliot police. Thank you for seeing me."

He sat down and waited.

"I've just investigated the sudden death of a guy called Nunziatta, an assistant driller at your mine. In his possession I found gold that has come from your strong room. Mr. Roberts was with me. I've given it to him."

Roberts slipped the bag out of the front of his coat and hoisted it onto Kemp's desk. Kemp frowned and picked it up. "You sure it's ours, Jim?"

"It looks like ours," Roberts said. I glanced around. Outside, the bullpen was busy and people were coming and going. I was afraid someone would see the gold. Gossip would kill my cover. There were vertical blinds on the windows and I closed them all.

Kemp watched me. "You're investigating this as a theft?" he asked, hefting the bag, then setting it down.

"Yes. But there's more to it than that. I've had a number of conversations with Mr. Roberts since last night. Has he told you anything about them?"

"He told me he trusted you and that you were going to take special precautions with our outgoing shipment tomorrow."

"It's more complex than that." I paused and thought for a moment. Every word I said was giving away my cover. If there was any leak, even gossip around town about my presence here, it could mean the end of my job at Elliot. Maybe even worse. If Harding was in this my life could be in danger. Kemp waited while I made my decision. In the absence of any guidance from Toronto I was going to have to press ahead on my own. The gold shipment would be the breakpoint. Either I was right or I was off this case.

I spoke carefully. "This is for your office only, please. I am breaking security because of the special circumstances here."

Kemp nodded and adjusted his glasses which had a habit of sliding down his nose. I laid out the facts as if I were giving evidence in court. "I'm on assignment from the Ontario Police Commission. My job is to investigate some unsubstantiated stories of corruption in the department here. I am beginning to think that only Sgt. Ferris was involved, but I'm not sure. I have reason to believe that the sergeant was planning something connected with your gold shipment tomorrow. My superior at the commission is out of reach until tomorrow, so I want to pursue the gold shipment to see if there is some connection to any improper conduct by anyone else in the department." All completely formal, no specific suspicions voiced. As neat as the story could get, I thought.

"Who else knows about your job here?" Kemp asked.

"My wife, of course. Also Dr. Frazer."

Now it was Kemp's turn to sit and think. He shoved his glasses again and looked at me, but blankly, the thousand-yard stare of combat fatigue. At last he said, "Thank you for taking me into your confidence. I must admit I've been less than happy with the conduct of the police in town, but I haven't mentioned it to our head office. I have to live here. The president doesn't."

"What do we do?" I felt a touch of relief at sharing the burden with him.

"I will keep everything secret until the shipment has reached the point where the Ontario Provincial Police become responsible," he said slowly. "That doesn't mean nothing will happen. You go five miles out of town and they take over. If somebody was planning something it could happen after that, but I can't allow the shipment to move any further without alerting the OPP to your concerns.''

"That's all I need,'' I said. "If you can pass the information to a high-ranking OPP officer with a request to keep the news from our chief, I might even be able to continue my investigation here.''

"Somebody's going to say you were here,'' he said. "Word may get back. What will you do about that?''

"I could tell the chief that Mr. Roberts needed a reason for taking so much time out of his working day.'' I turned to Roberts. "If you don't mind being made to look like a crybaby, Mr. Roberts. It would keep the investigation airtight.''

Roberts sighed. "If it has to be,'' he said.

Kemp nodded. "Thanks, Jim.'' He sat for a moment. Then he came back to his own problem, the gold.

"How'd you think this man got hold of the product?''

It was time for more honesty. "The head of your security here is married to the woman at the police office. There's a chance that she and Sgt. Ferris had worked together on this.''

"I've known Sheridan since I came here,'' Kemp said. "He's been given the highest possible clearance for our work.''

"I'm only guessing. It's a connection, that's all.''

"Pretty slim,'' Kemp said grimly. He shoved his glasses up, almost angrily. "But I guess you'd have to start somewhere. This stuff wasn't taken out in any other way that I could imagine.''

"What time tomorrow is the load moving?'' I didn't want Sheridan's history, just the facts on the gold.

"Seven A.M.,'' Kemp said. He was running his fingers over the little bars of gold under their plastic sheath. Suddenly he picked the bag up and turned his chair around. Behind him on the credenza there was a small brass scale. It had a plaque on the stand that supported it, a presentation from somewhere or other. "How many billets are there?'' he asked.

"Thirty,'' Roberts said quickly.

Without a word Kemp slipped off all but the bottom two of the weights on the scale and put the bag on the pan. The pan jiggled but did not sink.

"Something's wrong,'' Kemp said. "With the bag included this should weigh enough to lift the weights.''

None of us spoke as he removed one of the weights and re-placed it with something smaller. Then the pan sank and the weights lifted.

Kemp turned to look at me, his mouth a straight line. "This isn't gold at all," he said. "It's something lighter. A mixture of lead and something, I guess."

TWENTY-ONE

HE LOOKED at me with grim satisfaction in his face. "This makes things a lot easier to understand."

"How so?"

Kemp smiled, a relieved little flick of his cheeks. He was still intense but his early shock was over. "It hasn't been stolen from our storeroom. He must have made these up to sell to some gullible person."

"What about the color?"

"Paint, probably." He pulled a Swiss army knife out of his pocket and slit the evidence bag then took out one of the billets and scraped it. I leaned over the desk to watch. The metal was soft and it scratched easily, showing gray underneath. "Gold paint," he said and handed the billet to me.

"I guess that shoots down my theory about a gold heist tomorrow," I said.

Kemp nodded. "Yes, probably Nunziatta himself made these."

I nodded. "If you don't mind, I still want to keep tabs on your gold until it leaves our jurisdiction."

Kemp frowned. "Does this mean we won't be getting the escort we usually get?"

"Whatever I do will be extra. I haven't been told anything about escort duty. Do you usually speak directly to the chief?"

"Always," he said. He seemed stern. He wasn't comfortable with what I'd suggested and it was up to me to take his worries away.

"And he's been notified about this shipment?"

"Yes. I have no reason to expect it will be different in any way from our routine," he said.

"It almost certainly won't be different," I said. "But I'd like to watch as it moves, that's all."

He frowned. "Is that how you want it done?"

"Yes. I just want to add a little extra protection," I said. His probing was making me less and less sure of myself. I had nothing to go on but an *X* on a dead man's calendar. At three in the morning it had seemed important. Now I wasn't so sure. "If I can just ask you to keep it confidential, please. I'm not sure how long my cover story will stand up now but I can keep on for a while if you'll go along with me."

"Yes, I will," he said formally. He sat thinking for a moment until his phone buzzed. He picked it up. "Yes, Jennie?" Then he covered the receiver and said, "If you'll excuse me, sergeant, I have an important call here."

I stood up. "Thank you for your help, Mr. Kemp. I'll be looking out for your shipment in the morning."

"Good." He smiled a formal little smile and shook my hand.

I left alone and went out to the reception desk where I called the station and raised Levesque who was on patrol in town. He said he would come over and get me. I sat and leafed through back copies of *The Northern Miner* and waited.

The receptionist saw the police car coming up and she gave me a beautiful smile and pointed it out. I thanked her and left, zipping up my parka. It was not yet five but already it was dropping dark. The parking lot was emptying as the miners who had got off shift at four and showered were heading back to town.

Levesque stayed in the car and waited apparently without caring whether I was coming out or not. He didn't speak when I got in but drove away with great precision. I could tell he was reliving that last moment before he pulled the trigger. "You okay, Al?" I asked.

He nodded. "Yeah. I guess." He drove for a minute or so, then started to talk, almost to himself. "I never killed nothin' before. I don' even hunt."

"You had no choice with Harding giving the order." It wasn't quite true, but it was what he needed to hear.

He nodded, then turned his face to me, slowing the car. "You ever kill anybody?"

"I've had to," I said.

He looked ahead again and picked up the speed a little, both hands on the wheel, like a teenager taking his driving test. "Yeah. But you was in a war."

"And as a cop. It happens sometimes."

He wound the window down, letting in a knife edge of bitter air, and spat thinly into the slipstream. "In front of his god-damn wife an' kids," he said.

"Look, Al, it's done. If it helps, the guy was a lousy son-ofabitch. He was pushing drugs to schoolkids. He slapped his wife around. The only person regretting the fact that he's dead is you. And that's wasted worry."

"I'm gonna quit this job," he said. I didn't answer and he rambled on. "Like I always figured I was 'ard. You know. Fights? I love fights. I get in dere an' I fight an' love it. But I don' do it no more."

"You probably won't have to. People will respect you for what you did. Everyone knew he was pushing drugs. People will say you did a good thing."

He glanced at me again. "You t'ink so?"

"I can promise it."

"Well, I t'ink about what you say," he said. "I t'ink maybe I ask the chief for some leave. Take the wife back to Trois Rivières, see her folks."

"Just so you don't sit around town. If you do you'll feel worse," I said. "Don't worry, you're a good guy, Al. People know that. Tough but good."

"I finish bein' tough," he said and fell silent.

"My car's in front of Nunziatta's house," I told him. He nodded but didn't answer so I plowed on, giving him a preview of my story. "That guy Roberts was worried what his boss would say about him taking so much time away from his office. Had me go back with him and explain what had happened." I shook my head in disgust. "And he says he's an executive."

"I 'ear that guy Kemp, 'e's tough," Levesque said. "It was 'im set the rules, no booze in camp. Before that they 'ad a wet canteen. Guys could get a beer when they were done their shift."

I hadn't known anything about Kemp, and I followed up on the information, as much to keep Levesque's mind off his own sorrows as for the information itself. "How long's he been in charge?"

Levesque shrugged. "Six month' maybe."

I let it go at that and he dropped me at my car. I'd left Sam in the frontseat and now I allowed him a quick stretch while I started the car and ran the defrosters to clear off the ice that had formed on the windows from his breathing. Then I got Sam back in and drove to the station.

I took him in with me and set him down in the guardroom while I went into the chief's office. He was sitting there with his tunic unfastened, the first time I'd seen him looking less than rigid. I thought I could smell liquor, but except for the loose buttons he seemed normal. "What did you find out?" he asked.

"Nothing of any consequence. Nunziatta had five hundred in fifties in his wallet." I sat down without waiting for an invitation. "That guy Roberts is a wimp," I said.

"How do you mean?" The chief looked puzzled and a touch vague. I was right about the smell of liquor.

"He was nervous about taking time out from his office, insisted I go back to see his boss and explain what's going on."

"What did you tell him?" Harding asked quickly.

"I told him that Nunziatta was threatening his wife and kids with a rifle. We had to take him out. Period. The big thing I told him was that we wanted photographs for the inquest and that Roberts is the best guy in town to provide them."

"And that was enough?" Harding asked, more easily now.

"Yes, sir. He just wanted to know why his chief accountant was out playing cops and robbers when they've got a mine to run."

Harding sighed. "Okay. I guess that's fair enough." He sighed again, and this time I caught a solid gust of whisky in the air. "There will be an inquest, of course. I'll give a statement, so will Levesque. He was the one who pulled the goddamn trigger. Not me." He stared at me to see if I was going to argue. I said nothing and Harding went on. "What will you say, sergeant?"

"I'll tell it like it was," I said.

"And how do you think it was?" He had picked up the pen from a fancy presentation set on his desk and was playing with it. His knuckles whitened as he squeezed it. He was right on the edge.

"That Nunziatta had already fired a number of times, that he'd been using drugs, amphetamines probably. He was threatening his wife when the shot killed him."

Harding let the pen drop and leaned back. "Good. Why don't you type it up and then go home. There's nothing else to be done tonight."

"How about you, chief? Are you okay? It's been a tough day."

"These are the pressures of the office," he said.

I glanced at him to see if he smiled, but he was completely serious. This was the way he would talk at the inquiry. I wondered again whether he had the moxie to be involved with anything crooked. It must have been as much as he could do to get up in the morning and get dressed.

"Anything happening tomorrow?" I asked innocently. It was his chance to tell me about the gold duty.

"There's a special assignment first thing," he said. Then he checked himself as if stifling a burp. "But I always take care of it. No need to concern yourself."

"Whatever you say, chief." I stood up. "I'll type my report and leave it for you."

"Good." He nodded, not looking at me. I waited a moment, then walked back to the guardroom. I thought I heard a clink as I left but didn't look back.

When I'd typed out a bare-bones account of what had happened I took it back to Harding. This time he didn't bother hiding his glass. It was half full, sitting on the blotter in front of him.

"Here's the report, chief. I'll see you in the morning."

"Right." He frowned at me blankly, as if trying to remember who I was. I nodded and left.

Fred was her usual cheerful self when I got home. She came to the door and kissed me. I hung on to her and then she led me through to the kitchen. "You're getting a good healthy supper tonight," she said. "We've been eating too much red meat. I got a nice pickerel from the market."

"Sounds good." I patted her on the shoulder and slipped out of my parka, hanging it over the back of the chair.

She laughed and pointed at it. "Those brass things beside the back door are coathooks."

"Nag nag nag," I kidded and hung up the coat.

After I'd washed she asked, "So, how was your day?"

"Crowded," I said. "I guess you heard the scuttlebutt."

"About the man who was shot?" Her voice lost its lightness and I realized she had been acting for me. The brightness was all assumed.

"That was unnecessary," I said. "Listen, Fred, the more I see of this place and the guy in charge, the more I wish you'd head back to Toronto for a couple of weeks until I'm through here."

She went on tearing up lettuce, not looking at me. "I've considered it, Reid. But we're a team and no team has it easy all season."

I kissed her and she clung to me. "It's a bloody mess isn't it?" she whispered into my shoulder.

"Yes. I'm afraid it is." I squeezed her shoulders and then released her and she went back to the salad. "Just say the word and I'm gone."

"No." She was almost fierce with me and I realized, not for the first time, that she came by her Irish red hair honestly. "No, Reid. These are good people. They deserve proper police work, not the travesty they've had until now."

"Well, I think tomorrow is the breakpoint." I sat down at the table and she set down the salad and started serving the fish. "After this gold shipment in the morning I think my cover's blown. They've promised at the mine to keep it quiet until then. But someone will talk."

"What gold shipment?"

I remembered I hadn't given her the details and I apologized quickly.

"Sorry, love. I've been thinking about it all day. There was a note on Ferris's calendar for tomorrow and I find a gold shipment is moving. I want to see nothing happens to it. After that I think the mine manager will let it slip that I'm on the inside and I'll have to quit."

"Is it liable to be dangerous?" She dissected her fish carefully as she talked.

"I don't think so. But if something does happen I'll know who's to blame and we can call in the OPP and ride out of town."

"A gold shipment," she said carefully. She was looking at me and I noticed that she had the hint of circles under her eyes, something I had never seen there before. "A gold shipment is big time, Reid. Some very nasty things could happen if someone tries to steal it."

"Nothing I can't handle," I said. "I'm not going into this with my eyes closed."

She set down her knife and fork and folded her hands. "And what do you plan to do, husband mine?"

"I'm not sure there's much I can do except follow it to the edge of our jurisdiction. Then I just come home and go to work like any other day."

"That's all? Just follow it?" She frowned. "Doesn't sound very cunning. I thought you had some sneaky plan forming in that tiny mind."

"What else is there to do?" I shrugged. "Hell, I've never planned a heist. All I've ever done is act on tip-offs and been waiting around with a reception committee when it happens."

She picked up her knife and fork again and began to eat, but not with any enthusiasm. "Tell me how much you know," she commanded. "I don't have anything else to worry about tonight."

So I filled her in, giving her everything, including the phony gold that I had found on Nunziatta. She listened, nibbling at her dinner, and I sat back. "So I'm not sure what to do other than follow the van. What do you think?"

Now she said, "That's better. I hate it when you come on all strong and silent with me."

I held out my hand to her and she left her chair and came around the table to kiss me. "You have to understand that you're not the typical policeman's wife," I told her.

"I try not to be the typical anything," she said, "although it's getting harder to avoid the clichés these days."

I shoved my chair back from the table and pulled her onto my lap. "You want to explain that for a male chauv?"

"No." She laughed and stood up. "We'll see how good a detective you really are."

I was puzzled, but it seemed I'd been that way since waking up that morning, so I just helped her with the dishes and left, promising to be back soon. I had some checking to do.

My first visit was to the motel. There was no need to go in. A plain brown van was sitting on the lot. I stood on the back bumper and jiggled but the van hardly moved. Heavy-duty shocks and springs. Bingo. I'd found the gold truck. I memorized the license number and drove over to the old town and called on Wilcox. He was washing his supper dishes and offered me a cup of coffee. I thanked him but refused. That time of night coffee is death on sleep and I planned to get eight full hours before starting for the mine next morning.

He dried his dishes and sat down, "So what've you come up with?"

It didn't take long to fill him in. He listened carefully, rolling one of his cigarettes, then lit it and blew out a long pleasurable column of smoke. "So, Nunziatta was in on something. You think he was gonna pull this gold heist?"

"Could have been, but that chance is shot, if you'll excuse the joke. No, I think the only thing I can do is follow the van to the edge of town in the morning and turn it over to the OPP."

He nodded. "Yeah. I've been trying to think of something clever to do, but there's nothing. If we was to head off the van and get it away from the police escort it still wouldn't do us any good. We're not there to protect it, we're using it as bait." He mused for a moment. "Yeah, that's all, wait to see if some bastard tries to steal it, then see who they are."

"That could be hazardous to your health," I said.

He nodded and gestured with his cigarette. "So're these things, but I'm not about to give 'em up."

"Well, okay. How about I meet you at the mine site tomorrow morning, around six. The shipment's leaving at seven. We'll follow it in your car. The guys on the department would recognize mine. I've got my handgun back and we have your rifle."

He nodded slowly. "I'd like that a whole lot," he said. "I haven't used a rifle for real in most of forty-five years. Be good to use it again."

"Remember we can't take anybody out. We shoot only if we have to protect ourselves and we shoot to take prisoners, not to kill."

"Yeah. I'll remember that," he said. "What else?"

"There isn't anything else. Whatever happens tomorrow morning, I'm just about through here. There's no chance of my keeping on here much longer. Too many people know about me now."

"Then we better make it good," he said. "Now why'n't you go on home and I'll get a good night's sleep."

"Sounds good," I said.

"Right." He stood up. "See you in the morning. There's a pull-off on the road a little ways past the mine gate if you come out from town. I'll be there at six."

"Thanks." I shook hands with him and he asked, "Bringing that big mutt of yours?"

"He's earned his keep at times like this before," I said.

"Fine. May have to run some sonofabitch down in the woods," he said. "That's more'n I'm up to. Or this guy." He picked up his terrier and it yapped at me as he showed me out.

New snow was dusting down and I could see the tracks of a single car on the roadway. About usual for this time of night, I figured.

It was only nine when I got home and I sat with a book while Fred worked on the play she had selected, trying to decide which of her women would be best suited for which roles. She was concentrating so I didn't interrupt, finally closing my book and watching her with real pleasure. She looked up and caught my eye and winked at me. "Be right with you, sailor," she said.

At ten o'clock I stood up and put my book aside. "I want to be up early so I'm going to turn in. You want to work a bit longer?"

She yawned and stretched, like a cat. "Not me. I'm just starting to realize that producers really do earn their dollar."

"You go on ahead then. I'll put Sam out for a minute and join you." I clicked my tongue at Sam and he stood up. I touched Fred on the forehead lightly as I passed her chair, and she smiled at me, but somehow everything seemed a little strained and out of tune.

It was bitterly cold outside. I slipped my parka on and then my boots, not lacing them, and stepped out with Sam. The sky was clear and the stars were big and bright, even through the competition from the streetlights. I walked to the roadway and let Sam wander for a minute. There were a couple of cars parked on the street and I guessed they belonged to miners who hadn't felt like shoveling out their driveways now that the plow had been through, again, adding to the four-foot wall of dis-placed snow along the curb.

After a minute or two I patted my leg and Sam came back to me. We went indoors and I shut off the outside light. I hung up my parka in the front hall and settled Sam in the kitchen un-der the table. Then I went through to the bathroom, switching off the lights in the front of the house. When I got to the bed-room, Fred was already in bed. She put her arms around my neck as I got in alongside her. We kissed and I held her with-out saying anything. Finally she eased her arms out and we composed ourselves for sleep. Then she said suddenly, "Oh, I forgot to tell you. Mrs. Schuka says that Sgt. Ferris did have

one set of good friends in town—that woman who works at
your office and her husband. Sheridan, I think their name is."

"Suspicions confirmed," I said. "That would tie everything together neatly. He's in charge of security at the mine.
And Ferris was also tied up with Nunziatta."

"Down boy," she said sleepily. "Even Sherlock Holmes had
to rest sometimes."

She fell asleep first, breathing softly. I lay and counted her
breaths. I was up to maybe sixteen when my own eyes closed.

I wasn't sure how long I slept before Sam woke me with his
barking, a second before the crash. I sat up in bed and saw the
edge of the bedroom door outlined in light. Then the roaring
of flames.

I pulled the covers off Fred. "Up. There's a fire."

TWENTY-TWO

FRED SAT up, half asleep and foggy. "What?"

"Fire," I shouted, struggling into my pants and shirt. "Throw some clothes on and grab all your heavy clothes out of the wardrobe."

I put my back to the bedroom door and turned the handle, bracing myself. I had to get Sam out, but I knew there might be a smoke explosion if I let air into the blaze.

I was lucky. The flames were hot enough to eat up most of the smoke they were creating, and the door opened easily. Beyond it I saw the fire spreading like a liquid across the floor and I smelled gasoline. Sam was at the door. As I opened it he pushed through to my side, still barking.

Fred was half dressed. "Out the window," I shouted. I picked up the side table and threw it through the glass, then grabbed the counterpane and wrapped it around my arm and swept out all the shards of glass that still clung to the putty. One of them pierced the cloth and stuck in my arm. I pulled it out, working by feel, and grabbed Fred by the arm. She already had her slacks and sweater on and I hoisted her onto the sill. I knew it was about six feet above ground level. "Jump and roll," I shouted. "You'll be okay in the snow."

"What about you?" she half screamed.

"I'm right behind you." I let her sit on my arm in its protective counterpane and then prodded her in the back. "Jump."

She yelled and jumped. I took a moment longer to throw all the bedding out of the window, along with the clothes Fred had taken out of the wardrobe. Then I called Sam who was still standing by the door barking. "Up," I commanded, patting the windowsill. He leaped up and I shoved him out after the clothes. He landed and stood barking while I scrambled over the sill and jumped down.

Fred was already standing on one of the blankets, struggling into her thickest coat. "Good." I dug in my pocket for my keys.

"Start the car and turn the heater on full. Blast the horn until somebody calls the fire department."

"Where are you going?" She screamed it and clung to me.

"Downstairs," I said. "Mrs. Schuka's down there."

I picked up the same counterpane and wrapped my arm so I could punch in the basement window. Smoke rolled out of it, oily and poisonous. I took a deep breath and eased in over the sill, gouging my chest with another shard of glass. It was a long drop to the floor, and I had to brace in the window and swing my legs around to let myself down without injury.

The smoke was rushing out past me, but it was rising to escape. Down on the deck I could still breathe. There was carpeting under me, but I didn't know which room I was in. I lifted my head an inch or two and shouted. "Mrs. Schuka! Fire! Where are you?"

There was no answer, and I crawled on, keeping my nose against the carpet, breathing in shallow little puffs. I came to a wall and lay for a moment, remembering which way I had entered and where the door was likely to be. I figured it was to the left and edged over that way, keeping one hand against the wall until I found the doorjamb. I reached up but could not feel a hinge, so I took on as much air as I could and half crouched up, patting the wall beside the door until I found the light switch and clicked it on.

I dropped down again and opened my eyes. The light was glowing faintly, far away from me it seemed, dull brown in the smoke. My eyes watered, but I saw that this was the living room of the flat. I shoved the door open, seeing the smoke thicken instantly, almost totally blanking the light. I could hardly get any breath at all and was weakening with every move, but the heat was still not reaching me. Faintly outside I could hear the blaring of my car horn and then shouts. I gathered all the breath I could muster and called again, "Where are you?"

This time I heard a cough. It gurgled once and stopped but I could tell it was coming from the right, close to me. I crawled forward until I found a bed. It moved as I touched it, a convulsive shaking as if someone were writhing on it. Still keeping as low as I could, I reached up over it and found a form lying under the covers. I took in all the air I could in one convulsive gulp and crouched up to grab her, still swathed in blankets. I half stood and stumbled back the way I had come, following the ugly curling of the smoke that was pouring through the living-room door and out to the open air.

The woman squirmed in my arms and whined like a puppy, but I pushed forward, past the light, up against the outside wall of the house. Then a burst of flame erupted behind me, slamming me against the wall and letting me see for an instant which way the smoke was pouring out. It was six feet to my right. I reached it and stuffed my bundle out of the window, using up the very last of my strength.

I shoved at her feet, aware that there were people outside, shouting, coughing, reaching for the bundle of bedding. And then nothing. I passed out. Later I found that it had been only a few seconds, but all I knew was that I opened my eyes, feeling almost blissfully content. My face was against the wall, nose down to the carpet. There was air in the space there, lying under the smoke. I lay still, breathing gently, aware of the growing brightness on the wall in front of my eyes and of the noise, the roar of flames and the frenzied shouting of somebody above me. It must have taken thirty seconds before I understood where I was and what was happening. Then I slowly gathered myself together, overbreathing the foul-smelling air, preparing to stand up.

I knew it would be difficult. You can black out from standing up suddenly, and I was already in some kind of oxygen debt. The heat of the fire was clawing at my back.

Slowly I pulled myself up, allowing my body to compensate for the change until I was erect, open-eyed, facing the wall. The window was off to one side of me behind its curtain of roiling smoke. I stretched as far as I could until I found the edge of the sill, away to my left.

Someone outside shouted, and I felt someone touch my hand and start tugging my fingers. I eased over in front of the window, eyes tight shut against the smoke, not breathing. When I reached the window I realized it was at neck height. I had no strength to climb but suddenly another man grabbed my other hand. I felt myself being pulled out, bruising my chest on the sill, until I was able to gather new strength and brace my knees against the wall on the inside, arching myself to make their pulling easier.

Outside everything was a glare. I coughed and gasped as my rescuers dragged me clear, face down in the healing cold of the snow, then sideways, away from the column of smoke that had followed me out of the window like a genie from a bottle.

"He's alive," someone said. I heard Sam keening when he saw me, but I couldn't see him. I relaxed about him then. Cold doesn't bother him; he would curl down in the snow like a husky until I came for him later.

I was in shirtsleeves and the cold was cutting as deeply as the broken glass had cut. I shuddered and then found myself rolled into a blanket and carried like a carpet. I didn't move until they set me down, on something soft.

Instantly the blanket was pulled away and I found I was in a living room with two men unwrapping the blanket from me and Fred standing between them, leaning down over me, her face streaming with tears.

I pulled her to me and we both spoke in the same breath. "Are you all right?"

I squeezed her tighter. "You first. Are you okay?"

"Not a scratch," she said. "Oh Reid. How about you?"

"I'm okay." I let go of her and saw the blood on her front. "You're hurt."

"No, that's you. You're bleeding." She grabbed me again and unbuttoned my shirt with trembling fingers. When she saw the gouges she gasped and stood up. "You have to go to the hospital, Reid. You're hurt." She tugged at the arm of one of the men. "Can you take him, please? He's cut badly."

I tried to stand but a sudden wave of shock hit me, making a soft whooshing beat in my ears, clouding my vision. I sat back. "We all need to go to the hospital," I said softly. "You, me, and Mrs. Schuka. Was that her in bed? I didn't look."

"Yes." Fred was looking around frantically. "Where's your wife?" she asked one of the men.

"With her mother. I'll get her." He left the room, with Fred taking a couple of paces after him, then turning back on her heel to stoop over me again. The other man was looking around in the cupboard and he let out a little aha of delight.

"How about some of this?" He turned to Fred, holding a bottle of rum.

She shook her head. "No. Liquor is a depressant," she explained. Then, typically, she added, "But it's a nice thought. Thank you."

The man said, "Think I'll have a drop anyways."

A woman came into the room and Fred swooped over to her and they left, the woman staring anxiously at my chest which was leaking blood, probably on her living-room rug. She was back in a few seconds with a box of sanitary napkins. She ripped my shirt away and pressed a couple of the napkins over the cuts.

"Hold them in place," she told Fred. "I'll tear up a sheet for a bandage."

"I'm going to owe you," I said, but she brushed it aside.

"You pulled Mother outta that fire," she said. "You can have the top brick off our chimney." She got up, resting her hand on Fred's shoulder in a sisterly fashion, and walked out.

Fred had a tight, frightened look. She was concentrating very hard on my cuts, and I tried to josh her out of it. "Promise you won't tell the other boys what you're using on me," I kidded, but she wasn't amused.

"Quit being so goddamn macho," she said angrily. "You could have died in that basement."

"Sorry." I put my hand over hers as she pressed on my chest and she sniffled and pushed her head against my shoulder. The man who had found the rum bottle quietly left the room. We were alone.

"I'm sorry I'm being so crabby," she said, her voice muffled against my shoulder. "I'm just so worried about you."

I pressed her hands with my right hand, reaching around her shoulder with my left, hugging her to me. My eyes were closed, and a part of my mind was working outside my body, witnessing the start of the fire once more, seeing the puddle of flame spreading out over the rug in our rented house, smelling the gasoline and hearing Sam's fearful barking. As I lay there, holding onto my wife and relishing being safe and alive, I was coming to grips with the fact that someone had tried to murder us, both of us. And I knew what had to be done.

"Fred, I want you to do something important. It's unpleasant but there isn't any other way."

She moved her face back an inch or two from my shoulder, peering down into my eyes. "Don't tell me you want me to go away," she said fiercely.

"No. Just go along with me. I'm going to act."

I just got the words out before the other woman came back with long strips of bandage trailing from one hand. "How are those pads going?" she asked.

"One of them is leaking," Fred said. "Put another one on top."

The pair of them bent over me, concentrating on the gashes as if I were deaf and dumb, a wound rather than a man.

I groaned. Fred glanced at my face. "Are you all right, darling?" She never calls me darling. We both think it's a phony word. It was her cue that she was in character as I'd asked.

"Chest feels tight," I said weakly.

The other woman stopped pressing the pad on me. "Is it the bandage? Am I pressing too hard?"

I shook my head and said nothing. The woman quickly looped the bandage around my chest once more, then tore the end and tied it around my shoulder to hold it in place. "Keep him quiet," she told Fred and went out of the room.

I winked at Fred and gave her a tight little nod. She gave no indication that she had seen anything. Then the woman came back in with two men.

"He has to get to the hospital right now," she said. "Al, warm the car up. Pete, wrap him up in lots of blankets and then the two of you get him off to the hospital. Okay?"

"I'm going with him," Fred said.

"You can't go barefoot," the woman said. "What size boots do you take?"

"Eight," Fred said anxiously, then added, "please."

"No problem." The woman left the room. Fred bent over me. She licked one fingertip and wiped it over my face, then ran it over my lips. "They should be blue," she mouthed. "Soot will help."

She wrapped the blanket I was lying on around my shoulders, wiping my face with the end of it to smudge her finger marks. By the time the others came back she was well in character, sitting holding my hand, her finger on my pulse.

"Please hurry," she said to the men. "His pulse is awful fast."

"We'll be right there." One of them gripped me around the waist and hoisted me erect. "Take his weight," he said to Fred. "We have to make a seat."

I leaned against Fred, trying to make it look real without overdoing it. She completed the pantomime, and the men clutched their wrists to make a seat for me. Fred eased me back and they took my weight, leaning into me to support me.

The woman was bending down to help Fred on with a pair of snow boots and she ducked quickly to pull them on. I let myself relax as far as I could, but tried to miss nothing as we came down the steps of the house and went to the car at the end of the drive. I found we were across the street from the blaze. The fire engine had just arrived and the first man was hitting the fire with a hose while two others were uncurling another one. The fire was way out of control. Nothing would be saved—that was clear. There was a police car down the block, but I couldn't see the officer. Scott, probably, I thought. He was on night shift.

I let myself be lowered into the backseat of the car, then Fred scrambled in after me and the two men got in the front. As they tried to back out, the policeman appeared at the side window. I still couldn't see who it was but recognized Scott's voice and heard the driver's response. "We gotta get to the hospital. The cop from that house is hurt bad."

Fred leaned forward and half screamed out of the window. "Let us out. For God's sake. My husband's having a heart attack."

Scott must have stepped aside because the car jumped forward and sped down to the corner, leaning on the horn to blare his way through the crowd that had gathered.

"Hold on, buddy," the driver said over his shoulder. "Soon have you there."

Fred sat with her arm around me, whispering encouragement. "Not long now. Hold on."

I lay back and let it all happen. At the hospital I was whisked out and shoved into a wheelchair. I let myself droop slightly but sat tight until they pushed the chair into an examining room and the two men hoisted me onto a table. Fred thanked them, I didn't catch the words, and they both left.

She bent over me, mouthing, "You seem okay. Your pulse is close to normal."

"Keep the others away when the doctor gets here," I mouthed back. She nodded and waited, her unbound hair flowing down over her face.

The men came back with Dr. Frazer and the friendly nurse I had met before. Fred was on top of the scene, improvising to cover everything.

"Doctor, there was a fire. He's having a heart attack." Then she turned to the men. "Where's Mrs. Schuka? She should be here. Oh God. I'm sorry. You should have brought her as well."

They looked at one another startled. "Hey, yeah. Never thought about her when he started gettin' the pains. We better bring her in," one said.

"Right." The other one led the way out of the door. Fred followed them to it, calling out her thanks, then closed the door behind them.

Frazer looked at me, then Fred. "What happened to you? A fire?"

"Yes," Fred said. "I'm fine; I got out before the smoke got thick, but Reid was in it for ages, saving the landlady."

He went to her first, checking her pulse, glancing into her eyes. "You seem fine," he said. Chivalrous, I thought. Or more? Was he sweet on her?

Then he came to lean over me, putting his stethoscope into his ears. I held up one hand and sat up. As I did it I felt the cuts in my chest start flowing again.

"I'm cut, that's all doctor. But I need your help."

"Yeah, well lie down and you'll get it," he said, gently easing me back down. He held out one hand to the nurse and she slapped a pair of scissors into them, without waiting for instruction. He cut the bandage off and peeled back the dressing off my chest. "Extensive but not dangerous if we get you a tetanus shot," he said. "What happened?"

I looked at each of them in turn. "Somebody firebombed the house."

Frazer frowned. He looked more tired than I had ever seen him. "Are you sure?"

"Positive. My dog woke me up and I saw the fire spreading out across the rug and smelled gasoline. No doubt about it. They'll probably find the bottle in the morning when the fire's out. Only I have a feeling nobody on the police department will think to look for it."

"What you're saying sounds a little dramatic," he said. I opened my mouth to argue, but he held up one hand. "No, hear me out," he said, "or it would do, normally."

"These aren't normal times in Elliot," I said softly, containing my anger. I needed his help. I had thought from the talk we'd had earlier that I could count on it.

"I know," he said wearily. "Tell me, were you going to get some help in your plan?"

I hesitated and he said, "Okay, let me answer it for you. A man called Wilcox was in on this. Wasn't he?"

"Was?" I looked at him, noticing for the first time that he had a smudge of soot on the edge of his hospital-green jacket. "Why do you say 'was'?"

"I'm afraid you're not the only one who's had a fire tonight. I've just finished giving first aid to another guy, a Mr. Wilcox from the old town."

TWENTY-THREE

"You say first aid. How badly hurt is he?" I rolled my legs off the gurney and went to stand, but he pushed me back.

"He'll make it, but not by a hell of a lot. He's got bad burns over his hands and his legs. He wrapped a blanket around his head so his face is safe, but he's going to need proper treatment in Toronto before he's back in shape. It's going to be months before he's anything like normal. Another couple of minutes in that fire and he would have been finished."

I swore under my breath. "That's because he's working with me. I know it. I went to see him last night. Somebody had driven into the old town as I left. They must have seen I was visiting him, realized I was probably going to ask him for help, and tried to kill him as well as me."

"Well they didn't make it," Frazer said. "Only he's a lot older than you are and he didn't react as quickly as you did. He got burned badly."

I put my own problems out of my mind. "Can you get him to the hospital in Toronto?"

"He'll go out by air ambulance tomorrow morning. The guys here will take him to Olympia and from there he'll be flown to the burns unit at Wellesley." Frazer looked at Fred. "I'm afraid your husband's right, Mrs. Bennett. Somebody is seriously trying to kill him, and that puts you in danger as well." He scratched his forehead gently with the middle finger of his left hand. It looked studied, a gesture he would use when he had to break bad news to a patient.

"I want them all to think I'm dead," I said. "That way Fred will be safe. It's just for a few hours. It will put whoever threw that firebomb completely off guard. Will you go along with it for me?"

Frazer looked at me doubtfully, then at Freda. She spoke first, slipping down from her stool and coming over to me. "Isn't it time to quit, Reid? Can't you call in the OPP? You're not expected to take that kind of risk."

"I've thought about it. If I do that they won't be here before morning and in the meantime neither of us is safe." I reached out and squeezed her shoulder. She smiled crookedly.

Frazer persisted. "But that's what has to be done, surely. You call the OPP and wait here until they arrive."

It was as if he and Fred were ganging up on me. I didn't like that, but at the same time Fred in particular was entitled to know exactly what my reasons were. "I believe that the gold shipment is going to be lifted in the morning. Whoever is planning to do it knows that I intend to stop it. That's why they tried to cancel me out tonight."

Frazer and my wife exchanged looks as if they were both doctors studying a particularly frustrating case. Frazer did the asking. "And what do you intend to do about it?"

"I've made a plan to cover the shipment as far as the edge of town. I want to do it. If, as I think, the chief of police is behind all this, then I'll know it. My job here will be over."

Frazer pursed his lips, impatient with me. "And this job is that important to you?"

My chest and my arm hurt, my throat was painful from the smoke I'd breathed and I was weary. I didn't want to discuss this thing any further. I just wanted it over. I kept my answer simple. "Yes," I said.

The nurse came back in with a bowl covered with a cloth. Frazer smiled acknowledgment and pushed me gently down flat. I lay there while the nurse shaved my chest around the cuts. Then Frazer jabbed my chest with a local anesthetic and started stitching. Fred wanted to stand by but the nurse gently put her back on the stool, where she could not see what was happening.

Frazer glanced into my eyes as he worked. "Okay, Reid, I'll go along with it, but Judy has to know about this. She's going to be part of it."

"Know about what?" the nurse asked.

"Know that I'm going to pretend to be dead," I said, and she laughed.

"Wha's this, doctor? A new gimmick for a malpractice suit?"

Frazer chuckled, not looking up from his work on my chest. "I think you'd best let Reid explain it to you."

She laughed again but she was more angry than amused. I was upsetting her boss and that didn't sit right. "Just when I thought I'd heard everything," she said. "Go ahead."

I talked and by the time I was stitched up we had agreed on what was going to happen. Officially I was going to be declared dead, right here in this room. I would be wheeled to the morgue by the night porter. Fred would accept an invitation to stay overnight with the doctor and his wife, and they would go out to the car. At the same time, Judy would keep the porter busy at the other end of the building and I would slip out of the side door to the parking lot and go home with Frazer and Fred.

I glanced at Fred. She had said nothing while all the planning was going on. She looked pale. As soon as my chest was covered I stood up and went over and held her. "It's over as soon as the gold shipment leaves town," I promised. "There's enough going on that the OPP can investigate. Something is sure to shake out and the whole thing's solved."

She let me hold her but she was unbending in my arms. "If it's that straightforward, why don't you call them in now, Reid?" she asked, in a reasonable tone.

"Because if I'm right, the guys who did this to us will lift that gold in the morning and disappear. I want to stop them."

"You make it sound personal. That's not like you," she said.

And this wasn't like her, I thought. She had taken a lot of bad things in her stride since we'd been together. This time things were getting to her. The fire had shaken her worse than I had thought. I glanced up at the clock on the wall. It showed three-fifteen. "It is personal. They endangered you. I can't let them get away with that," I said. "Five more hours and it's all over."

She gave me a quick kiss. "I'm going to hold you to that."

Frazer and the nurse were standing back, looking at one another awkwardly. As soon as I let go of Fred they came to life. "Okay, Reid. I don't like any of this, but let's get it started," Frazer said. "Get on the trolley, please." I got back on and lay down. The nurse threw a sheet over me. "Don't sneeze and try not to make any movement as you breathe," she warned.

"Right." I lay very still and heard Frazer say, "Okay, Mrs. Bennett. Are you ready to play your part?"

Fred's voice was crisp. "Yes," she said. "Let's get on with it."

"Judy, go and get Mr. Tracy," Frazer said. "Come with me, please, Mrs. Bennett."

Everyone left. As the door swung softly shut I heard Fred's sobbing, low and believable. It filled me with disgust for myself and for a moment I almost threw off the sheet and abandoned the whole plan. But I reminded myself that this was the best way to keep her safe from whoever had thrown that Molotov cocktail through the window. I was their prime target but they had not hesitated to put her life in danger in their attempt on me.

The nurse was back a minute later, talking to a man who sounded elderly. "Doctor Frazer wants the body moved down to the morgue. I'll give you a hand."

"Who is it?" The obvious question.

"Bennett, his name is. He's a cop. There was a fire at the house, oil furnace, his wife thinks. He had a heart attack."

"Another goddamn fire? Two in a night," the man said. "Was he smokin' in bed or what?"

"His wife thinks the furnace exploded," Judy said. "'Parently he went back into it, pulled the landlady out. She lives downstairs."

I was glad to hear that story going the rounds, but it didn't seem enough to placate the porter.

"'Bout time he did somethin' good for somebody," he said, as the gurney started to move. "He stole that hooker's money and you can't tell me no different."

"Well, he'll never spend it now," the nurse said casually. The gurney bumped the doorway lightly and she gave a little cluck of concern. "Don't tip him off that thing, he's a big guy to lift back on."

"Don't worry. He can't feel it," the man said. He sounded as if he was enjoying slamming me around, punishing me.

I concentrated on breathing as little as possible, keeping my eyes closed and my jaw dropped, in case the sheet should slip from my face as we moved. We trundled down a long hallway and down the elevator, then out. There was a pause while Judy opened the door of the morgue, and then Tracy asked the question I'd been worrying about. "You want me to roll him offa this into a tray?"

She was perfect. "Naah. The funeral parlor guys will be here first thing. Let them take him off this. George keeps it cold enough in here. He won't spoil before morning."

The old man snorted a laugh and bumped the gurney against a wall. Judy said, "Oh, while I think of it, Mr. Tracy, can you bring your screwdriver and come and have a look at the desk on my station? There's a loose screw under the typewriter table. Young Lilian caught her knee on it yesterday."

Tracy gave a little chuckle. "Wants it kissing better does she?"

"She wants it fixed is what. It tore her stocking," Judy said. "You'll have to ask her about the knee."

They both laughed again companionably and left. The lock on the door was a simple Yale, and I heard them pull it shut as they went out, turning out the light.

I flicked the sheet off my face and lay in the dark, thinking what had to be done. My first needs were clothes. I couldn't protect anything before I'd protected myself against frostbite. My parka and overboots were gone in the fire at the house. I needed replacements before I could work in temperatures of ten below, Fahrenheit.

The second thing I needed was a weapon. My service revolver had been in the holster pocket of my parka. It was lost in the fire by now, twisted and ruined by the heat. The old Lee-Enfield rifle belonging to Mr. Wilcox was still on the backseat of my car. I shuddered and pulled the sheet around my chest as I thought hard about reclaiming my car. It was probably damaged. It had been parked in the driveway, close enough to the house that it may have lost its windows in the heat, or been damaged by the firemen as they worked around it. On top of which it wasn't appropriate behavior for Fred to trail back to the burning house in the middle of the night to pick up a car.

But there was also the other weapon—my best. Sam. He was still at the scene of the fire. Even as a bereaved widow, Fred could be expected to collect him. And if the car was drivable she could bring it back with her. I felt uncomfortable assigning her so big a part in the plan. I wanted her out of it, but at least with me supposedly dead, she should be safe.

It seemed hours before I heard footsteps outside the door and I was stiff with cold, doing my best not to shiver. For camouflage I threw the sheet back over my face and lay still as the door opened. It might have been Tracy coming back to gloat. But it was Frazer's voice that whispered to me, "Okay, let's go, Reid."

The doorway was outlined in the light from the corridor. I flicked the sheet aside and tiptoed out, moving quietly. Frazer was wearing a big down jacket. He looked at me as he pulled the door shut. "You'll need this, you're still in shock," he said and slipped out of his jacket.

"Thanks. I'm frozen." I pulled the jacket on gratefully, feeling my tight muscles slacken at once in the luxurious warmth. "You could store beef in that place."

"Kind of what we do," he said. "This way." He led me to the stairwell and up to the back door of the hospital. His car was parked there with Fred in the passenger seat. "In the back and lie flat," he told me.

I paused in the doorway to look all around. There were only two other cars on the lot and nothing was stirring, right back to the never-ending trees at the edge of the parking lot. Frazer went ahead of me, opening the rear door casually before getting into the front. I crossed the three paces to the open door and slid in, keeping low, hooking the door shut behind me.

"Good," Frazer said. "Let's get home." He turned the heater on full, suppressing a shudder. He drove off. Fred didn't turn around, but her left hand reached down between the bucket seats in front and she found my fingers and squeezed them.

"How're you doing?" I asked.

"Tragedy isn't my favorite," she said.

"The curtain comes down at breakfast time," I promised. "But there's one more scene to play in public. Can you do it, Love?"

"Sure." She gave my fingers a final press and then withdrew her hand. It was too much like the end of a relationship to leave me happy, but I planned to make up for it once this job was over.

"We have to get Sam back from the neighbors," I explained. "And if possible, get the car as well."

I saw Frazer glance sideways at Fred. The gesture looked anxious and I felt a tiny nip of jealousy. His tone of voice did not soften the impression. He asked her, "Will you be all right? I'll drive you over there when we've let Reid out at my place."

"It gives me a scene at center stage," Fred said. Her voice had a touch of its usual breeziness. It made the jealousy a little more real. Was she flirting with him?

He spoke to me next. "What's so important about the car, Reid? It might look a little suspicious. Your wife's supposed to be in shock. It isn't likely she'd worry about the car, not tonight."

I minimized my reasons. "There's something in it that I need for the morning."

"What is it? Maybe we can find a substitute." He kept his tone reasonable, too reasonable. I felt like a difficult teenager arguing with an understanding parent.

"It's a rifle." I laid the fact out for inspection. It didn't faze him.

"Then I can help," he said cheerfully. "When we moved up here I gave in to my daydreams of being John Wayne. I bought a Winchester lever action. I've fired it once and it's lived on the basement wall ever since. Will that do?"

"Absolutely. Thank you. But I'd still like to get Sam back, Fred, if you can manage it."

She exploded. "Dammit Reid. Don't keep asking me if I can manage it. I've taken this on and I'll work it through. I'm not a kid."

"Good." It wasn't what I wanted to say, but with Frazer in the car oozing concern and understanding from every pore, it was as close as I could get.

The exchange had chilled out the conversation and we rode in silence to Frazer's house. It was one of the two-story executive homes, stuck in the middle of the block, but it had one advantage. He used his garage, unlike a lot of the people in town. He had even cleared the snow so he could drive right in without problems.

He closed the door behind us and I sat up gratefully. My chest was getting painful again now, as the anesthetic was wearing off. Frazer switched on the light and Fred and I got out. She looked at me appraisingly. "You're pale as hell, Reid. You should lie down and rest."

"Okay, I will." I stood back to let her through the door into the house ahead of me. Frazer came last. The house was in darkness. He said, "Hold it a moment. There's stairs up to the main floor on your right, down to the basement on your left. Can you feel your way down, Reid?"

"Sure." I felt around for the handrail and moved on down the stairs. When I'd reached the door at the bottom Frazer switched on the light. "Okay, Fred. It's all right for you to go through to the living room. We never draw the drapes. I don't want the neighbor seeing Reid in there.''

"Thank you," Fred said. She called over her shoulder at me. "Sorry about that, dear. You have to use the tradesman's entrance."

I opened the door in front of me and went through, kicking off my shoes first, the way most Canadians do automatically in other people's houses. I felt carpet under my feet and I eased forward, making the most of what light spilled in through the doorway behind me until I found a couch. That was enough. I slipped out of the doctor's jacket and lay down, pulling the jacket over my aching chest.

I fell asleep almost immediately, but woke with a start when the light switched on. I sat up and faced Frazer standing at the door. "Mission accomplished," he said.

"Sorry. I dropped off. Combat fatigue." I sat up.

"Understandable," he said. "Your car's a mess, but we've got your dog safe and sound. I've had to leave him in the garage. One of my kids is allergic. I hope you don't mind."

"No. Not at all." I was getting my marbles back. I stood up. "Listen, I can't thank you enough for all the help. My wife's really upset, but I have to finish this thing off."

"She's going to be fine. She wanted to come down and see you but she's bushed. My wife took over and put her to bed in the spare room."

"Thanks." I felt like a bull in a china shop. Now the lights were on I could see I was in a beautifully finished recreation room furnished like something in a magazine. The couch I'd collapsed on was dark, fortunately, because my pants were coated with soot and they stank of the fire. "I shouldn't even be in here, dressed like this. I'm sorry. I didn't think."

"Forget it," he said. "Would you like a drink?" I was weary enough to hesitate a moment but he coaxed. "What'll it be?"

"Rye, please." I stood where I was and he made a gentle shooing motion with his hands. "Lie down again. You've been cut and you've got your lungs full of crud. Relax."

"But your furniture?" I am not a drawing-room animal at the best of times, and this wasn't it.

"It's for sitting on, not staring at. Sit." He went to the bar and pulled out a bottle of VO and two glasses. He sloshed about three ounces in each of them and brought them over to me. "Here's looking up your address," he said, holding one out to me. I took it and raised it to him. "Your health," I said and took a good slug of the rye. It went down like liquid gold.

He did the same, then set down his glass on the side table and went out of the door at the other end of the room. I waited and he came back in with a Winchester .3030, the kind you see in every Western movie. He flicked the lever down and passed the broken gun to me, butt first. I checked that it was empty and then cocked it and pulled the trigger, releasing the hammer carefully with my thumb.

"I've got one box of shells," he said. "Here." He took the box from under his arm. "One gone, that's all. Will twenty-four be enough?"

"I may not need any at all," I said. "But thank you for this. Just don't tell anybody about it in the morning when the gold leaves town without a hitch."

"I don't think that's going to happen," he said. "Not with somebody trying to kill both you and your partner. How are you going to manage now, on your own?"

"I'm not sure. But if something happens, I'll be there. They won't be expecting me to show up."

Frazer took another sip of his rye. He blinked one eye as he swallowed, like a young guy with his first bottle, trying to look macho. I don't think he did a lot of drinking. "Speaking as a professional, what would you say will happen?" he asked. "I mean, how will they go about trying to rip off the gold?"

"It depends on two things, their firepower and their determination." I finished my own drink in one swig and set down the glass. "If they're ruthless enough they'll stop the truck by blowing the top off it with an armor-piercing round of some kind. If they haven't got that much weaponry, which is likely, they'll force the truck to stop and kill or overpower the men in it."

"And how would they stop it?" He narrowed his eyes and bent forward, his elbows on his knees.

"The easiest way would be to sow the roadway with spikes—tear the tires off the vehicle to immobilize it. The driver will have to get out to change the tires and they'll hold a gun on him and force the guy in the back to open up and let the gold go."

Frazer sat back. "But what if the police car is ahead of them? Once it hits the spikes the gold truck will stop, intact and closed up."

"The police car will be behind them. It's policy when there's just one vehicle. You stay behind the load so you can see everything that happens."

"And where will you be?" The sixty-four-thousand-dollar question.

"I'll be bringing up the tail, back a hundred yards, looking like some innocent road user who's not in enough of a hurry to overtake them."

Frazer stood up, pausing to gulp down the last of his drink. He moved to the bar, picking up my glass as well and setting both of them on the countertop. "Okay. You're going to need help," he said. "You'll need outdoor boots and a toque as well as my jacket. And I think I can round up another man to come with you."

"Who?" I sat up very straight. "I don't want anybody else brought in. All I have going is surprise. I can't risk blowing that."

"Don't worry," he said. "I'm coming with you."

"No." I shook my head, suddenly fatigued again. "No. You're too important in this town. It's not your job. It's mine."

"I want to be there and see who does what," he said. "In case you didn't know it, I'm one of the commissioners of police for the town. If there's any wrongdoing, I want to see the proof of it."

I swore but he shrugged it off. "No sense arguing. I can be just as obstinate as you."

"In that case I won't waste time. I plan to be out of here at six."

"I'll set the alarm," he said. There was a chest in front of the couch, acting as a coffee table. He opened it and took out a couple of blankets. "Here. Use these for now, Reid."

"Thanks, that's great." I took them gratefully. I was chilly.

He stuck his hand out. "Shake, Reid. I want you to stay here and be our police chief when this is over."

I shook his hand. He had a good firm shake. "Does the offer hold regardless of what happens to the gold?"

"Yes." He backed away and reached for the light switch. "Personally, I don't see how anything can happen in the morning, but there's too much evidence to the contrary right now. Sleep tight. I'll call you at ten to six."

He switched off the light and left. I sat there, looking at the square of light from the doorway until he reached the top of the stairs and turned it off. Then I picked up the Winchester and the box of rounds. The chill of the metal against my fingers gave me reassurance, and I sat there in the dark, loading the gun, pushing six rounds into the magazine.

When the magazine was full I levered one up the spout and inserted one final round in the mag. And then my old Marine training took over. I laid the rifle beside me on the couch before covering myself with the blankets and lying back, willing myself to wake up at six.

TWENTY-FOUR

I WOKE as Frazer came down the steps. He was carrying a heavy sweatshirt and a thick wool sweater. "You're awake," he said. "Good. Here. Try these for size."

I sat up, feeling the stiffness of the bandage on my chest. I was going to be sore for a few days. Unless something worse happened over the next couple of hours to take my mind off it.

"Thanks. They look fine." I took them out of his hand and stood up.

"The can's behind the bar," he said. "I'll be upstairs making some coffee. Don't come into the kitchen. It can be seen from next door. Just call when you reach the top of the stairs."

"Thanks." I took the clothes and went into the bathroom. I would have liked a shower but settled for a brisk wash to get the sleep out of my eyes and the soot from my face and hands. With the clearheadedness of early morning I could smell the smoke on my pants and knew that Frazer's allergic little boy would be wrinkling his nose in disgust for months whenever he came down into the basement.

As I dried my hands the bathroom door opened behind me and Fred said, "Hello, Reid."

She was wearing a big loose flannelette nightgown, something they must have had in the drawer for visiting grandmothers. She was smiling, but she looked pale and shaky. I held up my hands to keep her back a little. "My pants are covered in soot," I said. Her huffiness of the previous evening was eating at me. For the first time ever I felt a little awkward around her.

"I don't care," she said. "Hold me, Reid. I'm scared."

We stood clinging to one another. Then she kissed me and whispered, "I'm sorry I snapped at you. After everything you'd done. I feel like a real bitch."

"Don't think about it," I said urgently. "I'm acting like a combat Marine again and expecting you to go along, and you've never been through boot camp."

We kissed again and then she squeezed my arms and pushed me out of the bathroom. "Take care," she whispered.

I was a little surprised and covered it with a crummy joke. "Is this an adieu in the loo?"

"Yes," she said urgently. "I'll see you soon. Take care."

I winked at her and left, taking the Winchester, the shells and the down jacket from the couch. Women, I thought.

Frazer was waiting on the landing with two traveling cups of coffee, the nonspill kind they sell in donut shops. "Black, right?" he asked.

"Thank you." I took the coffee and stooped to slip on my shoes, which were still lying on the little rubber tray by the back door.

Frazer said, "No, try these," and pulled out a pair of insulated snowmobile boots from the hall closet. They were a little snug but the insulation was soft enough that they would do for a short time without crushing my feet. I said "Fine, thanks," and laced them.

He held the rifle while I slipped into the jacket and filled the pockets with the remaining shells for his gun. Then he pulled on a heavy duffle coat over his sports jacket and pulled on a fur hat. He gave me a toque. I felt like a kid being dressed by his mother.

We went into the garage and Sam welcomed me, fawning around me like a puppy. I fussed him for about minute, then got in the backseat of the car and had Frazer open the garage door and let Sam out. He took a minute while Frazer started the car and then ran back and got into the front seat, twisting his head back to look at me as I lay across the rear seat, waiting to get clear of the house before sitting up.

When we were on our way Frazer asked, "Where are we heading?"

I told him and he asked, "Is some cop liable to see us there?"

"I wouldn't think so. They won't be expecting trouble. They'll drive into the mine site, they won't go past it to check."

"I hope you're right," he said. He began to whistle to himself, some little classical theme that I didn't recognize. He was psyching himself up. I could tell he was scared.

I stayed flat on the seat as we drove through town, then sat up, checking the terrain. It was still dark, of course, but I was able to see enough in the headlights to remind me of all the details. The road was straight except for one bend around the edge of a small lake. On one side was a sheer cliff, on the other, the ice of the frozen lake came right up to the road. There was nothing there when we passed but it seemed the logical place for an ambush.

We passed the mine gate three kilometers further on. It had a big streetlight outside it, the only light between here and town. Frazer drove past without slackening speed. Sure enough there was a plowed-out space, three hundred meters further, on the opposite side of the road from the mine gate. Frazer could park there almost hidden behind the banks of plowed snow and yet still see the mine gate from the driver's seat.

"Now we wait," he said.

"This is the hard part," I told him. "I'll come up front."

I got out and changed seats with Sam, who was much more relaxed to be in the back, able to see me. I reached over and patted him. "Easy boy. Nothing doing yet."

Frazer didn't talk. He sat staring down the road at the mine gate, whistling his little melody.

"The police car will probably come in soon," I said. "They'll most likely head through to where the truck is being loaded."

"If you say," Frazer said soberly. "It hasn't come in yet."

"It'll be here." I was tense myself and I took the precaution of checking the load on the Winchester, levering out the first round and replacing it in the magazine. Frazer watched me but said nothing. He had given up whistling now and was drumming his fingers lightly on the steering wheel.

"There's the police car," he said suddenly.

"How many people in it?" I asked.

"I couldn't see. It turned. I could only see the driver's side. I'll be able to check when he pulls back out." His voice was high and nervous.

"Don't sweat it." I looked down the road.

"You think anything will happen?" He almost squeaked the question out.

"Most likely not. But if anything does, it will be about three clicks down the road, at the bend. I figure that's where a pro would hit."

"And what do we do?" He had control of his voice now, dealing with facts rather than fears.

"The road bends to the left, coming at it from this direction. I want you to pull off the road to the right. I want to be able to see around the bend. Then I want you to get under cover. If there's anything going on, turn the car around and get back to the mine and call out their security people. If there isn't time for that, crouch down as low as you can in the front seat here, where the engine block comes between you and the scene."

"Doesn't sound like much to do," he said.

"It's enough. We don't have any more firepower and your safety is important to everyone in town. Don't forget that."

"What about yours?" He snapped it at me. "What about your wife?"

The same worm of jealousy gnawed at my heart but I said nothing. Instead I concentrated on what I might expect if an ambush happened. And I tried to resolve how I would overcome the biggest problem, the darkness, which would prevent me from seeing the sights of the Winchester well enough to line them up accurately.

I checked my watch. It was two minutes to seven. I sat looking at the sweep hand, not really seeing it, focusing instead on my breathing as I calmed myself down to be ready for whatever happened.

"There's a truck," Frazer said softly. "And there's the police car. Yes, there's a second man in the passenger seat."

"Let's go," I said. "Keep the pace down. Hang back far enough that they don't get suspicious."

"Right," he said. He let the little convoy get two hundred meters ahead of us before he pulled out, matching his speed to theirs so we trailed back, far away, like the last piece of paper on the tail of a kite. One vehicle passed us, going the other way. It looked like a small truck of some kind. As we approached the bend in the road, I told Frazer, "Pick it up a little, close us to a hundred meters, but be ready to hit the shoulder this side."

"Gotcha," he said. He was driving with tight control, both hands on the wheel, staring down the road ahead of us. The first light of dawn was brightening the sky to my right. It was enough for me to see that there was nothing waiting between us and the bend, no truck on the shoulder, no unexplained pedestrians. Then the gold truck passed out of sight around the bend.

The instinct of a thousand patrols made me flash a look behind me as we came up to the corner. And as I did, a Jeep-style vehicle roared by us with two men in it. They glanced into our car as they passed and I could make out only one detail in the dim light. The man on my side was wearing a ski mask, rolled down.

Frazer reacted with a start as the Jeep whooshed by us. "Drop back," I shouted. "Those guys are masked."

"What?" He shrilled out the word but he didn't lose control. He punched the brakes rhythmically so we wouldn't skid on the slick road, his eyes focused tight on the Jeep.

We were fifty meters from the corner. The police car was just rounding the bend when it slid sideways suddenly and stopped across the road. And then the Jeep jerked to a stop behind it. "Stop," I shouted and Frazer did, half skidding so that the right side, my side of the car, was almost flat on to the Jeep.

"Get back to the mine," I shouted. I rolled out, clutching the rifle and whistling for Sam. Ahead of me the driver of the Jeep was stepping down. I could see the bulk of a long gun in his hands. I lay prone, thumbing back the hammer, pointing rather than aiming the rifle, still unable to see the gunsights. "Drop that gun," I shouted.

He turned and fired, a round orange flash that filled my eyes and gave me the contrast I needed to line up the shallow rearsight on the blade of the foresight in its round protective tunnel. As the sound of his shot reached me, I squeezed the trigger and saw the man fly backwards, dropping the gun.

Ahead of him the doors flew open on the police car. A man jumped out of each side. At that distance in the poor light I couldn't recognize them but the guy in the driver's seat was wearing a parka, the one on the left was in a long topcoat. That was the chief. Then I saw the chief buckle at the knees and heard the quick popping of pistol shots, sounding almost playful after the crash of my rifle. The cop in the parka dropped to one knee and I saw the quick muzzle flashes of his return fire. Then the Jeep turned off the road and lurched over the drift left by the snowplow beside the road and out onto the frozen lake.

He was lost to me, in dead ground, below my sightline, but the cop in the parka stood up and fired again, rapidly. I saw one answering flash from the Jeep as it headed across the ice. I stood up, lining up on the back tire of the Jeep, making lightning calculations for distance and speed. I was lucky, he was driving directly down my line of fire. I didn't have to allow deflections. I squeezed off a shot, then levered another round and aimed again, but it was unnecessary. The Jeep had skewed to the left, his rear tire gone.

"Come," I called and Sam followed as I ran up the road to the policeman.

He stood there, pistol raised. I checked myself twenty yards from him and sank to one knee, covering him with the Winchester. "Reid Bennett. Identify yourself."

"Reid, for Chrissake! They said you were dead." I recognized the voice before he added his frantic, "It's Scott. What's happening?"

"Let's stop that guy," I said. "Come on."

"Right." He ran with me, awkwardly, trying to reload his pistol as he ran, scrambling over the snowdrift and onto the ice with its overburden of crunchy slush. Ahead of us the Jeep was making time still, its driver pulling hard to keep it on track, its three good driving wheels compensating for the torn tire. I crouched and fired again, aiming higher this time, letting the bullet slam through the back of the vehicle, but keeping to one side of the driver. He jinked but didn't stop.

"Don't let him get away," Scott shouted. He braced himself and aimed his pistol, using both hands, squeezing off six rounds without pausing.

The Jeep drove on, two hundred meters from us. I knelt and drew a long breath, letting half of it out, allowing myself a couple of meters lead and aiming high, at the center of the motor over the front tire. I squeezed off the shot and saw the front tire flapping.

The door opened on the Jeep and the man jumped out and ran. "Fight," I shouted and Sam bounded over the ice.

"Stop," Scott shouted. "Hold it or the next shot's through you."

The man ran on but he was tiring and Sam was getting closer with every bound. Then he turned and this time he pointed at Sam. I didn't hesitate. I pulled the trigger on the Winchester and the man spiraled away backwards and lay still.

I ran forward, gasping with the exertion, as Sam ran up to the fallen man and stood over him, barking into his face in his trained, threatening voice. Behind me I could hear Scott swearing as he ran, the frightened formless cursing of a man in combat for the first time.

The light was growing, seeping into the landscape like water into a dry garden. As I ran, my eyes grew more and more accustomed to the gloom, and from thirty paces off I saw the man ahead of me writhe and reach both hands down to his thigh.

I slowed to a walk and trained the gun on him as I came up. The ski mask I'd noticed in the Jeep was still rolled down over his face. Sam was still barking and snarling at him. I told him "Easy." He dropped back a step and fell silent, and I reached out and prodded the man in the chest with the muzzle of the gun. "Take that hood off."

He groaned but I ignored it, prodding him again until he raised one hand and pulled the ski mask up over his eyes. It was Berger, the owner of the Headframe.

"Don't shoot me," he whispered.

"Where's your gun?" I asked him. He moaned again and pointed off a few steps to the side. Then Scott came up, gasping for breath. He stood with his hands on his knees, bent over, looking down at Berger. Then he took a long slow gulp of air and straightened up. "Sonofabitch. What's going on?" he asked me.

"We'll know better when we've seen who the other guy is, back at the roadway."

"He hit the chief square in the chest," Scott said. "This is first-degree murder."

"Let's get this guy back to the road. The doctor came with me."

"Okay. I'll get his gun," Scott said. "That's evidence."

"It's over there someplace." I gestured with the rifle, then crouched to look at the wound in Berger's thigh. It looked bad. The big muscle was shrunken and the injured leg was shorter than the other.

The only thing I had to use as a bandage was the sweatshirt I was wearing, so I propped the rifle against my leg and slipped out of my down jacket to remove the shirt. As I unzipped the jacket Sam barked harshly. I glanced up and saw Scott standing off four paces, holding a pistol, aiming it at my chest.

I dived sideways, trying to shrug back into the jacket as I shouted "Fight!"

Sam barked and lunged and the pistol went off, the slug snatching at the hem of my unfastened jacket. Then Sam's bark changed to a growl and I knew he had Scott by the gun hand. I stood up and watched as Scott tugged and swore while Sam hung on, forcing the gun in his hand down almost to the level of the crusted snow. Scott looked up at me, then back at Sam as he yelled. "What's going on for Chrissake? He made the gun go off in my hand. I could've killed you."

It was the last straw. My anger boiled over and I strode up to him and punched him in the face, sending him flying backwards with Sam still anchored to his right hand.

He moaned and lay still. "Let go of the gun or I'll blow your goddamn arm off," I told him.

He groaned again but did it. I called Sam off with an "Easy boy." He dropped back, snarling quietly. I knelt down and fussed him, rubbing his head and telling him he was a good boy. Then I picked up the gun that Scott had dropped. It was an automatic, cocked, ready to fire. I held it on him and told him "Open your parka."

He did and I dug under his parka with my left hand, keeping the gun trained on him. He was holding his own hands over his bloody nose. I took his pistol first. It was useless anyway, he had fired all twelve rounds he had with him. Then I took the cuffs and snapped one of them over his right hand. I yanked lightly on his hand and he came to his feet. I twisted his arm behind him, firmly enough to show I was in charge, and led him back the couple of paces to the fallen man. Moving carefully I crouched, keeping Scott covered as I handcuffed his right hand to Berger's left. Then I backed off. "Right. Pick him up and let's go."

He looked up at me from his half crouch in the snow. "He's gotta weigh two hundred pounds," he protested.

"He ain't heavy. He's your brother," I told him.

He swore but did it, hoisting Berger over his shoulder in a fireman's lift. Berger groaned and I stood and took off the jacket, as I'd been intending, and ripped off the sweatshirt Frazer had given me. Then I put my jacket back on, picked up the Winchester and caught up with Scott. I levered out the last rounds from the rifle and used it as a splint for Berger's thigh. He passed out as I tightened it but the bleeding stopped almost immediately, and at least he was in no pain while he was unconscious.

By now it was bright and I could see Frazer standing on the edge of the road with a couple of other men. Up the road past the gold truck, facing towards it, was another car, the one they had come from, I guessed. Mostly likely it had blown a tire, like the truck.

Frazer and the men came down to meet us as we approached the edge of the ice. The doctor looked at Berger's leg, not interrupting Scott's slow walk towards the shore. "He's lost a lot of blood," he said. "We could lose him if we don't hurry."

"Right," I said. "Hold it there, Scott."

Scott stopped, sagging under the weight. The other man with the doctor took Berger's weight while I unlocked the cuff from his wrist and cuffed Scott's hands together.

"Now make a chair," I said. He didn't even swear. He locked his hands with mine and the others loaded Berger onto us. We set off faster over the snow and onto the road.

When we got to the road Frazer ran for his car. He drove it up beside me and jumped out to open the rear door. "I'll take him to the sick bay at the mine. It's closer than town and that road's blocked with spikes anyway. This chap says there's a dozen cars back there with their tires torn up." He pointed back at the two bodies lying on the road. "That's the chief of police and someone I don't recognize. There's nothing I can do for either one of them. I'll get the people at the mine to send their ambulance out."

"I know who that is," one of the other men said. "That's Jack Sheridan. He's head of security at the mine." He looked at me, then Scott. "What the hell's goin' on? Why's this cop in handcuffs?"

"For attempted murder," I said. "Help the doctor get this guy into his car, will you? Come on, Scott, in the patrol car."

We turned away as Frazer and the second man fed Berger's limp body into the backseat of the car and roared away.

I put Scott into the back of the cruiser, in the cage. He looked terrible. His nose had bled all over his parka and was still leaking. There were tissues in the glove compartment and I handed him the box before I shut him in. "Thanks," he said humbly. "I'm sorry, Bennett. I've been dumber'n hell."

"I'll get a statement later," I said. "Sit tight."

I left him there with Sam on watch outside the car as extra insurance, and I turned to look at the fallen men. The chief must have died instantly. He had two bullet holes in the front of his overcoat, heart shots. Blood had pulsed out in the last seconds of his life and the coat was matted with it in a stain the size of a dinner plate.

I stepped over him and looked at the man I had hit. He was sprawled backwards with a single neat hole in the front of the dark parka he was wearing. It was black-rimmed with seeping blood. Someone had pulled his mask up and I looked at him but did not recognize him. The two men who had helped carry Berger watched me without speaking. I ignored them, standing and rubbing my face, feeling the scrape of day-old beard against my hands, reliving that split second when my target had been the orange circle of the muzzle flash as this man had fired at me. Trying to do to me what I had succeeded in doing to him.

One of the men said, "The doctor told me what happened. Don't feel bad. This guy'd already killed your chief. He was bad."

I nodded, not speaking. I would have preferred to be on my own for a while, to get used to the idea of what I had done. But he didn't take the hint. "Good shootin' buddy," he said and stuck out his hand to me.

I looked at him, seeing the eagerness in his eyes, the blood hunger of a man with a war story to tell. "Are you with the gold truck?" I asked, just to change the subject.

"Hell no," he said. "The guy got out of the truck but he jumped back in when the shooting started. He's still there, I bet."

He led me on, the few yards more until we could see around the corner to where the gold truck was stopped, both front tires blown, kneeling like a camel waiting for a rider. I could see the white face of the driver at the side window. Beyond him I could see a half mile stretch down the highway. Along the whole distance there were vehicles, five or six, I didn't count, slewed each way, sagging sideways on flat tires.

I stood and worked out what had happened. The men in the Jeep must have driven towards the mine from town, sowing their spikes behind them as they approached the corner. They must have planned to take the gold away across the frozen lake in their vehicle.

I turned to the man beside me. "Listen. I don't feel so good. I'm going to sit down in the car. Just leave me, okay?"

"You sure you don't want somebody with you?"

"Positive, thanks." I touched him lightly on the shoulder. "But, hey, if you wanted to do the town a favor, maybe you'd take a look for the spikes they dropped on the road. Could you? Pick 'em up and save them for me."

"Sure," he said eagerly. "Hell, we ain' goin' nowhere with my front tires the shape they're in."

I turned away from him, nodding my head without speaking, and went back to the police car. I sat inside, putting Sam beside me on the front seat. Scott tried to talk to me but I held up one hand and he stopped. "Save it all up for the OPP," I told him. "They'll sort you out."

TWENTY-FIVE

THE KEYS were in the ignition and I started the scout car and sat there, ignoring Scott's snuffling from the backseat. After a while I picked up the microphone and called the station.

Levesque answered, his voice startled. "Who is this?"

"Reid Bennett, Al. I'm alive and working. I need some things done."

"They said you was kill' in the fire last night," he persisted.

"Rumors. Can you patch me through to Walker at his house, please?"

"Sure," Levesque said, but he had one final question. "Where's the chief? That's his unit you' usin'."

"He's dead. I'll explain later. Right now I want to talk to Walker, please."

"Sure," he said again. Thirty seconds later a woman's voice said, "Hello."

"Mrs. Walker?"

"Yes, who's this?"

"Reid Bennett. I have to speak to your husband, please. Is he there?"

He was right beside her, still in bed. "Hi. What's happening? Is there an emergency?"

"Yeah," I said. "The whole department's come unraveled." I filled him in briefly and he listened without saying anything.

When I finished he asked, "What can I do?"

"Please. There's some urgent things to be done."

He asked his wife for a pen. Then he said, "Go ahead."

I spelled what I wanted done. First, I wanted him to inform the OPP and have them send in a team of investigators. Second, I needed a man out at the site to assist me. Next I wanted a snowplow or a group of workmen out to the roadway to scoop up the spikes and open the road again. Finally I wanted him to go in to the police station and take charge until I returned.

That was the only order that he commented on. "Thank you," he said. "I'll call the OPP first, then the works people, then I'll go into the office. If you need me again I'll be there."

"Thanks." I hung up the microphone.

I left Sam on guard around the area of the scout car and the two dead men. Already some of the stranded motorists had strolled down to look at the bodies. They were standing off a little way, hands in pockets, puffs of frosty air gusting out of their mouths as they talked over the events. Some kind of professionalism from their own dangerous line of work had kept them back from the bodies far enough that they were not disturbing anything, but when I got out of the car they came over and showed me the spikes they'd found.

"Lookit. These were made special to tear tires up," one of them said. "Ever seen anythin' like that?"

I had, in the police museum in Toronto. They had been used to cripple police horses during a nailmakers' strike a hundred years earlier, four two-inch prongs of sharpened steel welded together so that one spike was always vertical no matter how they fell.

"Ugly," I said. "Did you get all of them?" They thought they had. One of them had cannibalized a wheel from a car similar to his own, making his car drivable again. They were about to head back to Elliot, if I was finished, they said. They were full of questions, but I told them the case was under investigation. One of them opened his thermos and poured me a cup of coffee. It went down well and I thanked him. "You're welcome," he said. "You stayin' on in town, are you? Now the chief's dead?"

"Nothing's certain yet," I said. "We'll see after the investigation."

He was a thoughtful, slow-moving man in his fifties. "Hope you are," he said. "This town needs a good cop."

"That's what you're going to get," I promised. "Thanks for the coffee."

While I waited for help to arrive I got the investigation kit out of the trunk. I chalked the outlines of the two bodies on the roadway, also the position of the shotgun that the guy I'd hit had been using. There was a slick of ice on the roadway and I had to scratch with my pocketknife to get down to the tarmac before I could chalk. But I did it. After that I paced off the distances to the bodies and the gun from the landmarks on the side of the road and noted them in my book with a diagram. Then I got back into the scout car and settled in to wait, leaving Sam to guard the bodies.

It was about a quarter of an hour more before the ambulance came out from the mine. By then all the stranded drivers had gone. I was torn whether to wait with the gold truck or follow them back to the mine site, but right on cue, Levesque came in, on foot, having jogged the last quarter mile from where the first car had its tire blown.

I briefed him and left him there while I drove the police car back to the mine, taking Scott and Sam with me. When I got to the mine site the gateman was expecting me. He directed me back to the security office where a young guy in uniform and a nervous-looking executive were waiting for me. The executive introduced himself. "My name's Lalonde, I'm the personnel manager. Security's my responsibility." He looked anxiously at Sam, who was sitting in the police car.

"Bennett," I told him. "I'm with the Ontario Police Commission. This man is under arrest for attempted murder and a bunch of other things. Do you have a cell?"

They didn't have a cell as such, Lalonde explained prissily. What they had was a "secure holding unit," which was a cell by a fancy name. It had a bunk and a toilet. It was not a cage, but it had no window in the wall and the door was steel with a shatterproof glass panel in it. I took Scott's cuffs off and put him into it. He tried to talk to me but I told him, "Just make yourself comfortable, please, and wait."

The executive was horrified by Scott's nose. "What happened to him?" he hissed at me when I'd shut Scott away.

"He ran into a reflex action," I said. "Would you instruct your man to sit here by the door and keep his eye on Scott? If he attempts to harm himself, he's to call. Not to go in there, but to call for me. Can he do that, please?"

"Sure. You think this man will try to commit suicide?"

"He's already tried murder. You can't tell," I said. "And there's another thing. Your gold is sitting on the side of the road about three K from here. Do you have a heavy-duty breakdown truck?"

"Yes," he said promptly. "Why?"

"Get them out there and tow the truck back inside. If you've got spare security men, arm them and send them along."

He looked at me, narrowing his eyes. He wasn't used to taking orders from people outside the company, but he nodded and picked up the phone.

Now the pieces were coming together. I could relax a hair. I went in search of Frazer and found him in the sick bay having a cup of coffee with a nurse. "Berger's going to be okay," he said as I entered. "His leg's a mess but a good orthopod'll fix it."

I didn't know whether an orthopod was a doctor or a truss, but it didn't seem to matter. "Have you called your house?" I asked him.

"Yes. I called a couple of minutes ago, told my wife to let yours know you were all right."

"Thanks. I'd like to speak to her. She's been a little shaken up by all this."

Frazer laughed. "Sometime soon she's going to have to sit you down for a nice quiet chat," he said.

I frowned. I didn't like other men making jokes around my family that left me on the outside. "What's your number, please?"

He gave it to me and I dialed. His wife put Fred on the line. She burst out, "Reid! Are you sure you're all right?"

"Never righter," I said. "Look, I can't talk now. There's people here. But you know what I want to say. I'll be there as soon as the t's have been crossed and the i's dotted."

"I love you Reid. I'll be here," she said.

It seemed a bit dramatic, but I was reassured. If something had gone wrong between us, it seemed fixable. I went back to the holding unit and waited. The uniformed man was watching Scott through the window as intently as if he were a hockey game. A couple of minutes later Walker phoned from the police station.

"I've got the plow out and a couple of guys on foot clearing the spikes," he said. "I've also had a call from an Inspector Kennedy at the Police Commission. He says he's on his way to Olympia by air. He'll be at the mine by ten or so. He's bringing a senior OPP investigation team from Toronto."

"Good. Levesque made it out to the site. See if you can dig out some diversion signs for him to put around the chalk marks I've made. He's to stay there until the OPP have investigated."

"Will do, chief," he said.

"You're jumping the gun. I'm just the sergeant."

"I'd rather you were chief," he said, and I guessed he was hankering for the stripes for his own sleeve. Well, a lot would happen over the next little while.

Scott was lying on the bunk in his cell with his eyes closed and his hands clasped. He seemed to be praying. I went looking for Lalonde again. He was on the phone. "Good," he was saying, "have them deliver the truck to the side door of security."

He hung up and nodded to me. "The tow truck's on its way."

"Fine. When it gets here, have your mine manager present. I want to check that load."

"Now listen." He bristled, standing up and doing his best to look important in his nice gray suit. "That's company property. It's nothing to do with the police."

"Two men died trying to steal it," I said. "Have your manager here or the OPP are going to wonder why you didn't."

He huffed but he sat down sulkily and after a moment he picked up the phone. He dialed and when it rang he swung his chair around so he was facing away from me. I shook my head and left him.

The gold truck arrived half an hour later. I put my parka back on and went out to check it. The executive came with me and then Kemp arrived, coatless.

"Why do I have to be here?" he demanded angrily when he saw me.

"I want this load checked," I said. "After what's happened, it's policy."

He pursed his lips but said nothing. The front end of the van was hoisted up, but the driver was still inside, looking out at us, not opening the door. I wondered if he intended staying there until he took his pension.

Kemp held up some kind of ID and the man peered at it, then unlocked and stepped down. "Tell your partner to open the back," Kemp said.

The driver leaned back into the cab and spoke into an intercom. There was a clatter at the rear door and it opened.

"You can get out," Kemp said curtly. "It's safe now."

The driver looked shaky. He was holding a shotgun and I held out my hand for it. He looked at Kemp, then shrugged and handed the gun to me. I stood and waited while Kemp stepped up onto the sloping floor of the van. I followed him in. The shipment was in a solid oak crate which was strapped to the bulkhead behind the driver. It was sealed. Kemp checked the seals and said, "It's fine."

"Open it up. Let's check the load itself," I said.

"What for? That load was put in under my supervision, yesterday," Kemp said.

"Call me nosy. I want to see that the gold is okay."

"By whose authority?" He was spluttering with anger now. He turned to call out to the executive outside. "Mr. Lalonde, I want this load replaced in the vaults, right away."

"Open it or I'll blow the seals off with this shotgun," I told him.

He turned now and bellowed at the executive. "This man's mad. I want him off the site."

He was trapped in the van. I was between him and the door. I reached back and pulled the door shut. "Open the box, Kemp," I said.

"You are mad," he said. But his voice was failing him.

"I think I know what's in there," I said. "Open it."

He reached in his pocket for his Swiss army knife. He opened it, looking at me as if he wanted to jam it into my stomach. I kept the shotgun pointed at the deck between us, bracing myself against the wall of the truck to compensate for the slope of the floor. Finally he opened a screwdriver on the knife and inserted it into the metal seal, twisting it open. Then he broke the other seal and stood back, bracing himself against the rear wall of the truck.

"Open the box and let's see the gold," I said.

He was past arguing. He pried up the lid of the chest and reached in. The contents were in small canvas bags. Each one was sealed. He changed to a blade on his knife and cut the seal off, tipping out the gold billets loose over the top of the other bags, not looking at them, looking at me. "Happy now?"

"Not quite. I want you to scratch one of them, like you did with the one in your office yesterday."

He locked eyes with me and then folded his knife and put it away. "No," he said. "This has gone far enough."

"Not quite." I raised the shotgun, keeping it trained on him as I reached down and picked up one of the billets of gold. I kept my eyes on him as I gouged it against the metal strap that had sealed the box. The gouge showed gray underneath. "Nice try," I told him. "Let's go into the office."

I opened the door and stepped down. "Lock this truck and seal it until the OPP get here," I told Lalonde. "Don't move it out of my sight. Mr. Kemp and I are going to wait inside."

The man looked at Kemp without speaking until Kemp nodded and turned away. I went with him, through to the office. The two security men from the truck came with me. I knew they were armed and I wondered whether Kemp might try to call on them, so I said, "I'm with the Ontario Police Commission. If you have sidearms, please put them on the table and sit down. The OPP are coming to conduct the investigation."

They looked at one another without speaking. I was still holding the shotgun, negligently, but up where I could use it if they played rough. The guy who had been driving said, "You got some ID?"

"Yes," I said but I made no move to get it out. He waited a moment then reached under his coat and pulled out an automatic. He laid it on the table and backed off a pace.

The other guy cleared his throat. "That shotgun is it for me."

"Thank you. The load you took out is intact," I told them. "I'd appreciate it if you could wait on the site here until the OPP team arrives to investigate."

The driver swore. "I wish I knew what was goin' on here," he said. "The hell with this job."

"Let's go get some breakfast," his buddy said. He looked at me sharply. "That be okay?"

"That would be fine. Just don't leave the site, please."

They nodded and walked out; I didn't mind. They weren't vital to the investigation anyway. Only Scott was, and Kemp.

I turned to Kemp. "The OPP are going to be here soon. Until they arrive you are in my custody on a charge of theft of gold bullion," I said. "I'm going to charge you and give you your rights but after that I'm afraid I can't let you talk to anybody until the other men arrive."

"Save your breath. This is all a mistake," Kemp said. But he didn't try to leave. He just sat down wearily in a chair across the room from me and settled in to wait. I stood up and collected the pistol the guard had put on the table. I put it in the pocket of my parka, then took off the parka and sat down.

It seemed endless, but Kennedy arrived a few minutes before ten. He had three other OPP men with him. The first thing I did was head for the john, then I came back and took Kennedy into the next room and laid out the whole sequence of events for him.

Kennedy listened and asked a few questions, then said, "We've got enough to go on for a while. Why don't you go get something to eat, maybe see Fred."

"I'd like that," I admitted. "I'll be back around one."

"Yeah." He slapped me on the shoulder. "Take your time. See if you can pick up some new threads without smoke on them. Being around you is like sitting next to a one-hundred-and-eighty-pound kielbasa."

"Thanks for the kind words." I winked at him and left, taking Sam with me.

Back down the highway I found Levesque still on duty guarding my chalk marks, but one of the OPP men was with him so I stopped to answer his questions and to give him the shotgun Sheridan had been using.

I pulled into the driveway of Frazer's house in the scout car and Fred burst out of the side door and hugged me. It was the first time in what seemed like years that we were back on the honeymoon footing we'd brought to town with us.

We hung onto one another while all the neighbors peered through their lace curtains, and then I said, "Let's go somewhere private. Where's your coat?"

"I'll get it." She craned up to kiss me and trotted up the steps. I put Sam in the cage at the back of the car and opened the passenger door for Fred. She came back out in her down jacket. It's some kind of green that goes great with her red hair. I felt as if my heart was going to burst my chest as she came down the steps. She kissed me again and got in the car. I shut the door and went around to the driver's side.

I backed out and drove aimlessly out of town. She didn't speak. She just reached over and held my hand. It was as if none of the horrors of the last weeks had happened. I squeezed her hand in return but said nothing until I'd driven out to the side road where Nunziatta had tried to kill me. I pulled into the same clearing, swinging the car around so it faced into the road. Then I pulled her to me across the seat and hugged her very tight.

"Look, Fred. A lot's been happening to put a strain on us. I'm sorry. I just want you to know that nothing's as important to me as you are."

She eased back from me, starting to smile, but I went on. "Can we get back to where we were, before all this happened?"

She went on smiling, then she tried to look stern. "Impossible," she said, in what I call her actress voice.

I could sense she was kidding but I was too shaken up with everything that had happened to be able to appreciate it. "Why?" I asked helplessly.

"Because you're going to be a father, you big lunk," she said. "There's going to be three of us to worry about."

"You're pregnant?" My mouth fell open as I realized how dumb I'd been. "I should have known. Sick in the mornings."

"That's the part I'm not wild about," she said. "But aside from that I'm ecstatic. How about you?"

I couldn't even answer. We just kissed again and then sat there hugging one another. Eventually I said, "Frazer knows, doesn't he?"

"Yes. He confirmed it, day before yesterday," Fred said. "All the time you two have spent together, I thought he might have told you."

"Everything but," I said ruefully. "I was starting to wonder if you two were, I don't know, shutting me out, anyway."

"Twit," she said softly. "I told you we're a team, Reid. Only now we're bringing in a new player."

I just shook my head at my own dumbness and Fred laughed again. After a while, because that's what you have to do, we drove back to town to get on with our lives.

She came with me to the town's only clothing store and picked out some clothes for me. The storekeeper didn't want to take anything for the clothes because of my antics in the fire, but we settled on a solid discount for me and a nice warm feeling for him. Then Fred and I went back to Frazer's house, where I had to take a tub. Showering was out for a while, until the cuts on my chest had healed.

After I'd cleaned up and changed I wanted to get back to the mine to check on the investigation, but Alice Frazer had prepared a fancy lunch and it would have been impolite to duck out. So we ate. Alice made nice noises about the baby and asked what we were going to call it.

"If it's a girl I refuse to call the poor kid Freda," Fred said firmly. "I've hated the name from the first time I heard it. I think we should call her Anne after my mother, or Louise, after Reid's sister."

"And if it's a boy?" Alice asked.

"It's up for grabs," I said. "I'd like to call him Jack, after my dad."

"Wasn't his name Reid?" Alice asked. "It's such an unusual name, I figured it must be a family name."

"It is, but not our family, except for me," I said, "My dad was a Brit. He served in their commandos with a guy called Tom Reid. They were in some hot spots together, and they made a pact. If one of them didn't come through it, the other one would christen his first son with his buddy's last name."

Fred reached out and held my arm. I looked at her and saw tears in her eyes. "You never told me. But that settles it. A son will be named Jack Reid Bennett."

TWENTY-SIX

As soon as I could, I went back to the mine. Kennedy had set up his investigation center in the security office. He was sitting at the desk Lalonde had been using, talking to one of the OPP guys. For once he didn't have his feet on the desk, but he was tipped way back in his chair as if he were flirting with the idea. When he saw me he said, "That's one hell of an improvement, Reid. Fred pick the duds out for you, did she?"

"What else?" I said.

Kennedy laughed, then made the introduction. "This is Bert Grange," he said, indicating the other man. "He's Detective Sergeant Grange, stationed in Toronto. He's their finance expert."

Grange was short for a policeman and excessively neat. He looked as if he could slip right into a banker's office without raising anybody's eyebrows. He stood up and shook hands. "Hell of a job you've done here, Reid. How did you guess about the gold being fake?"

"I wasn't sure." I sat down and put my feet up on Lalonde's desk. Kennedy sighed with relief and did the same thing.

Grange sat back down like a job applicant, back straight, knees together. He frowned as if in pain when he saw our feet go on the desk top, but he said only, "Why did you even suspect it?"

"Well, Kemp was awful quick to prove that it wasn't his gold that was circulating in Nunziatta's pockets," I said. "Weighing it like he did seemed like an extreme reaction. The evidence pointed to theft, and he didn't sit still for that. Instead he told me how easy it would be to make up a dummy batch."

"But why heist the goddamn stuff if it's phony?" Kennedy insisted. He fumbled in his pockets and came up with a pack of White Owl cigars. He took one out and unwrapped it pleasurably and lit up. There was no ashtray on the desk but he hooked the wastepaper basket closer with his left heel and dropped the match into it.

Grange answered the question. "That's easy," he said. "Kemp had been skimming the production, getting it out a few ounces at a time for months, him and that security guy of his. Now it was truth or consequences time. There was no way to cover what had been taken. And the moment the fake gold got to the mint the game was up. But if everybody thought it had been stolen, then Kemp and his buddies were home free. Why, they could even have gone on stealing and taken another six or seven million dollars' worth."

"Where would they have hidden it?" Kennedy knocked the ash off his cigar on the edge of the waste can. "They'd have had the same trouble as they would with real gold."

"No, that was the sweet part of the deal," Grange said. "They didn't have to find the stuff again, just lose it. According to Kemp, Sheridan had an ice fishing hut on the lake. They planned to drive out there in the Jeep and drop the 'gold' through the hole. They knew the chief would be dead and Scott would lead the chase off in some other direction."

"Your people would have seen the tire tracks in the snow on the lake," I argued.

"We wouldn't have been out there looking until later than this. By that time Scott would have muddied up the scene for them, running tracks all over the ice. We'd have searched as far as we could, but it would have been dark, and there's more snow expected tonight. They'd have been home and hosed after that." He paused, marshaling his other facts. "You have to remember that they were winging it, thanks to you, Reid. They'd counted on having four men to handle the snatch. Nunziatta was in on it. He was the one who had the mold to pour the phony billets for them. And Ferris was in on it as well. According to Scott, he was the one who brought him into the plan in the first place."

Kennedy parted his feet so he could look straight at Grange. "You got all of that in a statement?"

Grange nodded happily. "Two statements. Kemp sang his heart out as well. He told us that Scott killed the sergeant because the guy was chickening out. He wanted to turn the other conspirators in as part of a deal to get off that attempted murder charge. Kemp's afraid of getting charged with conspiracy to kill the chief of police. He says he didn't do anything wrong himself, except for the misappropriation of the gold. He wants to turn Queen's evidence in return for some light time. I've promised we'll do what we can for him."

"He'll probably get six years instead of twenty," Kennedy said. "Be out in a couple if he keeps his nose clean."

"I think Scott's the guy who's going for the big fall," Grange said. "He's facing the charge of trying to shoot you, Reid, plus maybe we'll find it was his gun killed Ferris, once the ballistics boys have checked it. He wouldn't offer anything on that, nothing at all. He says he figures that Ferris shot himself because he thought that hooker would testify against him."

"I think he shot Ferris, but it may be hard to prove. He could have used a throwaway gun," I said. I was enjoying myself. All the answers to everything that had haunted me in town were here in front of us, all we had to do was pick them out of the pile, one by one.

"Anyway, there's more than Ferris to worry about. There's that woman who was strangled," Grange said.

"Like I said, Scott says Ferris did that," Kennedy said easily. "Says Ferris was the big bad corrupt policeman and he was the little innocent who got swept up in it all."

"We may hear the truth when the woman comes out of her coma," I said. "But what else does Scott have to say about the corruption?"

"Not much," Kennedy said. "Not yet, anyway. He sang a couple of choruses, then asked to have a lawyer present. I figure we're going to have to spend a lot of time with him."

"The best guy to lean on might be Berger," I said. "He's in this deeper than anybody. It looks to me as if he and Ferris were in cahoots. That was even before he bought the hotel. In fact, he may be the reason why Ferris killed the previous bar owner. That's going to need looking into."

"It'll all come out," Kennedy said easily. He had reduced his cigar to a four-inch stub and he was enjoying waving it more than smoking. He gestured with it. "It's going to take time. I've started piecing it together. First thing I did was check the police chief's service record. Before he came here he was a chief in a small town down east. He kept the Chamber of Commerce happy, looking smart in his uniform and keeping the department on budget. But when they had a couple of murders in town he screwed up the investigation so badly they kissed him off. He'd been out of work six months when he took this job."

I yawned. "Dr. Frazer is on the police commission here. He'll know why Harding was hired. Probably because Ferris said it would be a good idea. Ferris would have wanted a tame chief, somebody who wouldn't interfere in the rackets he had going."

Kennedy rubbed his forehead with the hand holding his cigar butt. I'd never seen that done except on TV. "Lookit, Reid. You're the local guy. Why don't you go and check with the doctor? He's gone back to the hospital already. Find out what you can about Harding's being hired, and see if we can question the hooker. When you've done that, go home."

"Home burnt down last night. I'll be happier working until we've got this thing wrapped up."

Kennedy frowned. "Dammit, book into the motel. Put it on your expense account. Also all the stuff you lost in the fire. We'll be happy to pay it."

"Can't let an offer like that pass by," I said. "If you want me, try the station, or the Frazers' house." I gave him both numbers. "The Frazers are being very hospitable, but if Fred and I can break away we will stay at the motel."

"Lots more privacy in a motel," Kennedy said straightfaced.

"What we're looking for is peace and quiet for Fred," I told him and he chuckled.

"You make it sound like she's broody."

I gave him the news, and he tossed his cigar away and shook hands. "Listen, the hell with the investigation. Go to her," he said. "You've put in enough damn time on this project."

"I'll check the hospital first," I said. "See you later." I ambled out, feeling free for the first time since Fred and I drove into town.

In fact the investigation took most of a week. It slowed almost to a standstill the moment the lawyers got into the act. In the meantime, Dr. Frazer had done a great job on the woman in the hospital. She recovered completely and after a few days she even started to get her memory back. She was spotty at first. Most of the night she'd been hurt was a blank, but as the facts came back to her she gave us everything, including the inside story on the corruption in Elliot.

Ferris had been her contact. He had threatened to put her out of business and she had agreed to pay him, ostensibly for protection, when she and her buddy came to town. When Harding took over as chief he had been content to put a couple of men on guard for the girls. He must have been too green to know that it didn't happen that way in most northern towns and too embarrassed to raise the subject with any other police chiefs he had met.

She eventually made a statement that Ferris had been the one who had tried to strangle her. She had no way of knowing what else had happened that night, but the OPP investigators were satisfied that he had tried to frame me by planting money in my lunch pail.

The other good news of the week was that Wilcox turned the corner. Frazer had shipped him out as soon as he could to the burns unit at Wellesley Hospital in Toronto. They gave him a speakerphone in his room, something he didn't have to hold in his bandaged hands. I was able to talk to him there, and he was happy to tell me that his daughter had come to visit him. He also reported that the woman across the road from his house was taking care of his little dog. He laughed when I told him how much she'd hated it when I first spoke to her.

By the time the OPP had all of this, the ballistics results were back from Toronto and we knew that Scott's gun had killed Ferris. We had also uncovered most of the missing gold. There was close to seven million dollars' worth in all, enough to attract all the news media from Toronto and even from the States. It put Elliot on the map and made me a bit of a celebrity. The motel owner was happy. He did land-office business for a while.

Maybe because of this, he insisted on giving Fred and me the best accommodation he had to offer. We were glad to take it. The Frazers were very generous about having us there, but Fred was still being sick in the mornings and she wanted privacy. Aside from that she was fine. We were back to where we'd been in the good old days before we came to town.

A number of other good things had happened. A crowd of local workmen had rebuilt Mrs. Schuka's house. In that part of the country they're used to working in the cold. They had it done except for the siding in about three days. The townspeople had rallied around with furniture and money, so it was furnished better than it had been before the fire. Mrs. Schuka was anxious for Fred and me to move back in, but I'd been making excuses."

Finally, on the night before Kennedy and the OPP team were to leave for Toronto, Fred and I invited them and the Frazers for dinner at the motel. Fred was in solid with the cook, and she had been able to get the run of the kitchen so she could prepare the meal herself. It was the best dinner we'd had since the fire. Afterwards we all sat around the table with liqueurs and brandies, and soda water for Fred, and set the world to rights.

Frazer asked the big question. "What now, Reid? The police commission here wants you to stay on as chief. What do you say?"

"Well, the first thing is to say that Walker should be sergeant. He's honest and level-headed. He'll do a good job. In fact, he'd make a good chief. He hasn't had a lot of experience yet, but if you sent him down to the college he'd learn fast enough. And his local knowledge is invaluable."

"You mean the job doesn't attract you?" Frazer teased. I think he had already guessed what my answer was going to be, but we were all relaxed and he was kidding me.

"Thanks for the compliment, but no," I said. "I'll stay on for a couple of months, until Walker can take over, but not for keeps. Fred and I have discussed this and we've decided against it. She can put it better than me."

Fred sipped her soda and started slowly. "What's happening is like a play. It's been exciting and there've been all kinds of curtain calls. But now it's time to take off the greasepaint and stop being actors. For us that means having the baby and getting on with the business of being a family. I think we have to go home to do that." She paused and added, "Of course that's after I've put on the play at the community center. I couldn't leave all my people dangling."

Everyone at the table nodded approvingly and then Kennedy asked the big question. "Where is home going to be, Fred?"

Fred looked at me. "Shall I tell them?"

I nodded. "I wouldn't want anybody thinking I'd brainwashed you."

"That'll be the day," Alice Frazer said. "What have you decided, Fred?"

Fred smiled. "Well, Alice, according to your husband the expert, the newest Bennett was conceived while we were at

Murphy's Harbour. We would like him or her to be born there."

Kennedy looked at me and laughed. "Pretty sneaky, Reid. I didn't see your lips move through that whole speech."

"A mutual decision," I said. "You know how that works. You're married."

"Not just mutual," Fred said. "Let's not forget Sam. He wouldn't be happy in the city, any more than this guy I'm married to."

It wasn't quite true. I'm not big on cities. But right then I figured I would be happy just about anywhere, the way things were working out for me.

HOOKY GETS
THE WOODEN SPOON
LAURENCE MEYNELL

First Time in Paperback

HOOKY HEFFERMAN WAS MUCH BETTER AT GETTING GIRLS IN TROUBLE THAN OUT OF IT.

His passion for the fair sex and English pubs aside, he had been known to solve a crime or two as a private investigator, profiting from the idiocies of this comic adventure called life.

Now he's been hired to find a rebellious, poor little rich girl who has taken up with some unsavory characters. Dad isn't comfortable swimming the murky waters of London's underground. Hooky, however, feels quite at home.

He's never minded helping out a pretty face—and Virginia Chanderley is that—but young and angry, she's also easy prey for a professional crook planning to steal a priceless painting. In fact, lovely Virginia has got herself into more trouble than even Hooky Hefferman—London P.I. and soldier of fortune—knows quite how to handle.

"Laurence Meynell had a gift for creating recognizable characters and ingenious plots."
— *The Independent*

Available in August at your favorite retail outlet, or reserve your copy for July shipping by sending your name, address, zip or postal code, along with a check or money order for $3.95 plus 75¢ postage and handling ($1.00 in Canada) for each book ordered, payable to Worldwide Mystery, to:

In the U.S.
Worldwide Mystery
3010 Walden Ave.
P.O. Box 1325
Buffalo, NY 14269-1325

In Canada
Worldwide Mystery
P.O. Box 609
Fort Erie, Ontario
L2A 5X3

Please specify book title with your order.
Canadian residents add applicable federal and provincial taxes.

HOOKY-R

WORLDWIDE LIBRARY™

MURDER
HAS A PRETTY FACE
JENNIE MELVILLE

The raped man had drowned. No one claimed him. Nobody wanted him. Least of all, Police Inspector Charmian Daniels. Why did he have her name and telephone number on a card in his pocket?

Several large-scale robberies of furs and jewels and a mysterious, garishly made-up woman lurking about town add to the bizarre caseload. Charmian is convinced the crimes are connected—but how? A chance visit to a local beauty salon puts her on the trail of a diabolic gang of criminals—and leaves no doubt that even the prettiest face can mask a ruthless heart as cold as steel.

Available at your favorite retail outlet in September, or reserve your copy for August shipping by sending your name, address and zip code, along with a check or money order for $3.99 plus 75¢ postage and handling for each book ordered, payable to Worldwide Mystery, to:

    Worldwide Mystery
    3010 Walden Ave.
    P.O. Box 1325
    Buffalo, NY
    14269-1325

Please specify book title with your order. Sorry, this offer not available in Canada.

ONLY AVAILABLE IN THE U.S.

PRETTY-R

 **WORLDWIDE LIBRARY**
™

A SENSITIVE CASE
ERIC WRIGHT

AN INSPECTOR CHARLIE SALTER MYSTERY

THE BIGGER THEY ARE THE HARDER THEY FALL

The murder of masseuse Linda Thomas was a sticky situation—her clients included big people in high places. It was a case for Special Affairs Inspector Charlie Salter and his chief investigator, Sergeant Mel Pickett. They delicately kick open a hornet's nest of hostile, secretive suspects, including a provincial deputy minister, a famous television host, the tenants of the woman's building, a nervous academic, a secret lover and an unidentified man—the last person to see Linda alive.

A lot of people had a lot to hide—and even more at stake than their careers. To make things more difficult, Salter is worried his wife is having an affair.

It's a sensitive case, both at home and on the job. Charlie's doing a lot of tiptoeing around—with a killer lurking in the shadow of every step.

Available at your favorite retail outlet in November, or reserve your copy for October shipping by sending your name, address and zip code, along with a check or money order for $3.99 plus 75¢ postage and handling for each book ordered, payable to Worldwide Mystery, to:

Worldwide Mystery
3010 Walden Ave.
P.O. Box 1325
Buffalo, NY
14269-1325

Please specify book title with your order. Sorry, this offer not available in Canada.

ONLY AVAILABLE IN THE U.S.   SEN-R

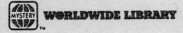 **WORLDWIDE LIBRARY**

BACKLASH
PAULA GOSLING

Winner of the John Creasey Award for crime fiction

THE TASK THAT FACED GENERAL HOMICIDE SEEMED MONUMENTAL

They had four dead cops from four different precincts, all shot through the head. The headlines were screaming cop killer. Rookies were making sudden career changes, while veterans of the force were anxiously eyeing retirement dates. Panic was growing.

For Lieutenant Jack Stryker, the pressure was coming everywhere: up from below, down from above, and in from the outside. And with each new death, the pressure increased. Was the killer shooting cops at random...or was there a more sinister reason for the murders?

But when Stryker is hit and his partner is almost fatally wounded...Stryker knows it's time to forget procedure and put an end to open season on Grantham's finest...before he becomes the next trophy of a demented killer.

"Gosling's novels have all met with critical acclaim."

— *Library Journal*

Available at your favorite retail outlet in October, or reserve your copy for September shipping by sending your name, address and zip code, along with a check or money order for $3.99 plus 75¢ postage and handling for each book ordered, payable to Worldwide Mystery, to:

Worldwide Mystery
3010 Walden Ave.
P.O. Box 1325
Buffalo, NY
14269-1325

Please specify book title with your order. Sorry, this offer not available in Canada.

ONLY AVAILABLE IN THE U.S.

BACKL-R

WORLDWIDE LIBRARY